YESTERDAY'S GONE

N. J. Crisp, a distinguished novelist and writer for television, lives in London. Leaving school in Southampton at the age of fifteen, he began work as a bank clerk. From 1943 to 1945 he served as a pilot in the RAF. After the war he held a number of jobs, from salesman to radio-cab manager, while writing his first novel. Since 1959 Mr. Crisp has been a full-time writer of magazine stories, novels, and television plays. In 1979 his first stage play, *Jet Set*, was produced in England. His novels include *The Brink* and *In the Long Run*, which will be available from Penguin later in 1988.

YESTERDAY'S GONE

N.J. CRISP

PENGUIN BOOKS

PENGUIN BOOKS

Viking Penguin Inc., 40 West 23rd Street,
New York, New York 10010, U.S.A.
Penguin Books Ltd, 27 Wrights Lane, London W8 5TZ
(Publishing & Editorial) and Harmondsworth,
Middlesex, England (Distribution & Warehouse)
Penguin Books Australia Ltd, Ringwood,
Victoria, Australia
Penguin Books Canada Limited, 2801 John Street,
Markham, Ontario, Canada L3R 1B4
Penguin Books (N.Z.) Ltd, 182–190 Wairau Road,
Auckland 10, New Zealand

First published in Great Britain by Macdonald & Co. 1983
First published in the United States of America by
Viking Penguin Inc. 1983
Published in Penguin Books 1988

LIBRARY OF CONGRESS CATALOGING IN PUBLICATION DATA
Crisp, N. J.
Yesterday's gone.
1. World War, 1939–1945—Fiction.   I. Title.
[PR6053.R497Y4   1988]   823'.914   87-7142
ISBN 0 14 01.0817 3

Printed in the United States of America by
Offset Paperback Mfrs., Inc., Dallas, Pennsylvania
Set in Baskerville

Author's Note

For his assistance with this book, I am deeply indebted to
Group Captain W. S. O. Randle, CBE, AFC, DFM. Like
myself, Bill Randle gained his RAF pilot's wings during the
Second World War at Number 3 British Flying Training
School in the USA, although Bill was on Number 1 course in
1941 – before America had even entered the war – while I was
there much later, on Number 20 course. (14,000 wartime RAF
pilots were trained in the USA.)

Bill Randle served with Bomber Command throughout the
war. He was shot down over Belgium, made his way through
France, across the Pyrenees into Spain, reached Gibraltar,
was flown back to England, and resumed operations.

In January 1946, he received a permanent commission, and
served happily in the Royal Air Force until 1972. He spent
three years as an exchange officer with the United States Air
Force, including a spell in Washington, and helicopter operations in Korea.

On leaving the RAF he became Keeper of the Battle of
Britain Museum, and then Director of Appeals of the Royal
Air Force Museum, and has travelled the world raising funds
on its behalf.

Bill Randle has also become an air historian who lectures
on various aspects of war in the air in both world wars, Korea,
and the brushfire campaigns, although his great love is the
Napoleonic Wars. He has acted as technical adviser on many
television series and feature films, going right back to the
movie *The Wooden Horse* in 1948.

He has, however, done much more than carefully vet my

manuscript, and make corrections concerning technical accuracy. He does not care for the myths which have flourished about wartime RAF air crew any more than I do. He gave endlessly of his time and knowledge in shaping the story before a word was committed to paper, and again while the book was being written. His suggestions were constructive and creative, and I am deeply grateful to him for his very considerable contribution to this novel.

I am also indebted to John Terraine for permission to quote from his penetrating study of the myths and anti-myths of war, *The Smoke and the Fire*.

N. J. Crisp.
LONDON.
1982

YESTERDAY'S
GONE

Chapter One

The log book which belonged to Squadron Leader David Kirby, DSO, DFC, is still in existence, its stiff blue cover faded and warped, the binding tattered and smelling of old, decomposing glue, the pages faintly discoloured with age, a relic of long ago, of a forgotten era, of another world with other values, of events receding into an ever more distant past, of dead men and dead boys, the one time thundering roar of engines recorded only in brief, neat entries and stilted phrases.

Pasted inside the front cover is a yellowing, printed sheet, headed 'British Flying Training Schools (USA). Instructions for compiling pilot's flying log book.'

Halfway down the sheet is a 'Sequence of Instruction (Elementary)', numbered one to twenty-eight. Number one is 'familiarization with controls', number twenty-eight is 'formation flying'.

In between come such exercises as 'Straight and Level Flight', 'Climbing', 'Descending', 'Taking off into Wind', 'The Approach and Landing', 'Stalling', 'Spinning', 'Steep Turns', 'Instrument Flying', 'Low Flying', 'Taking Off and Landing Out of Wind', 'Forced Landings', 'Action in the Event of Fire', 'Aerobatics', 'Night Flying', 'Pilot-Navigation', and many more.

The final summary for the unit, Number 9 BFTS, shows a total flying time on single-engined aircraft of 90 hours dual and 93 hours solo by day, and 12 hours dual and 14 hours solo by night. Instrument flying amounts to 27 hours, and link trainer 28 hours.

Inside the back cover is a page headed 'Record of Service'.

In the 'unit' column appear, ACRC, London; 7 ITW, Newquay; 9 EFTS, Ansty; ACDC, Manchester; 9, BFTS, Maranda, Okla.; 31, RAF Depot, Monckton; 7. ARC, Harrogate; 41, OTU, Chipping Wharton; 52. OCU, Thurston Moor, and number 545 Squadron, Woodley Common.

The opposite page is headed 'Aircraft Flown'. Five types are listed, Tiger Moth (DH 82A); Cornell (PT 19); Harvard (AT 6A); Wellington; Lancaster.

In the section of the log book devoted to squadron service twenty-nine operations over enemy territory are recorded. The first twenty-eight are against familiar targets, Stettin, Berlin, Hamburg and the like. The final raid is against a target so secret at the time that it scarcely appears in histories of the air war, and is lost to sight, forgotten, its tragedy hardly recorded, except in the bare statistics of those killed in action.

That one constitutes the last entry, and it is incomplete. There are no more. The remaining pages are blank.

'Kirby!'

He stepped forward smartly and stamped to attention, his hand swinging in the arcing salute which had been drilled into him at Initial Training Wing, longest way up, shortest way down.

'1432692. Sir.'

'Speak up, man,' the warrant officer standing behind the table said sharply, his boots and buttons glowing, apparently of their own volition. 'Can't hear you.'

He tried again.

'1432692. Sir.' He could hardly hear himself.

'Still can't hear you!' the warrant officer barked, frowning now. There was no such crime as dumb insolence in King's Regulations any more, a modern leniency the warrant officer considered a serious mistake, but if any of these cocky young upstarts thought they could safely take the mickey as a result, they bloody well had another think coming.

'I'm sorry, sir,' David Kirby whispered. 'I can't . . .'

The flying officer who was sitting at the table looked up at him for the first time.

'Why not?' he enquired wearily. 'Is something wrong?'

'My throat, sir . . .'

'Then report sick, for God's sake.'

'Yes, sir.'

There was no point whatever in trying to explain that he had already reported sick several times, to no avail. The bored young medical officer, the perfunctory examinations, the scribbled notes bearing the mystic phrase 'mist. expect. sed.'

'Should clear up soon. Medicine and duty.' Religiously swallowing the thick, strange-tasting stuff, which had no discernible effect.

Explanations were not required, called for, nor welcome, in this cold, cavernous place, where the damp chill nibbled through everyone's shivering flesh into their very bones, despite their heavy greatcoats, as they stood at ease in ranks of three, waiting for their names to be called, their turn to spring to attention, and march smartly forward to the trestle table, where NCOs deftly counted and made entries, and the flying officer, his shoulders hunched against the cold, super-vised, wishing to Christ that it was all over and he could get back to the comforting fug of his office at the end of a row of huts, and crouch over the coke stove until he unfroze. Behind the table, the warrant officer hovered suspiciously.

Aircraftsman Second Class David Kirby, 1432692, scooped the money on the trestle table into his left hand, saluted again, about turned, and marched back to his place in the ranks, where he would remain until Pay Parade was over. The warrant officer eyed him bleakly, still not entirely convinced that authority had not been slyly mocked in some fashion he could not prove.

Heaton Park was no more than a transit camp. The days were artificially filled out with parades, drill and lectures they had all heard before at ITW, where they had been delivered and listened to with considerably more keenness. Nothing really happened at Heaton Park. They were there to await their overseas drafts, no more. When his flight was finally dismissed for the day, Kirby made his way to his living quarters, one of the many hastily erected Nissen huts which were scattered around the park.

Roy Harrison, a large, cheerful, fresh-faced man older than David, was sitting on his bed, writing a letter. David nodded a reply to his greeting, sat on his own bed, polished his boots and buttons, and assembled his small kit ready for the morning.

Anyone who wished to report sick was obliged to present himself on Sick Parade at such an ungodly early hour that any sane man not genuinely unwell would much prefer the warmth, if not comfort, of his bed. Presumably, that was the idea.

Roy completed another page, and started on the fourth. He was wearing his greatcoat over his uniform.

'Shan't be long,' Roy said. 'I must finish this letter to Sylvia. There's a rumour we may be getting Christmas leave.'

'That's just shithouse gen,' David whispered sibilantly.

'Sure you feel like it?' Roy asked, writing busily at the same time.

'Better than hanging around this dump. I'm all right.'

It was freezing cold inside the Nissen hut, with its rows of RAF-issue iron beds. A cadet was squatting by the iron stove, trying to get it to burn and generate heat. The stove refused to produce anything but smoke, and the cadet was cursing it monotonously. The NAAFI would be equally inhospitable.

Greatcoat collars turned up against the bitter night cold, Kirby and Roy Harrison stood outside the gates of Heaton Park until the hooded, masked headlights of the bus appeared, the first trace of light in the blackness for minutes. They climbed on board, and rode through the grimy streets of Salford and into Manchester. The conductor gave Kirby two tickets and change for half a crown by the dim light of a small torch which he wore attached to his coat.

The blackout was absolute. Not so much as a chink of light showed from windows religiously shuttered or curtained with thick, heavy material. Such precautions were second nature. Patrolling air raid wardens would hammer on the doors of any offenders who allowed the faintest trace of light to seep from their homes.

There was no moon that night, and a thick layer of cloud shut out any residual dim starlight. Kirby, having been tested at the Air Crew Reception Centre in St John's Wood, knew that his night vision was excellent but, even so, when they got off the bus all he could see were occasional vague shapes, and he stumbled momentarily on a pavement which was unexpectedly uneven.

There was almost no traffic, even when they crossed a main road. The private motorist was non-existent. Only a few essential categories such as doctors, farmers and veterinary surgeons could obtain a petrol ration, and faced prosecution if caught using it for pleasure purposes. Taxis received only enough petrol for a few hours' work a day, and the drivers eked it out by picking and choosing their fares, and doubling up whenever possible.

Dimly, Kirby could just discern the faint shapes of the street lights suspended overhead, which had gone out on 3 September 1939, and seemed likely to remain out indefinitely. Memories of lighted streets and illuminated shop window displays, once taken for granted, belonged to an ever receding past. Darkness was the norm now.

In Manchester itself, the surviving pubs near the bomb-flattened central area of Piccadilly were busier and livelier than in industrial Salford.

In one of the noisy bars packed with servicemen, Kirby and Roy Harrison unfroze and, after a while, fell into conversation with a couple of girls. The presence of attractive females always brought a cheery grin to Roy Harrison's face and a wicked glint to his bright eyes, which most girls responded to, and the fair one obviously liked him. Kirby found himself huskily trying to communicate with the dark one, who was Joan Norris she told him, without much success, given the state of his voice and the din of conversation all around him, but she chattered on without requiring much prompting, and Kirby was quite content to nod and listen.

The pub was an island of warmth and cheerfulness, and when at nine o'clock the landlord put up the single bottle of whisky which comprised all the spirits he would sell that night,

Kirby by chance happened to be standing in the right place at the bar, and was triumphantly able to beat the mob which suddenly surged to the counter, and emerged with four singles, which happily turned into two doubles, since the girls did not like whisky.

The Scotch temporarily lubricated Kirby's throat, and made him feel better. They stayed until closing time, and then they saw the girls home. Roy Harrison and the fair girl had vanished into the darkness five minutes before and Kirby and Joan were alone when they arrived at the street where she lived.

She drew him into the blackness of a shop doorway. 'Let's say goodnight here,' she said.

Kirby discovered that, in two seconds flat, she must have undone the buttons of her coat. His right hand was guided on to a firm and extremely shapely breast. It could, he thought glumly, have been a lump of wet dough, for all the effect it had on him. The slim body under the dress was pressing itself against him urgently, her arms were round his neck, her lips were open and soft, her tongue inside his mouth. What Joan Norris expected, and wanted to happen next, was only too clear.

As well ask him to pole-vault over the rooftops. Embarrassed and useless as he was, Kirby felt dreadful. Her youthful, desirable flesh was his for the taking, yet he experienced not a flicker of answering desire himself.

He managed to extricate himself without, he hoped, hurting her pride too much, by stressing his unknown illness, how unwell he was now feeling, and the necessity of reporting sick long before dawn the following morning.

Joan buttoned her coat up, none too pleased.

The buses had stopped running, and Kirby set out on the long walk back to Heaton Park. The cheering effect of the whisky had worn off, and he was feeling more than a little sorry for himself.

At ACRC in London, there had been a widely credited rumour that 'they' were putting bromide in the tea. The evidence for this belief was empirical, and depended upon the common observation that youthful sexual urges had subsided into little more than nothing. In reality, this might have had rather more to do with the fact that the newly joined cadets were marched, drilled, exercised, bullied, harassed, vaccinated, inoculated, and generally kept on the go, usually at the double, from dawn to dusk. After this their time was their own, apart from boning obstinately dull boots until they shone like mirrors, polishing buttons, starching their white cap flashes, lining packs with cardboard so that they were square, enduring kit inspections and fire drills, scrubbing out their quarters, and sundry other devices to pass the time invented by seemingly sadistic NCOs, until at last they fell exhausted into bed, to be awoken by reveille at five-thirty the next morning.

Nevertheless, the legend of bromide in the tea persisted.

However, if the Royal Air Force was in truth administering drugs by stealth, it appeared to have little faith in its own subterfuge.

'Right, you lot!' the corporal had bellowed, as they stood at attention in the car park where they had been drilling all that Saturday afternoon. 'Listen to me. You've got the rest of the weekend off, except for Church Parade tomorrow, of course. Now I know what you randy buggers are like. You'll be trying to find a piece of skirt, and some of you'd put your cocks where I wouldn't put my walking stick. You just remember, any skirt that'll look at you, it won't be just second-hand or third-hand, there'll have been dozens before you, bloody hundreds more likely. Are you with me? Do you hear me?' The way he was shouting, Kirby thought, he could have been heard at Lord's Cricket Ground, and that was half a mile away. 'My advice to you is,' the corporal continued at full volume, 'keep your bloody pricks to yourselves. But if you can't, if you must shove it up between some disgusting tart's legs, then you visit the ET room as soon as you get back. And no messing. Is that understood? I don't want anyone in my flight going down with the bloody clap.'

The Early Treatment room was a cubicle just inside the main entrance of their billet. Formerly a block of mansion flats, it now housed air crew cadets, six or eight to each room, stripped bare of furnishings and floor coverings.

Inside the ET room were packets, on which were instructions on how to use the contents.

'Christ,' muttered one cadet, appalled as he took in what he was supposed to do to himself in the event of misadventure. 'It's enough to put you off the whole thing for life.'

But even during the exhausting rigours of ACRC, Kirby thought, as he entered the darkened Nissen hut and felt his way to his bed, even with the reiterated brutal directions to the ET room on his mind, if he had ever found himself alone with an aroused girl, he was positive that he would have felt something even if his mind had directed him to do nothing about it. Surely he should have felt *something*? Not just — nothing. As though he had been neutered.

Perhaps, Kirby reflected, as he undressed, he was more ill than he had imagined.

Roy Harrison was in bed and nearly asleep. 'Mine had a lovely little bum,' he muttered, with drowsy nostalgia.

The sky was still pitch black when Kirby walked, only half awake, across Heaton Park, early next morning. There were times, during those winter weeks at Heaton Park, when he felt like some troglodyte, who rarely glimpsed daylight, let alone the sun.

On Sick Parade, as usual, were a bunch of others with their small packs, who looked as wretched as Kirby felt. The medical orderlies wore the mien of men who were not deceived by such histrionics. The unspoken attitude appeared to be that anyone who reported sick was a malingerer until it was proved otherwise. 'Like by falling down dead,' the cadet next to Kirby said gloomily, *sotto voce*. 'If we were all sickening for the plague, they'd never believe it.'

The medical officer looked up as Kirby's turn came, and he went in.

'Haven't I seen you before?' he asked.

'Yes, sir,' Kirby whispered. The MO was about twenty-five, and must have joined the RAF straight from medical school.

Kirby had seen carbon copies of him before. They had sat lolling in hard-backed chairs, while he waited with other cadets in a seemingly unending line in the basement of Viceroy Court, opposite Regent's Park.

As each cadet advanced to the waiting doctor, the ritual was the same.

'Drop your trousers. Lift your balls up. Right. Next. Drop your trousers. Lift your balls up. Over there. Next. Drop your trousers. Lift your balls up . . .'

'Over there' meant going to an orderly who was armed with a large object like a drumstick with which he swabbed the inside of the victim's thighs with gentian violet, which fully lived up to its name. The purple stain took forever to fade from the skin, but it effectively dealt with sweat rash caused by constant exertion in their heavy serge uniforms.

The bored irritability of those young medicos was probably understandable. Having studied at such centres of excellence as Guy's, or Bart's, or the Middlesex, succeeded in qualifying and, stuffed with all the most up to date knowledge of modern medicine their distinguished professors could impart, having chosen to serve in the Royal Air Force, it must have been somewhat disillusioning to find themselves, not treating the shattered wounded of the front line squadrons, but obliged interminably to study the genitals of endless queues of healthy young men in search of sweat rash or venereal disease, however necessary that task might be.

'It's probably an old wives' tale,' the MO said, distancing himself from the ludicrous idea with a smile, 'but you could try sleeping with an old sock round your neck, I suppose.'

'I have, sir,' Kirby whispered. 'You suggested that last time.'

The MO sighed.

'Well, I don't know what the devil we can do with you,' he said, 'I really don't.'

'Perhaps, if I had a spell in sick bay, sir?' Kirby offered.

The young MO considered this daring proposal for several long seconds, pursing his lips doubtfully. Finally, he shook his head helplessly.

'Yes, I suppose so,' he said reluctantly.

When Kirby emerged with his chit, it was quite clear that the medical orderlies considered that their gullible, inexperienced medical officer had been grossly deceived, but regrettably there was nothing they could do about it.

Kirby caught a bus to sick bay, which turned out to be a large house converted into a small hospital, a mile away from Heaton Park.

There, to Kirby's relief, the attitude was markedly and reassuringly different. The squadron leader who meticulously examined him was considerably older, around forty, and gained David's instant respect, since he wore not only medical insignia on his lapels, but also the coveted wings of a qualified pilot on his left breast.

He smiled at his new patient, and listened intently to the whispered answers to his questions. His voice was quiet, and when he went into a huddle with the nursing sister, although Kirby strained his ears to hear what they were saying, he could not.

Finally, the sister nodded, and turned to David.

'All right, Kirby,' she said, briskly. 'Come with me.'

On the morning of the tenth day, the squadron leader perched himself on Kirby's bed, with one of his friendly smiles, and said, 'Well, old chap, how are you feeling?'

'Fine, sir, thank you,' Kirby said. 'What was wrong with me?' He had still not quite become accustomed to the sound of his own voice, to being able to speak normally again.

The squadron leader said, 'I know what it wasn't. It wasn't tonsilitis or laryngitis, among other possibilities.' He was referring obliquely to the diagnoses hazarded by the young MO at Heaton Park. 'As to what it was,' he went on, 'I could produce some long, impressive name, if you like, give you some gobbledegook, but that would be complete bull. The truth is, I don't know. Presumably some kind of relatively mild virus infection for which there's not yet a specific treatment, but there's very little the young, healthy body can't deal with, given rest.'

16

'It won't interfere with my training?' Kirby hoped, anxiously.

The squadron leader shook his head.

'No,' he said, firmly. 'No question of that, although I'm not prepared to send you back to Heaton Park just yet. So you either stay here for another week, or, alternatively,' he mused thoughtfully, 'if I thought you were well enough to travel I could send you on sick leave.'

Such a glorious possibility had never crossed Kirby's mind. It was 22 December, he realized. With any luck, he could be home that night. He willed his face to project an image of glowing, restored, perfect good health.

'I'm fine, sir,' he asserted. 'It's only a question of sitting on a train.'

Kirby dressed hurriedly, packed, said his grateful goodbyes to the sister and nurses, collected his authorization, and set out for Heaton Park, more tramping round, and a good deal of waiting, while his leave pass was made out, and his travel warrant and ration coupons issued.

'It's all right for some,' the flight sergeant grumbled sourly. He was not going on leave. Nor was anyone else, it seemed. The rumour about Christmas leave had been born only of fond hopes, and vigorously nurtured by wishful thinking.

By now, it was late afternoon, and growing dark again. The bus dawdled infuriatingly, but he just managed to get to the station in time to catch the last train which might make his connection. It was crowded with servicemen and women, there was scarcely standing room much less a spare seat, and he crammed himself into a corridor along with the rest of the human cattle, glad to be aboard and at least to have a partition he could lean against.

The train clattered, swayed, and bumped along, groaning in an apparent effort to gain momentum. Whenever it appeared to be in danger of working up speed, it creaked complainingly to a halt, sometimes at a station, more often in the middle of nowhere, and stood for minutes at a time, the engine hissing asthmatically, while the lucky ones with seats peered round blinds in the dimly lighted carriages at the impenetrable blackness outside, and speculated as to where they might be. It was the kind of journey they were all accustomed to.

The train was predictably late into Euston Station. Time-tables were more expressions of pious hopes than of serious probability, and David Kirby missed his connection at Waterloo, which left the so-called milk train. No one in their right mind travelled on the milk train if they could help it, and it was nearly six-thirty in the morning when the engine, wheezing with relief, finally clanked into Southampton Terminus station, just outside the Old Docks.

Kirby settled his pack on his back, and set out on the three-mile walk, through the bomb sites of East Street, Above Bar, and Commercial Road, along Millbrook Road where the bomb damage diminished, and into Foundry Lane near which he lived – named, he supposed, after some vanished, long forgotten piece of industrial enterprise. The first trams of the day were running now, and a trickle of bicycles, lights shielded as the regulations demanded, was building up, taking their riders to work in the remaining factories.

Edith Kirby was briskly shaking a mat outside the front door, when her son arrived. She looked at him, frowning in surprise.

'Hullo,' she said. 'What are you doing home?'

'Christmas leave,' Kirby said. 'Last minute. Didn't have time to send a telegram.' They had no telephone. None of the people Kirby had grown up with had a telephone in their homes. 'Hullo, Mum.'

He put his arms round her and hugged her, and received a reluctant peck on the cheek. He followed his mother indoors.

'I wish I'd known you were coming,' she complained. 'I'd have had some breakfast ready for you. As it is, I'll have to go in five minutes, and there's practically no tea left. You can have some toast if you like, but be careful with the margarine, it's nearly all gone.'

'Don't worry,' Kirby said, patiently. 'You go. I can look after myself.' Mrs Kirby worked at the British Restaurant, which had been set up underneath the Guildhall where meals including 'Shepherd's Pie' could be bought for a shilling or so.

The pie would consist of potato with a few traces of meat of dubious origin. Men and women who worked in factories with canteens had one extra main meal a day on top of their meagre food rations, and they could get by. British Restaurants were an attempt to provide a similar facility for office workers, and shoppers. 'You'd better have this,' Kirby said, handing over his ration coupons. His mother's eyes brightened. It was surprising what a difference even a few days' additional rations made. It was those who lived on their own who suffered most.

Mrs Kirby's weekly food ration comprised four ounces of bacon; two ounces of butter plus four ounces of margarine or lard; two ounces of tea; eight ounces of sugar; one shilling and tuppence worth of meat, which amounted to about thirteen ounces or less, depending on price; and a cheese ration which varied considerably during the war, but averaged around two or three ounces a week.

In addition, per month, she was entitled to one egg; one packet of dried eggs; eight ounces of jam; and twelve ounces of chocolate or sweets.

Milk was 'controlled' at around two or two and a half pints per person per week. Potatoes, bread and fresh vegetables were not rationed, but the latter were scarce and distributed on a controlled basis.

Tinned and packet foods were on 'points'. Mrs Kirby was entitled to twenty 'points' per four-week period. One packet of breakfast cereal, one tin of pilchards, half a pound of chocolate biscuits, one pound of rice, and one tin of grade three salmon, added up to twenty 'points', and so would exhaust Mrs Kirby's entitlement for a whole month. At twenty-four points for a one pound tin, stewed steak was a luxury available only to housewives with several ration books at their disposal.

For a nation of tea drinkers, the meagre ration of two ounces a week was probably the greatest hardship. Otherwise, the draconian rationing system equalized hunger, as it were; no one starved, and the health of the British people actually improved, which said much about the pre-war British diet, inequalities and deprivations of the unemployed and the poorly paid.

Kirby did not bother with weak tea or toast with a scrape of margarine. He went to his room, and crawled thankfully into bed, exhausted.

He had enjoyed the air force until Heaton Park, but now it was good to be home again, even if only for a little while. Although he would have to leave on New Year's Day, at least he would be home for Christmas, and he knew how much that would mean to his mother.

When he had been a small boy, he had gone through a period when he had thought that her manner, brisk at best, sharp to the point of harshness at worst, meant that she did not care for him, that he was unwanted. As he grew older, he realized that she was constitutionally incapable of showing affection in the way he witnessed in other boys' homes from other boys' mothers, that for good or ill she could not, and would never, allow her real feelings to show. There was probably, he supposed, some reason, but if so it was lost in the far off mists of her own childhood.

Over the years, he had adjusted, and he now knew that she did indeed love him deeply, even if that love would only ever be demonstrated by making his bed or sewing on his buttons, or cooking his meals, and never ever by means of words, or a careless, unforced embrace.

It was strange, Kirby reflected drowsily, for locked up in her somewhere was an urgent necessity to give and receive love, forever barred to her in its most natural form. He remembered some parent who had met her casually on a charabanc outing to the seaside, and whom he had subsequently overheard trying to identify her. 'The one in brown,' the man had said. 'The woman with the kindly eyes.'

That was where her love and kindness and concern resided, in her eyes, still a fine, pale blue, which had probably been her outstanding feature when she was a girl, although the only existing record of her youthful prettiness was a single, fading sepia, rather unnaturally self-conscious wedding photograph.

Now, her hair was greying, and her lined, weary face showed her age and her sadness. She was fifty-six years old. 'You were a surprise packet,' his father used to say jocularly. 'We weren't expecting you.'

That was when Charles was still alive. His father's jocularity had diminished after he died.

'Don't cry, Jim,' Kirby remembered his mother saying, helplessly. It was after the funeral. The handful of friends and relatives had gone. His father sat at the kitchen table, his shoes polished, his black tie neatly knotted, clutched his face suddenly, and burst into unrestrained, racking, heart-rending sobbing. The powerfully built, broad-chested man sat there and crumpled, the tears running down his face. 'Please don't cry,' Edith Kirby said again. She reached out her hand and almost touched her husband's shaking shoulders, but then hesitated and withdrew it. 'What's the use?' she said flatly. 'It doesn't do any good.'

David Kirby's father palmed the tears from his cheeks and stared at her with eyes which were already filling again.

'First of all it was the war to end wars,' he gasped, half choking. 'Now it's happening again. If only it could have been me . . . but not him . . . oh, Christ . . . not my son . . .'

Chapter Two

AC 2 David Kirby caught the tram into town, and got off in Above Bar, opposite the Regal Cinema, which was still standing, unlike a large part of the town centre.

During his absence, an improvised, temporary, single-storey shack had been erected on the cleared site of the bank.

The original premises had gone up in flames with the rest of the block during the blitz on Southampton in 1940. The reinforced strongroom, however, had withstood the weight of falling masonry, and survived intact.

They had burrowed in, and extracted the ledgers, forms, and cash, while Mr Stevens, the manager, had resourcefully rented rooms in the relatively undamaged building across the road, from which business was carried on as usual. Kirby pushed open the flimsy door, and went in. A counter had been built from hardboard nailed on to battens. Behind, was a motley collection of desks salvaged from somewhere. As ever, there were not enough stools to go round.

Kirby caught Lorna Barton's eye, as she raised her head from a ledger, lifted his hand in greeting and smiled. She smiled back, her eyebrows rising in surprise. Mr Stevens saw her expression, frowned slightly, and twisted his head, bird-like, to detect its source.

'Hullo, Kirby,' he said. Christian names were not in use in the bank, except between junior staff. 'On leave? You were enjoying yourself on the beaches of Newquay, the last time I heard.'

Mr Stevens cherished a fixed and unshakable belief that, by and large, those in the services were engaged in having a good time, leaving those unfortunate enough to be left behind, like him, to suffer unsung and unregarded.

Kirby withdrew ten pounds, pretty well his life savings, and asked after Hemmings, who had been a cashier when he was a junior. 'He came in last month,' Mr Stevens said. 'On leave *again*. He's in Coastal Command, a flight lieutenant. Running a car now, if you don't mind . . .' Air crew were entitled to a small petrol ration. Mr Stevens' Austin 10 had long since been laid up for lack of petrol, and was on blocks in his garage.

Kirby took his money, and went to a jeweller's which had only been half destroyed, and was operating from the remaining, boarded-up half.

Inside, he inspected the pitiful display. He really needed a new wristwatch. His own dated back to his school days, and was becoming erratic, but they only had three watches in stock, priced at eighteen, twenty-two, and twenty-five pounds. Such astronomical prices belonged to the land of dreams.

Instead he studied bracelets, and a few charms, but finally chose a brooch, a small, enamel replica of RAF pilot's wings, and a neat necklace of cultured pearls, which at least came in a halfway presentable-looking box. In search of some Christmas wrapping paper, he walked to the temporary Woolworth's store, reached over a kind of wooden foot-bridge from the pavement.

He went back to the bank and waited until Lorna Barton emerged. Lorna was nineteen years old. She had straight features, and shoulder-length, wavy brown hair, which somehow made an attractive combination. She had been his girlfriend since 23 November 1940, eight weeks after she had started work at the bank.

On that Saturday afternoon, Kirby, shopping in town for a new shirt, had run into Lorna by chance. When they came out of the store together it was dark outside, but there were crowds of homeward bound shoppers, and queues were forming outside the cinemas.

Apart from the blackout, the lack of street lights, it was much like a normal scene before the war. Trams creaked and clanked in line astern along their tracks, buses overtook them, there were even still more than a few motor cars around.

The air raid warning had moaned into life some minutes before but no one took any notice. Southampton had not been bombed since the summer daylight attacks during the Battle of Britain, when the German targets had been the docks, and the Supermarine works at Woolston, where Spitfires were built.

As winter set in, warnings at night had become frequent, and planes often droned high overhead, pursued by ineffective anti-aircraft fire, but they were always on their way to targets in the Midlands or the North. Hours later, they droned back again, on their way home, when there was finally the steady sound of the All Clear. The inhabitants of Southampton had taken to ignoring these intrusions. The only danger to them came from falling fragments of anti-aircraft shells. In due course, they would learn from the wireless or the daily newspapers where those bombers had been.

On the night of 23 November 1940, the warning had sounded earlier than usual, and the approaching anti-aircraft fire seemed to be heavier, but Kirby and Lorna hardly noticed. They had reached the Junction, when it suddenly became clear that tonight was going to be different.

An eerie, harsh light, almost approaching the intensity of day, illuminated the town centre. For a fraction of a second, Kirby blinked, not immediately comprehending why the blackout had suddenly been lifted, why he could see every detail, passing trams and buses grinding and squealing to a halt, the expressions on the faces of everyone around him momentarily frozen, like his own. Then, as though a cine film had begun to roll again, he saw them. Clusters of brilliant flares, leisurely descending from on high. Moments later came the whistle of the first falling bombs.

'I think we'd better find a shelter,' Kirby said. He gripped Lorna's arm, and hurried her across the road.

Shelters had been erected and dug all over the town. Some were brick-built structures on the surface, others, in the parks,

were half below ground, their entrances shielded from blast by
sandbags.

Kirby had never consciously noticed the one in the park
behind the Cenotaph, but he remembered it now. He guided
Lorna along the path, and inside.

Soon it was jammed to overflowing.

'Standing room only inside,' called the inevitable wag to
breathless new arrivals.

They sat on the slatted wooden seats, crushed up against
each other, listening to the cacophony outside, the incessant
guns, the deeper slam and whoomp of high explosive bombs
and, quite soon, the sinister sharp crackling of raging fires.

'Incendiaries,' someone who was near enough to the
entrance to be able to glimpse what was happening outside
reported, unnecessarily.

From where Kirby was sitting, halfway along that shelter
shaped like half a concrete cigar tube, he could see nothing
but the faces of those around him, the intent expressions as
they listened, trying to determine what the jumble of sounds
outside meant, all of them hostile and menacing, none of them
reassuring; the nervous scratch of matches as cigarettes were
lit; the cheerful fathead who tried to get a sing-song going. A
notable omission, compared with the daylight raids, was the
absence of machine-gun fire coupled with the roaring zoom of
diving, manoeuvring fighters. Where the hell were our night
fighters? There appeared to be none whatever up there in the
clear night sky. Didn't we have any? The Germans were
bombing at their leisure, untroubled by any effective opposition.

Whenever that rising, deepening whistle of falling bombs
kept on coming, gaining in unnerving intensity as though
targeted on them personally, the ones near the entrances
abandoned their bravado and crouched down, instinctively
covering their heads, and when the explosions were near
enough to shake the very ground in which the shelter was set,
Lorna shuddered, and turned her face into Kirby's shoulder.
He put his arm around her, protectively.

It seemed as though it would never end, but at last the

drone of the Junkers and the Heinkels slackened, became intermittent, and finally receded. The guns stopped firing. All they could hear was the steady, busy crackle of burning buildings.

For a while, they sat where they were, listening suspiciously, not convinced that it was really over. Then, starting low, rising to a steady pitch of relief came the All Clear.

Stretching, they stood up, easing aching limbs, only then realizing how cramped and stiff they were. Kirby had no idea how long it had lasted. His watch had stopped. He thought it must be about midnight.

Outside, even the inevitable wag was silenced. A gas main in London Road had been hit, and the flames leapt and scorched high into the air like some giant blowtorch. A nearby department store was blazing, and there was a crash and a rumble as the roof fell in. Silent trams stood among the rubble where they had been abandoned. One had been flung on its side, crushed and crumpled like a toy. The whole town seemed to be on fire. Above Bar was blocked, but Kirby glimpsed ambulances and fire tenders trying to inch their way round collapsed masonry. His father would have a busy night, he thought. He hoped he was all right, but there was no way of finding out. He could only wait. Meantime, he must get Lorna home. She lived in Shirley, only about half a mile from him.

They walked through the park and along Commercial Road. The pavement was a carpet of broken glass from shop windows, which crunched and splintered under their feet. Somehow it was that, trudging across glass too thickly strewn to be able to kick aside, trivial enough in itself compared with the fires and wrecked buildings and blocked streets they were walking away from, but it was that which finally brought home to David Kirby the unnatural, topsy-turvy nature of the world in which he was now living. The reality of war – it was walking on broken glass.

At the top of Four Post Hill, they turned into Shirley Road. Ahead of them it was dark again, like walking into a black tunnel, and it became clear that the whole of the town had not been destroyed after all.

Kirby took one last glance behind him. There were smaller fires scattered about in a random fashion, but he could now see that the raid had been largely concentrated on the town centre which, from here, looked like some vast bonfire, from which evil, swirling clouds of black smoke were rising.

From that moment onwards, it was taken for granted that Lorna was Kirby's girlfriend.

When he arrived home, his front door was open, the hall light off. Mrs Kirby was standing there.

'I was beginning to wonder where you'd got to,' she said. The house was undamaged. She had spent the raid sitting in the Anderson shelter in the garden.

'Any sign of Dad yet?' he asked.

Mrs Kirby shook her head.

'You go to bed,' she said. 'I'll wait up for him.'

'I'm not tired,' Kirby said, truthfully. 'Any tea going?'

It was six o'clock in the morning before the front door slammed, and Kirby's father came in, and sank into a chair. His eyes were bloodshot, his face blackened with smoke, exhaustion written into his creased cheeks.

'I reckon I'm too old for this lark,' he said.

'I told you that in the first place,' Mrs Kirby said, acidly. 'But you wouldn't listen, would you? I expect you want something to eat. And take those boots off. They're filthy.'

Before the war, Jim Kirby had been a driver with a firm which ran limousines for weddings, and funerals, and, less frequently, taking rich Americans disembarked from the *Aquitania* or the *Mauretania* on tours of the countryside.

When tips were good, Kirby's father sometimes brought home as much as four pounds in a single week, but such affluence was rare. More often it was nearer three and, during slack periods, less. Then Mrs Kirby's lips would tighten, and she would be prone to wonder aloud how she was expected to make ends meet.

'Think yourself lucky I'm not on the dole, my girl,' Mr Kirby would tell her.

But things were easier after Kirby's elder brother thankfully left his elementary school when he was fourteen, and started work on a milk round. Unlike David, Charles had no interest in school whatever. Cars were all he cared about. At fourteen, Charles knew more about the internal combustion engine than David ever learned years later in the air force.

As soon as he was old enough, his father taught Charles to drive, and then badgered his boss into giving him a job. Proudly, Charles donned the regulation black suit, the white shirt, the black tie, and stood before his father, similarly attired, on his first day at work.

His father chuckled.

'Tweedledum and Tweedledee,' he said.

When he was old enough to look back and see those vanished years in perspective, David Kirby thought that they had probably been the happiest in his father's life. He and his elder son were working for the same firm, both doing a job they enjoyed. They talked about the same things, they thought the same things, they had everything in common. They were more like brothers than father and son. The little house was a cheerful one and, with Charles paying for his keep and a bit more, Mrs Kirby could indulge in occasional luxuries, and was more relaxed, easy-going and smiling than Kirby could ever remember her.

Those days finally came to an end on the day war was declared, when they learned that Charles, who had been ordered to report to his unit, would not be coming back after all. Normal life had ended.

Like many people, the Kirbys could not afford to buy a wireless set, but Charles, to his father's wonderment, had built one, from a give-away plan in a magazine.

It was on that that they listened to the prime minister, his voice coming from the plywood fretted speaker, announcing that a state of war existed between this country and Germany.

'Well, that's it,' Mr Kirby said, switching the wireless off. He looked at his wife, who was silently peeling potatoes. 'I'd better see about joining the AFS, I suppose.'

For months now, the Auxiliary Fire Service had been advertising for volunteers. The regular fire service would never be able to cope on its own with the kind of air raids which were expected in the event of war.

'There's no need for that at your age,' Mrs Kirby said, sharply. 'You did your bit in the last war.'

'There's no point in arguing about it,' Mr Kirby said. 'I've made up my mind.'

David Kirby stood in the gallery overlooking the Assembly Hall, listening to the headmaster reading out the travel arrangements. The school was to be evacuated to Bournemouth.

'Aren't you coming with us, David?' his form master asked, surprised. 'Why not? You're exactly the sort of chap we want in the Sixth Form.'

When Kirby was ten years old, he had won a scholarship from his elementary school to a grammar school. His father viewed this achievement with some bewilderment. Grammar schools were for the sons of posh people, he obscurely felt. This was far from the truth. Nearly all those at David Kirby's school were scholarship boys, but there was always a certain lack of comprehension mixed up with his father's pride.

David had passed his school certificate examination with matriculation exemption, and until now he had seriously contemplated trying for one of the handful of scholarships to university.

'I shall get a job for the time being, sir,' he said, 'and then volunteer for the air force as soon as I can.'

'Well, perhaps you'll change your mind,' his form master sighed. 'You have considerable academic ability, David. It seems such a waste.'

The following week, David Kirby saw an advertisement in the local newspaper, answered it, and started work at the bank. His commencing salary was sixty-five pounds per annum.

On the nights of 30 November and 1 December 1940, the Luftwaffe attacked Southampton again, in even greater strength. It was on 30 November that the bank was burned down. David Kirby spent those two raids in the Anderson shelter with his mother.

The anti-aircraft fire was as enthusiastic and noisy as ever, the searchlights scoured the skies above the placidly floating barrage balloons, but Kirby, peering out of the shelter from time to time, came to the conclusion that, at night anyway, the guns were of little use, except perhaps to assure the population that they were at least trying. He saw the occasional bomber caught in the searchlights, but none were hit. Again, there were no night fighters.

Numbed and tired after the second consecutive night assault, they sat waiting for his father to come home. It was eight o'clock in the morning before the door knocker banged sharply.

Mrs Kirby knew as soon as she opened the door, and saw the fire officer standing there. Her lips tightened.

'Come in,' she said, and held the door open wide for him.

For the second time that year, Kirby stood beside his mother in Hollybrook Cemetery after a burial service, and watched a coffin being lowered into the ground. He turned, and led the way with his mother along the path, their feet crunching on the gravel, towards the funeral car, which had been provided free by Jim Kirby's former employer. Friends from the AFS were there, offering awkward, halting condolences. Mrs Kirby nodded her thanks, dry-eyed.

The body had remained in the mortuary until the funeral.

'Don't let her see him, son,' the fire officer had said to David Kirby, quietly. 'The roof was on fire when it fell in, and . . .' He gestured vaguely. '. . . well, it'd be best if she didn't see him.'

That night, Mrs Kirby busied herself in the scullery. She scoured saucepans, scraped and cleaned the oven of the gas stove, and finally got down on her hands and knees and commenced to scrub the stone floor.

Kirby hovered uneasily, looking down at her.

Mrs Kirby moved the bucket, sat back on her haunches,

and stared up at him. 'David, go somewhere else. You're getting on my nerves, standing there.'

An hour later, Mrs Kirby came in, sat down opposite him, and folded her hands in her lap.

'There's only you and me now,' she said, 'but there's still the rent to be paid, food to be bought, gas and electric money to find. Your wages won't keep us. I shall need to find a job. It'll have to be cleaning or washing dishes. I can turn my hand to that at least.'

Kirby wished that he could disagree, that he could offer some alternative, but he could not.

'It might not be for too long, Mum,' he said, encouragingly. 'When I'm in the air force, on a pilot's pay, I should be able to . . .'

'That's another thing,' his mother interrupted. 'You can stop there. I've lost a son and my husband. I think that's enough for any woman. Neither of them were obliged to do what they did, but now they're both dead, and you're all I've got left. Now I know what's in your mind, but you can be in the air force without flying. They can't make you fly. With your education, you could get into accounts or some ground job where you'd be safe. And that's what I want, David.'

She gazed at him, her face set and firm, but there was a moistness in those pale blue eyes which made Kirby's stomach turn over in pity.

'Mum,' he said, 'I think I'd promise almost anything except that. I can't tell you why I want to fly. I can't put it into words. I have to, and that's all I can say. I suppose I'm like Dad, I want to do the most I can. Not leave it all to other people.'

Mrs Kirby sighed, and shook her head in despair.

'Life never held too much for me and your father. But I had him to look after, and I had Charles, and I had you.' She shrugged helplessly. 'Now, all I've got left is you. If anything happened to you, David, I'd have nothing.'

'You don't have to worry about me, Mum,' Kirby said. 'I shall come through it all right.'

'That's what Charles said before he went to France,' his mother said. 'Near enough word for word.'

Kirby said, 'I'm sorry, but if they'll have me, I'm going to fly.'

Later, when the time came, he was called to the Air Crew Selection Centre in Oxford, and soon afterwards informed that he had been accepted for air crew training. But there would be a delay, caused in fact by bottlenecks in the training programme which was being hurriedly expanded and improvised in the face of steadily mounting losses.

Weeks dragged into months and David, still working at the bank, chafed impatiently. Mrs Kirby was relieved by what was, to her, this reprieve, although the news bulletins on the wireless upset her.

By then, Bomber Command's night assault on Germany was uncertainly gathering strength, but German defences against night attacks appeared to be more efficient than the British had been during the Blitz of 1940.

'Last night,' the level voice said from the loudspeaker, 'a strong force of RAF bombers attacked targets in Essen . . . thirty-one of our aircraft failed to return . . .'

'. . . Hanover . . . twenty of our aircraft failed to return . . .'

'. . . Frankfurt . . . twenty-nine of our aircraft failed to return . . .'

Mrs Kirby's lips would become pinched, her cheeks would pale, and she sought refuge in scrubbing, dusting, polishing, anything to take her mind off those fearful figures. Every time she heard them, as the dreadful toll was intoned night after night, she saw David in one of those burning, exploding bombers.

When David Kirby was finally ordered to report to Lord's Cricket Ground, his mother brushed some fluff off his jacket before he left to catch the train.

'Well, I'll say goodbye then,' she said, briskly. 'Take care of yourself.'

Chapter Three

Mrs Kirby had decorated the living room with holly and paper streamers, and from someone at work she had acquired a small Christmas tree. Some other contact had come up with a chicken, and she had even managed to conjure up sufficient dried fruit to make a Christmas pudding.

It had been their custom to open presents first thing on Christmas morning, and Kirby was up as early as his mother.

'Happy Christmas, Mum,' he said.

'And you, my son.'

As always, she accepted his kiss reluctantly, her body taut, instinctively, if slightly, pulling away from him. David gave her a smile, squeezed her shoulders, and picked up the parcels, which he had left beside the Christmas tree. Nothing was ever going to change her now.

'Two presents?' She was astonished. 'Both for me? I hope you haven't been spending too much money though, David.'

'No, Mum,' Kirby said patiently. 'Just open them.'

She was delighted with the handbag.

'Exactly what I need most,' she said. 'My old one's falling to pieces. Well, I never. How did you know?'

'Lorna suggested it,' Kirby admitted.

She studied his second present with rather more reserve.

'Yes, very nice,' she said, neutrally. 'But perhaps Lorna should have this, not me.'

Kirby said, 'I'm your son. It's so that people know what I'm doing.'

'Well, if that's what you'd like . . .' She pinned the enamel replica of RAF pilot's wings on to her jumper, and peered

33

down at her bosom for a moment. 'It's not that I'm not proud of you, I hope you know that, it's just . . .' She broke off, and handed him a package. 'This is yours,' she said. 'Something useful.'

Kirby opened the small box, and stared at the contents.

'Mum . . . good God . . . where on earth . . . ?'

'I knew you needed one,' Mrs Kirby said, pleased with herself.

The case was stainless steel, but the wristwatch was Swiss made, and of good quality.

'It must have cost the earth,' Kirby said.

'It's second-hand,' his mother told him. 'One of the cooks at work, it was her husband's, and he wanted to sell it.'

'It's marvellous,' Kirby said, sincerely. 'Mum, thank you. Thanks very much . . .'

'Yes, well I can't stand about chattering,' his mother said. Expressions of gratitude always embarrassed her intensely. 'Dinner won't cook itself.'

Later, Kirby gave himself a whisky, and managed to entice her to have a glass of Ruby Port. He had managed to persuade the local off licence to disgorge the two bottles from under the counter.

'It doesn't seem quite right in the middle of the morning,' she said, doubtfully. 'Still, I suppose it is Christmas Day, after all.'

She made no mention of going to morning service. Her church-going had just survived Charles' death, but had ended when his father was killed. She could not reconcile those two brutal, random deaths and the constant fear she felt for her younger son with the concept of a gentle, loving and merciful God.

'That was wonderful,' Kirby said. Only a few chicken bones remained on his plate.

'There's plenty left to have cold tomorrow too,' Mrs Kirby said. 'I refuse to open a tin of Spam on Boxing Day, not for Hitler or anyone else.'

Kirby had discreetly kept her glass of port topped up, and she was relaxed, something approaching a smile on her lips.

She said, 'I shall be getting quite tipsy.' She sipped the stuff, which he found unbearably sweet and sickly, and watched David pour himself another Scotch without comment. 'It is good to have you home, David,' she said, her tongue loosened by Ruby Port. 'It would have been a miserable old Christmas without you, I can tell you.'

'And for me at Heaton Park,' Kirby said.

'But you'll be starting your flying soon, I suppose,' she sighed. 'Where do you think they'll send you?'

Kirby said, 'Canada, South Africa, Southern Rhodesia. Shan't know which till the last minute.'

Flying training to wings standard was carried out abroad, away from the dangers of unpredictable English weather, and intruding German fighters.

As the afternoon wore on, and the Ruby Port wore off, Mrs Kirby became silent and withdrawn. Kirby tried to rekindle her previous happier mood, but she merely sat there staring blankly at nothing, without answering.

Finally, she said, irritably, 'I'm thinking, David. About other Christmases when we were all together. Your father, well, at least he was fifty-five. He'd lived most of his life. But Charles, with the best years still before him . . .' She shook her head. 'And why? He could have gone into munitions. I know lots of men of his age who've done that. Still living at home, and making good money too, more than they've ever earned before in their lives.'

Charles had come home in the spring of 1939, with the news that he had signed on for the Territorial Army. Mrs Kirby had looked at him as though he had suddenly gone mad.

'What on earth possessed you to do a thing like that?'

'It's only a question of a few drills in the evenings, and summer camp every year,' Charles told her, reassuringly. 'It'll be fun, and a bit of extra money too.'

Summer camp never materialized. The Territorial Army was mobilized before war was declared. A few weeks later, Charles was in France with his unit.

When the Germans struck with their Blitzkrieg in 1940 and

the British Army retreated towards the Channel ports, Charles was seriously wounded by strafing German fighters.

They got him to the beaches, where he received such makeshift medical attention as was possible under the shelling and bombing, and eventually, delirious with pain, on to a boat, and back to Dover. But by then, many days had passed since those low flying Messerschmitts had suddenly roared across the hedgerows, and he had uselessly dived for cover. His wounds had become gangrenous. He died in hospital.

There had been a twelve-year gap between David and Charles. They were almost of different generations. David had just been really getting to know his elder brother as a fellow human being, when he put on his khaki uniform, and said, 'Goodbye, kid brother. Be back when this lot's over.'

Just the same, David had learned enough to know that he admired his brother, his strength, his simplicity, his kindness.

Kirby said, 'I know how you feel, Mum, but brooding over it won't change anything.'

'You don't know how I feel at all,' his mother said, her face and body angular. 'Otherwise you wouldn't have insisted on this flying nonsense.'

'Hazel and Maurice have decided to get married,' Lorna said, as they walked along. It was Boxing Day. She was wearing the string of cultured pearls he had bought for her.

Her sister was a year older than Lorna, and had been engaged to Maurice for eighteen months. Before Kirby joined the RAF, they had sometimes gone out together as a foursome.

They were heading for Lordswood, a quiet area of gorse and trees with rambling footpaths, behind the municipal golf course. On past summer days, they had often strolled along those unpopulated paths. Kirby glanced at the gates of Hollybrook Cemetery as they walked past. On Christmas Eve, he had laid flowers on the two graves, for all the use that was.

'I haven't thanked you properly for my present,' he said, lightly, putting his arm round her. Lorna had given him a pair of cuff-links. She accepted his kiss, but her lips were closed and cool. He let her go, and they walked on.

'You'll soon be posted abroad, I expect,' she said, thought-fully. 'How long will you be away?'

'About eight months,' Kirby said.

'There's something I ought to tell you before you go,' Lorna said. 'I want to be straight with you.'

Kirby listened. He was not too surprised. He had half guessed already from the tenor of her letters, the slight, almost indiscernible distance which had been between them, since he had unexpectedly walked into the bank, and raised his hand in greeting.

Over the past few months, Lorna had been doing voluntary work at the military hospital at Netley. There, she had met a soldier, a Canadian, recuperating after being wounded.

'He loves me,' Lorna said.

Kirby nodded. He understood perfectly. Early on, he had discovered that Lorna wanted to be loved. Nearly all the films they went to see together were about love, romantic splendid love, usually at first sight, consummated eventually with a kiss, on which THE END was superimposed.

That was what Lorna craved, that kind of immediate rhapsodic, beautiful love.

'He loves me,' Lorna said, again. 'And you never have, David, not really. You do understand, don't you?'

'I hope it works out for you,' Kirby said, truthfully. 'I hope you'll be happy.'

He was, he realized, somewhat relieved. The war was grinding on relentlessly; within a year or so he would be flying in an operational squadron. Best if there was no one else to worry about his safety. His mother was enough.

On New Year's Eve, he was lying on the Victorian sofa, an ugly but supremely comfortable object on which to read.

He was halfway through Dostoevsky's *The Idiot*. When he was a boy, his mother had continually complained, 'You've always got your nose stuck in a book' and 'Don't read when you're eating. It's rude.' Now, she had become accustomed to it, or given up, or both. Kirby had been much impressed by

Crime and Punishment, having found his way to it via Tolstoy's *War and Peace*.

Mrs Kirby drew the blackout curtains, switched the single overhead light on, and looked at the clock.

'If you're going out with Lorna tonight, you'd better get yourself ready,' she said.

'I'm not,' Kirby said. 'We shan't be seeing each other any more.'

'Oh,' Mrs Kirby said. 'I'm sorry to hear that. She's called in to see me nearly every Sunday while you've been away. I shall miss her little visits. It'll be more lonely than ever for me now, if I can't look forward to seeing Lorna now and then.'

She gazed at Kirby reproachfully, and retreated to her own private haven, the scullery.

It was late in the afternoon of New Year's Day when Kirby arrived back at Heaton Park. He was trudging across the parade ground when a deep authoritative voice hailed him.

'Hey, Dave. Just a minute!'

Kirby turned and waited, as Smithy approached him. Graham Smith was one of the several former policemen in his flight, a heavily built, burly man with a moustache, who must have been an impressive figure on the beat. He wore the lanyard which denoted that he was a flight leader.

'We're on the next draft,' Smithy said. 'But your name's not on the list. It all happened while you were on leave.'

Trust the bloody air force, Kirby thought bitterly. He had been hanging around for weeks, and as soon as he turned his back . . .

'Where are you going?' he asked.

'America,' Smithy said, grinning broadly.

'Are you serious? America? It's not Canada?'

'The good old USA,' Smithy said. 'That's us. Still, I reckon you'd rather wait for the next draft,' he said slyly.

'Up yours, Smithy,' Kirby said. 'But thanks for the tip.'

The lethargy which this dump imbued suddenly gone, Kirby raced across the parade ground, to try and persuade the flight sergeant to restore his name to the list. He shot an anxious glance at his new wristwatch as he ran, and prayed that Chiefy would not have sloped off early, which he often did.

Something was happening at last. Kirby could not bear the thought of not being on the next boat.

'Be there, you fat, lazy bastard,' he muttered to himself, and banged open the door to the Flight Office.

Chapter Four

The logistics involved in putting several hundred bombers over a target in Germany were formidable: repairing and servicing aircraft, replacing dead crews, bombing up, fuelling, meticulous briefings, and countless other precise details which called for exact compliance by thousands of men and women of many different trades, from the chief of air staff to the humblest erk emptying the Elsan toilets.

For a service capable of such warlike efficiency, the Royal Air Force, Kirby reflected wearily, not for the first time, made remarkably heavy weather out of moving a few hundred men a short distance from A to B, in this case the thirty-five-odd miles from Manchester to Liverpool.

This feat was finally achieved in something over ten hours, from parading at dawn to arrival on the dockside. Here at least they could look at the ship which was to take them, the *Andes*, which would sail unescorted, relying on her speed for safety.

When his flight's turn came at last, Kirby shouldered his kitbag and followed the others, clattering up the creaking gangway on to the former luxury liner, and then down one stairway after another to their mess deck. There were no portholes, so it was presumably below the waterline. It contained nothing but tables and benches fixed to the deck. There were hooks in the ceiling from which to sling the hammocks in which they would sleep.

There was the constant humming of generators in the air which, Kirby was to discover, was an ever-present feature below decks.

An officer arrived and assigned duties, on a 'you, you and you' basis, recording names as the cadets answered. 'Whitney, sir.' 'Jackson, sir.'

A few others besides Kirby escaped being given on board duties, but not many. Later, he felt slightly guilty about avoiding the torments which most of the others suffered, but not for long. After a couple of days, he blessed his good luck.

That night, he slung his hammock and peacefully fell asleep. The ship was under way, and the relentless *grunt grunt* of the engines was a soporific.

At first, he could not quite understand why he had woken up again. The lights in the mess deck had been dimmed, and it was four o'clock in the morning.

Then he realized that the enclosed metal box of the mess deck, that collection of bulkheads, was moving in more planes than one, and his hammock was swaying to and fro in sympathy. The big liner was not only rolling, it was pitching as well in an evil, unending corkscrew motion. There was the constant groaning and creaking of metal plates with hammer-like thuds interspersed as the bows fell into each succeeding solid wall of water.

Others besides himself were awake now. Some clambered out of their hammocks and hurriedly stumbled, swaying as they went, into the adjoining wash room, from which came the unpleasant sound of helpless retching.

Kirby was feeling distinctly unwell himself, but he was determined not to give way. He fought off his queasiness that night, although he lay wide awake until reveille. On the second night, he succumbed.

By then, the winter storm into which the *Andes* was heading was even fiercer, the erratic pounding even more violent. Kirby stuck it for as long as he could, trying to ignore the noises from the wash room, the ashen shakiness of those returning, but finally he reasoned that since he was not sleeping anyway, it would make more sense to be within easy range of a WC. Perhaps a drink of water might help too. He would try that.

Whatever sea legs might amount to, he had not yet acquired

them. He reeled and staggered as he made his way to the wash room. There, he discovered that a good many of his messmates had been unable to restrain themselves. All the wash basins were full of foul-smelling vomit. Pools of vomit slopped back and forth on the floor. His stomach finally and irrevocably revolted. He just contrived to get into the nearest WC, and stayed there until the thought of dying or being torpedoed came to resemble the notion of a merciful relief.

Kirby spent all of his daylight hours on deck. He found a huge coil of rope and, curled up inside that, he was somewhat sheltered from the storm force gale. Even with his hands gloved and the collar of his greatcoat turned up, it was still bitterly cold, but at least in that retreat of rope, which he came to regard as his own personal territory, he did not feel ill. The clouds were low and unbroken all the way, but so long as he could see the horizon he was all right, even if that horizon consisted of looming, mountainous waves. One thing, he thought, as he often found himself actually looking upwards at the foam-whipped cold green waves, they must be safe from U-boats in this. No submarine could possibly bring its periscope to bear in such foul weather.

There was a kiosk on deck from which he could purchase bars of Hershey chocolate, without having to hand over ration coupons as well as money, which was a novelty after years of sweet rationing.

Guard duties were assigned to cadets whose names did not appear on the lists of those perspiring in the kitchens or cleaning lavatories, so Kirby found himself on guard during several of those endless nights when no one was allowed up on deck, which he did not mind at all. It was better than lying, swaying, in that hammock, listening to the moaning and cursed complaints of those around him.

Kirby had no idea what he was supposed to be guarding, or who from. Guards were mounted, and that was that. Kirby had stood outside the cliff top hotel in which he was billeted in peaceful Newquay, at two o'clock in the morning, although the only living creatures he ever saw were a couple of stray dogs, the guard commander, and his relief. He had guarded

Heaton Park, his bottom cautiously perched on a dustbin for support, ready instantly to spring erect, and cry, 'Halt! Who goes there?' should the familiar figure of the guard commander appear. Guarding the passageway of a ship, busy with crew members going about their duties, made quite as much sense as that.

When they finally sailed into still, calm waters it seemed, for a while, unnatural. It was twilight, and had become much colder, twenty degrees below freezing, although the chill in the air was dry and invigorating.

Standing on deck with everyone else, Kirby watched the skyline of New York grow closer, a sight with which he was already familiar from dozens of films. It looked exactly the same, the Statue of Liberty, the towering skyscrapers. What came as a shock were the lights. The entire city seemed to be ablaze with light from every window of those soaring skyscrapers. After years of total blackout, the sight was like a fairyland of forgotten normality.

There were no welcoming bands on the quayside. They were marched off the ship, on to a waiting train, and that was the last they saw of New York.

As the train rumbled north across New England, snow was lying thickly on the ground. Again, as they stared from the windows of the train at this country which had been the background for most of the movies they had ever seen, but which none of them had ever visited before, it was the amount of sheer light which made the deepest impression, the blazing headlights, unhooded, of passing cars, lights streaming from the windows of houses, street lights strung like criss-cross ropes of glowing pearls in the small towns they passed through from time to time.

The train journeyed through the night, crossed into Canada, and finally arrived at Monckton, in New Brunswick, where after a few days they boarded yet another train.

The three days which the journey took merged into a kind of limbo. There was nothing to do but sleep, eat, talk, play cards, read, join in sing-songs, and sleep again. Kirby found it quite agreeable, mostly perhaps because they were finally on their way.

From Chicago, the train headed south across the prairies of the mid-west, passed through Kansas City, and a few hours later, came to a stop at their ultimate destination, Maranda, Oklahoma, where Number 9 British Flying Training School was situated. They would constitute Number 8 course.

First, brief impressions as the bus swept through Maranda on its way from the railway station to the airfield three miles outside of town, were favourable. Maranda, population 9,000 they later discovered, was laid out in a geometrically precise grid pattern. The long Main Street was lined with parked cars and trucks, including a sprinkling of ancient Model T Fords. It looked a bright, clean sort of place. A few people on the sidewalks waved and smiled in greeting as the bus drove by, and then they had left the town behind.

The flying school too was cleaner, brighter, and more comfortable than anything they were used to. It comprised a collection of long, low, wooden buildings, all recently erected by the look of them, set round a square of well-kept grass, crossed by immaculate paths. In the middle of the square was a flagpole, from which the RAF flag was flying.

The mess was another revelation. It was cafeteria style, but with a large choice of appetising food, limitless in quantity, and served by cheerful, smiling American civilians. The tables were spotless, the chairs comfortable, the outlook through the large windows agreeable, the air warm despite the January cold outside.

Their quarters positively sparkled with cleanliness. Number 8 course learned with astonishment that there would be no fatigues. A janitor did all the cleaning.

There were stout, wooden two-tier bunks and every man had his own locker cum wardrobe in which to stow his kit.

'I've been in worse hotels than this,' Smithy said, although he was not referring to the barracks room which would house the majority of 8 course. Smithy was examining the small separate room which would be occupied by the course leader and the flight leaders, appointments which tended to go to ex-policemen, used as they were to discipline and handling men. Smithy had his eye on that, and his optimism was well founded. He became course leader and, provided he passed out successfully, almost certain to be commissioned.

Number 8 course assembled to hear an address of welcome from the commanding officer, Wing Commander Sinclair. He was a square-set man in his forties, with a brown, creased face, and a neat moustache. He wore the ribbon of the Air Force Cross, and was a regular officer.

They were, he told them, guests in a foreign country, the Royal Air Force would be judged by the way in which they conducted themselves, and he expected them to behave accordingly. The fact that Oklahoma was a dry state would no doubt assist them in this endeavour. However, the CO added before getting on with his pep talk, they would shortly have their first taste of local hospitality. A dance at the high school had been organized to welcome them to Maranda.

As Kirby studied the smiling, well-scrubbed girls in the arms of their new-found partners, it occurred to him wryly that this process was repeated every two months. Those bright-eyed girls had no doubt bidden fond farewells only a few days ago to the graduates of Number 7 course, and would be here again to welcome Number 9 course when it arrived.

Roy Harrison, a smooth practitioner of the waltz, the quickstep, and the foxtrot, danced with the same girl all evening, a young teacher at the High School. Her name was Lois Webster. Roy Harrison became close friends with the Webster family, and spent much of his free time with them.

'He's got himself fixed up fast enough. Not that that's difficult, if you don't mind plain bits of skirt,' Smithy observed, morosely, although Lois Webster was in fact a pleasant-faced girl, with striking auburn hair. Smithy's advances had been politely repulsed by the young beauties of Maranda, who could pick and choose, and did. Smithy never did have any luck in Maranda, although later on, he claimed to have encountered plenty of willing crumpet in Joplin, Missouri, and points further north.

Elementary training was carried out at a grass satellite field, to which they travelled daily by bus. Apart from the aircraft, there was only a hut on that desolate, wind-swept field where they clustered to try and keep warm in between flying, with the omnipresent ambulance, known as the Blood Wagon, parked alongside.

Four cadets were assigned to each of the flying instructors, all of whom were American civilians, whose backgrounds ranged from civil aviation to circus flying.

Kirby found himself with Roy Harrison, Don Shepherd, and Ralph Whitney. Roy Harrison, twenty-four years of age, had been a skilled and highly qualified engineer, in a reserved occupation. He had volunteered for air crew several times, and been refused, it being maintained that he was of more use in the factory, building tanks. Roy had argued, appealed, pulled whatever strings he could find, and finally made such a nuisance of himself that he had reluctantly been released.

Ralph Whitney too was an older man, the only genuine intellectual among them, who would soon find himself editing the unit magazine, and running the debating society. He had won a scholarship from his public school to Cambridge, and had acquired a First in history. Perhaps because of his academic prowess, he had been appointed their flight leader, a role in which he did not prove particularly distinguished. Ralph's undoubted brains were allied to an easy-going, tolerant temperament, which was just as well, in some ways. Coming from a different background to most of the others, he was the first target for horseplay. It was Ralph who found himself being chased, set upon and debagged, and finally sought refuge by climbing on to the roof of the flying hut, where he sat shivering in his underpants, until the ring-leaders, Smithy prominent among them, relented, and gave him his trousers back.

Don Shepherd had escaped into the air force as soon as he could from his local Town Hall where he was a junior clerk. Don was introspective and quiet, but the naturally glum, dour cast of his features would sometimes be lightened by a warm, almost impudent, smile.

Kirby thought that they made up a pretty good bunch, who would get on well together.

Their flying instructor was Mr Severn, an immensely tall, lanky Texan, who flew in a leather, fur-lined Irving jacket and high-heeled cowboy boots, and looked and drawled like someone out of a Western movie, although his voice sometimes fluted high in exasperation as he addressed them like recalcitrant buffalo.

'Goddamit, Kirby, stop heaving on the fucking stick like that. You can fly this aircraft with your thumb and forefinger. Try and get the feel of the fucking thing, for Christ's sake. OK,' wearily, 'now relax, and try again. Don't let the nose drop. You're supposed to be flying straight and level, not weaving about all over the fucking sky. Now you're over-correcting. Imagine the stick's a woman's tit. You stroke the fucking thing, you don't grab it and heave it about. Well, maybe you do, but . . . watch your nose! And don't bury your head in the cockpit. If you want to fly into some other bastard, I don't. Watch your horizon, and keep the nose on that, for Christ's sake. You've got rudder on. She's yawing. You don't have to fly this machine, Kirby, she'll fly herself, if you'll only let her. Take your hands and feet off the controls. Come on. Right off. There. You see? OK. I've got her. Let's go home.'

Despite the flying suit and gloves which Kirby was wearing, it was bitterly cold in the open cockpit, but he was sweating from sheer tension when he climbed out, and Roy Harrison climbed in.

He would later appreciate the truth of every one of Mr Severn's colourful words. The Cornell, or PT19, was a docile monoplane, obedient to every touch. But for some time, to him, it bore more resemblance to a bucking bronco with a rebellious mind of its own, which obstinately refused to do what he wanted it to do.

He seemed to have forgotten everything he had learned at Grading School on Tiger Moths, the 'feel' of which was quite different to that of the Cornell anyway, and he began to worry as the hours of dual went by, five, six, seven, eight, and still Mr Severn's remorseless drawl nagged at him through ear-

47

phones in his flying helmet. A hurdle was fast approaching which would have to be surmounted, that of his first solo on Cornells.

Should a cadet prove incapable of flying solo, or fail the course at some later stage, he would be sent back to Canada, and remustered as a navigator or a bomb aimer. Kirby did not wish to follow either trade, which definitely meant serving in a heavy bomber squadron. He wanted to be a pilot, preferably a fighter pilot. But if he could not even solo . . . he tried as hard as he knew how.

'You're trying too fucking hard, Kirby,' Mr Severn complained into the intercom. 'Relax.'

The first cadet to go solo, after eight hours dual, was Stan Jackson, a small chirpy, black-haired Londoner, a former apprentice, unusual in that he had never got to grammar school, much less passed School Certificate. But Jacko was a natural pilot. It was his element from the first moment the wheels of his PT19 left the ground. He took to the air like a fledgling bird, rapidly gaining in skill and confidence after the first few, awkward flutters.

Others followed. Roy Harrison soloed after nine hours, Ralph Whitney after nine and a half. Smithy surprised everyone, and himself most of all, by making it at the same stage, the first of the ex-policemen to fly solo.

Kirby consoled himself with the thought that, from his accounts, Don Shepherd seemed to be having even more trouble than he was. But Mr Severn climbed out, and waved Shepherd off after ten hours.

Twelve hours was regarded as the deadline. At the end of his eleventh harrowing hour, Kirby made his approach, and landed. The thump as the aircraft stalled on to the grass told him that he had held off rather too high, but at least it was a three-point landing, he thought moodily, seeking what consolation he could from that.

Mr Severn heaved himself out.

'You stay there,' he bawled above the noise of the idling engine. 'One circuit, keep a good look out, don't let your speed drop on finals. OK. Off you go.' He stepped back, and clamped a large cigar between his teeth.

Now that it had happened, Kirby could not believe it. His stomach was suddenly empty. His hands were trembling – or was that imagination?

Instinctively, he went through the check which had been painfully drilled into him. T.M.P.F.F.

Trim in take off position. Mixture not applicable, the PT19 had no mixture control. Nor was Pitch. She had a fixed propellor. Fuel, on. Flaps in take off position, fully up.

He paused at ninety degrees to his take off path, and studied the sky. None on the final approach. None on the crosswind leg. One on the downwind leg at 1,000 feet. No need to wait for that.

He turned the aircraft into wind, and opened the throttle.

He was on the downwind leg before it really hit him. There was no bulky, broad-shouldered figure in that front cockpit. *He* was flying the aircraft. He was alone.

Kirby found himself singing raucously from the sheer joy of it.

When, half dazed by his achievement, he taxied to a stop and switched off, Mr Severn came towards him, with his rolling cowboy gait, trailing blue cigar smoke behind him.

'I've seen worse landings,' Mr Severn said. 'But not fucking many. OK. Now let's go fly some more.'

Chapter Five

A timeless kind of routine developed, as though they were going to spend the rest of their lives at 9 BFTS.

Half of each day was spent flying, or hanging about waiting to fly, and the other half in Ground School where the subjects, taught by a mixture of American civilian and RAF instructors, included Navigation, Theory of Flight, Airmanship, Engines, Aircraft Recognition, Meteorology and Gunnery.

David Kirby discovered that Aircraft Recognition was his weakest subject for some reason, which bothered him. To achieve his aim and become a fighter pilot, he must be able to distinguish instantly between a Mosquito and a Messerschmitt 410, a Focke Wulf 190 and a Thunderbolt. When the images were projected on the screen for several seconds, he could manage it, just, but when it came to one-second flashes from the epidiascope, he was uncertain at best, and guessing at worst. In the evenings, he took to studying carefully all the various silhouettes and ordering his brain to memorize them. He improved, but it still did not come easily. He envied Stan Jackson who could effortlessly and infallibly tell the difference between a Hurricane MK 2 and an Me 109F even when they got to flashes of only one tenth of a second's duration.

Kirby's flying settled down somewhat and progressed, if in fits and starts. Just when he felt that he was mastering the aircraft, Mr Severn relentlessly, and not without a degree of sly relish, moved on into some new and unfathomed procedure – such as spinning.

In truth, the docile Cornell practically had to be bullied into a spin and would probably come out of one of its own accord were hands and feet simply to be removed from the controls, without the 'full opposite rudder, stick fully forward, ease out of the dive when the aircraft stops spinning, and open full throttle' which was the proper recovery procedure.

Just the same, the first time Kirby found himself bucketing earthwards, staring at the ground which appeared to be approaching uncomfortably fast and rotating viciously at the same time, his stomach contracted in the face of this new and petrifying experience. He was not much reassured when he was told that he had got even the initial stages wrong.

'For Christ's sake,' Mr Severn's Texas drawl said, tinnily, in Kirby's earphones, 'that wasn't a spin, it was a fucking spiral dive. You've got to bring the fucking thing to the stall before you kick on full rudder. OK. Climb up and do it again.'

They did. Many times. Kirby's breakfast remained in his stomach that morning, but it was a near thing.

Kirby's aerobatics were on the ragged side too. He found it hard to become accustomed to hanging upside down in the open cockpit during inverted flying with nothing between him and the ground five thousand feet below. No matter how tightly he pulled the lap strap beforehand, it always seemed to shift a little when he turned the aircraft on to its back, leaving him groping anxiously for the stick and rudder. For the same reason, he rarely accomplished a good slow roll. But he practised assiduously, his loops became firm and confident, and Mr Severn even complimented him – once – on his roll off the top, the manoeuvre known in the First World War as the Immelmann turn, after the German fighter pilot who had introduced it and baffled, for a time, with deadly results, the Allied pilots who found themselves the pursued instead of the pursuer.

Kirby's navigation was good from the start. The only difficulty he found was in controlling the map strapped on his knee, which tended to flap about disconcertingly in the slipstream which always invaded the open cockpit. He was rather pleased with his new-found skill, although he did not really perceive at that time how easy map reading was in the sparsely populated vastness of the Middle West where it would have been difficult to confuse the widely separated small towns, where a single isolated factory was marked on the map as a pinpoint, where the long straight ribbons of the highways were invaluable guides, woods were uncommon enough to provide a useful fix, and the fields, as in the days when Oklahoma was first settled, were still laid out in one-mile-square sections, their boundaries running precisely north, south, east, and west. Moreover, the visibility was crystal-sharp. There were occasions when Kirby could pick out the first turning point on his cross-country flight within five minutes of taking off. A compass was hardly necessary.

Just the same, as his hours accumulated, Kirby began to feel that he was becoming the master of the aircraft rather than it of him. This comfortable illusion was shattered when he started night flying.

Suddenly, he was as deprived of the familiar daytime terms of reference as a man abruptly afflicted with partial blindness. The satellite field miles from anywhere possessed not a glimmer of light apart from the row of paraffin flares which comprised the flarepath. Once in the air, the horizon by which he had become accustomed to judge his attitude in daylight, was either only dimly perceivable or, on really dark nights, completely invisible. The Cornell boasted no artificial horizon or gyro compass. There were only the primary instruments to guide him through the blackness, the altimeter, air speed indicator, flickering compass, and the turn and slip indicator, which to the harassed Kirby appeared to possess a wayward unpredictable mind of its own.

The flare path, Kirby learned, did not, as he had once imagined, illuminate the ground. Only the apparent change of angle of the flares showed the embryo pilot where he was as he brought the aircraft in to land. If the flares appeared far apart, he was high. If they seemed to be close together, his wheels were near the ground. There was also a glide path indicator which was visible on the final approach. According to the height of the aircraft, the pilot would see either red, green, or amber. Red, logically enough, indicated that he was dangerously low. Mr Severn, understandably, laboured the point in his usual vivid way.

'. . . are you fucking colour blind, Kirby? . . . we're in the fucking red . . . more throttle . . . if you want to wrap the fucking thing round the fence, I don't . . . Jesus Christ, now we're too high, you stupid sonofabitch . . . keep the fucking wings straight, god dammit, you want to land on the fucking flares? Shit, now you've got too much speed on . . . it's no use holding off now, you half-witted bastard, we'll run out of fucking flare path before you get the thing down . . . go round again . . . overshoot, for Christ's sake . . .'

A third of the way along the flare path was a pair of double flares which indicated that by then the plane should be on the ground. Kirby had already floated past these double flares. He banged the throttle wide open, and the Cornell rose unevenly into the blackness ahead. It was quite a while before he began to enjoy night flying.

The weather changed with a suddenness unusual to English eyes. There was none of the slow, unsteady advance from winter to spring, increasingly milder days erratically reverting to unexpected frosts and the chill of cold north-easterly winds, while daffodils and crocuses bloomed, and trees gently blossomed, marking the onward march of seasons, forecasting the summer to come.

Here in Maranda, it was cold and sharp one day, demanding the use of fur-collared flying suits, the next it was sunny and warm, and the temperature continued to rise over the weeks until it became blazing hot, and stayed that way. Somehow, the stark, bare branches of the trees without so much as a bud or a leaf looked odd under the blue skies, as though they too had been taken by surprise and needed time to adjust.

Flying suits were abandoned but, like the foliage, the Royal Air Force worked to a calendar which took no account of the actuality of the season, according to which it was not yet time to change into summer uniforms. The cadets continued to perspire in their heavy blue serge for another month before orders decreed they should change into cooler shirt and slacks.

Others besides Roy Harrison had begun to receive hospitality from the local people. Quite the most popular cadet on Number 8 course with American families was Bert Bagley, of humble origin from Bradford. 'Come on, Bert,' they implored him, 'say something else. Just talk.' And the amiable Bert would grin, ponder judiciously, and finally make some laconic remark in his thick Yorkshire accent, while they listened with delighted incomprehension.

As the primary course approached its end, there was an unexpected announcement. They were to receive five days' leave. Much excited discussion ensued about where to go.

Some decided on Texas and the chance of crossing into Mexico. Some opted for the oil city of Tulsa. Smithy and three other ex-coppers plumped for the bright lights of St Louis where, they confidently believed, anything went. A few, more ambitious, hoped to hitch their way by air from the nearest American air base to Hollywood where, it was widely rumoured, film stars would provide lavish hospitality on a sumptuous scale for visiting RAF cadets. Whether this rumour had any basis in fact, none of them ever found out, since they failed to get any closer to Hollywood than Denver.

Don Shepherd and Kirby counted their dollars, calculated bus fares, and settled for Kansas City. Roy Harrison changed his mind about going with them.

He had been invited to spend his leave with the Webster family, he said, at the small, secluded holiday place they owned on one of the lakes.

Chapter Six

Smithy and the fellow ex-coppers who had headed for St Louis had, they made plain, enjoyed the fruitiest experiences, as befitted older men of the world, who knew their way around.

They had booked into the plushest hotel they could find, and their extravagance had been richly rewarded.

'There were some chorus girls staying on the same floor,' Smithy said, significantly. 'Need I say more?'

The general consensus was that he should, preferably in great detail.

'What's St Louis like, anyway?' asked Bert Bagley, anxious for more mundane information. Armed with his camera, Bert had hitch-hiked to Tulsa, where he had been scooped up by a couple convinced that he would enjoy a quiet few days in the bosom of an American family which consisted, in their case, of themselves, and a brash and amorous teenage daughter. Nothing would ever drag him back to Tulsa, despite the pressing invitation he had received, and the spoilt daughter's ardent advances. Bert was not interested in girls, or rather only in his own girlfriend back in Bradford to whom he religiously wrote daily. They planned to get married when he returned to England, with his wings.

'What was St Louis like?' Smithy feigned deep thought before replying. 'It's no use asking me. We never left the hotel, day or night. What? With all that crumpet along the corridor?'

The nods and winks and broad hints sketched in an impressionistic outline of booze, naked women, and writhing bodies, a more or less continual orgy, interrupted only by the occasional T-bone steak to refuel.

This stirring account of He-men on the loose rampaging in and out of hotel bedrooms was only slightly marred when it emerged that Smithy and Co. had run out of money after two days, and been obliged to scrounge a lift back to Maranda where they had spent the remaining three days in camp, playing poker and pontoon for matches.

'Girls like that expect you to spend a bob or two on them,' Smithy explained loftily to the less initiated. 'And that forty-eight hours was worth every penny, believe me.'

Kirby threw a towel over his shoulder and padded off naked towards the showers. He could not help wondering if Smithy and the others had not been chucked out of the hotel for making a nuisance of themselves.

With Don Shepherd he had received a surfeit of generous hospitality in Kansas City from the warm-hearted American family with whom they had stayed. Kirby felt pleasantly refreshed, and ready for the next stage. His advanced training.

The Harvard, or the AT6A as the Americans called it, had one unmistakable distinctive characteristic – its earsplitting roar as it flew overhead. It must have been one of the noisiest machines of its kind ever produced.

This was not because of its Pratt and Whitney 550hp air cooled radial engine, although that had a grating bark of its own and was not exactly quiet. But the propeller was not geared down, with the result that, in normal flight, the tips of the propeller were rotating at close to the speed of sound. At full throttle, in a dive, the racket was appalling.

The Harvard cruised at 160mph indicated airspeed, had a top speed of 180mph straight and level, something approaching 250mph in a dive, and made its final approach to the runway with flaps and undercarriage down at 90mph.

The Harvard thus reasonably approximated to the performance of most operational aircraft then in use.

From now on, they would fly from the main airfield, with

its single north-south runway, and its looming hangars, topped by the glass box of the control tower.

Kirby, Ralph Whitney, Don Shepherd and Roy Harrison would continue to share the same instructor who was now to be a Mr Morrisey.

'Hi, fellows,' Mr Morrisey said, shaking hands with each of them in turn. 'Glad to know you.'

Neither Kirby nor Don Shepherd were especially tall, but both found themselves looking down at Mr Morrisey. They were to find that this was not his only contrast to the lanky, drawling Mr Severn from Texas.

Mr Morrisey was a quiet man, with the almost self-effacing manner of one who had long since mastered his trade, and knew it. He did not shout or hector, and no swear word ever left his lips. Only the occasional rise in his tone of voice showed when he was pent up. Normally, when in the air, he called his pupils by their Christian names. When he used surnames, they knew they were in the doghouse and had done something exceptionally clumsy or stupid, which, however, Mr Morrisey had a gift for analysing concisely and with perception. He lived in Maranda, and had a wife but no children.

'OK, fellows,' Mr Morrisey said, looking at his watch, having allowed three minutes precisely for the courtesies, 'let's go look around the airplane, and then we'll do some flying.'

Kirby was not exactly nervous as he stood with the others on the tarmac in the sun, and listened to Mr Morrisey. He had envied those who flew the Harvard too long for that, but he was certainly decidedly apprehensive. The Harvard looked such a big, heavy, powerful beast compared with the small, delicate Cornell. But when it came to his turn for his first dual flight – '1. Familiarity with cockpit layout. 4. Effect of controls. 6. Straight and level flight. 10. Medium turns. Flight duration 32 minutes' he later wrote in his log book before replacing it in the log book rack on the flight line where it was 'to be kept at all times' – he felt distinctly more at ease in the Harvard than he had anticipated.

To some extent, this was because, in the Harvard, the pupil sat in front of the instructor, whereas the reverse was the case with the Cornell. Kirby felt more in the 'driving seat' as it were, and the psychological boost of being more apparently, if not actually, in control was considerable. The drawback to this arrangement lay with the instructor, whose field of vision was severely restricted, especially when taxiing and on the final approach. Even the placid Mr Morrisey was prone to emit nervous squeaks concerning real or imagined dangers which he could not see from where he sat.

Mostly, though, Kirby responded to Mr Morrisey's laconic yet exact style of instructing, which suited his temperament. It was a relief not to have a more or less continual flow of largely abusive rhetoric ringing in his ears.

Just the same, flying the much less forgiving Harvard was, in the early stages, hard work, and Kirby began to worry about that renewed obstacle which lay before him again, the first solo.

He was surprised but delighted when Mr Morrisey packed him off on his own after six and a half hours dual, which was sooner than Kirby had expected.

He was told to leave the circuit, and practise some climbing and gliding turns before he came back – which may or may not have been a mark of confidence on Mr Morrisey's part, but Kirby chose to interpret it as such.

Forty minutes later, he was making his final landing check, muttering the initials which he could repeat in his sleep, and probably did. U.M.P.F.F. Undercarriage – down. Mixture – fully rich. Pitch – fully fine. Fuel – on the correct tank. Flaps – in landing position, half given the light wind.

When he levelled out and held off in his landing attitude, the bulky nose of the plane rose, obscuring the runway in front of him, and from then on he could only judge his line and height from the ground from his angled view of the edge of the runway to his left. Back on the stick . . . back . . . back . . . it seemed a long time before the moment when the stick went slack as the aircraft stalled, but then the Harvard hit the runway, and he was down. Not perhaps with the gentle kiss which Mr Morrisey's practised fingers induced, with a decided thump and some squealing of tyres to be blunt, but it was still one of the best landings which Kirby had yet contrived to make, and he was quite pleased with himself.

Mr Morrisey had, of course, been watching. It was his job to get his fledglings off on their own as soon as possible, while yet being reasonably confident that they would not kill themselves in the process. Weighing the conflicting probabilities could give a sensitive man ulcers. Mr Morrisey was always nervous when he sent one of his pupils solo for the first time, and the rare smile on his face showed his relief.

'That was OK, David,' he said. 'Though it looked to me as if you were a little high on the crosswind leg, and tried to dive it off on your final turn.'

'I think I did, sir,' Kirby admitted.

'That meant you were coming in too fast,' Mr Morrisey said. 'Which is why you had to hold off for so long before she stalled. Me, I'd have gone round again. We'll do some work on that tomorrow.'

Almost imperceptibly, the driving rhythm of the course began to accelerate. Those who were not going to make it had been eliminated during the primary stage. The survivors were expected to get their wings, and were pushed ever harder accordingly, both in their flying and their programme of ground studies.

Many evenings were spent in the Link Trainer, flying complex instrument approach patterns, guided only by staccato morse dots and dashes in their earphones, and a cone of silence to show when they were over the beacon. The progress of the imaginary aircraft was recorded by a device which crabbed its way across a perspex-topped table in front of the Link instructor. When the student began to get the hang of it, the instructor fed in rough air which sent the instrument needles flickering wildly, or told the pupil to lock his gyro instruments, and fly on primary instruments only. And, later on, both.

It was not only possible, it was quite easy to become completely disoriented in that dark interior, straining to visualize what those increasing or diminishing dots and dashes meant, peering at the phosphorescent glow of the instruments, trying to guide the dummy trainer on its fictitious way by the 'feel' of stick and rudder bars which had no feel, which were dead compared to those of a real aircraft.

Kirby climbed out tiredly one night, and gazed in disbelief at the loops and twirls recorded on the table, a shapeless mess which resembled a tangled cat's-cradle of wool rather than the exact pattern round the beacons which an aircraft on an instrument approach should have followed.

'I don't know what the hell you thought you were doing, Kirby,' the Link trainer instructor said, dryly. 'I let you get on with it, so that you could see for yourself. Care to explain it to me?'

'I don't think I can, sir,' Kirby said, embarrassed. 'I must have got a bit confused.'

'You and me both,' the instructor said. 'The damned crab nearly fell off the table at one point. If you'd been doing it for real, you'd have been coming in to land ten miles away from the field. You think about that. It's been known to prove kind of fatal.'

More evenings were spent sitting in a sort of airless box while perspiration dripped from foreheads and ran down forearms, a navigation version of the Link Trainer. Here, Kirby plotted courses allowing for wind so that the 'aircraft' followed the correct track, making his calculations with the simple but effective standard computer. This was dead reckoning navigation, relying solely upon speed, course, and the occasional fix. Instructors kept themselves awake during these exercises and tested their pupils by providing fixes which showed that the 'aircraft' was not on track. This in turn indicated that the wind had changed, and it was the student's task to calculate what the new wind was, allow for it, and provide a fresh course which would take the 'aircraft' to its proper destination.

Real life navigators were supposed to keep a D/R plot going at all times. A complex system of radio beams and beacons normally told the navigator where he was, but that system was dependent on wireless communication, which could be affected by circumstances, such as enemy action or adverse weather conditions or simple malfunction in the aircraft itself.

In that event, lacking the more sophisticated aids, old-fashioned dead reckoning navigation was the only way an aircraft was going to find its way home.

From the beginning, Kirby made few mistakes inside the navigational sweat box, and rapidly improved. Interpreting the three-dimensional picture of an aircraft's progress through the air came easily to him. He already knew that he was good at map reading, and he felt that the combination boded well for his ambition to fly single-engined fighters, where the pilot was his own navigator.

Forty years later, the ink in the log book which belonged to Squadron Leader Kirby, DSO, DFC, is fading. The red ink used to underline night flying, or first solo on new type, as laid down in 'Instructions for compiling pilot's flying log book', is almost invisible, little more than a thin line.

Evidence for the growing, imperative tempo of the course can be gleaned from the entries. The steadily increasing amount of solo flying. The appearance of new exercises, altitude test, formation flying, air to air gunnery, air to ground gunnery.

Cross-countries using pilot navigation become more frequent and longer. The fading ink records a litany of turning points and destinations. Ponca City. Bartleville. Chanute. Eureka. Harrison. Ozark. Fort Scott. Carthage. Monmouth. Lafontaine. Lockwood. Arcadia. Lamar. Eyrie. And more. Little mid-western towns where, perhaps, men and women going about their business in the summer heat once heard the familiar approaching snarl of an aircraft engine, and

looked up indifferently for a moment, as the silver plane
with its red engine cowling far above them, banked and
turned on to its new course.

Small, remote places, far away in a distant country.

When night flying, once again Kirby found himself more at
ease in the cockpit of the Harvard than in the Cornell. The full
instrument panel, and the absence of a distracting slipstream
when the canopy was closed helped; in addition the main
airfield was considerably easier to fly in and out of at night
than the dark satellite field, with its single row of paraffin
flares.

At Maranda, the apron in front of the hangars was floodlit
by a blaze of light, and although there was a flarepath
alongside the runway, it required a conscious effort to use it in
the proper manner. There was sufficient reflected light to
enable a pilot to see the surface of the runway and make a
daytime landing, a point which considerably exercised Mr
Morrisey.

'Look at the flarepath, not the runway, Kirby. You won't be
able to see the ground when you're on operations back in
England.'

Leaving the circuit, and flying off into the darkness, presented few problems either. The clusters of lights which
indicated the small towns below were so far apart that there
was little doubt about which was which. And there was the
comforting knowledge that on top of the control tower was the
airfield beacon, continually flashing its welcoming identification signal visible, on most nights, from forty miles away. It
was impossible to get lost. Even Smithy, whose navigation
and map reading was largely guesswork, always found his way
home safely.

There was an air of excitement about night flying; the rows
of planes standing ready, silver fuselages gleaming and glinting
under the floodlights; the barking cough as engines were
started; the almost invisible circle of idling propellers as
cockpit checks were carried out; the thunder of planes taking
off overhead; the bursts of throttle as aircraft taxied, zigzagging

so that the pilot could see what was ahead of him; the squeak of brakes protesting and the final engine roar as someone pivoted his plane in an arc, manoeuvring into his parking position on the line.

The cacophony of noise had become familar to Kirby, and exhilarating too. While waiting for Mr Morrisey, he was carrying out part of the pre-flight check, inspecting the control surfaces, wings and fuselage for damage, making sure that the pitot head – which provided readings for the altimeter and air speed indicator – was uncovered.

While concentrating on what he was doing, Kirby was at the same time aware of all that was happening around him, and savouring it.

Stan Jackson had commenced the long zigzag taxi to the far end of the runway. Smithy and his instructor had climbed into a nearby aircraft, the starter motor whined to an ever rising pitch, the engine burst into life, and settled down to idling speed.

Bert Bagley had finished forty minutes' circuits and bumps. He switched off, his engine sighed, his propeller slowed, kicked, and came to a stop.

Wearing his flying helmet, Bert climbed out, strapped into his parachute, and jumped awkwardly down from the wing. He unbuckled his chute, and slung it over his shoulder.

Kirby was crouched over his undercarriage checking valves and making sure the tyres were fully inflated when it happened. He not only saw it but for a second or two beforehand, he knew, with ghastly inevitability, that it was going to happen.

Bert Bagley was walking towards the despatcher's office, where he would check in and be given his flight time, skirting Smithy's plane as he did so.

Whether Bert caught sight of one of his friends and half turned to call out to him, or whether, ears muffled by his flying helmet and thinking of something else, he was momentarily unaware of the shimmering disc which was Smithy's idling metal propeller, no one knew and would never know.

Kirby straightened up, screaming urgently at the top of his voice.

'Bert! Bert!'

But Bert Bagley did not hear him; with his flying helmet on and the constant background of engine noise, could not hear him. The next second, his body was hurled sideways, as if sliced down by some whirling, frightful, inhuman axe, and lay prone under the spinning propeller.

Kirby ran like a madman, grasped Bert Bagley's feet, and pulled him away with gasping desperation. His action was reflex and instinctive. And also useless.

There were agitated shouts now, more people running, converging on the young Yorkshireman who lay on his back on the floodlit apron. Smithy's puzzled face peered round the side of his open cockpit canopy, as he realized that people were gesticulating and yelling, and wondered why. His instructor slammed open the rear canopy, screaming an order. Smithy switched off, and his engine stuttered and died.

Ground staff bundled Kirby aside, and bent over Bert Bagley. Smithy had climbed out on to his wing, and was standing there, gazing down with horror, white-faced.

'What happened?' he kept asking. 'What happened?' No one took any notice of him.

The ambulance was already on its way, tyres screeching, but Kirby did not wait. Bert Bagley did not need an ambulance. Bert's face had disappeared, his skull was split open, and in the trail of blood which lay behind him on the tarmac were glinting smears and globules, like grey jelly.

Kirby walked stiffly back to his plane, and leaned on the fuselage, shaking. There was a foul taste in his mouth. He doubled up, and retched violently in dry, racking heaves, his eyes watering. He spat out the bile in his mouth, and straightened up.

The ambulance had gone. Ground staff were hosing down the tarmac, and sweeping away the blood which had once belonged to Bert Bagley, with stiff bristled brooms.

Mr Morrisey had been standing a little way off, watching Kirby, and waiting. He walked across.

'I've checked the aircraft, sir,' Kirby said.

'David, suppose we go sit down for a while, and have a quiet cigarette?' Mr Morrisey suggested.

'I'm all right,' Kirby said.

'You sure?'

Kirby nodded.

'Well, I guess we may as well go do some flying,' Mr Morrisey said.

Cadet pilot Kirby picked up his parachute, slipped it on, buckled it, climbed up on to the wing, and into the cockpit.

Chapter Seven

Letters for Bert Bagley, addressed in a round, girlish hand, continued to arrive for another week, and then they stopped. Ralph Whitney took them to the adjutant, who sent them back.

Bert Bagley was buried in Maranda cemetery, where nine cadets from previous courses already lay in neat, well tended graves. No one ever talked about Bert. Even his close friends did not refer to him again. It was as though he had never lived.

Day followed day; flying, Ground School, Link Trainer, poring over notes and manuals in the evenings, the occasional cricket match for recreation. Weekly instructor's flying checks marked the onward passage of time.

During air to air gunnery, one Harvard acted as a target plane, and the others carried out interceptions, coming in on a diving curve of pursuit, using the illuminated gunsight to try and achieve the correct deflection. As with clay pigeon shooting, which had formed part of their Initial Training Wing course, it was necessary to aim in front of the moving target in order to hit it. Kirby had become adept at clay pigeon shooting, but in the air there was an additional complication – the gun platform he was flying was moving too.

The Harvard was fitted with camera guns, and after each exercise, as soon as the film was developed, they sat in the darkened projection room, while Mr Morrisey analysed their marksmanship.

'Your deflection's OK, David,' Mr Morrisey said. On the flickering screen, the ring of the gunsight hovered the correct distance in front of the target Harvard. The trouble was that the film also recorded Kirby's turn and slip indicator, the bottom needle of which was pointing in the wrong direction. 'But look at your turn and slip indicator,' Mr Morrisey went on. 'You're holding on rudder like crazy to stay in the turn. That means you're skidding sideways, and that means your bullets would be skidding out of line too. If that was a real dog fight, you'd have missed him by a mile.'

Kirby tried hard correctly to co-ordinate rudder and ailerons to achieve that smooth curve which would send bullets or cannon shells accurately into the target, and finally managed to bring it off sometimes, but not with any degree of certainty.

Predictably, Stan Jackson's results were perfect. Even Mr Calder, his manic instructor, allowed that he was impressed.

'That boy's a born fighter pilot,' Kirby overheard Mr Calder telling Mr Morrisey one day.

Kirby loved low flying. Skimming across the wooded, hilly wastes of the Ozarks at fifty feet, with no sign of human habitation except for the occasional isolated shack, was his idea of pure enjoyment.

His air to ground gunnery, diving in, firing at a fixed target, pulling out at the last moment, became practically faultless. These skills, he felt, should counterbalance his erratic, less than brilliant performance against aerial opposition. After all, Spitfire squadrons were used now on low-level sweeps against ground targets in the occupied countries of Europe, and that role would presumably become even more important once the Second Front started. Not that there was any sign of a Second Front yet, but the American soldiers, being despatched a division at a time across the Atlantic in great liners like the *Queen Mary* and the *Queen Elizabeth*, were not being sent to camps in England for nothing.

One cadet pilot, Gordon Frazer, an introspective Scot, nineteen years old, failed to pull out of his dive when practising air to ground gunnery solo, and flew his Harvard dead into the target.

Gordon Frazer was buried in Maranda cemetery.

The course moved swiftly towards its conclusion. The Wings

Cross Country, during which cadets took it in turns to act as pilot and navigator on alternate legs, took place, and Number 8 course flew north, Maranda to Des Moines, Des Moines to Scott Field, Scott Field to Madison, Wisconsin, a total of just over six hours' flying time, sufficiently tiring for most not to need the awful warnings concerning what would happen to them were they not back inside the US Air Force base where they were quartered, before eleven o'clock that night.

Kirby, Roy Harrison, and two or three others spent the evening in an agreeable open air beer garden, and were back in time. There was no sign of Smithy, last seen purposefully following a pair of high-heeled legs into a none too salubrious looking bar.

Kirby woke up when Smithy stumbled into the end of his bed, and swore in an undertone. It was 3 a.m. The main gate had been manned by beefy, alert, armed and suspicious American military police.

'Hard luck, Smithy,' Kirby said, sleepily. 'Bang goes your commission.'

'Balls,' Smithy said, quietly. 'I wasn't a copper for nothing.' He sat on Kirby's bed and eased his shoes off.

'Those guards have never seen a uniform like ours before,' Smithy said. 'So when this jerk scowled at me, and said, "Where the fuck do you think you're going, soldier?", I pointed to those B17s parked near the fence, put on a posh accent, and said, "Now look here, my good man, I've just flown one of those Forts in from England today, and I'm tired. Kindly step out of my way".'

It was a passable imitation of a nasal, clipped, English public school voice, of the kind affected by a good many officers during the war who had never been near a public school. It was also how a lot of Americans still believed that Englishmen spoke, unless they were Cockneys born within the sound of Bow Bells.

'What did he make of that?' Kirby asked, amused.

'The silly bugger saluted, and said "Sorry, sir".'

The following morning, they took off and flew from Madison

to Columbus, Columbus to Malden, and Malden to Maranda. On the middle leg, Kirby flew as navigator to an RAF officer, whose task it was to mark his performance, and felt that he had acquitted himself reasonably well.

Kirby flew his Final Instrument Check, his Final General Flying Check, and his Wings Low Level Cross Country when, without a map, the object was to fly precisely by memory out from Maranda to a series of turning points and back.

Ground School examinations loomed, and finally arrived. Kirby experienced a moment of panic when he examined one paper and discovered that he knew less about airmanship than he had imagined. He groaned inwardly, and fell back on examination techniques learned at school, first answering those few questions he knew, then those about which he had some foggy idea, thus leaving the maximum available time to invent, with a combination of imagination and desperation, enough about the mysterious remainder to fill four pages.

That was a bad afternoon, and only Smithy's gloomy, baffled expression offered some consolation – although not a lot.

When the final results were posted on the notice board, everyone crowded round anxiously. Kirby was on the fringe, craning his neck.

Ralph Whitney elbowed his way out, grinned, and said, 'Well done, David.'

Kirby discovered the reason for Ralph's congratulations when he struggled close enough to be able to read the various sheets of paper.

As he had rather anticipated, his flying results were about average, leaving him half way down the list, but in the overall Ground School results, he had come a close second to Ralph Whitney, who was top. Some of his inventions for that airmanship paper must have been truly inspired or, more probably, extremely lucky guesses.

Also, Kirby had been awarded a commission, along with Ralph Whitney, Roy Harrison, Smithy and the other ex-coppers. He was now Pilot Officer Kirby.

Stan Jackson, although he had headed the flying list by a mile, was promoted to sergeant pilot, like the remaining cadets.

The flights marched on to the apron in front of the hangars, now serving as a parade ground, heads held proudly high, arms swinging stiffly in perfect time, to the strains of an American military band.

There was an exhibition of drill and counter marching before they formed up in ranks. Hundreds of spectators from Maranda and further afield were there, the hospitable friends they had made since they all arrived in America. There was a collective determination to impress, to put on a good show. Ralph Whitney's flight responded to his hesitant commands with instant precision. Kirby remembered that first drill corporal at St John's Wood, as he attempted to ram the rudiments into his latest collection of civilians, the way he bellowed, 'Swing those arms, you miserable shower! You look like a bunch of bloody schoolgirls. Let's have some bloody swank!'

There was plenty of swank on Wings Parade that day in Maranda, in front of the watching girls and women in their summer dresses, the fathers and husbands perspiring under the sun in their lightweight suits.

The moment came when they were formed up in ranks, facing Wing Commander Sinclair. The band had stopped playing. There was silence, except for the thin sound of the adjutant's voice as he called out each name in turn.

Kirby waited, motionless as a rock, while the adjutant worked his way through the first half of the alphabet.

'Kirby!'

Kirby sprang to attention, stepped forward, a smart right turn, quick march, halt. A left turn, stamping his right foot, as laid down in the drill book.

He was facing Wing Commander Sinclair. He saluted. The CO returned his salute, a small smile nestling under his moustache. He reached out and pinned pilot's wings on to the left breast of Kirby's shirt.

'Congratulations, Kirby,' Wing Commander Sinclair said. 'Well done.'

'Thank you, sir.'

A pace back, a salute, left turn, back to the ranks. At last he wore the wings of a pilot in the Royal Air Force.

Chapter Eight

The Atlantic was in a bland and peaceful mood, there were no ferocious white-capped waves, and the deep green waters merely heaved, so lethargically and gently, as if breathing peacefully in some deep sleep, that the liner ploughed steadily forward in the upright posture of a ship on a leisurely pleasure cruise.

The *Ile de France*, 'inherited' by the British when France fell in 1940, was an ageing, stately vessel which, even in its best days, had never been remotely in the running for the Blue Riband of the Atlantic.

Few were able to suppress the reflection that, in smooth seas and good visibility, this somewhat ponderous ship must rank as a U-boat skipper's dream come true.

Certainly, the crew look-outs were comfortingly alert, and could be seen continuously scanning the placid ocean through their binoculars, and the optimists among the newly qualified air crew argued that the first trace of that tell-tale wash from a rising periscope would be instantly visible. Those of a more pessimistic turn of mind opined that by then, since the submarine would be in a position to fire, it would be a bit late, and even if it were not, no such comfort could apply at night, when a disconcertingly large moon rode high in cloudless skies, and the solitary liner would form a textbook silhouette against the horizon.

Meanwhile, those who were newly commissioned officers had the privilege of occupying cabins, rather than mess decks. The cabins, stripped of their former furnishings, and now equipped with plain wooden bunks in two tiers of four, were less than luxurious for eight men and all their kit, in a space designed for two passengers with an eye to economy. At least they were not sleeping in the hated hammocks, which would always be associated in Kirby's mind with a stomach in revolt and vomit on the floor.

Kirby and Roy Harrison spent much of their time on deck, sitting in sheltered corners, or leaning on the rail, pock-marked with the initials of servicemen who had stood there before, staring out over the endless wastes of the ocean.

They talked in inconsequential snatches, about this and that, flitting from one subject to another, including their hopes for the immediate future, which for Kirby meant his Spitfire squadron. Roy Harrison was wavering, uncertain whether to opt for fighters, or whether to try for day bombers.

'I've sometimes wondered about you and Lois Webster,' Kirby said, late one afternoon.

They leaned over the rail, gazing in silence at the churning green, foam-flecked water passing them by below, and listened to the ponderous *thump thump* of the *Ile de France*'s elderly engines.

'We were friends,' Roy Harrison said, finally. 'Lois is a very nice girl. If I'd met her in different circumstances, say if I hadn't been married, it might have been different. But I am married. Lois understood.' He turned his back to the sea, looked up at the funnel, and smiled ironically. 'We talked about things in a roundabout kind of way,' he said.

There were four alarms when everyone dashed to their boat stations struggling into lifejackets, but each time, after hanging about for a while, they were stood down again. Whether they were boat drills, or whether a lurking submarine had been detected, no one ever told them. When the first Catalina flying boat appeared from the east, and circled overhead, they felt safe. From now on, they would be under the protective wings of Coastal Command.

The *Ile de France* dropped anchor in Gourock as darkness was approaching. They disembarked into tenders and, once on shore, boarded a waiting train, which meandered overnight to the inland spa town of Harrogate where the pleasantly old-fashioned hotels now housed air crew returning after overseas training. They were back in the land of rationing and blackout.

The grand old firm of Moss Bros must have been booming, deservedly so in view of their efficiency. Within days, Kirby had spent his uniform allowance, and was kitted out with his officer's uniform, peaked cap, forage cap, barathea service dress, greatcoat, raincoat, black socks, black shoes, air force blue poplin shirts, and a couple of black ties, with enough money left over to indulge in some decent underwear and pyjamas as well.

They handed in their airmen's uniforms and kitbags with no regret. From now on, their kit would be packed in suitcases. The wartime variety were made of fibre, but Kirby found some second-hand leather ones, which were well used and battered, but still sturdy and serviceable.

The first preoccupation of most of the new officers was to remove the wire stiffener from their peaked caps. The best course of action then, some maintained, was to fill the cap with beer, when the crown could be moulded easily, and in drying, would set nicely. There was an unwritten custom that officer air crew bent their peaked caps into a shape which, consciously or otherwise, resembled that worn by the Luftwaffe. It differentiated them from mere admin officers and those in other ground trades, who did not fly. Authority turned a blind eye to this particular breach of the dress regulations.

Smithy was one of the exceptions. Like a few others, it was his keen ambition to become an instructor. Smithy kept his wire stiffener in his peaked cap, which would, he hoped, make a good impression at the interview.

The police force was a reserved occupation but, as the war dragged on, the age of exemption rose until it was the turn of those in their middle and late twenties to register for call up.

Such men were mostly married, including Smithy, with homes of their own to go back to, settled domestic lives, and wives who urgently preferred live bread-winners and fathers of children, to dead heroes.

By definition though, they were physically fit men, accustomed to responsibility. If Smithy had registered for the army, he would have been liable to find himself, in pretty short order, serving in some unit such as the Tank Corps. Smithy had wondered if he could scrape together enough educational qualifications, pondered deeply, and reflected that pilot training was lengthy, well over a year before operational flying loomed and, should the war not have ended by then after all, well, who could be better equipped to become a flying instructor than a sober, responsible, disciplined fellow like an ex-policeman?

Smithy coveted a flying instructor's course avidly, followed by the beguiling possibility of a posting to Rhodesia or South Africa, far from the scene of any actual fighting.

Like the others who were itching to fly operational aircraft, Kirby viewed Smith's brand-new, stiff, flat-topped peaked cap with bewildered although uncritical amusement. Instructors were necessary, and they might as well be men with a wife and kid to think about, like Smithy.

There was much talk of disembarkation leave. Smithy maintained that they were bound to get some before their postings. Kirby too felt that a week or ten days' leave would not come amiss. He had written to his mother, giving her his temporary Harrogate address, and enclosing a photograph of himself in his new uniform which he thought she would appreciate, but his presence for a while would mean more, he knew that.

Kirby was interviewed by a wing commander who, since he repeated the process with newly qualified pilots in an endless stream, all day long, day in and day out, looked understandably jaded.

'Your first choice, Kirby, would be . . .?'

'Fighters, sir,' Kirby said. The great moment had come.

'Not a chance,' the wing commander said, flatly. Kirby stared at him, hardly able to believe that his cherished preference was to be rejected without even a token discussion. 'Fighters are out. We've more than enough fighter pilots. Forget it. Second choice?'

'Day bombers, sir,' Kirby amended, deflated. 'Bostons.' The

Boston was a twin-engined, up to date American light bomber, and the RAF had several squadrons of them. Kirby had looked round a Boston at Madison, Wisconsin, and thought it a sleek, good-looking aircraft.

'Your preference will be taken into account,' the wing commander said, wearily.

And that was it. Kirby stood up, replaced his cap, saluted, and left.

A few days later, the postings went up on the notice board in what had once been the foyer of the hotel where they were billeted.

All of them had been posted to various night bomber Operational Training Units. None had been selected for fighters, not even Jacko, the 'born fighter pilot'. None were to be sent on flying instructor's courses.

The postings were immediate. There was to be no disembarkation leave.

'You'd think they could have let a few of us off,' someone grumbled rebelliously. 'Surely they can't need everyone for night fighter fucking fodder. Things can't be that bad. Can they?' The loss rate was running high on night bombers, and they all knew it.

Smithy stared long and hard at the list, like a man who could not credit what he saw, before he turned away. Kirby walked up the stairs with him towards the room which they shared with Roy Harrison and Ralph Whitney.

'Well, it's the heavy stuff for us after all then, Smithy,' Kirby said.

'No surprise to me,' Smithy said, belligerently. 'It's what I asked for. They tried to persuade me to go on an instructor's course, but I said no, I wanted to go on operations.'

In their room, Smithy sat on his bed, removed the wire stiffener from his peaked cap, and began to massage the crown into the standard drooping shape. His face was set.

Kirby and Roy Harrison had both been posted to Number 41 OTU, Chipping Wharton, near Lechlade in Gloucestershire, which proved to be a permanent RAF station. The Officers' Mess, although overcrowded by peacetime standards, was a vast improvement on the Nissen huts they had expected. They unpacked their belongings in a comfortable room they were to share.

'Really makes you feel like an officer and a gentleman,' Roy Harrison said, approvingly. 'I wonder if we get a batman?' They did, they discovered, but the hard pressed airman had so many officers to look after, that his services amounted to little more than a cup of tea in the morning, and pressing their uniforms occasionally if they were lucky.

There were ten crews on the course. They would fly Wellingtons, known affectionately as Wimpeys, after that redoubtable cartoon character, J. Wellington Wimpey, with his passion for hamburgers.

The Wellington was a twin-engined aircraft, which had been the mainstay of Bomber Command until the heavier four-engined bombers, Stirlings, Halifaxes, and Lancasters, came into service. Capable of carrying a 4,000lb bomb, the Wellington had the reputation of being able to absorb a great deal of punishment, due to its geodetic construction. Now obsolescent, it had become the standard training aircraft at OTUs.

The next day, Kirby met the crew who had been assigned to him. They were all sergeants. None of them dreamed of calling him 'sir', nor did Kirby expect them to. Sergeant air crew, even at the OTU stage, did not regard officer air crew as superior beings.

Kirby shook hands with them, the bomb aimer, the navigator, the wireless operator/air gunner, and the air gunner who would man the rear turret, known as the tail arse Charlie. A flight engineer would join the crew when they moved on to their Operational Conversion Unit.

As they chatted, Kirby tried to sum them up. If they were to operate efficiently together, a working and personal bond must be forged which would bring these men he had never met before closer to him, perhaps, than any other beings on earth.

His new crew were engaged in the same kind of speculation. They would have preferred to find themselves assigned to a sergeant pilot, someone who messed with them rather than an officer who, no matter how chummy, lived and ate in a separate mess, when they were not flying together.

There was an initial suspicion, which Kirby sensed, and strove to overcome. After a while, they began to relax a little, as it became clear that at least he was no public school twit.

But he had yet to prove himself in their eyes. This blue-eyed young officer with the lean face and the rather serious expression was not only to be their pilot who, every time they took off and landed, would literally hold their lives in his hands. He would also be their skipper, the captain of the aircraft, the one who took the split-second decisions. According to the correctness or otherwise of those decisions, they would get back home in one piece, or they would not.

'Pilot Officer Kirby?' a voice enquired.

Kirby turned, and saw the flight lieutenant pilot who would be his instructor. Later he found that he would also instruct Roy Harrison, a sergeant pilot called Derek Clark, a pale-faced Londoner, and two or three others.

Kirby managed to resist the ingrained instinct to salute. Pilot officers did not salute flight lieutenants, only senior officers – squadron leaders and above. He supposed that he would become used to his new standing eventually.

'John Trent,' the flight lieutenant said. He offered his hand.

'How do you do?' Kirby said.

Trent could only have been in his twenties, but he looked considerably older. There were two unnatural, irregular red patches on his face. He wore the ribbons of the DFC, and the DFM.

The instructors at OTUs, navigation, gunnery and so on as well as pilots, were known as 'screened instructors', men who had completed a tour of thirty operations, and were now enjoying six months' 'rest' before they returned to operations for a second tour. It was not a popular chore among veteran air crew. Instructing at an OTU could be nearly as dangerous as flying on operations.

'Don't worry about not having any twin-engined experience,' Flight Lieutenant Trent said. They were walking towards a parked Wellington. 'The Wimpey's an obedient old thing. You'll soon get the hang of it. Quite simple really.'

Kirby had diligently read the Wellington Mk 3 Pilot's Notes from beginning to end, several times. From that mass of flat, stodgy, fact-filled prose, there appeared to him to be nothing simple about it, from starting procedure onwards. He could never, he felt, commit all that to memory. And yet he must, so that it became second nature, automatic.

Kirby eased himself into the left-hand seat. Flight Lieutenant Trent sat beside him.

'All the instruments and controls you're used to on the Harvard,' Trent said. 'More of them, that's all. Plus a few extra bits and pieces. OK, let's get familiar with the cockpit layout . . .'

An hour later, Trent said, 'Right, now you know your way round the cockpit, let's start her up and try a circuit or two.'

Kirby donned his leather flying helmet. Everything was foreign and unfamiliar, even down to the microphone, which was part of the dangling oxygen mask. In America, he had always flown with a throat microphone.

He soon realized that the days of careful nursing were behind him. Flying school had been just that, a school, the pupils analogous to schoolboys, assiduously watched and coached. Now, although increasingly conscious of how inexperienced he was, how little he knew, he wore the wings of a qualified pilot, and was expected to be capable of converting on to a new type without undue fuss or delay.

After a little over two hours' dual flying by day, he was sent solo. A few circuits sufficed to check him out by night.

Much of the few remaining hours he flew with Flight Lieutenant Trent was spent mastering the mysteries of asymmetric flight, feathering one engine, controlling the off balance thrust which this created, and trimming to take as much pressure as possible off the controls.

'Good,' Trent's voice said in his earphones, metallically. They were flying at ten thousand feet. Kirby had successfully feathered the port engine, kept the aircraft straight and level, and was maintaining height. 'If an engine goes at cruising speed, that's all there is to it. If it happens on take off, that's another matter. All you can do then is follow the book. Keep your safety speed, feather, clean up the aircraft, wheels and flaps, and you should be all right. If you lose one below critical speed, you've no option but to try to keep her level, and go in straight ahead – and pray to God.'

Kirby's remaining flying time at OTU was mostly spent with his crew on board, carrying out crew training. The real shock for him was not the Wellington, as he had anticipated. Flight Lieutenant Trent was right about that. After he had become slightly accustomed to the sheer size of the aircraft, the unnatural height which he seemed to be perched above the runway in his cockpit, the heaviness of the controls compared with those of the Harvard, and the ponderous way, with a sort of inbuilt time lag, with which the Wellington answered to the control column, he found that flying the machine was not as difficult as he had expected.

The rudest awakening, the aspect which churned his stomach in nervous spasms during those early days, was simply flying over England.

Gone were the blue skies of Oklahoma, the ability easily to identify a pinpoint from twenty or thirty miles away. Instead, there were mists, low cloud, poor visibility. Here, there were no section lines running due north and south, no wide open spaces. Without a glance at his gyro compass, Kirby had no idea what his heading was. The ground, even when it could be clearly seen, was a confusing patchwork of fields and woodland, intersected by roads which twisted and turned erratically, indicating nothing. Towns were shapeless dark sprawls, either so close to the next that it was easy to confuse one with another, or joined together in one huge urban sprawl.

Kirby had rather prided himself on his map reading ability, but that had been in the vast continent of America. Densely packed England was a very different matter. He remembered the stories he had heard about the highly trained, confident, American Flying Fortress crews who had arrived in England, taken off on familiarization flights, and promptly become hopelessly lost, unable even to find their way back to their own airfields. This was regarded by the RAF as a good joke, but Kirby did not laugh now. For the first time, he sympathized.

There were occasions, even in what passed for daylight, when Chipping Wharton appeared to have vanished. That was before the confusing, misty jigsaw below began to take form and make sense. It did not quite happen to Kirby, more by luck than any good judgement he felt, but some on his course put down at airfields as far apart as Scotland and Kent, with not the faintest idea where they were, anxious only to get their wheels safely down on the first runway they could find.

The nearest Kirby came to that was when, with only a few hours' experience on the Wellington, he took off on a particularly filthy day. Visibility, in a drifting drizzle of rain, decreased, and after only a short flight, he could not find the airfield. Nothing below made sense, there was no feature he recognized. He controlled the moment of sheer panic, gritted his teeth, and told himself that he could not possibly be more than a few miles away. The damned place had to be down there somewhere. Finally, with relief, he spotted the dim shape of the hangars away to starboard, and was able to request permission to join the circuit without the humiliation of being obliged to call up and ask the tower for a bearing home. But it was a bad few minutes.

At night, of course, it was even worse. Below, under the overcast cloud, was nothing but blackness. It was like flying in a dark void. Once away from the circuit, he was dependent on his navigator to get him back again. Even that was not the same as being safely on the ground.

Chipping Wharton was equipped with an operational flarepath. The lights beside the runway were only visible to an approaching aircraft in a narrow arc. Until a plane was lined up on its final approach, there were no runway lights to be seen, only the scattering of red obstruction lights on the tops of hangars and buildings which were switched on with the flarepath.

The system was designed to make it difficult for intruding German night fighters to locate aerodromes where aircraft landing and taking off would present easy pickings. Fledgling

OTU pilots sometimes found it hard to pick out the runway too, until they worked out that those scattered red obstruction lights could provide a guide when in doubt.

Early on in the course, one pilot officer, another former bank clerk like Kirby, evidently became completely disorientated and flew his Wellington into a pylon a mile away having, it could only be surmised, continued to descend in search of that elusive runway, and failed to keep an eye on his altimeter. All his crew perished with him.

Nine crews left.

Kirby was not the only member of his crew who found flying over England confusingly daunting. Both his bomb aimer, whose duties included map reading, and his navigator had been trained over the Western prairies of Canada.

'A trapper's hut, and you knew where you were out there,' Ted Hollis, the bomb aimer said. He was holding an empty pipe. Sometimes he filled it and smoked it, but not often. 'Sorry about today, David. I didn't have a clue.'

'Nor me,' Kirby said.

'Don't you worry, my old son,' Maurice Howard said. 'Me and the magic box, we'll always get you home again.'

'Talk about bullshit baffles brains,' Ted Hollis said. 'Who had us flying a reciprocal course until the skipper enquired politely if that wasn't Swindon coming up ahead?'

'I was just going to give him the new course,' Maurice Howard said loftily. 'The wind had changed.'

'Bollocks,' Ted Hollis said, briefly, and with deliberation. He was a deliberate man to the point of slowness, deliberate, or slow, in thought, speech and action. Now in his middle twenties, he had been a lathe operator before the war.

'My glass is empty,' Maurice Howard said, pointedly.

'My round,' Vic Butler said. He gathered up the beer glasses, and went to the bar.

On most of their free evenings, they drank, as a crew, in the crowded, nearby village pub. Tonight, they had been lucky enough to bag a table.

Already, Kirby reflected, they were all friends, as though they had known each other for years. As individuals, he liked and responded to each of them. On a different level, which he kept concealed, he was trying, as a new aircraft skipper almost entirely lacking in the necessary experience, to assess where the strengths and weaknesses of this crew of his might lie.

His wireless operator/air gunner was, it was immediately apparent, on top of his job. Arthur Wood seemed never to have perused the pages of anything except wireless magazines since the day he learned to read. In the air, he was precise and efficient, never at a loss. On the deck, something seemed to happen to him. He withdrew into himself, became almost invisible. Possibly that was because, before he volunteered, he had been an assistant in a men's outfitters, where the manager, obsequious to his customers, bullied his staff mercilessly and treated them like dirt.

No, they were a good bunch, Kirby thought. The rear gunner, Vic Butler, seemed a bit nervous in the air when he spoke on the intercom but then he occupied a physically and psychologically isolated position, confined in that rear turret, which Kirby did not envy in the least.

Maurice Howard had certainly made one or two boobs, or so it sometimes seemed, but who was Kirby, with his slender knowledge of navigation, to judge? Maurice was always full of confidence. To be fair, it had usually worked out all right in the end, and the navigator's job was a taxing and complex one. In the Luftwaffe, so Kirby had heard, the navigator was sometimes the captain of the aircraft, which showed with what respect the Germans regarded the trade. Yes, once Maurice, like Kirby himself, had fully adjusted to the different conditions prevailing in Europe, he would be fine.

It was over Ted Hollis that a query hovered in Kirby's mind. There were times when he could not decide whether the man was not just slow, but thoroughly dim. He would have to watch Ted, likeable though he was.

'Ted,' Maurice Howard said. 'Wakey, wakey.' He drained his glass, and banged it on the table.

'M'm? What?' Ted Hollis was poking about inside the bowl of his pipe. He looked up enquiringly.

'It's your bloody shout, that's what,' Maurice said.

'Is it? Oh, right.' Ted laid his pipe down carefully and began what appeared to be the painstaking task of placing empty beer glasses on the tin tray they had acquired. It was no use going to the bar without glasses. There was a shortage of glasses.

'Time, gentlemen please; the landlord bellowed above the hubbub. 'Come on now, time, please.'

'Too late,' Ted Hollis said. 'Have to be some other evening.'

'Marvellous,' Maurice Howard said, shaking his head in wonder. 'There's poor old Ted, dim as a Toc H lamp, needs two sheets of paper to work out what time of day it is, but when it comes to keeping his hand out of his pocket, he's a genius. I don't know how he does it.'

Ted Hollis grinned placidly.

Flight Lieutenant John Trent DFC, DFM, had the kind of operational record which excited instant respect from aspiring operational pilots who had yet to see action. He had fought in the Battle of Britain as a sergeant pilot, and gained the DFM after his sixth kill before being shot down in flames by an Me 109.

Badly burnt, he had been one of Sir Archibald Macindoe's 'guinea pigs', and had his face more or less restored. It was a lengthy process, but after convalescence and sick leave, the red blotches did not prevent him from being fit to fly again.

He converted on to multi-engined aircraft, joined a newly formed Halifax squadron, was one of the only two crews who survived their tour of thirty operations, was awarded the DFC and a commission, and was now over half way through his period of rest as a 'screened instructor' at an OTU.

Off duty in the mess, he was an uncomfortable companion. He rarely went out anywhere but, when he was not night flying, he drank steadily, with no visible effect whatever, from after dinner until bedtime. He did not impose himself, he was quite happy to be left alone, but he was also perfectly willing to talk to any of the new young officers who sought his company.

In the beginning, they were eager to drink with Trent, as an heroic, much admired figure. But he did not conform to their preconceived ideas of a hero. His cynicism undermined the received notions with which they faced their futures, and with it was interwoven something close to callousness, which made them uneasy. After a while, instead of seeking him out in the mess, they began to avoid him. If Trent noticed, he quite evidently did not care much.

One evening, after waiting for the fog to clear, night flying had finally been cancelled. Kirby and Roy Harrison decided on a drink in the mess.

Kirby found himself elbow to elbow with Flight Lieutenant Trent, who was impassively contemplating his glass.

'Scrubbed, have they?' Trent asked. 'Can't think why. Missed a good chance to write off a few more.'

As ever with Trent, Kirby did not know whether he was supposed to smile or not. It had been a bad week. On Monday, a Wellington had crashed on landing. The crew, now in hospital, would live, but the screened navigator on board had been killed.

On Tuesday, another aircraft had failed to return from bombing practice. It simply disappeared. It had not landed elsewhere, no wreckage had been reported. Flying with the crew was a screened bomb aimer, Warrant Officer Miller who, Kirby knew, had been one of the only other surviving crew on Trent's squadron.

Seven crews left.

'Well, Dusty's fish food,' Trent said. He raised his glass. 'Cheers.'

'They could still turn up somewhere,' Kirby said, uneasily.

'Got lost, ran out of fuel, came down in the North Sea,' Trent said. 'Happens all the time. There won't be any dinghies floating around either. A thirty knot surface wind Tuesday. No sprog pilot's going to be able to ditch in those conditions.' He eyed the single thin rank marking on the shoulder of Kirby's battledress. 'No disrespect,' he said absently. 'Just a fact.'

Kirby visualized the conditions, the whipped up seas, heard the pilot's order in his head, 'Dinghy, dinghy, prepare for ditching', and could not disagree.

'That's why the figures are all cock,' Trent said, pursuing his own line of thought. Kirby glanced at Roy Harrison.

'Pissed as a newt,' Roy murmured softly.

'Losses,' Trent said patiently, 'are what is all cock. Casualties in training, losses at OTUs, they're ignored for a start. As for ops, the way to arrive at the best approximately accurate figure . . .'

Carefully, Trent lit a cigarette, blew out a cloud of smoke, and peeled a shred of tobacco from his lips.

'Listen to the German radio,' Trent said. 'They're methodical bastards. They've counted all the bits and pieces, human and mineral. Then add ten per cent for crashes on take off and landing that they don't know about, and we prefer not to mention. Then you've got the real loss figure, near enough.'

As usual, they were listening to heresy. It was a well known fact that the BBC told the truth, and German radio told lies concocted by Doctor Goebbels.

'Oh, come on, John,' Roy Harrison said. 'The Jerries always exaggerate the number of planes they shoot down. They're just trying to boost morale. Their figures are only propaganda.'

Trent laughed, a soft, gentle sound of honest amusement.

'Remember the day we won the Battle of Britain?' he asked. 'When we shot down 185 of theirs, and we only lost 30 odd?' Kirby nodded. He recalled the blazing headlines, the excited discussion at the bank, Mr Stevens' triumph. 'Bullshit,' Trent said. 'I reckon they lost about 60, and we lost about the same.'

Kirby found it hard to believe that someone, somewhere, had calmly multiplied Luftwaffe losses by three, and halved the RAF fighter losses, in order to persuade the nation that a great victory had been achieved. This time, Trent's cynicism, induced perhaps by his own terrible experience, flew in the face of the fact that the Luftwaffe had been beaten.

'But soon after that,' Kirby argued, 'the Jerries switched to night bombing. That was a tacit admission that they'd failed to destroy Fighter Command. They'd lost.'

'Quite true,' Trent said, nodding. 'But they only lost because the finest fighter in the air at that time could only spend five minutes over London. Its duration was too short.'

Roy Harrison frowned. Trent was not making sense.

'The Spitfire?' he queried, bewildered. 'Only five minutes over London? That must be wrong.'

'I'm talking about the Messerschmitt 109,' Trent said, patiently. 'That was the best. If they'd been able to carry more fuel, Jerry would have knocked us out of the sky. As I know to my cost, having tangled with a few of them.' He smiled, and unconsciously stroked one of the ugly red patches on his face. His smile was lopsided.

'Yes, but you were flying Hurricanes, John,' Roy Harrison said. 'They were slower . . .'

'There is a myth,' Trent said, 'that the Battle of Britain was won unaided by a handful of Auxiliary Air Force officer pilots, with red satin linings to their Savile Row uniforms. I expect the press found them more glamorous than the sergeant pilots, mostly ex-apprentices like me, regular airmen. But there were a damned sight more of us flying. And there were a lot more Hurricanes than Spitfires. You add up the kills by NCO pilots and work it out one day.' He sighed. 'Never mind,' he said. 'We were all like you two once. You'll learn.' He pushed his empty whisky glass aside, and looked at his watch. 'Time to crawl into my pit,' he said. 'Am I flying with you tomorrow, Roy?'

'I don't think so,' Roy Harrison said.

'Oh, no, that's right. Sergeant Clark. Got the makings, Nobby, like you two.' The throwaway compliment was the more welcome for being a rare item. 'Not too sure about his navigator though,' Trent said. 'I'll tell you what I've told Nobby. If the time ever comes when you're not satisfied with any member of your crew, you're entitled to get shot of him. Don't hang about. Do it. It's not just your neck, it's the entire crew. If you remember nothing else I say, remember that.'

Kirby and Roy Harrison promised that they would.

'See you,' Trent said. 'Good night.' He walked out of the bar with the easy tread of a man in complete control of himself.

That was the last they ever saw of him. The wreckage of the Wellington was found on the side of a Welsh mountain. The navigator's charts survived, and showed that they had been letting down through thick cloud, in the belief that they were over the Bristol Channel.

Six crews left.

'I'm beginning to think it might be safer on operations,' Roy Harrison said.

Others too pondered the spendthrift way in which lives were being expended. One of the sergeant pilots decided that he had had enough, and went LMF.

All air crew were volunteers, and could not be ordered to fly. However, those who changed their minds, like the sergeant pilot, were deemed to have shown 'Lack of Moral Fibre'. LMF was a nagging, continual problem for Bomber Command both during operational training and on the squadrons.

The Sergeant Pilot would be sent to Uxbridge in disgrace, where he would be stripped of his rank and flying badge. Thereafter, his future would be at best uncomfortable, ordered about and despised in some greasy, steaming kitchen, an object of contempt.

The sergeant pilot did not much care what happened to him – so long as he did not have to fly any more.

His crew were withdrawn from the course, and would start again with a replacement pilot.

Five complete crews left.

The course was approaching its conclusion when Pilot Officer Roy Harrison took off as dusk was falling. At almost the same moment, without warning, his port engine failed.

The aircraft wallowed, wings providing scarcely enough lift to hold it uncertainly in the air, the controls were slack and floppy.

Roy Harrison did everything right. He feathered the port engine at once, to eliminate drag from the idling propeller, and immediately retracted his undercarriage, he kept the nose down, the wings straight and level, but he simply could not attain his safety speed.

Ahead were fields where he could make a belly landing. But in a direct line, in between him and those fields, was a house.

Rightly, Roy Harrison did not attempt to turn. The first dip of one of his wings would send him crashing into the ground. The aircraft was juddering now, on the point of stall. He tried to hold the little height he had just long enough to ease over the chimneys of that house.

The Wellington was stalling when it hit the roof. It smashed through tiles and timber, went through a hedge a hundred yards further on and skidded across the meadow beyond. A tree ripped off the starboard wing, the Wellington spun round on its belly, and came to a stop.

Four complete crews ended the course, out of the original ten.

Chapter Nine

The musty pages of the log book which belonged to Squadron Leader David Kirby, DSO, DFC, record his presence at Chipping Wharton. Most of his hours with another captain were flown with Flight Lieutenant Trent. Later on, entries show that he flew twice with a Flying Officer Pierce.

The final entry is countersigned by a wing commander, whose signature is indecipherable. It reads:

Summary for 31 Course – 41 OTU
Aircraft Type – Wellington Mk 3

	Day	Night	Total
At controls (with captain)	9·55	3·30	13·25
At controls (without captain)	37·40	32·55	70·35
Crew training	37·35	31·15	68·40
Grand total at OTU			84·00

Roy Harrison was propped up in a hospital bed. He had suffered a fractured sternum, a broken nose, and a sprained wrist.

'Christ, you were lucky,' Kirby said.

'Luck nothing,' Roy Harrison said, beaming. He was in a chirpy mood. He felt that since he had one crash under his belt, and had got away with it, he would be all right from now on. 'Pure skill. If it hadn't been for that bloody house, none of us would have been scratched even.'

Roy had already been visited by the wing commander, who felt that he had put up a jolly good show. At least no one was dead. The house had been empty, the fortunate occupants having decided to go out for the evening.

'It's a bind having to go back a course, and do it all over again, that's all,' Roy Harrison said. Four of his crew had got off as lightly as he had, but his navigator had suffered a fractured pelvis. The pilot and the navigator were key personnel, and if either were killed or incapacitated, the remainder of the crew were obliged to repeat the course with the replacement.

'You'll be the best trained sprog skipper in Bomber Command,' Kirby said. 'Look at it that way.'

'I'd rather be coming with you,' Roy Harrison said. 'Where are you posted?'

'51 OCU,' Kirby said. 'Thurston Moor, Yorkshire somewhere. No leave yet, though.'

Roy Harrison said, 'Perhaps I'll catch you up later on. Let me know which squadron you end up with. You never know, I might be able to swing the same posting.'

'I'll do that,' Kirby promised. 'Oh, I had a letter from Ralph Whitney. He's been put back, his navigator went LMF. And Smithy pranged, but he's not hurt, and Ralph says it wasn't his fault.'

'Ralph always was a kindly, gullible soul,' Roy Harrison said. 'How about Jacko and Don Shepherd? Are they all right?'

'Don't know,' Kirby answered. 'Haven't heard.'

As an officer, Kirby received a first-class travel warrant, but he preferred to sit with his crew in their third-class compartment.

The crowded train ambled in a generally northerly direction. After a couple of hours, the talk became less general. One by one, they began to doze off in the smoke-filled carriage.

Kirby closed his eyes too, but for some time his mind remained active. OTU had shaken him more than he would have cared to admit to anyone else. He was glad that his was one of the only four crews to get through unscratched, but he was far from sure that there was any special merit to be claimed. It seemed to be largely a matter of luck.

Looking back, it was now clear what a sunshine honeymoon flying school had been. That honeymoon was definitely over. He had entered an entirely different world. He had not known quite what to expect, but it had certainly not been this. Nor, he supposed, was it likely to improve.

He went over, in his mind, the crews who had not completed the course, most of whom he had known but slightly.

Five Wellingtons written off. Four men slightly injured, five men seriously injured, and sixteen dead, plus three 'screened instructors'.

All in the course of completing only eighty hours' flying each.

It seemed such a gratuitous waste, after all the previous lengthy, expensive training for so many to have died without ever getting near the enemy.

Even to Kirby's inexperienced eye, the cause was clear enough. Flying aircraft with which they were not familiar, they had been thrown into hazardous conditions for which their training to date had not adequately prepared them.

Was that mere blind stupidity on the part of the RAF? Or was it, for some reason, necessary, inevitable? Why take such careful pains to train air crew, and then chuck them into conditions where many would die or be seriously injured before they ever reached a squadron?

Thurston Moor was as desolate as its name, a bleak, lonely, Nissen-hutted place, its quarters cold and dank, in sharp contrast to the warmth and comfort of the permanent buildings of Chipping Wharton. There was a running shortage of coal in the shared huts, and they were lucky to be able to scrounge enough to keep the clumsy cast-iron stoves alight for an hour or two in the evenings. Sheets and pillow cases were damp to the touch. Only in a restricted area around the stove in the officers' mess ante-room was it genuinely warm, an area usually commandeered by the permanent staff.

It was immediately apparent that the flight engineer who

joined Kirby's crew, Len Bellamy, was going to be a great asset. Len was a regular, a former boy apprentice. Trained at Halton as a skilled fitter, he had later volunteered for air crew. Len never flapped, he was precise, he knew exactly what he was doing. Perhaps Kirby and the rest had learned more than they imagined at their OTUs. At 51 Operational Conversion Unit, the task was to convert on to their operational type, the four-engined Lancaster, and this was achieved with relative smoothness.

The Lancaster possessed excellent flying characteristics, and was powered by four Rolls Royce Merlin engines, initially 1280hp each, later 1460hp or 1640hp.

It had a gigantic and unobstructed bomb bay, which enabled it to deliver a bomb load of up to 22,000lbs.

The wing span was 102 feet, its length 69 feet 4 inches, its height 20 feet 6 inches. The maximum take-off weight was 68,000lbs. At a height of 15,000 feet, the Lancaster cruised at 200mph. With a 7,000lb payload, its range was 2,530 miles.

The aircraft was defended by a front turret housing twin Browning ·303in machine-guns, a mid upper turret also housing two ·303 machine-guns, and a rear turret with four ·303 machine-guns. All the turrets were power operated.

Over 7,000 Lancasters were built and delivered during the Second World War.

In heartening contrast to Kirby's OTU, only one crew was lost. During a night interception practice, a Hurricane slid into position on the Lancaster's tail. The Hurricane pilot was about to reach for his switches and flash his navigation lights when, to his horror, the dark silhouette in front of him suddenly and unaccountably began to grow so large as to fill his windscreen.

The Lancaster crew had decided to try something the next time a fighter was spotted moving into position. The pilot had cut his throttles, and lowered his undercarriage and flaps.

The Hurricane pilot yanked back on his stick as soon as he realized what was happening, but his propeller chewed up the rear turret, together with the air gunner inside it, and chopped off the tailplane.

The Hurricane pilot managed to bale out. The crew of the spinning Lancaster did not.

But, after OTU, only to lose one crew during the course seemed a great step forward.

Kirby was sitting in his hut, writing up his log book.

'Grand Total for OCU – 82·00.'

He was wearing his greatcoat, the collar turned up. There was half a bucket of coal, but that was being saved for the evening, unless it was pilfered by the occupants of some other hut in the meantime.

They were to go on seven days' leave, after which he and his crew were to report to 545 Squadron at Woodley Common, which was north of Chelmsford.

After 388 hours' total flying time, he was now fit to become a squadron pilot, the captain of a four-engined bomber which would fly across Germany against the best and most sophisticated night fighter and anti-aircraft defences in the world.

There was a cursory tap on the door, and Sergeant Vic Butler came in. Kirby looked up.

'Hullo, Vic,' he said, a little surprised. He examined Vic's face more closely. It was set and strained. Vic licked dry lips. 'What's up?' Kirby asked. 'Something wrong at home?' It was the first explanation which leapt to his mind, a brother reported killed or missing, parents taken ill, a home bombed . . .

Vic Butler shook his head.

'I can't take it any more,' he said in a flat, quiet voice. There was a silence. Vic met Kirby's stare. 'I've thought it out,' Vic said. 'Nothing's going to make me change my mind. But I reckon you've got a right to know first. So . . .' He gestured vaguely. '. . . here I am.'

'You know what they'll do to you,' Kirby said. It was a statement not a question. The question was in his own mind about himself: Why the hell didn't I see this coming? Vic Butler's nerviness he had noted, but thought it no more than normal apprehension. Kirby cursed himself. This was partly his fault. Earlier, he might have been able to do something. Now, it was too late.

Vic Butler said, 'I just can't take flying any more, and that's it. Stuck back there in that turret . . . I get sick every time you turn on to the runway, and open the throttles, and the tailplane lifts off the deck, and me with it. I've started shitting myself every time we take off. I'm not kidding. The number of stinking underpants I've washed . . .' He managed a shaky, apologetic smile. 'That's it, you see. I'm shit scared. And, Christ, we haven't even been on operations yet . . . anyway, now I've told you, I'll go and make it official.'

Kirby stood up.

'Would you like me to come with you?' he asked.

'No thanks,' Vic Butler said. 'Thanks for the offer, but from now on, it's all downhill. They can do what they like.'

Kirby held out his hand.

'Well, good luck, Vic,' he said. 'I hope it works out for you.'

Vic Butler's hand was clammy, despite the cold.

'I'm sorry to let you down like this, skipper,' he said, subdued. 'But there's nothing I can do about it. There's no one I'd rather fly with . . . except I haven't got the fucking guts,' he said.

In war, only one kind of courage was recognized, that required to keep on going in the face of likely death. Many did so because, paradoxically, they were afraid to do otherwise. Openly to admit to 'cowardice' and accept the consequences took, perhaps, a special variety of courage of its own, valuable in peacetime but, unfortunately for its possessors, of little use in fighting a war of any kind, and even less so one which simply had to be won. Vic Butler was entitled to make his decision, which was far from being an easy one. But it still meant that another man would have to fly in his place.

Kirby left it for an hour, and then walked through the icy wind to the group of Nissen huts which comprised Station Headquarters.

'You've heard about your rear gunner?' the wing commander enquired.

'Yes, sir,' Kirby said. 'He told me. I was wondering, since my crew's now incomplete . . .'

'Go on leave as arranged,' the wing commander said. 'A new gunner'll be assigned to you at Woodley Common.'

Kirby walked back to his hut, and started to pack, ready for the morning. He noticed that someone had swiped the half bucket of coal in his absence.

He could not suppress an irritated resentment nudging hostility. Damn the man. Just when they were really getting used to each other, and beginning to function as a truly effective crew. He paused over that. Were they? So far, despite all the anxieties, it had not been for real. He was still not certain how the slow, placid Ted Hollis would respond under operational conditions. And he could not rid himself of a lingering unease about Maurice Howard. There had been more than one occasion when he suspected that when the landfall which Maurice had confidently predicted duly arrived, a few miles to starboard, or four minutes late, it had been due more to guesswork and luck than accurate navigation.

Now, in addition to his private reservations about Maurice and Ted, he would take off on his first operation with a rear gunner on board, charged with guarding them against night fighters, whom he had scarcely met, and with whom he had never flown before. Kirby slammed a drawer closed in annoyance.

Still, that was over a week away, his first op.

Mrs Kirby was on the doorstep when Kirby climbed out of the Standard 14 taxi, which he had been lucky enough to find at Southampton Central Station.

'Hullo, David,' she said, and pecked him on the cheek.

'Hullo, Mum,' Kirby said, and for perhaps four seconds she allowed him to hold her thin body close against his, before she broke away, briskly.

Indoors, she insisted on unpacking for him.

'What beautiful shirts,' she said, inspecting one with admiration. 'I'll give them all a good wash.'

'Mum, they're clean,' Kirby said. 'They've been laundered.'

His mother sniffed.

'I can see that,' she said. 'It's a crime to send shirts like these to a laundry. I'll wash and iron them properly for you.'

She hand-washed his spare underwear, socks, pyjamas and handkerchiefs too. She washed everything in sight, clean or not. She eyed the scent which he had brought back from America for her with something approaching a glow in her eyes, before putting it away.

'I shall keep that for special occasions,' she said.

That meant never, as Kirby well knew. He sighed inwardly, but said nothing.

She had, it transpired, taken a week off work, not having had a holiday during the summer.

'I thought I'd save it for when you were home,' she said.

'Yes, well, we must go somewhere,' Kirby said. He tried to think where, in the middle of a war. He supposed they could catch the train to Bournemouth, where the big stores were still standing, even if they had little to sell. The beaches would probably still have barbed wire on them, but that hardly mattered. It was not beach weather anyway. And there were restaurants in Bournemouth where they could have a meal . . .

'I don't want to go anywhere,' Mrs Kirby said, firmly. 'And I don't want bad food in some restaurant when I can cook good food for you at home. I've been saving my points for months, for when you came on leave. No, I shall occupy my time giving this house a good clean from top to bottom, and you can go out and see all your old friends.'

The house was spotless already, as always, but it was fruitless to argue. He made the rounds, as his mother suggested, but his friends from school days were in the army, or the navy, or the air force, and none of them was on leave.

'Why don't you go and see them at the bank?' Mrs Kirby asked. She was on her hands and knees with a dustpan and brush. She stopped brushing, and rocked back on her heels, gazing at him.

'I don't feel like listening to Mr Stevens' trials and tribulations,' Kirby said.

'Lorna will be disappointed. I saw her not long ago,' his mother said. 'She's still got a soft spot for you.'

'She's engaged to some Canadian,' Kirby said.

'She told me things,' Mrs Kirby said, cryptically. 'I think we'll find that was all a flash in the pan. A chap in a strange country far from home, girls are attracted to the uniform, things like that don't last.'

The idea had its appeal. He was no monk. Lorna was more than attractive and he had always liked her. Perhaps she would indeed be glad to see him, and ready to start again. It was that thought which decided him. Within days he would join his squadron. He thought of John Trent. Of the others. No. Leave it. Perhaps later. Not now.

On his last evening, Mrs Kirby said, 'Well, a week soon goes, doesn't it. Back to work on Monday.'

Kirby had been thinking. As an AC2 he had allotted his mother one shilling a day from his three shillings a day pay, increased it when his pay rose to seven shillings a day, and again now that his pay as a pilot officer was fourteen shillings and sixpence a day (out of which he had to pay his mess bills, and maintain his uniform). But it was still not enough for what he had in mind.

'I don't like to think of you working in that place, Mum,' he said. 'If I were to send more, which I could manage as soon as I'm made up to flying officer . . .'

'I'd rather work, thank you, David,' his mother said. 'What would I do sitting at home all day, with no one to look after? If you were home, it would be a different matter.'

'Well, I'll send more as soon as I can anyway,' Kirby said.

'If you do,' she said, 'I shall only put the money away for you.'

'Mum,' Kirby said, 'there are times when you're bloody impossible.'

'Don't swear,' she said automatically, but there was a smile on her lips. 'Oh, you haven't given me your new address.'

Kirby had written it down. He passed the slip of paper to her. She read it carefully, and then looked at him.

'This 545 Squadron . . . does that mean . . .?'

'Flying Lancasters,' Kirby said.

'I see.' She folded the piece of paper neatly, and tucked it into her handbag. 'Do be careful, David,' she said. 'Don't do anything silly . . . for my sake . . .'

Woodley Common was another wartime aerodrome comprised of Nissen huts. The control tower was the only permanent-looking structure in sight. Lancasters were dispersed all around the perimeter, each on its own patch of hard standing. Kirby wondered which one would be his.

His billet was a Nissen hut half a mile from the officers' mess. It was divided into single cubicles, each just large enough to hold a truckle bed, a chest of drawers, and a battered single wardrobe. A batman was assigned to each hut. The wash house was fifty yards away.

Kirby dumped his kit, walked to the officers' mess, booked in, and wandered into the bar which was part of the ante-room. A separate games room housed a billiard table, and two table-tennis tables.

He felt somewhat ill at ease, an outsider, patently a new boy, out of place among all these people who knew everyone else except him. The packed bar rang with animated conversation and loud bursts of laughter.

He sidled his way into an inconspicuous corner, ordered a beer, and was sipping it when someone touched his arm.

'You must be Kirby,' the someone said. Kirby turned. 'My name's Gale. You'll be in my flight.'

Kirby shook hands with his flight commander. Squadron Leader Gale wore the ribbon of the DFC, and appeared to be little older than Kirby himself.

'As you may gather, we're not on ops tonight,' Gale said, smiling. 'You're the second new arrival today. Our new CO took over this morning. Wing Commander Norgate.'

'What happened to the previous one, sir?' Kirby asked.

'He bought it last week,' Squadron Leader Gale said. 'No need to use "sir" in the mess, old chap. Except to the CO, I add hastily, because he's coming over.'

Kirby stopped leaning on the bar, and stood up straight, as Squadron Leader Gale introduced him.

'Pilot Officer Kirby, sir,' he said. 'Replacement for "A" Flight.'

Wing Commander Norgate nodded distantly in Kirby's general direction.

'A word with you, Squadron Leader,' he said, and drew Gale aside.

Kirby studied his squadron commander from a distance with deep respect. Wing Commander Norgate was in his late twenties, medium height, slenderly built. His prominent cheekbones gave him a severe expression, his blond hair was neatly parted, and brushed flat. He wore a slight frown, and the DSO, DFC and bar, and the DFM.

Kirby had never actually seen anyone with so many decorations before, except on the newsreels. His admiration was to grow to something approaching awe when it was learned that, not only was Norgate commencing his third tour of operations, but that his second tour had been on Stirlings.

The Stirling, the first of the British four-engined bombers, was underpowered. It flew slower than the later bombers, and its ceiling was considerably lower.

Halifax and Lancaster crews were prone to rejoice when a few squadrons of Stirlings formed part of the bomber stream. Flying several thousand feet below them, the Stirlings served to attract more of the shit from anti-aircraft guns.

Anyone who completed a tour of ops on Stirlings was a rare specimen, and the chances were that he was not only remarkably skilful but had access to so much luck as to be practically immortal. Kirby was buoyed up, pleased with his own good fortune in landing up on a squadron which would be led by such an intrepid and able commander as Wing Commander Norgate.

Next morning, he reported to 'A' Flight Office, and was reunited with his crew. They were talking about their respective leaves when a short NCO elbowed his way into the group.

'Your name Kirby?' he enquired, aggressively.

'Yes, Flight,' Kirby said. 'What is it?' He did not much like this swaggering individual's tone of voice.

'I'm Ron Ferris,' he said. His expression was surly. 'Seems you're short of a rear gunner.' His lack of enthusiasm could not have been plainer. 'Seems I've got to take his place.'

'Delighted, Ron,' Kirby said, sincerely. 'Couldn't be more pleased.' He held out his hand. Ferris took it reluctantly. 'I'm David,' Kirby said. 'This is Ted Hollis . . .' He introduced Ferris to the rest of his crew.

Like Kirby, they fell over themselves to be polite, to make Ferris feel welcome, asking him solicitous questions, to which he replied in an offhand manner, only barely, if at all, short of rudeness. None of them minded. They treated Ferris with the gentle care and respect due to an object of inestimable value.

For Flight Sergeant Ferris sported the ribbon of the DFM under his air gunner's badge, which identified him at once. He was a second tour air gunner.

'Lancs,' Ferris said, answering Len Bellamy. Ferris possessed light ginger hair, and very pale eyebrows. 'Had a skipper who knew what he was about,' he said, addressing some point in space above Kirby's right shoulder. Arthur Wood asked the follow up question. 'Just done my six months' instructing at OTU,' Ferris said. 'They offered me a commission. I told them what they could fucking do with *that*.' His gaze focussed pointedly on Kirby's rank markings, with disdain.

Kirby felt no resentment. No telepathic ability was required to discern what was in Ferris's mind. 'Jesus, lumbered with a bunch of sprogs, still wet behind the ears. Just my bloody luck.' Ferris took out a packet of cigarettes.

'Have one of mine,' Len Bellamy said, hastily. Ferris examined the packet suspiciously before he took one.

Kirby could sympathize with Ferris's scarcely veiled contempt but, he joyfully thought, fate was certainly on his side, if not Ferris's.

Rear gunners were even more liable to wind up dead than the rest of the crew. Exposed in their rear turrets, they were in line to collect the first burst of fire from any attacking night fighter which was anywhere near on target. Many a damaged bomber limped its way back home with a dead or mortally wounded rear gunner on board.

One like Ferris, who completed a tour of ops, had to be good at worst, and probably shit hot. When someone had chanced to assign him to Kirby's crew, Kirby had won a lottery at his first attempt. He wondered how Ferris had won his DFM.

'Dished out with the rations,' Ferris said, sarcastically. Pressed further, he finally admitted that it might have had something to do with two Me 110s and a Ju 88 he had claimed, one of which had been confirmed. The other two were officially listed as 'possibles'. 'I bet their fucking crews'd be glad to hear they were only possibles,' Ferris said. 'One was burning, and the other was in a spin the last time I saw the bastards. What happened to *your* rear gunner, anyway?'

'He went LMF,' Maurice Howard said.

'I see,' Ferris said. 'One of the yellow variety.'

'Vic was all right,' Kirby said, defensively.

'You reckon?' Ferris said. 'Me, I'd shoot the buggers.'

Courting Ferris, Kirby reflected, who was not only prickly but was nursing a grievance, was not going to be an easy task. But it had to be done, and without further alienating the man who, with his record, could reasonably have expected to be assigned to an experienced crew, and had some right to feel aggrieved. Somehow, though, he had to be persuaded 'into' the crew, an integrated member, whole-heartedly part of it, and not an acerbically cynical, detached and critical outsider.

The process was interrupted by Squadron Leader Gale, who took Kirby into his office.

'I expect you know,' Gale said, 'that you won't go on ops with your crew straight away. First, you'll fly as second pilot on a couple of trips with experienced crews. Two dummy runs if you like, give you an idea what it's like. You'll fly the first one with Warrant Officer Harding. Be a good idea if you made yourself known to him. OK?'

When Kirby rejoined his crew, Ferris was not among them.

'Where's Ron?' Kirby asked. 'I thought we might take him out for a drink tonight.'

'I suggested that,' Len Bellamy said. 'He gave me the brush off. Said he had some letters to write.'

Kirby sighed.

Before Kirby took off to fly for the first time over Germany, Wing Commander Norgate had begun to dissipate the initial goodwill which his gallant record had immediately inspired.

All pilots were summoned to a meeting. 545 Squadron consisted of sixteen Lancasters, divided into two flights, 'A' and 'B'. Officer and NCO pilots stood up with a scraping of chairs as Wing Commander Norgate strode into the room, his bearing stiff and erect.

Norgate mounted the rostrum.

'Sit down, gentlemen,' he said. They sat down. Norgate surveyed them in silence. They stared back at him, waiting. 'You may as well know right from the off,' Norgate said, 'that I am regarded as a bullshitting bastard.'

There were cordial smiles, and a few scattered titters. It was good to know that their new squadron commander had a sense of humour.

Wing Commander Norgate smiled thinly in return.

'545 has a good record,' he said. 'On that, I congratulate you. It provides a firm foundation on which to build. But I would remind you that there are a handful of squadrons in Bomber Command which are regarded as outstanding. 545 is not yet among them. I see no reason why it should not be.' The smiles before him had seeped away. They gazed at him uneasily. 'If we can achieve that in a spirit of co-operation and good humour, splendid,' Wing Commander Norgate said. 'But make no mistake, gentlemen, that is the aim we shall now pursue. I do not regard that as a subject for levity, and nor should any of you. Let us understand each other from the start. I want 545 to be a squadron which I am proud to command, a squadron to which you will be proud to belong. Not just a squadron in Bomber Command, but an elite squadron in Bomber Command, one of the chosen few.' There was no doubt about it now. The man was in earnest. 'There is a belief in some quarters,' Wing Commander Norgate said, 'that discipline is something to which air crews are not subject. It is not a belief to which I subscribe. I shall require not only the self-discipline which any good bomber crew must possess, but squadron discipline as well and if, to achieve that, some of you may be obliged to change your ideas, I shall be on hand to assist you. When you take off to attack a target, you are not flying as individuals, but as part of a Bomber Command force, and within that, as members of 545 Squadron. We shall fulfil each task with the maximum efficiency and effectiveness. We shall press home every attack with the utmost vigour. Never forget that you belong to 545 Squadron. No one will turn back before reaching the target unless it is absolutely imperative, and I *mean* imperative. I am not a man who likes excuses. You are not merely pilots, you are in command of your crews. It is *your* job to ensure the highest standards of navigation, bombing, communications and the defence of your aircraft, from those you command. No slackness will be tolerated. Between us, gentlemen, we shall transform 545 into the finest squadron in the Royal Air Force . . .'

Wing Commander Norgate carried on in similar vein for another five minutes before stepping down from the rostrum. His audience stood up. Norgate strode out, looking neither to left nor right.

Kirby had never been addressed in such a fashion before, but nor had the others either, judging from the snatches of conversation he overheard, as they shuffled disconsolately out of the room.

'He thinks he's in the sodding army . . .'

'No one will turn back . . .' An imitation of Norgate's precise, neutral accent, his rather thin voice. 'Jesus . . .'

'What does he expect? Berlin on two engines.'

'That one's out to make a name for himself,' Warrant Officer Harding forecast, glumly.

'The Charge of the Light Brigade . . . that'd be right up his street . . .'

The general mood was sullen and resentful. The previous

CO had been well liked, 'one of the boys'. They resented Norgate's implied criticisms, not only of themselves, but of the man who had previously led them.

They were also alienated, in the exact sense. The concept of a squadron as analogous to a regiment in the army was alien to them. The first loyalty of a bomber crew was to each other, the men with whom they would fly, and live or die. Despite Norgate's harangue, they *did* fly as individuals. Once having taken off into the darkness, the sixteen aircraft of any one squadron were soon dispersed and absorbed into the massive night bomber stream, comprising several hundred aircraft.

The squadron was an administrative unit, providing a place to eat and sleep, quarters and a mess in which to drink with friends, a machine to order rations, issue leave passes, and travel warrants. It was not a fighting formation as such, with the exception of a very few squadrons such as 617 Squadron.

'Doesn't he realize he's not leading the bloody dam busters,' Kirby heard a flight sergeant enquiring, as they began to walk away in twos and threes.

'Half a chance, and he'd be in there,' Warrant Officer Harding said. 'And us too. He's one of your death or glory types.'

'More like death and bloody glory, by the sound of it.'

With Warrant Officer Harding at the controls, they took off. All the crew had swallowed a benzedrine tablet, and Harding advised Kirby to follow suit. 'Makes you sharper. More alert.'

After briefing the bomb aimer had least to do, and it was Harding's bomb aimer who had collected the two benzedrine tablets issued to each crew member before every operation, along with the in-flight rations, a flask of coffee, biscuits, chocolate, and when they were in luck oranges. Kirby made a mental note to adopt the same procedure.

He watched all Harding's actions, listened to every word on the intercom, anxious to assimilate as much as he could. There was an eerie combination of familiarity with what was going on, and nervous apprehension. Kirby had done all this before, but only in training. It was the difference between sparring in the gym, and ducking under the ropes into the ring, against a determined opponent with a knockout punch. Like the ring, this was a venture into the unknown.

At four thousand feet, climbing, they entered cloud. Kirby had attended briefing, and listened to the met forecast.

'Met's bang on,' Harding said approvingly.

Cloud cover was predicted to within fifty miles of the target. They were part of the main force. The smaller force, which would carry out a diversionary raid to the south, would not be so fortunate. They would face clear skies once they crossed into Germany.

At sixteen thousand feet Harding levelled out. They were still in cloud.

'Looks good,' Harding said, glancing at Kirby. His crinkled eyes indicated a smile. They had been on oxygen since 10,000 feet, and Harding's mask concealed his features.

Over the North Sea, Kirby heard the brief rattle, as first the rear gunner and then the mid upper gunner cleared their guns.

'Guns OK, skipper.'

'OK, Terry.'

'Guns OK, skip.'

'OK, Wilf.'

They flew on in the dense cloud, the wings invisible. They could have been alone in the whole wide world, flying unseeing and unseen in that comforting, protective blanket of cloud, which searchlights might probe as they crossed the enemy coast, but would not penetrate.

Kirby could not repress a start when, suddenly, the flashes of exploding heavy anti-aircraft shells appeared in the cloud first below them, then to starboard, then ahead and above.

'Crossing the Dutch coast,' Harding said. 'Check, Mac.'

'Spot on, skip.'

'New course?'

'Steer one six five.'

The flashes pursued them for a while, and then ceased to appear.

'Cloud's beginning to break up ahead, skipper.'

'OK, Johnny, seen it too. We'll keep going for a while, and take a look-see.'

The cloud thinned and became wispy. Kirby strained his eyes, peering into the darkness ahead, trying to put himself in Harding's place. To starboard, the sky seemed to be clear, but to port was a cliff of cloud rising a thousand feet or more above them.

'If we go port, Mac, we could stay in cloud for a good bit longer. That cause any problems?'

'Could run into more flak that way, skip.'

'Sooner chance guns than night fighters.'

'OK, steer one five five. That might keep us clear with any luck.'

The aircraft banked, and a minute later re-entered cloud. Soon, flashes which turned into balls began to appear, some near enough to make the heavily laden aircraft bump and dip.

'They're getting bloody close back here, skip.'

'Yes, not sure this was such a bright idea, Terry. Still, we're stuck with it now.'

'Hang on . . . I think they've found some other bugger . . . I can see the bursts way below now.'

'Praise the lord for Stirlings.'

Abruptly, the cloud vanished behind them, and at the same moment, Kirby could see the fires burning fifty miles ahead.

The conversation on the intercom became more staccato, intense and jumpy. They were in night fighter territory.

As they came closer to the target, from which came a spreading glow, Kirby realized with a shock that they were not alone in the sky after all. The air was full of planes, Halifaxes and Lancasters to either side of them, ahead and a little above, the dark shapes of Stirlings silhouetted far below.

'Watch out for that Lanc starboard, skip.'

'Got him, Johnny.' The aircraft rose and banked, and a Lancaster slid diagonally below them. 'Silly sod.'

Harding turned on to his bombing run, flying absolutely straight and level now into the maelstrom of shells and searchlights spouting from the burning city towards which they were heading. His only deflections from now on would be in response to the bomb aimer's instructions.

The entire bomber stream of some five hundred aircraft would bomb within twenty minutes, with the object of overwhelming the defences. More than half the stream had already bombed. Aircraft could be seen ahead turning for home. Far below, there was a carpet of fire, with scattered flowing pinpoints outside the periphery, where incendiaries had missed the main target area. Mini volcanoes heaved and spouted as 8,000lb bombs descended into the flames and exploded.

Kirby's heart was pounding rapidly. He was both awed and appalled by the spectacle around him. Whatever was happening in that hell on the ground, the defences were far from overwhelmed. The phrase 'war in the air' took on a meaning he had never anticipated in his darkest forebodings. Here, all around him, a full-scale battle was being fought, sixteen thousand feet above the ground.

He glimpsed, away to starboard, flashes of light – a night fighter's cannons firing at its target. He saw, a moment later, tracer cutting lines across the sky – the reply from the rear gunner of the bomber being attacked. Just the guns firing. He could not see the aircraft concerned, he never knew the result of that engagement to starboard.

He saw a thin, blue, radar-controlled searchlight as it flicked on to and held a bomber which was immediately coned by several conventional searchlights. The bomber dived and weaved uselessly, in a dance like a butterfly's on a summer's day. Exploding shells cocooned it. The bomber blew up in a great ball of flame.

He looked down. Silhouetted against the raging fires below was a Lancaster with part of its tailplane missing. It commenced a leisurely spin, rotating slowly on its vertical downward axis. No parachutes appeared. In his earphones, Kirby only half heard the bomb aimer's instructions.

'Left, left, steady . . . right, steady . . .'

They seemed to be flying into a hail of heavy anti-aircraft fire, in which nothing could conceivably survive. Warrant

Officer Harding ignored it, calmly intent only on his precise, deliberate changes of course.

Over that burning city, Kirby discovered things he did not know about anti-aircraft shells. If he looked down, he could see the light flak falling away, several thousand feet below, where the Stirlings were. Up where he was, inside the heavy anti-aircraft barrage, when the shells came close you could *hear* the muffled thud of the explosion above the constant thunder of the Lancaster's four engines.

And when they got really close, you could not only hear the explosions, you could *smell* them, you breathed in the sour, acrid stench of cordite.

Chapter Ten

'How about Bishops Stortford or Chelmsford?' Kirby said to Ferris.

Kirby was still trying to woo his recalcitrant rear gunner. He had now flown twice over Germany, the second time with a Flight Lieutenant Abel, and the next time the squadron went on ops, Kirby would not be there merely for experience. It was mid afternoon, and nothing had gone up on the notice board in the Flight Office, but this might be the last night before they all flew together on operations for the first time.

Kirby had gained a considerable amount of status with his crew, who questioned him with anxious interest about what it was like, the real thing. Kirby had been where they had not, passenger or no.

The natural exception was Flight Sergeant Ferris, who yawned openly as Kirby recounted his experiences, and wore an incipient, patronizing sneer. As Ferris remarked to a fellow old hand on the squadron, he had spent more hours on the bloody Elsan than had his sprog skipper over Germany.

'Stortford's a dead hole,' Ferris said, dismissively.

'OK, so it's Chelmsford,' Kirby said. 'That's on. We'll see if we can find a decent pub.'

'There's one just down the road from the Wrennery,' Ferris said. 'They get in there sometimes, if anyone fancies that sort of thing.' Ferris had an encyclopaedic grasp of such important details.

'Too true,' Maurice Howard said, his eyes lighting up. 'Lead me to it. I like crumpet with a bit of class.'

Ferris eyed him contemptuously.

'Stuck up lot if you ask me,' he said. 'They all come from bloody Cheltenham or Kensington, and talk as if they had plums under their tongues.'

Ferris was prone to sweeping judgements, but it was true that, unlike the other women's services, girls were not conscripted into the Women's Royal Naval Service, and not all who volunteered, in some cases perhaps because of the attractive uniform, were accepted. As with any group composed solely of volunteers, including air crew, there was a tendency to regard themselves as an elite.

'It's those black stockings,' Maurice Howard said, longingly. 'Who cares how they talk? Black stockings on lovely white thighs. I can't wait.'

'You'll be lucky,' Ferris said. 'Professional virgins, all of them.'

The pub in question was on the outskirts of Chelmsford. It was patent that Ferris was obstinately preserving his critical air of distance, and had no intention of becoming one of them. Kirby was beginning to despair. If there was some way to get through to Ferris, he had not yet found it.

'Always smoke a pipe, do you?' Ferris enquired. Ted Hollis nodded, and puffed in calm slow motion. Ferris eyed him judicially. 'One big advantage to a pipe,' he said. 'No one expects you to hand the fucking thing round.' Ted Hollis smiled absently.

When it came to Ted's turn, Kirby noticed that his bomb aimer was walking away towards the lavatory. His timing, as ever, was perfect.

'My shout,' Kirby said, collecting the glasses.

'It bloody ain't,' Ferris observed.

Kirby returned from the bar, and put the tray down on the table. Ted Hollis had come back.

'Don't he ever buy a bloody round?' Ferris demanded.

'It's against his principles,' Maurice Howard said.

'I pay my share,' Ted Hollis said. 'It all evens out. I don't drink as much as you lot.'

'Only at someone else's expense,' Maurice Howard said.

'Ted's a saver,' Kirby said. 'How much is it you've got in the bank now, Ted? Five hundred?'

'Nearly,' Ted said. 'I'm aiming for a thousand quid by the end of the war.'

'Bloody hell,' Ferris said. A thousand pounds was a fortune. 'What for?'

'Capital,' Ted Hollis said, vaguely. 'I want to have some capital behind me.'

'Capital?' Ferris was incredulous. 'You're just starting a tour of ops, and you're thinking about capital?'

'Plus interest,' Ted Hollis said. 'Put it on deposit, you see, and that way it works for you.'

'Well, listen, John D. Rockefeller,' Ferris said, 'if you want to be the richest bloody bomb aimer in some cemetery, that's your lookout. But you're not accumulating capital at my expense. This lot may stand for it, but not me. I'm keeping count from now on, chum, and you owe me a drink.'

Just after nine o'clock, four Wrens arrived, and stood in a group in the far corner of the bar. Maurice Howard eyed them, and held a conference in undertones with Arthur Wood. The latter looked nervous and doubtful.

'You don't have to say anything, Arthur,' Maurice Howard told him. 'Just stop looking like a dead sheep, and play the strong, silent type. Come on.' He stood up. 'Shan't be long,' he promised. 'We'll bring 'em over in a minute, so don't let anyone pinch these chairs.' They set off on their quest.

'That's all I need,' Ferris said. 'Forking out on gin and its for toffee nosed Wrens who think they're sitting on a gold mine.'

'Let's go into the public bar,' Kirby said. Ferris seemed a bit surprised, but he stood up willingly enough. So did Ted Hollis, moving quite swiftly for him. 'You stay where you are, Ted,' Kirby said, firmly. 'You heard Maurice. Keep those chairs vacant.'

The public bar was mostly populated by locals, with a sprinkling of army privates. A darts match was in progress. Kirby and Ferris propped up the quieter corner of the bar.

Kirby's two trips had left him with a mass of impressions,

mostly confused. He had formed a profound admiration for the sheer courage of Warrant Officer Harding and Flight Lieutenant Abel, and their crews. He found it hard to imagine himself performing those tasks as coolly and efficiently, in that inferno high above a target.

But as he had gone over those hours spent watching how it was done, reliving them again and again in his mind, he had come to feel, if a little uncertainly, that his baptism ought to lead to rather more than merely copying how other men did it, no matter how skilful they were. He was not Harding or Abel, he was himself, David Kirby, with a mind of his own, which pointed tentatively towards conclusions of his own, and not theirs.

The idea of forming slightly different assessments in this way worried him more than a little. Surely it was safer simply to follow in the well-tried footsteps of such experienced pilots? Who the devil was he to question the routine they adopted? It seemed presumptuous in the extreme. And if it was, Ferris was certainly the man to tell him so in no uncertain terms.

'I'd like a bit of advice, Ron,' Kirby said.

'Oh?' Ferris was lighting a cigarette. He blew out the match, and gazed at Kirby non-committally.

'Two trips with someone else doing all the work means damn all, I realize that,' Kirby said. 'But it's all I've got.' Ferris said nothing. His gaze shifted to the dart board as someone scored a treble twenty, and a cheer went up. It was hard to tell if he was listening or not. Kirby ploughed on. 'The night I flew with Flight Lieutenant Abel, it was clear skies all the way,' Kirby said. 'Over the North Sea, we cleared our guns.' Ferris inhaled deeply, blew out a stream of smoke, and flicked ash on to the floor. 'Others were doing the same,' Kirby said. 'I saw one of them, oh, five or ten miles away. Just flashes from the gun muzzles, but I could see them. Now I know that's all routine,' Kirby said, 'and I've no idea if German night fighters patrol out over the North Sea or not. But it struck me that if I could see those guns firing, so could any Jerries around.' Ferris screwed his cigarette into the ashtray. 'It's just a thought,' Kirby said, lamely.

'I don't trust any bleeding armourer,' Ferris said. 'Once he's finished, I check and double check. I know my guns are in perfect working order before I ever leave the ground. Mine don't need clearing upstairs.'

'Arthur Wood's a first-class wireless operator,' Kirby said, 'but he doesn't know as much about Brownings as you do. Nor does Ted Hollis.'

'They would if I had a few sessions with them,' Ferris said.

'So we scrub clearing our guns,' Kirby said. 'That all right with you?'

'Suits me,' Ferris said indifferently. But Kirby was encouraged. He felt that marginal progress was being made. Ferris's pale eyebrows lifted in enquiry. 'Is that it?'

'Not quite,' Kirby said. 'On the intercom, both crews, Harding's and Abel's, used Christian names all the time, Len, Fred, Mac and so on.'

'So?' Ferris lit another cigarette.

'So have we, all through training,' Kirby said. 'It seemed the natural thing to do, we all know each other's voices, I could always tell who was speaking. But after we left the target with Warrant Officer Harding, we nearly got jumped by an Me 110. There was a lot of chat going on, and Tim Harding thought his rear gunner had spotted this Messerschmitt. But it wasn't. It was his mid upper gunner, and Tim turned the wrong way, which put the Me 110 bang on our tail. As it happened, his first burst missed us, Tim took evasive action, managed to get into cloud, and we lost him. But it made me think about Christian names and too much chit-chat.'

'If you want to play it safe, up to you,' Ferris said.

'One for the road,' Kirby suggested.

'Don't mind if I do,' Ferris said. 'Have a fag.'

'Thanks,' Kirby said. He ordered two halves of bitter. Ferris lit his cigarette for him. 'I know you've got thirty ops behind you, Ron,' Kirby said, 'and we're only just starting. But is there anything I can do to help you? I mean, the way I fly . . . well, I don't know what I mean really . . . just anything which might make life easier for you.'

Ferris pursed his lips doubtfully.

'Depends if you want to go to a lot of trouble,' he said.

'I'll tell you what I don't want,' Kirby said. 'I don't want to get shot down.'

'I can see at night like nobody's business,' Ferris said. 'I was born that way. I'm like a bloody owl. But the Jerries have got something, Christ knows what, and it hits you before you know it's there. You must have heard about it.'

Kirby nodded uneasily. 'Planes suddenly blowing up for no reason. It's true, then? It's not just a yarn?'

'It's true,' Ferris said. 'Blokes flying peacefully along, no flak, no sign of night fighters, nothing. Then, boom, they explode. Blown out of the sky.' His forefinger tapped Kirby's uniform. His face was serious. 'But there's got to be a reason. It can't just happen. Maybe they've developed a fighter powerful enough to climb up on us and attack from underneath . . .'

'It'd need one hell of a rate of climb for that,' Kirby said, doubtfully.

'Or maybe it's just a manoeuvre we haven't cottoned on to,' Ferris said. 'I don't know. It's a fucking mystery. But whatever it is, it can't be invisible, and the more I get to see, the better chance we stand. If you can fly in a sort of slow corkscrew all the time, so that my turret rotates in a kind of arc, *then* I get to see below, as well as behind and above and to the sides. If you can do that, no bugger's going to catch us unawares. Besides which, it'll confuse any fighter's radar operator, put him off his stroke.' Kirby sipped his beer, and stared into his glass. 'It makes it hard work,' Ferris said. 'Must be hell's own delight to fly an accurate course that way. No time to relax and sit back. Perhaps it's early days to think about it. Let's see how it goes. Get a few trips under your belt first.'

'People get shot down on their first few trips,' Kirby said.

'That's when most of them buy it,' Ferris said, comfortingly. 'Before they know arse from elbow.'

Kirby was thinking that it would have to be a pretty flat corkscrew. It would not do to lose too much height. Fully laden with bombs, the Lancaster would not easily regain lost height.

He said, 'We couldn't do it if we were in the main stream. Too much risk of collision.'

'Whatever recommended height we get at briefing,' Ferris said, 'we'd have to fly well above it.'

'Well, I asked you what you wanted,' Kirby said. 'It wouldn't work if everyone else did it though.'

'Everyone won't,' Ferris said. 'They're too fucking idle. Rather sit on their bums and hope for the best.'

'We'll give it a go,' Kirby said.

'Getting through a tour of ops,' Ferris said, 'you need a lot of luck. Nothing the finest crew in the world can do without that. If you've eliminated every chance you can think of, and you still get the chop, hard luck. I'm just not in favour of sitting up and begging for it, that's all.'

When the three-ton truck disgorged its passengers back at Woodley Common, Kirby took his crew to one side before they dispersed to their billets.

They stood in the darkness, shivering, greatcoat collars turned up against the cold. In the Wrens' company, Maurice Howard had taken to gin as well as beer, and the mixture had made him bellicose.

'For Christ's sake, David,' he said, 'just because you're an officer, you don't have to come all this Navigator to Pilot crap. That's all bull, and you know it.'

'I've explained why,' Kirby said. 'You'll get used to it.'

'And how the hell you expect me to navigate with you weaving about all over the the sky . . .'

'I'll worry about flying the correct heading,' Kirby said. 'Anyway, there'll be no problem until we're out of Gee range, and after that a mean course'll be accurate enough until we can see the markers.'

'Well, don't blame me if we get lost,' Maurice Howard said, aggressively.

Kirby said, controlling his irritation, 'We'll give it a try, and see how it works out.'

'On your say so,' Maurice Howard said, slurring his sibilants somewhat. 'Don't try pulling rank, David Kirby, just because you're a bloody pilot officer.'

A match flared, Ferris sucked on his cigarette, threw the match away. 'You're too pissed or too stupid to understand what he's told you,' Ferris's voice said in the darkness. 'Either way, just fucking belt up. He's the skipper, and he's got the right to have things his way.'

'Oh, sod off,' Maurice Howard said, and lurched away into the darkness.

Kirby's first operation was a fiasco. Take off was delayed several times, due to weather. It was the early hours of the morning before the squadron finally received the go. Transport dropped Kirby and his crew off at dispersal, and they climbed aboard K – King, 'their' aircraft from now on. The station call sign was 'Castle' and the squadron call sign was 'Horseman'.

Kirby had started his four engines, and tested his magnetoes. Len Bellamy quietly confirmed that all engines were functioning normally.

'Engineer to Pilot, everything OK.'

This was it, the moment it had all been leading up to. Kirby released his brakes, rolled forward gently, tested them, and came to a stop, waiting his chance to take his place in the queue of aircraft which was forming on the perimeter track, indicated by dim, spaced out pinpoints of light.

'Rear Gunner,' Ferris said, 'there's some WAAF behind. Seems to be watching us.'

'Seen her,' Kirby said. 'She turned up five minutes ago.'

He glanced over his shoulder. She was still there, a shapeless figure merging into the darkness, battledress trousers below her greatcoat, a scarf muffling her face, woollen gloves on the hands which were gripping the handlebars of her bicycle, as she stood motionless in the long grass beside the circle of hard standing they had just left.

Kirby eased forward into the queue, brakes squeaked as he turned on to the perimeter track, and came to a stop behind the Lancaster in front.

'Still there,' Ferris reported. 'She must be bloody freezing.'

117

Ahead of Kirby were the dull shapes of Lancasters, squatting, waiting, propellers spinning. The first one turned on to the runway, and received the green lamp signal from the caravan parked to one side.

Throttles opened in a roar which Kirby could hear above the noise of his own idling engines, and L – London, flown by Wing Commander Norgate, moved forward along the runway, and gathered speed.

The queue inched forward and came to a stop again as the second aircraft turned on to the runway.

'She's just given us a wave,' Ferris said. 'I reckon she's come to see us off. Anyone know who she is?'

'Her name's Kay,' Kirby said.

'How do you know that, skip? She a friend of yours?'

'No,' Kirby said. 'But I like to go and see my own parachute being packed. If I ever have to use the thing, I want to know it's going to open. She's the WAAF who packs my 'chute. We've just passed the time of day, that's all.'

Ferris said nothing more. He eyed the girl, Kay, who must have cycled two miles from the WAAF quarters to reach dispersal, and wondered if she was fat or thin, pretty or plain. Impossible to tell under all that heavy clothing.

K – King moved forward again, the tail wheel below Ferris's turret bumping on the tarmac. Behind, the first of the following Lancasters closed up. Before its fuselage obscured the girl, she lifted her right hand high once more in a final gesture of greeting. Ferris gave her a thumbs-up gesture for good luck, although he doubted if she could see him now.

Aircraft were taking off to Ferris's left at intervals, roaring along the runway, tailplanes lifting into the air as they gained speed. K – King rumbled forward. One more to go, and it would be their turn. The first operation of Ferris's second tour.

So far, Ferris thought, his green young skipper had made all the right noises. Ferris approved of his concern for detail, such as taking time out to make sure that his parachute would open if the time ever came to bale out. David Kirby was dead right about that, Ferris thought, who followed the same routine himself. You would only get the one chance, and if the fucking

thing didn't open then it was too late. The WAAF who had
packed his 'chute was a dumpy bit of skirt called Wendy,
offhand, but efficient. He supposed that Kay could have been
around there somewhere, but if so, he had not noticed her.

Moving forward again now, turning on to the runway. The
next few hours would tell what Kirby was made of. Making
the right noises was one thing. Anyone as bright as Kirby
undoubtedly was could fly a perfect operation over a glass of
beer in a nice safe pub. 'Right, you bloody novice,' Ferris
thought. 'Now let's see if you've really got what it takes.'

In the final few seconds before the throttles opened, and the
rumble of the four engines ascended into a deafening roar,
Ferris carried out the ritual which never varied.

He wriggled his behind one last time, settling into the seat
which he would not leave for the next several hours.

He conjured up a particular face in his mind, held it for a
moment, said, 'Good night' to it, 'see you soon', and let it go.

Thirdly, and finally, a believer in the rule of three, Ferris
groped under his heated flying suit, and touched the hard
shape of the silver plated cigarette case which he had slipped
into the left-hand breast pocket of his battledress, a final check
that it was actually there. The cigarette case was a birthday
present, and Ferris never used it. He only ever carried it when
he flew on operations. One of these days, it might serve to
deflect a shell fragment from his heart. You never knew.

The same ritual had seen Ferris safely through thirty
operations. He would faithfully repeat it every time they took
off for Germany, in the hope that fate would continue to
acknowledge and accept the bargain.

His turret juddered and bounced as K – King gained speed.
Ferris watched the tarmac runway unrolling behind him. He
had done all he could. Now, it was in the lap of the gods, his
own keen eyes, his guns, and the remainder of the crew, five
unknown quantities up front.

Ferris searched the receding airfield away to his left as K –
King left the ground, but even his eyes could not make out her
small shape in the dense blackness below, if indeed she was
still there. He wondered if her presence at their particular

dispersal was a good sign. He hoped so. Instinct told Ferris they were going to need every particle of luck which could be recognized, accumulated, treasured and hoarded.

K – King entered cloud at five hundred feet. When Kirby levelled off at 16,000 feet, they were still in cloud, dark, dense, impenetrable. Bad weather was predicted all the way, with the chance of a break over the target area. Conditions for landing were expected to have improved by the time they returned.

'Navigator to Pilot,' Maurice Howard said, his tone oozing obvious irony. 'You don't seem to be flying that slow corkscrew you were so keen on.'

'Pilot to Navigator, there's no need in this shit,' Kirby said, tartly.

'Roger D, Captain,' Maurice Howard said.

'Pilot to Navigator, we're still on climbing course,' Kirby said, pointedly. He told himself that Maurice was merely being his usual self, his idea of being funny.

'New course coming up.' There was a long silence. Kirby fretted. Dear God, what the hell was Maurice up to?

'Pilot to Navigator, what's the problem?' he enquired finally.

'Gee seems to be on the bloody blink . . . hang on . . .'

Gee was one of their two navigational aids. Linked to slave transmitting stations in the UK, it provided a lattice work of bearings which, given accurate interpretation by the navigator, indicated the aircraft's exact position. The drawback was that its range was limited, and did not extend much further than Holland.

'No, sorry, the damn thing's definitely packed up. Can't get anything at all.'

'Pilot to Navigator, we must be towards the limit of Gee anyway, so carry on with your D/R. I've given you steady courses since take off.'

'Navigator to Pilot, I haven't been able to verify my D/R plot for the past thirty minutes.' Maurice Howard had stopped being jokey. 'In effect, I shall be restarting it from the last Gee fix, which was quite a way back.'

'Pilot to Navigator, fine. Let me have a new course as soon as possible.'

What difficulties this presented, Kirby could not imagine. He stood the silence for as long as he could, and then flicked his microphone switch on.

'Pilot to Navigator, have you got that new course yet?'

'Navigator to Pilot, one five zero.'

Kirby banked gently, watched the dial of the gyro compass rotate, began to ease out of the turn at 145 degrees, and the gyro compass settled comfortably on 150. He could hear the noise of gentle breathing in his earphones.

'Someone's got his microphone on,' Kirby said. There was a click, and the breathing stopped. Time went by. The engines were running perfectly. They were cruising at correct speed and altitude. Locked in black cloud, visibility was zero, there was nothing to see.

Kirby shifted restlessly, and glanced at his watch. He had schooled himself to keep a mental plot going in his head. It could not be more than a rough estimate, but it was some sort of check.

'Pilot to Navigator, shouldn't we have crossed the enemy coast by now?'

'The wind must have changed, affected our ground speed a bit. We're OK. Hold your present course.'

Minutes passed. Kirby was beginning to understand how it was possible to become completely disoriented. Apart from the faint phosphorescent glow of the instruments before him, there was no guide to their attitude. He had the unreasoning feeling that they were flying in circles, yet the artificial horizon, gyro compass, and altimeter told him that they were straight and level and on course. He glanced at his magnetic compass again; gyros sometimes went wrong, but the compass needle between the parallel bars was vibrating gently on 150.

The air speed indicator showed a steady 140 knots but since they were flying at 16,000 feet, that was equivalent to 250 knots ground speed, if the wind were nil. If the wind had changed as, if Maurice Howard was right, it must have done, by how much? Until they got a fix, there was no way of knowing.

'Pilot to Navigator, did you allow for the extra time we were flying on climbing course, before we turned?' He was getting screwed up, and he knew it.

'Navigator to Pilot, no need to panic,' Maurice Howard said, resigned. 'We can't be far off now. Two or three minutes at most. I'm switching on the H2S.'

Kirby let that go. H2S was an airborne radar device which provided the contours of the ground below on the navigator's radar screen. But it could only be used in brief snatches. Once switched on, it enabled German night fighters to home on to the aircraft using it. Still, in this filthy muck, they should be all right for a few minutes.

Without warning, the balls of exploding anti-aircraft shells glowed in the black murk around them. Kirby was almost glad to see them. The aircraft lurched, and then steadied. Maurice Howard was triumphant.

'There you are. Just crossed the Dutch coast now . . . got a good fix, too . . . I was right, the wind's shifted . . . steer one three five.'

Kirby altered course. His spirits lifted. The anti-aircraft shells receded behind them, and died away.

'Rear Gunner, that didn't look like Dutch flak to me,' Ferris said, gloomily, the Cassandra in the tail end.

'For Christ's sake,' Maurice Howard said, 'we crossed twenty miles south of Rotterdam. The contours couldn't have been bloody plainer.'

That night, the main force was attacking Berlin. 545 squadron formed part of the smaller, diversionary force, which was to bomb the secondary target, also deep inside Germany, but well to the south and west of Berlin.

They would not fly a direct course, but in a series of dog legs, with the object of concealing the target from the German defences until the last moment.

From now on, they were dependent on dead reckoning navigation, only occasionally using H2S when they should be approaching some feature, such as a river, which would show up on the radar screen.

They encountered no further flak which, at first, Kirby welcomed. After a while, he found its absence almost eerie. It made him uneasy. He also became uneasy about Maurice Howard's constant corrections, whenever he secured a fix on his H2S.

'Pilot to Navigator, are you sure about all these wind changes?'

'There's a trough extending diagonally right across Europe from the south-west,' Maurice Howard said. 'If you remember,' he added, but his tone showed tension, rather than his usual haughtiness when his calculations were queried. Maurice was getting screwed up too.

'I know that, Navigator,' Kirby said, refraining with some difficulty from adding 'I was at the bloody briefing too'. The narrow predicted trough, hundreds of miles long, meant that the winds they would encounter, although fairly light, would shift 180 degrees as they flew across Germany. 'But according to you, every forecast wind has been wrong.'

'Listen,' Maurice Howard snapped, 'I can only give you what I see on the fucking radar screen, and I'm fucking telling you . . . let me do my job and you do yours, all right?'

'Pilot to Navigator, take it easy,' Kirby said. 'Just tell me how late we'll be over the target.'

The remainder of the diversionary force of eighty bombers would have encountered the same wind changes, and should also, of course, be equally late. Many, like K – King, were carrying incendiaries. Even in this shitty weather, some reflection of the fires below should penetrate the thick layer of cloud.

As they approached their revised ETA, Kirby peered ahead, searching for some indication, balls of flak in the cloud, the dim glow of a burning town on the ground, anything. There was nothing but complete blackness. The bomb aimer and rear gunner reported that they could see nothing either.

'Bomb Aimer to Pilot, suggest we bomb on ETA,' Ted Hollis said.

'Pilot to Bomb Aimer, we haven't come all this way to bomb fuck all,' Kirby said. 'Perhaps this cloud's too thick. I'm taking her down a bit, so keep your eyes open.'

Flying in a wide circle, Kirby lost height. At 12,000 feet he levelled out. Any lower than that, and they ran the risk of light anti-aircraft fire, although so far there had been none of any kind. And still . . . nothing . . .

'Where the hell is the damn place?' Kirby muttered, to himself.

Ted Hollis and Ferris spoke simultaneously. Kirby had seen it too. A faint flickering glow, oozing up through the cloud, away to starboard.

'Rear Gunner to Pilot, that looks like fires.'

'Bomb Aimer to Pilot, there it is.' Ted Hollis sounded almost excited for once.

'OK, Bomb Aimer, got it.'

Kirby turned starboard, and they bombed the flickering glow.

'Bombs gone.'

'I told you.' Maurice Howard was jubilant. 'Spot on. Exactly where I said it was.'

Well, at least they were going home now, but after his initial excited lift when he had first glimpsed that faint glow far below, Kirby developed a sense of uncertainty. If that had been the target, why had there been no anti-aircraft fire? Perhaps the preceding bombers had knocked them out. Yes, that must be it . . .

But he could not shake off the nagging instinct that something was seriously wrong. They still had to get down in one piece. He wondered what the weather was like over England.

The homeward-bound flight seemed even longer, locked as they still were in anonymous blackness. Kirby shifted in his seat. He was becoming stiff and tired. He thought about swallowing another benzedrine tablet, but if he did that he would be in no condition to sleep, and in less than two hours now they should be back at Woodley Common.

'Navigator to Pilot, wind's changed again . . .'

Kirby could not quite decide whether Maurice Howard was displaying masterful confidence, or utter confusion.

'Pilot to Navigator, where the hell are we?'

'Over the North Sea now.'

'If we've already crossed the coast, why wasn't there any flak?'

'We must have just struck lucky. That new wind's taken us further north than we should be.'

'Pilot to Navigator, are you dead certain about our position? We'll have to start letting down through this bloody shit soon.'

'No question. Got a perfect fix on H2S as we crossed the coast. You can start letting down now.'

Kirby glanced at his watch, made some quick calculations, and decided to leave it for another five minutes to be on the safe side. After that, there would be no doubt about it, they must be safely over water. They could not be all that far off track.

He began to let down at five hundred feet a minute. At four thousand feet, he thought for a moment, with relief, that the cloud was thinning. Then he realized that it was not, that the very slight lightening, the ability to see for the first time that night the inner engines, was because, somewhere high above the cloud mass, night was receding. For the moment, he had forgotten how late they had taken off.

He slowed his rate of descent to three hundred feet a minute. At one thousand feet, he levelled off. They were still in cloud, although he could now just see his own wingtips.

'Bomb Aimer, Rear Gunner, can you see anything?'

Even Ferris could not detect the sea, which should be not far below them.

'Navigator to Pilot, you can keep on going,' Maurice Howard urged.

Kirby resumed his descent, inching cautiously down through the cloud at one hundred feet a minute. If the pressure had changed along with those winds, his altimeter would not be showing the correct altitude.

The needle crept past five hundred feet . . . four hundred and fifty . . . four hundred . . . there was perspiration on

Kirby's face. His hands were clamped on the control column like vices. He took a deep breath, and tried to relax . . . three hundred and fifty feet . . . he dare not take the machine much lower . . .

And suddenly, they were below cloud, racing close above cold green water in the first murky light of the day.

'Bomb Aimer to Navigator, coast coming up.'

'Navigator to Pilot, right on time,' Maurice Howard was exultant. A textbook piece of navigation. 'We should be coasting in just south of Norwich. Alter course to 225 when crossed.'

'Pilot to Navigator, damn good. Well done.' Kirby was highly relieved. Later, after they had landed, he would apologize to Maurice properly.

He altered course to 225, and flew inland. Again the feeling that something was wrong took hold of him. Somehow, in the first light of day, the countryside did not look like East Anglia.

'Bomb Aimer to Pilot, that looks like an airfield coming up,' Ted Hollis said.

Kirby's reaction was instinctive. He flung the huge Lancaster into a steep banking turn as if it were a Harvard. The starboard wingtip seemed almost to be brushing the ground below. He too had seen the airfield. He had also picked out the big letters on the side of a building which spelt DUN-LOAGHAIRE.

Maurice Howard's stomach compressed unpleasantly in the G of the steep turn.

'What's going on?' he demanded, uneasily, unable to see outside from his compartment. 'What have you turned round for?'

'Pilot to Navigator, because I don't fancy getting shot at by the Irish,' Kirby said. 'You nearly took us over Dublin Airport, you stupid bastard.'

'What? Don't be bloody silly,' Maurice Howard said. 'That's impossible.'

'Rear Gunner to Navigator,' Ferris said. His tone of voice was peculiar. 'I'm looking at bleeding Gaelic, pronounced Dunleary, at a guess. As for where we've been . . . Christ.'

Maurice Howard said nothing. Nor, for a while, did anyone else. The perspiration on Kirby's face had gone cold, and his lips were dry. He could see the map and its contours in his head. In the belief that they were over the North Sea, he had been letting down across the Welsh Mountains. If he had started his descent when Maurice Howard told him it was safe to do so, the Lancaster would now be a heap of shattered wreckage on some bleak hillside, and they would all be dead. Even as it was, he wondered by how much they had missed the ground, and his body shivered involuntarily. It could have been by a mere few feet. He would never know.

'Pilot to Navigator,' Kirby said, 'we're now approaching Bristol. You can show that on your charts as the point where we got a fix. I don't feel like explaining why we nearly flew over Dublin Airport.'

Maurice Howard said, almost humbly, 'I'm sorry, David. I can't think what happened, honestly I can't, unless the H2S is on the blink as well.'

'Never mind that now,' Kirby said. 'When you've cooked your plot, come up front, and help map read home. I'd rather keep the ground in sight from here on.'

'Flight Engineer to Pilot, we're low on fuel,' Len Bellamy said. 'You'd use too much if you tried to climb. We'll be lucky to make it back anyway.'

'We'll reduce speed,' Kirby said. 'Let's have a go. You tell me if we have to divert. There are plenty of places we can put in if we have to.'

There was no dangerously high ground between them and Woodley Common. They flew back across England, skirting north of London, well clear of the barrage balloons.

Kirby called Woodley Common on R/T, and received permission for a straight in approach. He thought he detected a note of surprise in the controller's voice.

Flaps and undercarriage down, he came in over the perimeter fence, and tyres squealed as he eased back on the control column, and the Lancaster stalled on to the runway.

He taxied to his dispersal point, and switched off the

engines. After the constant, unending roar, silence in itself seemed like a sudden palpable wall of sound.

'Well, we made it, Len,' he said.

'The traditional spoonful left, skipper,' his flight engineer said wryly.

They climbed out, and stood in the morning chill beside the perimeter track, waiting for transport. Arthur Wood's face was parchment pale, and he kept swallowing.

'Are you all right, Arthur?' Kirby asked.

'A bit queasy, that's all,' Arthur Wood said. 'I'll be OK.'

He wandered a few yards away into the long grass, stood still for a few moments, and then bent double, and vomited.

Ferris unearthed a crumb of comfort.

'That WAAF was there when we came in,' he said. 'She must have a chum in Air Traffic Control, told her we were coming back.' Kirby nodded. As the runway had broadened and flattened in front of him when he made his approach, he had seen the muffled up figure with the bicycle. 'Maybe she's adopted us,' Ferris said, hopefully. 'WAAFs do that sometimes, pick on a particular crew, see them off, there when they get back. Perhaps she's decided to be our lucky mascot.'

'If last night was anything to go by,' Len Bellamy said, 'she's a damned good one. I hope she's there next time. Every time, come to that.'

'Me too,' Ferris said. He eyed Maurice Howard, a pale, hard stare. 'We're going to need luck by the fucking ton, if you ask me.'

They were the only crew in the debriefing room.

'We thought you'd had it,' the intelligence officer said. 'You've been posted missing, along with Warrant Officer Harding.'

'Isn't he back yet?' Kirby asked.

'No,' the intelligence officer said. 'OK, let's get on with it. I expect you chaps are ready for bed.'

Warrant Officer Harding never did get back. Eventually, through the Red Cross, it was learned that his navigator and rear gunner had baled out, and were prisoners of war. The remainder were presumed killed.

Kirby woke up ten minutes before his batman called him, and lay in bed, thinking. By the time he had washed and dressed, he had made his decision.

At two o'clock, he walked to the Flight Office, and looked at the notice board. No operation was scheduled for that night.

'Glad you got back, David,' Squadron Leader Gale said. 'I gather it didn't go too smoothly though.'

'It was a shambles,' Kirby said. 'From beginning to end.'

Squadron Leader Gale smiled.

'We've all cocked one up,' he said. 'Don't worry about it. But the CO wants to see you.'

'Well, as it happens, I want to see him,' Kirby said.

Wing Commander Norgate sat in his office behind his desk. He had read all the debriefing reports, including Kirby's. He had also had words with the Squadron Navigation Leader who, after every operation, collected all the navigators' charts, and studied them.

Norgate looked up at Kirby, who had entered and saluted, and was standing at attention before him. Norgate had no intention of inviting him to sit down or to stand at ease.

'According to your debriefing, Kirby,' Norgate said softly, 'you encountered no anti-aircraft fire over the target. And yet every other crew reported heavy flak, and my own aircraft and two others were slightly damaged. How do you account for that?'

'Looking back, sir,' Kirby said, 'I don't think we bombed the target at all.'

'Then why did you bomb if you weren't over the target?'

'We thought we were, sir,' Kirby said. 'We saw what we imagined were fires. Perhaps they were German decoy fires, or perhaps reflected searchlights . . .'

'Or perhaps you just dumped your bombs at random,' Norgate said.

'That, sir, is not true,' Kirby said.

Norgate stared at the young man in front of him. Kirby had already come to his attention in a way he did not much like, and nor did he like the unblinking gaze directed at him. It looked like defiance to Norgate, almost insolence, and he wondered if that was founded on some private knowledge which Kirby had.

'If it is not true, Kirby,' Norgate said, 'you conducted one of the most incompetent operations I've ever come across. Your navigator's charts are a mess from beginning to end. They're either pure fiction, or they don't make sense. And don't trot out the failure of your Gee as an excuse.'

'I wasn't about to, sir,' Kirby said. 'But I had already decided to . . .'

'I haven't finished,' Norgate interjected sharply. 'Where you went last night, God only knows, and probably not even Him. You wander all over Europe, you turn up over Bristol instead of East Anglia, I don't know what damned country you bombed, never mind which place, and you've practically no fuel left in your tanks. I don't expect miracles from an inexperienced pilot, but even for the first operation this one is quite appalling.' He slapped the papers on his desk. 'Well?' he demanded.

'I can only agree, sir,' Kirby said.

'I'm glad to hear it,' Wing Commander Norgate said. 'But I'll be keeping an eye on you from now on, and if anything like this happens again, God help you. All right. That's all.'

'I'd like to make a formal request before I go, sir.'

'What? What request?'

'I want my navigator replaced, sir,' Kirby told him.

'You want your navigator replaced,' Norgate repeated. All his doubts about Kirby, temporarily soothed by the young man's apparent acceptance of criticism, returned.

'Yes, sir. He's not up to operational standard, and I don't think he ever will be.'

Wing Commander Norgate laughed, a mirthless, contemptuous sound.

'And you're an authority on operational standards, are you?' he enquired.

'No, sir,' Kirby said. 'But he's a member of my crew, and I want him out.'

'Don't waste my time,' Norgate said. He bent over his desk, and reached for the paperwork which kept piling up. Kirby stood where he was, motionless. Norgate looked up. 'Do I have to translate?' he asked. 'I told you to get out of my office.'

'Sir,' Kirby said, steadily, 'I'm sorry to have to insist . . .'

'Insist? Who the devil do you think you are, Kirby?'

Kirby ploughed on. 'I quite realize that I should have asked for a replacement before, during our crew training, when I first had doubts about him. But after he went to pieces last night, I've no alternative but to . . .'

Norgate said, icily, 'Don't try and hide behind your navigator, man.'

'The responsibility is mine, sir,' Kirby agreed. 'I've already apologized for not accepting it before. But I have to think of the rest of my crew, and Maurice Howard could kill us all. I don't think he should be flying at all, but that's up to someone else, not me. I just don't want him in my crew any more.'

'If you think this is a way of keeping yourself off operations for a while,' Norgate said, 'you're very much mistaken.'

'That's not my intention, sir,' Kirby said.

'You'll have a replacement navigator within twenty-four hours,' Norgate said. 'And that's a promise.'

'Thank you, sir,' Kirby said.

Wing Commander Norgate watched the serious-faced young man with the withdrawn manner as he saluted, and left the office. Norgate drummed his fingers on the desk thoughtfully, and decided to speak to an individual he could trust. He did not trust Pilot Officer Kirby. He lifted his telephone.

'You lousy shit,' Maurice Howard said, white-faced.

'I'm sorry, Maurice,' Kirby said. 'But there was nothing else I could do.'

'Oh, yes, blame me because things went wrong,' Maurice Howard said, almost spitting with fury. 'Sod the fact that more than half of it was because you can't even steer the courses you're given, oh no. You go crawling to the CO, and tell him it's all my fault . . .'

Kirby let him rage on. They both knew the truth. It would have been nice if they could have parted cordially, with a handshake over a drink, but if it did anything to restore Maurice's damaged self-respect to swear at him, so be it. Kirby believed that he had done the right thing. He could not be certain. The rest of the crew were pretty boot-faced about it. Except Ferris. He did not know what Ferris's reaction would be. Ferris was not around for some reason.

'Sit down, Flight,' Wing Commander Norgate said, cordially.

Ferris crumpled his forage cap, and slouched in a chair. Ferris's salute when he entered the office had been decidedly negligent. Even Ferris could not avoid saluting senior officers now and then, although the result was so casual as to come close to a silent 'up you'.

Wing Commander Norgate, who would have torn a strip off any of his officers who behaved in such a way, did not mind in the least. He knew all about rough, tough, cynical second-tour air gunners, and admired them. He offered Ferris a cigarette.

'Thanks,' Ferris said, and groped for a match.

'You're an old hand, Flight,' Norgate said. 'What the devil went on last night?'

Ferris blew out his match, leaned forward, and flicked it expertly into a distant ashtray. Norgate moved the ashtray to the edge of his desk.

'It was a cock up,' Ferris said, briefly.

'This talk about seeing fires, and bombing on that . . .'

'I thought they could have been fires,' Ferris said. 'Couldn't see anything else.'

'Ah, so there was something . . .?'

'Like we said at debriefing,' Ferris said. From anyone else, that would have been impertinence. From Ferris, mere cheek, and Norgate nodded.

'Do you know that Pilot Officer Kirby has been to see me?'

Ferris shook his head. Norgate told him of Kirby's request. 'He didn't discuss it with you?'

'No,' Ferris said. 'But if the skipper wants to get shot of Maurice Howard, good for him.'

'I see. You fee. that Sergeant Howard was largely at fault?'

Ferris said, 'He ballsed it up right from the off.'

Norgate smiled at Ferris. 'Thank you, Flight. You've been most helpful.'

After dinner that night, Kirby searched the mess for Wing Commander Norgate. He found him propping up the bar with a couple of visiting brown jobs from the Glider Pilot Regiment, a major and a half colonel. Kirby stood a few feet away, pointedly waiting.

'I lost three rear gunners during my last tour,' Wing Commander Norgate was saying. 'They had to be scraped out of the turret with teaspoons.' He had noticed Kirby, but ignored him.

The conversation shifted to before the war. The pongos had haw haw Sandhurst voices.

'God, I was poverty stricken in those days,' the major said. 'Well, one is in the services, without a private income. How did you find things?'

'Oh, I managed,' Wing Commander Norgate said. 'I was making about fifteen hundred a year.'

'Fifteen hundred? Good God!' They were astonished. 'You must have had a hell of a good job.'

'I was in business,' Norgate said. 'Travelled a lot.'

'Ah, business, that's where the money is. And all those expenses, eh?'

'Actually,' Wing Commander Norgate said, 'I only made about five hundred a year from my job.'

'Ah, so you do have private means.'

'No,' Wing Commander Norgate said. 'I made the rest betting at the dog tracks.'

The brown jobs roared with disbelieving laughter at this obvious jest. Norgate smiled at them thinly. He sipped beer from the personal engraved silver tankard, which was his own property and, when not in use, stood prominently behind the bar, ready for the barman to fill it at once whenever he saw the

CO coming. His eyes rested directly on Kirby for the first time. In Norgate's mind, Kirby was more or less vindicated, so what the hell was he hanging about for?

Kirby stepped forward. His expression struck Norgate as distinctly odd.

'I'd like to speak to you if you please, sir,' Kirby said.

'Not now,' Norgate said, mildly irritated. 'In the morning.' He turned back to the two soldiers, about to resume the conversation.

'I'm sorry, sir,' Kirby said. 'It's important.' Norgate sighed impatiently. His eyebrows rose. 'In private, sir,' Kirby said, glancing at the pongos.

Norgate's lips tightened. Kirby followed him away from the bar to a quieter corner of the ante-room. Norgate turned and faced him.

'Well?' Norgate enquired quietly, his voice cold. 'I have guests, Kirby. Make it quick.'

'I understand you questioned Flight Sergeant Ferris about last night,' Kirby said. His normally even-toned voice had a rough edge underlying it.

'That subject's closed,' Norgate said. 'As it happens, your rear gunner confirmed your version.'

'I had already told you exactly what happened,' Kirby said. 'If there's any implication that my word can't be accepted, I have to tell you that I resent that, sir. Very much,' he added.

Norgate realized what was odd about Kirby. The young idiot was seething with anger. A flush of answering anger burned Norgate's cheeks.

'Your word didn't make sense, Kirby,' Norgate said softly, but dangerously. They were standing inches from each other, face to face, voices pitched low. 'I still think you were covering up something, but after I'd seen Ferris, I was prepared to let it go. In view of your present conduct, I'm not so sure. This is neither the time nor the place. You could see that I was entertaining visitors.'

'You're entitled to ask me anything you like, sir,' Kirby said. 'But you are not entitled to interview members of my crew behind my back, and without me being present. In future I'd be obliged if you'd question me if you're dissatisfied with anything, and not my crew.'

'You're treading on very thin ice, Kirby,' Norgate hissed. 'I don't like trouble-makers, and I won't have insolence from pipsqueak know-alls scarcely out of short trousers.'

'If I've been discourteous, I'm sorry,' Kirby said. 'But at least you know how strongly I feel about it.'

'I'll deal with you in the morning,' Wing Commander Norgate promised ominously.

'My apologies to your guests, sir,' Kirby said.

Norgate turned away and walked back towards the haw-hawing pongos.

The morning passed without any summons from Wing Commander Norgate, but in another respect, he was as good as his word. Late that afternoon, Kirby's replacement navigator arrived, Pilot Officer Alan Russell.

'Suppose we go down to the pub in the village tonight,' Kirby suggested. 'And you can get to know the rest of the crew.'

They arrived at opening time, and managed to bag a corner for themselves. The local pub quickly became jammed to the doors every evening.

Ferris would have preferred an NCO navigator. One officer in a crew was enough, and usually too much in his opinion, but at first he was prepared to give Alan Russell the benefit of the doubt, even if they were lumbered with another sprog who had yet to fly on his first operation.

Still, Russell seemed a decent sort of bloke for an officer, quiet, straightforward, a bit earnest perhaps, but with occasional flashes of dry, quirky humour. His rather bony, angular face had a studious look about it, and the way his hair was already receding at the temples made him look older than he really was.

Ferris's incipient suspicions of any officer, never far below the surface, were reawakened, however, when it transpired that Alan Russell had been at a teachers' training college.

'That what you want to do?' Ferris enquired, incredulously. 'Clout a lot of snotty-nosed kids round the earhole?'

Alan Russell smiled.

'I want to teach, yes,' he said. 'But as for clouting them, no. I don't believe in corporal punishment.'

'Jesus,' Ferris breathed. But he abandoned the subject for the time being, in favour of a much more important one which he had just remembered. 'Here,' he said. 'I've worked out why that WAAF's adopted us. It's obvious. Her name's Kay, right? Well, we're K for King. That's why she picked on us.' He grinned broadly with satisfaction at the intellectual rigour of his deductions. A further strand fell brilliantly into blinding place. 'Another thing,' he said, excitedly. 'The skipper's name, Kirby, begins with a K. That's it. The rule of three. By Christ,' he said, 'I'll bet a million quid, that if she's there to see us off every time, we'll get back home safe and sound.'

'You haven't got a million quid,' Ted Hollis said, a stickler for detail.

'All right, everything I've got in the fucking world.' Ferris searched his wallet. 'Nine pounds ten. I'll give you ten to one.'

'There's no point,' Ted Hollis said, sucking his empty pipe thoughtfully. 'If you lose, and we buy it one night, I couldn't collect my ninety-five quid anyway.'

'That's immaterial,' Ferris said, impatiently. 'A bet's a bet. Who says I'm wrong?'

None of them contradicted him. His hypothesis was not only plausible and beguiling, it was as elegant in its simple perfection as Einstein's $E = MC^2$.

'Here's to Kay,' Len Bellamy said, lifting his glass. 'May she be there every time.'

Solemnly, they drank to Kay.

'The trouble is though,' Arthur Wood said, worriedly, 'we can't be sure, can we? I mean, just because she's been there once . . . how do we know she'll be there next time? We've still got twenty-nine trips to go,' he said glumly.

'David knows her,' Len Bellamy said. 'He could have a word with her.'

'No, no, he mustn't do that,' Ferris said, with some agitation.

'If anyone asked her to be there, it'd kill the charm. It wouldn't work.' He looked at Kirby, and chewed his lip. 'It'd be nice to know, though, skip,' he said.

'I'll talk to her casually, without actually asking her,' Kirby promised. 'See what she says.'

'Marvellous,' Ferris enthused. 'And I'll bet it'll be all right. I'll bet.'

There were no takers. They were all convinced, with the possible exception of Alan Russell who said nothing but wore a somewhat sceptical look, that in Kay they had discovered the unlooked for magic key. That somehow, through her, fate had chosen them, that they were destined to survive.

Ferris was so euphoric that he did not even object when Ted Hollis developed a fit of coughing, and went outside for a breath of fresh air, thirty seconds before his turn finally arrived.

'I'll get them,' Ferris said largely.

His euphoria evaporated soon after he handed the drinks round. During his absence at the bar, the conversation had taken a turn which Ferris found deeply distasteful.

'You mean you're a pacifist?' Len Bellamy was asking. He could hardly have been more astounded if Alan Russell had announced that he was a Martian in disguise.

'I said I was,' Alan Russell said. 'I read so much about the Great War, *All Quiet on the Western Front*, Robert Graves's *Goodbye to All That*, Richard Aldington, the poets like Siegfried Sassoon. It seemed such a useless slaughter, a complete waste of human lives. I couldn't believe that anything justified that. When this one broke out, I decided that when my turn came, I'd register as a conscientious objector.'

'You *what*?' Ferris enquired, peering at him slit-eyed.

'It wasn't until later that I changed my mind,' Alan Russell said.

'That was big of you,' Ferris observed.

'But why choose to volunteer for air crew?' Kirby asked, interested in the twists of Alan Russell's conscience. 'If you believe killing is wrong, you could have served on the ground staff.'

'The education branch,' Ferris said, sarcastically. 'Just the job.'

Alan Russell shook his head.

'I either had to say "all war is morally wrong, even this one", or I had to take the same chances as anyone else. I volunteered as a pilot in the first place, but I failed the flying course, and remustered as a navigator. That's why I'm late getting on operations.'

Kirby was rather impressed by the thoughtful way in which Alan Russell had approached and made his decisions. It was, he thought wryly, a far cry from his own original vague feeling that he would like to fly, without any real conception of what, in the end, that would mean. He could dimly perceive the agonized doubts which must have tormented Alan Russell, and felt that he had shown a strange and unusual kind of courage.

It was not a view shared by Ferris.

'Jesus wept,' he muttered. 'A fucking conchie for a navigator. That's all we need.'

Chapter Eleven

Cyril Barry Norgate was born into a pleasant, middle-class home in the Thames Valley, not far from Reading. He did not attend the kind of state elementary school, populated by boys with grubby knees wearing thick woollen jerseys, from which Kirby had won his scholarship to a grammar school.

Norgate senior had begun his working life as a shop assistant, and painfully built up his own business the hard way. As he prospered, he joined Rotary, and the golf club, and stood for the local council, but while he was accepted as a self-made man within the ranks of the Conservative Party, he was not a gentleman, and knew that he never would be. His only son, however, would.

At the age of five, Cyril Barry Norgate went to a fee-paying day preparatory school, where he wore a grey flannel school blazer edged with pink piping, and a cap sporting the school crest, and was jeered at by the jersey-clad rabble from the nearby elementary school.

When he was old enough, Cyril Barry Norgate went away to a public school. It was a minor public school. Norgate senior would have preferred one of the great, prestigious public schools such as Harrow, or Eton, or Winchester, but such establishments tended to look askance at the sons of drapers, which in truth was what the Norgate emporium really was, and Cyril Barry Norgate, although undoubtedly clever, was not brilliant enough to secure entry to Winchester as a scholar.

Minor league or not, however, it was still definitely a public school, and attended by a sprinkling of the sons of minor gentry, as well as the sons of arrivistes like Norgate senior. All would emerge in the same mould, with the right accents, the right attitudes, the right connections, the old school tie – which attributes automatically qualified them as natural leaders and gentlemen, fitted to command their less fortunate countrymen. Cyril Barry Norgate took all this for granted, and approved.

Cyril Barry Norgate remained at his public school just long enough to polish his accent, hone it into the one instantly recognizable by other public school men, the one which inspired instant deference in head waiters and club servants. At the age of fourteen and a half, he left. Norgate senior had gone bankrupt.

Cyril Barry Norgate never forgave his father for this disaster, in which, perhaps, he showed some lack of compassion. Finding school fees since the age of five had been a contributory factor in Norgate senior's downfall, admittedly combined with spending too much time in the council chamber and on the golf course, instead of in the shop. Nevertheless, Cyril Barry Norgate could find no pity for his abject, bewildered and penniless father, unable to cope with debts and yet more debts.

The house had gone, everything had gone. They were living in shabby rooms. Suddenly, shillings were vital. Shillings would buy food. Cyril Barry Norgate found himself, with no educational qualifications, obliged to work for shillings, instead of becoming a gentleman, and he bitterly resented it.

He resented nearly as much his mother's foolishness in choosing his first Christian name, which had been her father's, on whom she doted. He had soon learned at prep school and even more at his minor public school, that 'Cyril' attracted mockery, and lent itself to being said with a sneer. Cyril Barry Norgate fought a number of schoolboy brawls with his tormentors, and since he was an aggressive fighter, who did not care if he got hurt provided he could damage the other fellow nearly as much, and preferably more, the sneers, at least to his face, diminished markedly. But he could hardly go on punching people for the rest of his life.

He took to signing himself C. Barry Norgate, and by dint of persistence, this device finally worked. Over the next few years, as his former acquaintances dropped away and out of his life, the hated Cyril was successfully discarded, except when it came to filling in forms, and he became known as Barry.

Norgate's first job was with a large firm of accountants, as an office boy, salary fifteen shillings a week. There were two office boys, who sat in the draughty outer office, licking stamps and running menial errands. The other was called Cullen, two years older than Norgate. Cullen had been to a grammar school, and achieved the fairly unusual feat of failing every subject in his School Certificate Examination.

Cullen speedily initiated Norgate into the fiddles open to an office boy, the main one being making fictitious entries in the postage book, and pocketing the money for the unused stamps from the petty cash. Provided they were not too greedy, this practice was unlikely to be detected. They settled for half a crown a week each. It was a small, though welcome addition to Norgate's insignificant income, most of which went to his mother anyway, and he felt no compunction as he weighed an envelope on the scales, priced it at 4½d instead of 3d, and made the appropriate enlarged entry in the postage book. It served his employers right for being so stingy.

The young Norgate hated his lowly status, being constantly at the beck and call of men who were no cleverer than he. For Norgate had a gift for mathematics, and he knew instinctively that, given the training, he could do their job better than they could. And being an accountant had a certain standing, it was at least a profession, and well paid too, once a man was qualified.

There were a number of pupils in the office, young men with fathers who could afford to pay the premium for them to be taken on, and support them until they passed their final examinations. Thanks to Norgate senior's feckless incompetence, that route was irrevocably closed, but there was an alternative, longer and harder, but still open to a youngster with sufficient determination. When the senior partner sent for him at the end of his month's trial period, he was ready.

The senior partner was an arid, elderly, distant man with a wispy, sepulchral voice.

'Well, how do you think you've been getting along, Norgate?' he enquired, dry-washing the parchment skin of his hands. An almost equally ancient black gas fire, its elements cracked and lopsided, popped and hissed an accompaniment in the background.

'Very well, sir,' C. Barry Norgate said, confidently. 'I like it here very much,' he said, adopting a tangential route to the truth. 'So much, in fact, that I'd like to become an audit clerk. I'm very good at maths, sir,' he said, pressing the point, in the face of the senior partner's blank, empty old eyes. 'Had I not been obliged to leave school I'd certainly have gained a distinction in matric. You can see that from my school reports.' He took out the envelope containing those documents with which he had prudently armed himself.

Audit clerks were a lesser breed, unqualified, who did most of the spadework when the accounts of various businesses were audited, but the good ones knew as much as most accountants. Moreover, it was possible, by means of a correspondence course which entailed studying evenings and weekends over a period of years, to acquire the necessary paper qualifications. C. Barry Norgate had decided on that course of action to retrieve his fortunes.

The senior partner waved away the proffered envelope.

'I'm afraid that will not be possible, Norgate,' he said, his words falling gently through the air like dry autumn leaves. 'At the conclusion of your trial period, I have to inform you that you are not regarded as a suitable employee. You will take one week's notice. Thank you, Norgate,' he said listlessly. 'That will be all.'

C. Barry Norgate was stunned, and remained stunned. He could not understand it. In what way was he not suitable? No explanation was ever offered. The obvious one was that the discrepancy in the petty cash had come to light, but since Cullen was not dismissed too, that could hardly be the case.

C. Barry Norgate could only put it down to the observable

fact that the world in its entirety was against him. No one could be relied upon or trusted, but himself.

It was only much later that Norgate wondered idly if the postage fiddle had in fact been detected, and if Cullen, when confronted with the shortage and required, as the senior office boy, to account for it, had succeeded in laying all the blame on Norgate. But by then it no longer mattered.

C. Barry Norgate left his first job in life with a reference which was guarded, to put it mildly, and the only work he could find was in the despatch department of a biscuit firm. His fellow workers closed ranks against this intruding outsider with the posh, stuck-up accent, and treated him with hostile derision. Norgate clung to his accent at that time, nonetheless. For one thing, it was natural by now, it was not assumed. It was also the badge which indicated where he truly belonged, and whence he would some day return. But when he left the biscuit factory in search of more money, it was only to become a warehouse porter, heaving crates and boxes on and off lorries and trolleys.

C. Barry Norgate had an ingrained dislike of manual labour. He detested getting his hands dirty. At the very least, to put it at its lowest, he urgently needed to get out of overalls, to find something, anything, where he could wear a collar and tie, and a suit, the bottom line necessary for some slight degree of self-respect. He wrote endless applications for clerical jobs, any clerical job, but he was rarely even interviewed. Hard-headed employers were impressed more by his complete lack of educational qualifications than the name of the minor public school he had briefly attended.

C. Barry Norgate was twenty-one years old before he began to make his escape. He read an advertisement in the local newspaper which called for young men of good presence, bearing and appearance; promised opportunities and income limited only by the successful applicants' drive, ambition, dedication, and willingness to work long hours; stipulated the ability on the part of applicants to organize their own working day and display initiative, and, for this incomparable opportunity, no formal educational qualifications were required.

Finally, in addition to commission and bonus, a car allowance would be paid. The words 'car allowance' appeared, to C. Barry Norgate, to stand out from the surrounding newsprint in glowing letters of gold.

He put on his one presentable suit, his single white shirt and starched collar, brilliantined his hair, and caught a bus to the hotel where interviews were being held.

His appearance went down well, his minor public school was thoroughly approved of, and his accent was positively relished. C. Barry Norgate was accepted at once, and four weeks later, after a period of training under the guidance of his area manager, who made it all seem remarkably easy, he started work, fully fledged, on his own, driving a second-hand Austin 7 on which he spent every pound he had painfully saved from his hours of overtime.

The territory to which he was assigned was centred on Salisbury and covered a wide area. Norgate left his unhappy parents to their own debt ridden devices with relief, and rarely returned to the dingy rooms in which they contemplated their unhappy fate. The money he posted regularly, he felt, more than discharged his responsibilities.

C. Barry Norgate had become a vacuum cleaner salesman.

By comparison with the cess pit of personal humiliation from which he had emerged, it was an improvement, if but a modest one. He felt nothing but contempt for the gullible housewives whose initial caution as they suspiciously peered round their front doors was so easily dissipated by his well-scrubbed appearance, the charm and flattery, the tools of his trade, with which he anointed them. When C. Barry Norgate set out for a day of cold calls, he gained entry more often than not. From then on, it was downhill work; compliments to the good lady of the house; discreetly open personal admiration if appropriate, or alternatively, for those in the upper age bracket, the adept adoption of a surrogate son role; the convincing demonstration with the specially beefed up machine with which his company thoughtfully provided its salesmen and never on any account to be sold; the cordial cup of tea or coffee; and the arrangement to come back that evening when the man of the house would have returned home from work. Usually, the sale was successfully clinched that night.

C. Barry Norgate despised what he was doing, but he was a good vacuum cleaner salesman, although his earning potential, he came to realize, was limited by the far-flung nature of his territory. As time went by, he was obliged to forage further and further afield in search of new prospects, and spent a lot of time just travelling. Even so, he was soon making what, by pre-war standards, was a considerable income, probably twice as much, he sometimes reflected with grim satisfaction, as most of those to whom he peddled his machines.

And if at heart he regarded his occupation as disreputable, there were compensations, apart from money. There was an illusion of freedom, no one told him what to do or when, he was virtually his own master. He was not obliged to dirty his hands, his overalls had been thankfully thrown away, he wore good clothes, and he enjoyed being well dressed and clean. Most of all, there was the car. A car of one's own was a very considerable status symbol, even an Austin 7. And girls found a well-mannered chap with a car highly attractive.

The girls changed pretty frequently. Having been persuaded to give their all in the sand dunes behind some secluded beach, or in a lonely sun-dappled clearing in the New Forest, locations virtually inaccessible at the time except with the aid of an invaluable car, too many were tediously prone to turn their minds to the romantic subject of love and the practical subject of marriage. C. Barry Norgate did not debate these points. Instead, he would concentrate his working and social efforts elsewhere. Working a far-flung territory had its advantages.

C. Barry Norgate was not interested in marriage, and certainly not to one of the shop assistants or typists whose voices grated on his nerves even while he was undressing them. When he married, at thirty or possibly thirty-five, it would not be to one of their kind, but to a girl with the right social background, a girl with breeding. That presupposed no longer being a vacuum cleaner salesman. Somehow, he must evolve again, acquire the social cachet and standing which would put him on a par with the young lady, whoever and wherever she was now, who would become Mrs Barry Norgate, and who would have been educated at a girls' boarding school, and come from a county family, or have a father who was something in the City. He had met their like briefly, the sisters of some of the boys at his minor public school. He knew how they looked, how they talked, how they held themselves, the ingrained superiority with which they regarded the world and its inhabitants.

Quite how he was going to inspire respect on the part of such a creature was far from clear to C. Barry Norgate, but he had every faith in his ability, somehow, to achieve it, mainly because he could not contemplate any alternative. In the meantime, he had money in his pocket and, quite soon, rather more.

At first, passing through the turnstiles of various dog tracks had been no more than whiling away an hour prior to, or in between, evening appointments. But there were several dog tracks within Norgate's large territory, and it soon occurred to him that the greyhounds travelled around as well as himself. His mostly unused mathematical flair also told him that certain discrepancies in the local odds were thrown up from time to time, which a peripatetic punter like himself might turn to advantage.

Norgate was a good gambler, cold and careful. He respected the odds, but was not intimidated by them. He was a consistent winner and, since he played several tracks, he did not become known to the bookies he was outwitting.

Later, when privately mocking people whom he no longer respected, taking inward pleasure from their stupid haw-hawing disbelief, he tended to exaggerate his gains for effect, but he made enough to replace his car with a more practical one. The Austin 7 was too small inside to permit satisfactory sexual activity when it was raining, even for the supple and determined. The Standard 12 which he bought in its place, if thirstier on petrol, was larger and more accommodating. However, while his financial and physical needs were more than adequately filled, he still lacked that indefinable status which he knew to be his rightful due.

C. Barry Norgate became intensely interested in the Royal Auxiliary Air Force, the 'weekend' flyers. Organized in squadrons, all the pilots were officers. Many of them were destined to die in the Battle of Britain or soon after, but in pre-war peacetime, although they served a serious military purpose as was later demonstrated, the squadrons were also exclusive clubs for young gentlemen, who tended to be upper class or professional middle class, and public school boys almost to a man.

The more C. Barry Norgate thought about it, the more he liked the idea. There would be difficulties, major ones, but against that he had many of the right assets. He was certainly fit, he knew himself to be clever, he had the right appearance, the right manner, the right accent. His public school might have been a minor one, but it was tolerably well thought of, and would certainly make a far better impression than would, say, the grant aided schools, which were also technically public schools.

There would certainly be some awkward questions, best avoided, and the phrase 'family misfortunes' rose into his mind. He liked its timbre, its solemn ring. It was suitably vague, and yet it delicately indicated the sort of disaster such as crippling death duties which would be familiar to the kind of men he would be meeting, entirely acceptable. In any case, they would be decent chaps with the good manners of their kind which would inhibit them from probing into implied personal tragedy with questions which they would regard as impertinent, and bad form.

There were other problems to be faced and overcome, but the prize was great, almost priceless. If he succeeded in joining such a squadron, he would have crossed that invisible barrier which at present excluded him, he would have re-entered that England where the right school and a particular station in life mattered more than money. He would not only meet the right people, and mix with the right people, he would *be* one of the right people. Moreover, the friends he would make would be young men of influence, and a word in the right place could work miracles. His father used to remark sagely, in better days before bankruptcy overtook him, 'It's not what you know, son, it's who you know.' If C. Barry Norgate could bring this off he would know people who could secure a position for him, say in some family owned company or partnership where nepotism counted and not qualifications. A mere recommendation on an old boy basis could remove him for good from his present socially unacceptable occupation. *That* would have to be kept tucked well out of sight, but Norgate could see ways of achieving such an aim. Fortunately, his employers, in some initial burst of grandeur, had chosen to christen themselves 'Sales International Home Marketing' and the trade name of the vacuum cleaner did not appear on their impressive notepaper, should a reference be required, a document which Norgate could type out for himself anyway since he possessed stocks of notepaper and a portable typewriter.

C. Barry Norgate's head positively swam with excitement as he contemplated the splendid vista which, as near as dammit, was within his grasp. The main thing was simply to get an interview with one of the squadrons. Once face to face with chaps who spoke the same language, he was confident that he could bring it off.

Norgate resisted the impulse to shoot off a letter that very day, and made some quiet enquiries first, which was just as well. He discovered that no applicant stood a serious chance unless he could produce a letter of recommendation from someone who carried weight.

Momentary despair gripped C. Barry Norgate. He knew no one who would carry weight with a Royal Auxiliary Air Force squadron. He pulled himself together. Think, man. Think. And then it came to him. A half-forgotten friend at his minor public school, one of the few he had made. Had his father not been a serving officer in the Royal Air Force? That was years ago now, he had not been in touch since he had been humiliatingly obliged to leave school, but after all, that surely was what having been at a public school was all about.

Norgate wrote to his former friend, care of the school. Back

came a cordial reply. Norgate telephoned, and they arranged
to meet. Out of that reunion, laced with half truths, vague
generalizations, and a few highly necessary lies, Norgate
emerged triumphant, with a warm, written commendation
from his friend's buttered-up father, who had since retired
from the air force, regretted that his son, being myopic, could
not follow in his footsteps, and heartily approved of Norgate's
ambitions, or at least those he chose to state.

A letter from a retired wing commander should do the trick,
and Norgate sent it off, together with his application, to the
nearest auxiliary squadron, based near Marlborough. Back
came a reply, inviting him to an interview.

Norgate chose his clothes with care. He bought a smart new
blazer, dark blue with chromium-plated buttons, together with
a new pair of grey flannel bags. He considered wearing a
cravat with an open-necked shirt, but rejected that in favour
of his old school tie, the colours of which nicely matched the
light blue shirt made from sea island cotton which he also
bought. Norgate studied himself in his full-length wardrobe
mirror, and was pleased with the effect.

On the appointed Saturday, he arrived at the airfield, and
parked his Standard 12 outside the squadron office. Until
then, Norgate had been rather proud of his car, but now he
studied the others with some concern. His was practically the
only saloon there, and certainly the only mass-produced
saloon. Most were tourers or sports cars or drop head coupes,
Bentleys, Lagondas, Morgans, and a number of MGs.

Once he had joined the squadron, he would have to buy an
MG, Norgate thought, he could run to an MG. Thank God he
had got rid of his Austin 7, at least.

There was some flying going on, and Norgate stood for a
minute or two watching the planes taking off and landing. A
completely unexpected thrill shivered through his body,
strange, foreign, yet tantalizingly familiar, as though he had
experienced it before somewhere. It took him a moment or two
to identify the comparison, and then it came to him. It was a
similar sensation to that which he felt as he caressed some
girl's shapely body before lowering himself on to her. It was a

kind of lust, an itch. In those few seconds, Norgate realized something he had not known before. He not only wanted to fly, nothing would ever satisfy him now until he did fly.

'Do sit down,' one of his interlocutors said, the squadron leader with the sandy hair. The other one was a flight lieutenant. Both were clean shaven.

'Thank you, sir,' Norgate said, relishing the man's accent, knowing his was the same. It was like being back home after years in the wilderness. He sat in the indicated chair. Outside the squadron office, a plane roared low overhead, its engine crackling.

'I'm James, and this is Dicky. We're all pretty informal here. What does the C. stand for?'

'Cyril,' Norgate said, uncomfortably, 'but . . .'

'I see. Well, Cyril, Wing Commander Spranger seems to think well of you, which is jolly good, of course . . .'

'Actually,' Norgate said, 'I acquired the Cyril to please my maternal grandfather, for some extraordinary reason. In fact, everyone always calls me Barry.'

'Yes. Quite. Amazing what parents get up to, isn't it?'

Norgate returned the easy friendly smile.

'I desperately want to fly,' he said, anxious to share his remarkable discovery. 'The way the Germans are carrying on, war seems to be pretty well inevitable, and if so, I feel I should be in a position to play my part right from the beginning.'

'We do rather take all that for granted, old chap.'

'Of course,' Norgate said. 'I quite realize that. What I was really getting at was how long it takes to train a pilot up to squadron standard. How quickly one might go solo, and so on.'

'We'll come to all that later. Just like to put the odd question first, matter of form, you know. Let's see . . . your school . . . Dicky's elder brother was there actually, left before your time, but Dicky tells me it's a decent sort of place.' Norgate shot a look of gratitude at Dicky, who smiled, locked his hands behind his head, and leaned comfortably back in his chair. 'You seem to have left rather early though, as far as one can gather.'

'Family misfortunes, I'm afraid,' Norgate said. 'No alternative.'

'Ah. Sorry about that. Death duties, I suppose, or something of the sort.'

'That kind of thing,' Norgate said.

'Yes, well, these things happen. What did you do then? Go to a crammer or some such?'

'I had to help my father sort out the mess,' Norgate said. 'It took rather a long time. Young as I was, he rather relied on me. After that, I did a few odd jobs, a taste of what real life was all about, if you like, before taking up a career in business.'

'Ah, business. Closed book to me, I'm afraid. Dicky's the expert on that.'

'Not really,' Dicky said. He was gazing dreamily out of the window. 'My father happens to be a barrister. I seem to recall that his opinion was sought not long ago. Sales International Home Marketing, isn't it? Been involved in litigation, I believe.'

'I don't know,' Norgate said, truthfully. If so, it was news to him.

'Something about alleged infringement of patent,' Dicky said. He yawned and rocked back in his chair. 'On a vacuum cleaner,' he said drowsily. 'That is what they do, isn't it? Sell vacuum cleaners?'

'It's one of their products,' Norgate said. Damn and blast the man to hell. How could he possibly have anticipated this chance piece of random knowledge?

'Occupation, Technical Representative,' the squadron leader said, glancing at the papers in front of him. 'Is that what they call it? Selling vacuum cleaners?'

'It's part of one's executive training,' Norgate said. Perfectly true. The original advertisement had promised the prospect of management status. Norgate had recently been told that he could well be in line for the next area manager's job to fall vacant. 'One has to know how the chaps in the field operate.'

'But that is what you do for a living, Barry? Foot in the door stuff? What does it feel like? I mean, when some female slams the door in your face? Can't be very pleasant, surely?'

'You may have servants to do your cleaning for you?' Norgate said. 'Most people don't.' He remembered the time when a maid had been employed in his father's house in the Thames Valley, and a woman had come in daily for the heavy work. 'Vacuum cleaners make life a damn sight easier, and we supply them. Is there something wrong with that?'

'Certainly not. Please . . .' the squadron leader said, back-pedalling hurriedly, '. . . no offence intended, I do assure you. Just trying to fill in your background, no more.' He glanced at Norgate's application again. 'What does your father do, exactly?'

'He's retired,' Norgate said.

'I see. What *did* he do, then?'

'Local politics and golf mostly,' Norgate said, producing the rehearsed phrases automatically. 'The money came from a department store in Reading he owned at the time.'

'Dull sort of place, Reading,' Dicky said. 'As ditchwater.'

'The family home was in the Thames Valley,' Norgate said, another of the pre-planned phrases. 'Rather a nice outlook, secluded, fun in the summer, we had our own tennis court . . .'

'I can't pretend to know Reading terribly well,' the squadron leader said, 'but I used to drive through a lot at one time, oh years ago now, I had a girl friend lived near Maidenhead.'

'Highly appropriate,' Dicky said. 'Nothing like exploring virgin territory.'

'Now then, Dicky. Down, boy.' He turned his drooping tolerant smile on Norgate. 'I seem to recall a place as one left the town centre. Looked like a draper's shop. Stays in the window. Corsets. Pink things, boned, with suspenders attached.'

'Sounds ghastly,' Dicky said. 'Evidently more fat women around who wish they weren't than one imagines.'

Norgate stood up decisively.

'I think I've taken up too much of your time,' he said.

'Not at all. Thank you for coming, Barry,' the squadron leader said, agreeable. 'It's been a great pleasure to meet you. We're seeing a number of applicants over the next week or two, but we'll let you know in due course.'

'Don't bother,' Norgate said. 'You've had your fun. You can stuff my application up your dirty arses. You two,' he said distinctly, 'are patronizing, ill-mannered, brainless louts. As far as I'm concerned, you and the Auxiliary can fuck yourselves. And next time you feel like being clever,' he added, 'you might try and grasp the idea, if you're not too stupid, that when you want to shit, you both drop your trousers like anyone else.'

Norgate turned and left. At least the smiles had been erased from the faces of the two young men, both of whom were destined to die in August 1940, and had been replaced by expressions of shocked distaste at his appallingly vulgar, coarse behaviour. But it was small consolation.

For a while, as he drove back towards Salisbury, teeth set, hands clenching the steering wheel, Norgate was simply numb, as though afflicted with mental paralysis.

By the time he parked his car, that had been replaced by a cold and bitter anger which, like the flame of an oxy-acetylene torch, was almost invisible, and the more dangerous for that.

From that moment, Norgate deliberately discarded the public school accent he had prized for so long. He fashioned his speaking voice into a clipped but neutral, classless accent. He would still get there, somehow, but without sounding like *them*, who from then on he despised and hated. That afternoon, he had endured one humiliation too many, and Norgate was not a forgiving man.

The itch to fly, however, did not go away, in fact it was enhanced, if only to show *them*. Norgate applied to join the Royal Air Force Volunteer Reserve, and was accepted.

The well-equipped squadrons of the Auxiliary Air Force saw no possible comparison between themselves and the VR. The pilots of the VR tended to resent their lesser standing, and affected to regard Auxiliary officer pilots as public school twits who needed the right Daddy because between their ears there was nothing but empty space.

Norgate learned to fly Tiger Moths at the weekends, attended lectures during the evenings, and went to summer camp for a fortnight's intensive training.

When war was declared, he was mustered into the RAF as a sergeant pilot. His first operational type was Blenheims, twin-engined day bombers which were becoming obsolescent, but performed valuable service in North Africa. There, Norgate flew his first tour of operations, and his determination, coolness, skill, and courage soon attracted attention. Halfway through his tour, he was awarded the Distinguished Flying Medal. Soon afterwards, he was commissioned. On his thirtieth operation, he was awarded the Distinguished Flying Cross for 'exceptional gallantry' in pressing home an attack, during which his squadron suffered heavy losses.

Flying Officer Norgate returned to the UK and, after his 'rest' from operations, converted on to Stirlings. At the end of his second tour, he was one of the few in the squadron who had survived. He had been awarded a bar to his DFC, and the Distinguished Service Order. Sheer attrition, apart from his own ability, meant that he had become one of the flight commanders, with the rank of squadron leader.

Bomber Command suited Norgate. He had the tenacity and stamina as well as the cold courage and endurance required of a bomber pilot. Bomber Command's war, at squadron level, was fought essentially by operational air crews who were civilians in uniform. They had become professionals but, had it not been for the war, few would ever have flown or had the chance to fly. Surviving regular officers mostly held high rank by then. Most of the operational crews were NCOs, and one of Norgate's eventual weaknesses as a commander was that he always felt closer to his NCOs than to his officers, whom he instinctively distrusted. It was perhaps a paradox that he had also come to regret being awarded the DFM which indelibly indicated his own NCO origins and, he felt, could hinder his own advancement, but Norgate was not an especially consistent man.

When he was appointed to command 545 Squadron, he felt that his life was on track at last. Through the accident of war, his dreams were within reach. With his DSO, DFC and bar, and his DFM, he was one of the more highly decorated pilots still alive. He felt a twinge of resentment that, despite his gallantry awards, he was not a public figure, he was not one of those whom the press picked up and wrote about, those heroic individuals selected to symbolize bravery and the will to win, 'names' known to everyone throughout the nation. But there was time for that to change. The war was still in full swing. And now, he had his own squadron. Given one more piece of luck, he was in a position to manipulate events.

Wing Commander Barry Norgate had no idea what that essential piece of luck might be, but he had every faith that, somehow, it would turn up in due course. When it did, he knew that he would recognize it at once, when most men would not, and ride it ruthlessly, when others would hesitate and flounder.

His first aim was to turn 545 from just another squadron into one which stood out as unique in some way, not only in the minds of the senior officers at Group but, in the perfect world, in the mind of Air Marshal Sir Arthur 'Bomber' Harris himself, at Bomber Command Headquarters.

For that, he would need the special piece of luck he could grab at. It would come along, Norgate knew it would come along, everything was going his way, but he could only wait his chance, and snap it up when it did.

Given that, given the opportunity to lead his squadron on some unusual operation and, it went without saying, to a successful conclusion, and given also his present array of medals, Norgate believed that there was only one remaining decoration he could be awarded for conducting such an, as yet unknown, enterprise. And that was the Victoria Cross. When his DFM would cease to be a potential hindrance.

With the VC, Norgate would join the ranks of the Leonard Cheshires and Guy Gibsons, become a public figure, with his photograph in all the newspapers. He would almost inevitably be promoted to group captain, still just short of thirty years of age. He would successfully have buried his past.

And when it was all over, Group Captain Norgate, VC, DSO, DFC and bar, DFM, one of the great heroes of the war, and moreover one who had shown the crucial ability to command, why then he would certainly be offered a permanent commission in the Royal Air Force. And with a record like that, there were no heights to which he might not aspire.

C. Barry Norgate would have pulled it off and what was more, through having a 'good war', by his own courage and his own efforts, with no help from anyone, least of all the old school tie brigade. And if those who had mocked him, laughed at him, and humiliated him, were now dead, that did not diminish Norgate's hatred of their kind by one iota.

Such were Wing Commander Norgate's private thoughts as he remained on the alert for his chance. Pilot Officer David Kirby was the only potential piece of grit in the smoothly oiled machine which was carrying Wing Commander Norgate towards distinction and fulfilment.

Norgate had glanced at Kirby's documents before they ever met, and a frisson of apprehension ran through him when he noticed the young pilot officer's home address. The western half of Southampton had been part of Norgate's territory in that past which he had imagined was now safely decaying in its grave.

Norgate could not recall the actual street, but he knew the district, and took what comfort he could from that. He was certain that he had never made any cold calls *there*. While not a slum, it was a poor area, where pay packets were counted out to meet necessities like food and rent, with nothing left over for vacuum cleaners, even on the beguiling hire purchase terms about which he had once waxed so enthusiastic.

But the fear would not go away, a fear more intense than anything Norgate ever felt over the target, or when cannon shells ripped out chunks of his aircraft, or members of his crew died in agony, or he crash-landed a practically uncontrollable machine.

Norgate was not one of the tiny handful who were brave because they knew no fear. He lived with it, every time he took off. Often, he was gripped with more than fear, sheer downright terror. But he could control that. He remained cool and calculating, he overrode fear or even terror, took rational decisions, no matter what. He possessed that kind of will-power.

Perhaps he had used up too much of that will-power. David Kirby continued to worry him, no matter how firmly he told himself that it was so unlikely as to be almost impossible. Kirby might have had friends in the nearby, rather better off district of Shirley, which Norgate had canvassed extensively. He *could* have seen Norgate lugging his equipment up some-one's garden path one day. He *might* remember that. It was *not* out of the question.

However unlikely it might be, the short hairs on the back of Norgate's neck itched as though insects were crawling through them, and sweat ran down from his armpits at the idea that one of his squadron pilots and, what was worse, a fellow member of the officers' mess, might know that he had once been a vacuum cleaner salesman.

Was that why David Kirby was able to stand firm and look him in the eye, not out of any inner convictions, but with private, derisive impertinence? Because of that secret inward knowledge? Was Kirby daring Norgate from contempt, ready to spread the story round the mess if Norgate came down hard on him?

Norgate could feel the perspiration soaking into his shirt.

Chapter Twelve

Kay's heavily muffled, shapeless figure was there again. It was Kirby's second operation with his crew. With a half moon riding high, it was a bitterly cold night. The forecast was for clear skies all the way, the destination was Berlin, 'the big one'. Ferris was exultant.

'We've definitely been adopted,' he said, giving the girl a cheerful wave.

Kirby too was relieved. He had spoken to Kay while she was repacking his parachute, but he had decided not to 'check up' yet, as his crew desired, in case it broke the spell. But she had turned up again of her own accord, without prompting. Reason told him that the strengthening feeling that her presence lent them special protection was without foundation, mere superstition. His guts, the immediate surge of optimism, told him the reverse. To hell with reason. He too smiled and waved in her direction. It was so clear under the cold moonlight that he knew she smiled back when she lifted her hand in reply, even though her mouth was concealed behind the thick woollen scarf pulled up over her face. He could see the way her eyes crinkled at the corners. This was going to be almost like flying by daylight. The German night fighters would scarcely need their radar tonight.

Half an hour out, still climbing, Len Bellamy spoke on the intercom, quietly and precisely.

'Flight Engineer to Pilot, starboard outer's overheating.'

'Pilot to Flight Engineer, any chance it'll cool off when we level out?'

'Flight Engineer to Pilot, won't wash. Could be losing oil

Pressure's falling. We'd better shut down now before she seizes up.'

Kirby feathered the starboard outer propeller. Speed dropped, and the rate of climb slowed. He glanced at the stationary propeller, clearly visible, upright, like a knife. Some four and a half hours to go, there and back. They could make it on three engines . . . but if another one failed, that would be that. The main problem though was that, cruising more slowly, they would fall behind the main stream, cease to be a part of it. Like deer, the chief protection for a bomber was to remain part of the herd.

'OK, we'll call it off,' Kirby said, reluctantly. They would have to stooge around for a long two hours or so, burning up fuel, to reduce the all up weight before landing.

'Bomb Aimer to Pilot, better dump our load, hadn't we?' Ted Hollis enquired.

Kirby levelled out. With the moon behind now, he could see the glint of the North Sea far below, a convenient receptacle for a harmless explosion.

For one wild moment, he considered not jettisoning. In some airless, blacked-out factory, men and women sweated and worked overtime producing these bombs. Should he take them back for use another time?

But common sense quickly told him that the gesture would be not only melodramatic, but would end in bathos.

The 8,000lb 'cookie' they were carrying in addition to armour-piercing bombs was little more than nearly four tons of high explosive packed into a container. That container had a thin skin. If they crashed on landing, the 'cookie' would explode on impact, and blow all of them to hell in unrecognizable shreds of fleshy fragments and splintered bones.

Kirby was still inexperienced, and a night landing at maximum all up weight on three engines would be difficult enough. The Control Tower would ask Kirby about his aircraft's condition. If he still had his 'cookie' on board, threatening Woodley Common in the event of accident, he would be ordered back to the North Sea, and regarded as a fool for not jettisoning in the first place.

'Pilot to Bomb Aimer, yes, we'll jettison now.'

More than two hours later, Kirby made a wide, deliberate circuit at 1,000 feet, the dark sprawl of hangars and Nissen huts away to his left. He flew further downwind than he normally would. On his orders, Len Bellamy selected half flap, and then undercarriage down. Kirby felt the pressure on his controls, and retrimmed. Time to turn, ears strained to pick out the first imminent falter from any of the remaining three engines.

On to the long final approach now, the perspective of the runway lights shifting as he came in, suddenly conscious of speed, lights racing towards him, of the sheer mass and size of the great aircraft.

Time to level out . . . holding off . . . straining every nerve and sinew, every tense reaction, to kiss nearly twenty tons of bomber on to the runway, as delicately as if it were a Tiger Moth.

A bump, the squeal of tyres biting tarmac, a jar in Kirby's spine. Not as feather-light as he would have wished, but they were down. Plenty of runway left, use it all, brake gently, take no chances now. Slowing down nicely, the end of the runway coming up, ease brakes off, moving at little more than walking pace.

Kirby turned on to the perimeter track, and taxied towards dispersal. He became aware that he was sweating, and palmed his face.

'Well done, skipper,' Ferris said, gratefully. 'Bloody good. And you know what?'

'She was at the end of the runway,' Kirby said.

'She must have a private line to her mate in Air Traffic,' Ferris said, delighted. 'She keeps tabs on us, God bless her.'

They reported to the intelligence officer, but the operation would not count.

Kirby said good night to his crew, walked to the mess, and read newspapers and magazines in the deserted ante-room. The benzedrine had not worn off. He might as well wait up until the rest of the squadron came back.

He was walking along the moonlit path towards the debriefing room when the first returning Lancaster came in. There was another one in the circuit.

Kirby sat in a corner out of the way, as the crews came in, one by one. He listened to them talking to each other, exchanging anecdotes while they waited to be debriefed, and he gathered that it had been a rough night.

Wing Commander Norgate was the fourth to arrive in. He flicked a glance at Kirby, but then ignored him. At last, all the crews were back, debriefed, and away to their traditional egg and bacon breakfast, with one exception. Squadron Leader Gale's aircraft was missing.

Wing Commander Norgate lit a cigarette as he glanced through the debriefing reports. He still had some hopes that Squadron Leader Gale had landed at some other airfield, and a phone call would soon come through. Kirby stubbed out his own cigarette, and stood up to go. He was feeling sleepy now.

'Just a minute,' Norgate said. He walked across to Kirby and studied him for a moment. 'Your starboard outer failed, I see,' he said softly at last.

'Yes, sir. Half an hour after take off.'

'We all knew it was going to be nasty tonight,' Norgate said. 'We'll see what Maintenance have to say. That engine had better be U/S, Kirby.'

'Goodnight, sir,' Kirby said.

In the morning, Kirby walked to the huge cavern of a hangar. It was even colder than the night before. Frosty grass crunched under his feet as he took a short cut.

He looked up at K – King. Half-frozen mechanics, standing on a gantry, were working on the starboard outer engine.

'Much wrong with it, Chiefy?' he asked.

'Buggered,' the flight sergeant in charge said. 'We're replacing it. Good job you came back when you did.' He was an older man with greying hair, and he looked tired. Patching up operational aircraft and keeping them in flying condition strained the endurance of ground crews to the limit. He eyed Kirby quizzically. 'The CO's been on the blower about it, for some reason,' he said. 'Christ knows when he ever sleeps. I told him the same thing.'

Kirby made his way to the Flight Office, and looked at the notice board. Flight Lieutenant Abel had been appointed flight commander 'A' Flight, and promoted to acting squadron leader.

No one ever found out what had happened to Squadron Leader Gale, DFC, and his crew.

The blue-black ink in the log book which belonged to Squadron Leader David Kirby, DSO, DFC, has soaked deep into the pages over the years, and the neatly printed entries now appear slightly blurred, but can still be read without difficulty.

Avro Lancaster R5868 Self Crew War Ops – Stettin.
        8000lb plus AP target attacked in good
        visibility – heavy opposition.
                        6 hours 50 minutes

'The CO wants to see you,' Squadron Leader Abel said.

'Oh, for Christ's sake,' Kirby said. 'What am I supposed to have done wrong now? Farted in the mess?'

Squadron Leader Abel was a large, leather-faced Australian, with a diminutive sense of humour.

'He didn't say,' he told Kirby, the leather uncracked.

Wing Commander Norgate was, confusingly, a different man.

'Come in, David. Sit down. Have a cigarette.' He was positively purring, all smiles, as though no threatening word had ever passed his lips. Kirby cautiously lit the proffered cigarette. Suddenly, he was 'David' for some reason, having previously come close to being accused first of imcompetence, and then of cowardice. He could not account for it, unless – the possibility crossed his mind fleetingly – Wing Commander Norgate was slightly mad.

'A first-rate photograph you brought back the other night,' Norgate said. 'One of the best I've ever seen.'

Having released its bombs, each aircraft was supposed to

continue on the same steady course with bomb doors open until a photograph of the result was obtained. The camera in the bomb bay was triggered by flares released with the bombs. Good target photographs were not too common. The camera could be prematurely triggered by someone else's flares. They might be bombing through cloud. While all aircraft had to overfly the target anyway – it was too risky to turn across the bomber stream in a sky full of aircraft – there was a strong temptation to get those bomb doors closed quickly in readiness for that blessed moment when, the target behind, they could bank and head for home.

That minute or so before the bomb doors should be closed seemed endless. Target photographs were coveted by planners and strategists. For crews being shot at over the target, delivering bombs was the object of the operation. Bringing back photographs seemed less important than getting themselves back.

'Tremendous,' Norgate said. 'Group are delighted. Here.' He handed Kirby a glossy print. 'Show it to your crew, I'm sure they'd like to see it. Let me have it back, of course. Congratulations, David. Keep it up.'

Kirby stubbed out his cigarette. He could find no good reason why a mere photograph should attract so much glowing approval. He could only suppose that his bombs had landed dead on target, and yet Norgate had made no reference in his paean of praise to accurate bombing, or even mentioned, much less applauded, Ted Hollis, the bomb aimer.

In fact, Kirby had been the unwitting means which had taken Norgate a small but satisfying step along the path towards the end which he so deeply desired.

The air officer commanding had telephoned personally from Group. Norgate's pleasure had expanded during the brief conversation.

'Not often we see anything as excellent as this,' Air Vice Marshal Farleigh had said. '. . . the pilot concerned, one of your old hands? . . . a new boy? . . . really? . . . well, he's a credit to you . . . perhaps we should give him some recognition, encourage him . . . I think Bomber Command might like to see this . . . chalk one up for 545 Squadron, eh? . . .'

Norgate had made suitably modest noises, but when he hung up, his cheeks were flushed with pleasure. Everyone stood to gain credit, including Group, which was why the AOC proposed to forward the photograph to Bomber Command where, more than likely, it would be studied by Air Marshal Harris himself. Norgate pictured the print, with the typewritten flimsy attached: 'Stettin. K – King, 545 Squadron.' He saw 'Bomber' Harris's face as his eyes registered the squadron number.

The AOC had been half inclined to recommend Kirby for a Mention in Despatches, but had finally discarded the idea, to Norgate's relief. That would have been going altogether too far. Just the same, perhaps young Kirby had the makings after all. Norgate decided magnanimously to let bygones be bygones.

Crowding together, shoulder to shoulder, Kirby and his crew peered through the magnifying glass at the print. The clarity was astonishingly good.

'Evidently it's quality that matters, not results,' Kirby said eventually.

Kirby's 8,000lb 'cookie' was frozen as it exploded low down into the side of a tall block of flats in the centre of Stettin. The whole building had already begun to collapse. The markers which had been accurately planted on the target area, the docks, and at which K – King had aimed, were not on the photograph. Kirby estimated that the bomb must have landed about two miles from the target markers.

The 'cookie' somewhat resembled a giant dustbin. It had no ballistic characteristics. Once released, it could land anywhere within a five-mile radius of the aiming point.

Alan Russell pushed the print aside with a sweep of his hand, and stood up. His face was set.

'I wish I hadn't seen that,' he said.

'Why, for Christ's sake?' Ferris demanded.

Alan Russell said, 'We aim at a military target, and what do we hit? A block of flats. Probably a shelter underneath. God knows how many civilians, women and children, buried alive.'

His face was pale, the tiny muscles round his mouth taut. 'And everyone thinks it's marvellous, congratulations all round because we've got a perfect picture. All right!' He swung round on Ferris, who wore a mirthless smile. 'I'm not stupid. I know what we're really doing. Usually, though, we don't see, we never know, and I don't want to know.' He waved at the discarded print, tiredly. 'I just don't want my nose rubbed in it, that's all,' he said.

They were all looking at him, silent in the face of this embarrassing outburst.

Ferris took in a deep, rasping breath.

'Still a bloody conchie, you are, all right,' he said. 'You bleed for the bastards like some soppy schoolgirl, if you want to, but not me, because they're trying to blow me out of the sky, and I don't give a fuck.'

'Don't talk cock,' Alan Russell flared back. He stabbed a finger at the photograph. 'We're not killing soldiers or airmen. That's just my point.'

'Listen, mate,' Ferris said, with the weary impatience of a teacher attempting to drum simple truths into a backward child, 'it doesn't matter a fuck what we hit or who we kill. Women, children, sodding babes in arms, it makes no difference. For one thing, they're all fucking Jerries anyway. For another, we're tying down Christ knows how many guns and planes that'd be knocking shit out of the Russians otherwise. Not to mention firemen, rescue workers, buggers in Civil Defence all over Germany, there must be a million of them or more. They've got to make fighters instead of bombers, anti-aircraft guns instead of anti-tank guns, and these civilian casualties you're so upset about, they need doctors, nurses, hospitals, bloody gravediggers come to that. All that lot, they can't do any fighting, because of us. Jesus, it's so simple,' he breathed, exasperated.

'Because something's simple in your simple mind,' Alan Russell said, 'that doesn't make it right.'

'Simple-minded am I?' The sudden rush of blood into Ferris's face turned it dark.

'Knock it off, you two,' Kirby said, sharply. 'Pack it in.'

'Just one more question for our navigator, skipper,' Ferris said. 'A simple one,' he said, guilelessly. 'There's still no Second Front. What were we supposed to have done since 1940, if we hadn't bombed the bastards? Sit back and let the Russians do all the fighting? And they didn't come in until they were attacked, any more than the bloody Americans did. We're helping to win the war, and that's all that matters,' Ferris said. 'And if you're so squeamish you can't take it, then piss off. Go LMF or something.'

Ferris's was the authentic voice, if expressed in more colourful language, not only of 'Bomber' Harris, but of the British government. He also spoke for the vast majority of the crews in Bomber Command. What was the alternative?

The effects of the German heavy bomber raids on London in 1918 were vastly overrated by both sides. The British Handley Page 1500 was designed to attack Berlin, and by the end of the First World War it was a widely held belief that the future lay with the bomber. This theory was embraced in the 1920s, by authorities on both sides of the Channel, and in America, which claimed that the bomber would be a war-winning weapon that was unbeatable. 'The bomber will always get through.' The British Air Staff needed no convincing. It was their belief that:

'The strategic air offensive is a means of direct attack on the enemy state with the object of depriving it of the means or will to continue the war. It may in itself be the instrument of victory, or it may be the means by which victory can be won by other forces. It differs from all previous kinds of armed attack in that it alone can be brought to bear immediately, directly and destructively against the heartland of the enemy.'

The RAF saw the bomber as a strategic weapon, operating primarily independently of ground and naval forces whereas, in the rapidly re-arming Germany, the doctrine of application was switched more towards a tactical co-operation with other arms.

In Britain, it was not until 1936 that specifications were

issued which eventually led to the building of heavy bombers. On 14 July of that year, Bomber Command was formed.

On the outbreak of war, Bomber Command was not equipped for the role which many saw for it. It had five operational groups, mainly equipped with Battles, Blenheims, Whitleys, Hampdens, and Wellingtons, all light or medium bombers, although the Wellington was later modified, and became capable of carrying a 4,000lb bomb.

The Germans had demonstrated the effectiveness of air/ground operations, but there was a reluctance in Bomber Command to commit their 'strategic' force to combined tactical operations. This reluctance was reinforced when ten Battle squadrons of Number One Group were detached to France, and suffered very heavy losses in a series of un-coordinated attacks on the Meuse bridges.

At that time, Bomber Command did not have the right aircraft, either in type or quantity, for the cherished strategic bombing offensive and, moreover, there was a general unwillingness to start an 'all out' air war against a superior equipped power.

In the early months of the war, except for the Battle squadrons detached to France for a short period, Bomber Command confined itself to leaflet dropping by night over Germany, mostly carried out by Whitleys, and daylight attacks, principally by Wellingtons, on German shipping.

The Wellingtons suffered appalling losses, as high as 50 per cent on one or two occasions. Whitley losses, by night, were far less. This was one factor which led the RAF to favour night bombing – to reduce losses.

When Winston Churchill became Prime Minister, on 5 May 1940 he authorized bombing east of the Rhine. That night, 99 bombers attacked oil and rail targets in the Ruhr. The Strategic Bombing Offensive had begun, although for some time it remained faltering and uncertain.

Until late 1941, Bomber Command operations were varied, but generally small-scale and ineffective, despite the new aircraft which were coming into service, Stirlings, Halifaxes, and Manchesters – but they all had their problems. The

Manchester was a twin-engined 'heavy', which soon evolved into the Lancaster, the most effective heavy night bomber of the war. The Halifax too, after modification, became a successful aircraft.

One of the major difficulties was bombing accuracy. Bomber Command tried to attack small targets at night, but its aircraft lacked accurate navigational aids. At this time, the exponents of strategic bombing were optimistically claiming an average error of 1,000 yards. An enquiry, based on air photographs taken during and after raids, suggested that only one bomber in three dropped its bombs within five miles of the target. Service critics of Bomber Command and the whole concept of strategic bombing, argued that the massive resources which would be required, were it to continue and increase, would be more effectively used elsewhere, and should be switched forthwith.

1942 was the turning point for Bomber Command. Air Marshal A. T. Harris was appointed C-in-C. Harris was convinced of the value of the offensive, but recognized that, not only did the morale of the Command badly need a boost when its fortunes were at a low ebb, but that his political chiefs needed something not only persuasive, but dramatic.

Harris planned a '1,000 bomber raid'. The target was the city of Cologne, the date 30–31 May 1942. By scraping together every possible aircraft and crew, including crews still in training, a force of 1,046 bombers took part in the attack.

Fortunately for Harris and Bomber Command, if not the citizens of Cologne, the raid was a success. Large parts of the city were destroyed, while British losses at 3·7 per cent were reasonably low.

This success silenced most of the doubters among the service chiefs. Through Bomber Command, Britain was perceived as striking back at last, inflicting a major blow on Germany itself. The government was more than ready to be convinced. If not bombing – then what? Bomber Command was allocated a higher priority for aircraft and, more importantly, scientific development of navigational aids and radar.

'Gee' came into service in 1942, but the system had a limited range. Late in 1942 came the better 'Oboe' with an improved though still limited range, and the Pathfinder squadrons took priority. Even late on, many front line squadrons had to make do with 'Gee'. In January 1943 H2S radar was introduced.

Also in January 1943, the Chiefs of Staff Conference met in Casablanca. Arising from that meeting, Bomber Command were given a new directive.

'Your primary objective will be the progressive destruction and dislocation of the German military, industrial and economic system, and the undermining of the morale of the German people to a point where their capacity for armed resistance is fatally weakened.'

The careful wording of that brief directive provided carte blanche. Bomber Command was to operate without any restrictions whatsoever. Total war was enshrined as official policy. It was a clear invitation to the advocates of strategic bombing to prove their case. Air Marshal A. T. Harris could have asked for nothing more.

In March 1943, Bomber Command launched a sustained attack on Germany. The first part was the 'Battle of the Ruhr', aimed at destroying vital war industries in that vast conurbation. The assault succeeded in causing serious damage, although this was quickly repaired by the Germans.

In late July and early August, Bomber Command and the US Eighth Air Force, acting in conjunction, carried out a series of attacks by day and by night on the city of Hamburg. During these extremely heavy and accurate series of raids, an estimated 50,000 of the population of Hamburg died, mostly burned and suffocated in the firestorm which had been created. Goebbels said of the resulting damage that it was a 'catastrophe, the extent of which simply staggers the imagination'.

For a while, the Allied Air Forces believed that they had discovered a new and deadly form of devastation which bombers could inflict, the ultimate weapon. But despite several subsequent attempts, they never succeeded in creating again the freak conditions which had given rise to the Hamburg firestorm (until Bomber Command attacked Dresden, when the war was almost over).

The third part of the offensive was the 'Battle of Berlin', which began in November 1943.

Bomber Command had demonstrated the destructive power of large numbers of heavy aircraft. Nevertheless, continued improvements in defence took a heavy toll. In May 1943, at the Washington Conference, a policy was declared proposing the destruction of the Luftwaffe and the German aircraft industry by daylight American raids, and Bomber Command by night. Not before time, it had been realized that air superiority was a basic prerequisite for successful bomber operations.

From early 1944 onwards, the Rolls-Royce-engined Mustang provided daylight cover to the American bombers, all the way to their targets and back. American losses declined. No equivalent night cover was available to the RAF.

At the beginning of 1944, Bomber Command had 1,600 front line aircraft, nearly all heavy bombers, except for the squadrons of Mosquitoes. Soon after, the offensive against German cities was diverted to softening up German defences, and disrupting lines of communication as part of the build up to the projected Allied invasion of Europe.

Fresh targets for Bomber Command emerged: the new and formidable weapons which Germany had developed, and which posed a serious threat to Allied plans.

Even at the height of the war, a few lonely voices publicly attacked British bombing policy. In the House of Lords, Bishop Bell of Chichester condemned 'area' or 'carpet' bombing, aimed at cities and civilians, labelled it as 'indiscriminate bombing', and called for its cessation.

In reply, the government lied with a straight face. The RAF was not bombing indiscriminately. The Royal Air Force always aimed at specific targets.

The bishop's campaign generated little support. The British public believed that bombing was the most effective means of prosecuting the war. They did not much care whether Bomber

Command was bombing discriminately or indiscriminately. They were bombing the bastards, and that was all that mattered. Anyway, the Germans had started it all with their night bombing raids on London. No one seemed to remember that initial attack on the Ruhr in May 1940, or the bombing of Berlin, ordered by Churchill at the height of the Battle of Britain in August 1940, and if they did, such niceties were brushed aside.

545 Squadron did not fly on operations every night. Sometimes, it was only once or twice a week. Kirby began to realize that his tour of thirty operations would take months to complete.

That was not to say that they did not fly. They flew almost every day on intensive squadron training, with the object of drastically improving bombing accuracy. The other side of the Channel, ramps were being erected from which, months later, V1s would be launched against London – 'flying bombs'. In order to damage those ramps, squadrons would have to plant their bombs much more precisely than they were accustomed to. Two crews were lost during training, when their aircraft collided.

Kirby walked into the mess one evening, and stared disbelievingly at the three new but very familiar faces.

'Well, I'm damned,' he said, grinning. He shook hands warmly with Roy Harrison, Ralph Whitney, and Smithy. 'It's good to see you again.' It was even good to see Smithy. 'How the hell . . .?'

'We all got stuck in the pipeline,' Roy Harrison said, beaming. 'Landed up at the same OCU.'

'We knew you were with 545,' Ralph Whitney said.

'Must be the first time in history anyone's been given the postings they asked for,' Roy Harrison said.

'What's it to be? This calls for a celebration.'

Over that round and several succeeding rounds, they brought each other up to date, and the newcomers asked questions about 545 Squadron. Roy, Ralph and Smithy had been on leave twice, waiting for courses.

'It was good to get it regularly again, I can tell you,' Smithy said, with feeling.

'I thought you always got it regularly, Smithy, wherever you were,' Kirby remarked.

He waited, smiling affably, for Smithy to react to this oblique challenge to his veracity and virility, his assertions that there was always a constant supply of willing crumpet only too eager to oblige. But the heavily set man did not respond. Under his clipped moustache, a sheepish grin merely appeared.

'My shout,' Smithy said. 'Same again?'

It dawned on Kirby that there was a slight but definite shift in the attitude of all three of them, even the formerly patronizing Smithy, even his close friend Roy, while Ralph Whitney, for all his superior brain power, was not only courteous, which was his nature, but almost unnaturally polite.

No doubt most of that would soon wear off, but Kirby knew the reason. He had only done five ops, but they had done none. By chance, he had become the senior, the one with experience, the one who knew what it was like. And he would continue, with a five ops start, to be more experienced until the end of his tour, unless something went wrong, and . . . Kirby surreptitiously touched the wood of the bar, an exorcism against that particular thought, and pushed it out of his conscious mind. But it had begun to lurk, somewhere in the background . . . as if slowly gestating . . . waiting . . .

'What's the CO like?' Ralph Whitney asked.

Kirby said. 'Press on regardless at all costs.'

'Just Smithy's cup of tea,' Roy Harrison said.

'Bang on,' Smithy said. 'Just the job. Good show. Wizard.' He grimaced, and they all laughed. The catch phrases attributed to RAF air crew appeared less frequently in their conversation than those who made stilted films about them imagined. Kirby reflected that Smithy seemed to have improved somewhat.

'We ran into Jacko and Don Shepherd,' Roy Harrison said. 'They're going to try for 545 Squadron too.'

'The CO'll never know how lucky he is,' Kirby said. 'He's dying to have an élite squadron.'

'That's us,' Smithy said. 'The élite.'

'What's it like, David?' Ralph Whitney asked. 'Flying your first operation?'

Avro Lancaster   R5868   Self   Crew   War Ops – Hesdin.
        8000lb plus AP. First attack on missile
        sites in Pas de Calais. Doddle.
        Queueing to bomb.   2.55

Avro Lancaster   R5868   Self   Crew   War Ops – Pas de Calais.
        8000lb plus AP. Missile site. Aborted
        due to weather. Long stooge to reduce
        AUW for landing with bombs. Jettison
        not possible. (Operation does not
        count.)   5.00

Each time they came back, Arthur Wood walked away as they stood waiting for transport at dispersal, and vomited into the long grass.

'There's Arthur, at it again,' Ferris said, cheerfully. 'Puking his fucking guts up.'

It was part of the routine, like the figure of Kay, waiting for them to land.

Smithy and Ralph Whitney had been assigned to 'A' Flight, Roy Harrison to 'B' Flight. Jacko and Don Shepherd were supposed to be on their way, but had not appeared yet.

'Why don't we buy a car between us?' Roy Harrison suggested. 'No need to rely on squadron transport then.' They were sitting companionably in Kirby's small room. 'We could drive to London, if he gets a 36-hour pass . . .'

'What happens if one of us gets unlucky?' Kirby enquired.

'Like a joint savings bank account,' Roy Harrison said. ' "Either or survivor".' He grinned. 'It's a damn good scheme,' he said.

Kirby thought about it. His assets were negligible. Somehow, his mess bills were always more than he had anticipated. He was remitting more to his mother . . .

On the other hand, he had just been promoted to flying officer, and was now being paid the princely sum of eighteen shillings and twopence a day. The idea of a car was appealing. He was tempted.

'I can't drive,' he temporized. He had never learned.

'An hour's dual from me, and you will,' Roy Harrison said, dismissing that. 'What do you say?'

'Depends how much it'd cost,' Kirby said, doing some mental arithmetic.

On a free afternoon, they hitch-hiked into Chelmsford, courtesy of a friendly lorry driver. After some fruitless tramping around, they found an otherwise empty showroom tucked away at the back of which was a 1933 Ford 8.

'Forty quid,' the garage owner said. 'First-class condition . . .'

'Too much,' Kirby said, hurriedly, visualizing his last bank statement. 'Thirty.'

Roy Harrison drove halfway back to Woodley Common. On a long, straight stretch of empty road he established that the small car could just about manage 55mph, throttle flat on the floorboards, downhill, with a following wind. There was considerably more sensation of speed than when flying.

'I reckon safe cruising's about forty-five,' Roy Harrison bellowed above the racket of the clattering, straining little engine, as the car bucketed and rolled. 'Shouldn't be heavy on petrol though.'

'I still think we were done,' Kirby shouted back.

'So do I, but it's too late now.'

Roy Harrison slowed down and came to a stop. At idling speed, the noise level of the engine declined to something approximating nuts and bolts being rotated in a vibrating tin can.

'Your turn now,' Roy said.

Kirby had already obtained a driving licence. There were no driving tests. He simply filled in a form, and was given an

'All Groups' licence, which entitled him to drive a motorcycle, a tractor and a steamroller, among other vehicles.

The gearbox suffered for a while, its synchromesh either being rudimentary, or sadly worn, but by the time he parked outside the mess at Woodley Common, he was getting the hang of it. It was the only driving lesson he ever had.

Ralph Whitney, it emerged, intended to return to America after the war. They were playing billiards, and Kirby was winning easily, although he was neither very good, nor in practice. Ralph Whitney was simply terrible at billiards, as he was at cricket or football, or anything, come to that, which involved a ball of any kind.

'You remember the navigation instructor at Maranda?' Ralph Whitney asked, missing an easy cannon.

'Mr Lindsay, yes,' Kirby said. 'A nice chap.' Mr Lindsay was darkly good-looking with unruly black hair, an academic, unfit for active service, who had taken a post as a ground school navigation instructor as the next best thing.

'We were very friendly,' Ralph Whitney said, watching Kirby go in off the red, and respot the white. 'We had a lot in common. He'll be going back to the University of Illinois after the war. We used to talk about teaching in the same faculty one day, but I didn't take it too seriously. Now he's written to say that he's been in touch with Illinois, and they're willing to offer me a post. I've accepted, sent the letter off this morning. It's the kind of chance I never thought would come my way, and now it has. War seems to have certain advantages, after all.'

Kirby potted the red, and racked his cue. 'That's it. A hundred. Come on, you owe me a beer.' They walked into the bar. 'I'm not sure if you know,' Ralph Whitney said, 'but I met a girl out there. She lived in Baxter Springs. We write to each other. That's another reason!'

The target was Berlin.

Ralph Whitney was the last to take off. He had had some difficulty in starting one of his engines. When it finally fired, it seemed to be running smoothly. Ralph worriedly checked with his flight engineer, but they decided it was OK. Ralph Whitney was not anxious to distinguish himself by aborting while still at dispersal.

Shortly after take off, the same engine failed. Fully laden with fuel and bombs, the Lancaster wallowed, lost flying speed, and stalled into the ground, half a mile from the end of the runway.

The 'cookie' exploded, detonating the armour-piercing bombs as well. There was nothing left of the aircraft or its crew, except fragments of twisted, tortured metal scattered around a huge crater.

The explosion shattered windows in the guard room, and the WAAF quarters.

It was Ralph Whitney's second operation.

Chapter Thirteen

Avro Lancaster R5868 Self Crew War Ops – Berlin.
              Full load incendiaries. Attacked cross-
              ing Germany by EA. Lost port inner.
              Load jettisoned. Attempted landing at
              Manston on 3 without hydraulics. Air-
              craft total write off. Crew safe.   3.50

Manston was much used by returning aircraft in trouble, due to its size and its position on the south-east tip of England, the first airfield where a crippled plane on the way back from Germany could try and put down.

Kirby and his crew had something to eat, and dozed fitfully in armchairs until the lift home they had been promised finally materialized. The Dakota was being ferried to Yorkshire, and would land at Woodley Common on the way. Kirby had heard about Ralph Whitney when he telephoned Woodley Common to report that he and his crew were unhurt.

Ferris twisted himself into a position where he could look out of one of the windows during the Dakota's final approach. He winked at Kirby, and gave him the thumbs up. Kirby nodded.

The Dakota landed, turned off the runway, and taxied towards the control tower. Normal speech was now possible.

'She's a bleeding wonder,' Ferris said. 'Now she can look after us by remote control. I reckon she deserves taking out for a few strong gins, or whatever her tipple is. What do you say, skipper? Kind of a big thank you from all of us.'

All the crew knew Kay now, and smiled at her when they

were in the Parachute Section, but by unspoken consent communication with her was left to Kirby. That was a part of the superstition, that was how it had started.

They jumped down from the Dakota, and stretched stiff limbs. Wing Commander Norgate emerged from the Control Tower, and walked towards them, as spruce, upright, and alert as if he had slept soundly all night and had just soaked in a leisurely bath, rather than having flown to Berlin and back, waited until all his crews were accounted for, risen after four hours' sleep, carefully gone over the debriefing reports in detail, and held a meeting with his flight commanders.

Kirby was beginning to understand Norgate's apparent need for little sleep. In Kirby's case, when he finally got to bed, he fell asleep at once, but a few hours later found himself unwillingly coming awake again, his mind focussed on what might be posted on orders in the Flight Office.

And Kirby was only on his first tour, well short of the halfway mark. For Norgate, on his third tour, and with the responsibilities of squadron command, it must be that much worse.

'Glad to see you're all more or less fighting fit,' Wing Commander Norgate said. His welcoming smile was stretched, as if it were an effort, but it was a smile, nevertheless. 'Your replacement aircraft is ready for you, but there's nothing on tonight, so have a good rest. You deserve it. Splendid to have you back safely.' He smiled again. 'Right, off you go,' he said. 'Oh, Flying Officer Kirby, a word if you please.'

Kirby half expected an inquest on his crash landing at Manston, but Norgate did not mention it. They walked side by side in the direction of the squadron office.

'They're shaping up into a good crew,' Norgate said. 'I have my doubts about Russell, though. Peculiar sort of individual. Some very funny opinions. He doesn't seem to fit in. Something of an odd man out.' He glanced sideways at Kirby enquiringly.

'He's a good navigator,' Kirby said. 'That's all I care about.'

'We'll see,' Norgate said, dubiously. 'He hasn't had the chance to prove himself yet, one way or the other.' Kirby thought that he would have a long, hot bath before he fell into bed. 'Two NCO pilots have arrived,' Norgate said. 'Shepherd and Jackson. I gather you were at flying school with them. How do you think they'll make out?'

'Don Shepherd's a determined sort of chap,' Kirby said. 'It doesn't come easily for him, but he never gives up. Stan Jackson's a natural. If he doesn't prove to be one of the best pilots you could wish for, I shall be very surprised.'

Wing Commander Norgate nodded.

'Good,' he said. 'They sound very likely material in their different ways.' He glanced at his watch. 'Care to join me for an early lunch, David?'

'If you'll excuse me, sir,' Kirby apologized, 'I'm not very hungry . . .'

'I know,' Norgate said. 'Sometimes, bed's the best meal there is. Another time.'

He walked off.

Kirby made his way along the road to his billet. The air was cool, but there was a pleasantly fresh tang to it. Spring was on the way.

What a contradictory man Norgate was. With a head start bestowed by his astonishing bravery and skill, he nevertheless seemed incapable of acquiring that easy respect on an informal, personal level, which a good commander should have.

Kirby had fallen into conversation in the mess one night with Norgate's bomb aimer, a flying officer. 'Flying with him is great in some ways,' Norgate's bomb aimer had said. 'He's so on the ball, so good, you know he'll get you back home again every time. You just know it. And you're dying to like him for that, but he won't let you. I don't expect him to be chummy, that's not his style, but if only he'd relax just a bit – but he never does. He's a cold fish, and the atmosphere up there, he behaves like the captain of a destroyer or something, expecting his crew to do everything at the double.'

Yet Norgate *was* attentive to his crews; in his own way, he *did* make an effort, as he had done today. And Kirby's crew had appreciated it, despite his wooden manner. If only he were consistent they would accept him fully, but just when they thought they knew where they stood, he would spoil it with some petulant outburst, some harsh decision which struck everyone as unjust, for reasons which remained mystifying and obscure, incomprehensible to anyone but Norgate himself.

Vanity, perhaps, Kirby speculated? Was that it? He was deep in thought when he strolled quietly into the corridor of his Nissen hut, and he had passed the closed door of the room which had belonged to Ralph Whitney, before the slight sounds registered in his mind.

Kirby stopped and listened. Softly, he moved back to the door, placed his fingers on the handle, paused, and then flung the door open, with a crash.

Ralph Whitney's open suitcase was on his bed. The wardrobe door gaped wide. The two airmen in the room stared at Kirby, transfixed. Kirby could hear them breathing in the silence, almost felt their hearts beating with sudden fright.

One of them was bending over the suitcase. The other was crouched beside the open bottom drawer of Ralph Whitney's chest of drawers. Ralph's gold wristwatch was in his hand. A wallet protruded from his right-hand trousers pocket.

Kirby recognized neither of them, but he knew who they were. Air crew left all personal belongings behind when they flew on operations. They were forbidden to carry anything which might, however indirectly, betray which squadron they belonged to, should they be shot down, taken prisoner, and interrogated. The only means of identification which they flew with was their identity discs, which were impervious to fire.

The two airmen were members of the Ghoul Brigade. Those who ransacked dead air crews' belongings before they could be sent home to their next of kin.

Kirby thought of Ralph Whitney, the lousy billiard player who had planned to start a new life at the University of Illinois, and who had been writing to a girl in Baxter Springs.

'Sir,' one of them managed at last, 'I'm sorry, we . . .'

'Shut up, you bastard,' Kirby said. 'Batman!' he shouted. 'Batman!'

There was no response. The batman would have gone to lunch.

'All right, you two, outside!' Kirby ordered.

'Please, sir,' one of them said, 'we were only . . .'

'I said outside,' Kirby replied. 'And don't put anything back,' he told the other one. 'You took it, you can bloody keep it.'

The two airmen walked miserably ahead of Kirby along the road which scythed between rows of Nissen huts towards Station Headquarters.

The younger of the two airmen stopped and turned. His face was ashen. It came out with a rush.

'Sir, this is the first time, honestly. It's never happened before. We'll never do it again, if you let us go, I swear to God.'

'No, you won't,' Kirby agreed. 'Because you two are going to be court-martialled.' He caught sight of an NCO fitter ambling between huts. 'Sergeant!' he shouted peremptorily. 'Here! Double quick!'

The sergeant's forage cap was tucked into the shoulder strap of his battledress. Hurriedly he removed it, and settled it on his head. He was not used to being shouted at by hatless young air crew officers in flying overalls. He doubled towards Kirby, came to a halt, and saluted.

'Sir.'

'Take these men to the guard room, and have them placed under arrest for stealing,' Kirby said. 'Orders of Flying Officer Kirby.'

'Sir,' the sergeant said. 'All right, you two. Quick march. Left right, left right . . .'

Kirby took his hot bath, but he did not lie in it for long. His rage had been replaced by cold fury. He would not be able to sleep now.

He dressed, walked to Squadron Headquarters and saw the squadron adjutant, who completed the formal charge against the culprits. Subsequently, after a period under close arrest, a summary of evidence was taken, and the two airmen were finally court-martialled and sentenced to six months' detention with hard labour.

Leading Aircraft-woman Kay Dunn was not in the least

shapeless when not muffled up in a greatcoat. Her hair was a
rich dark brown, and she wore it rolled up, tight against the
nape of her neck. Regulations decreed that WAAFs' hair must
not touch their uniform collars. Her eyes were green, and
looked out from a heart-shaped face which, given her smooth
skin, straight nose, and well-moulded mouth, might have
attracted instant attention from any quarter, had it not been
for the withdrawn expression of reserve which she habitually
wore, and behind which, perhaps, she hid.

Only when a smile, normally little more than formal, turned,
if rarely, into one of genuine amusement, revealing regular
white teeth, and causing her green eyes to light up, was the
intangible shield dissolved, and a quite uncommon kind of
beauty briefly revealed.

The WAAFs' quarters comprised a complex of Nissen huts,
flanking a narrow lane, just outside the airfield perimeter. She
was waiting beside one of the paths. Kirby slowed the 1933
Ford 8 to a creaking halt. He had never before seen her
wearing a skirt, only battledress trousers. In a detached way,
he observed that, even in flat shoes and lisle stockings, she
possessed agreeably shapely legs. Kay opened the passenger
door and got in.

Kirby had proffered the invitation which Ferris had suggested, but Kay had shaken her head.

'I won't, if you don't mind,' she had said.

Kirby realized that she probably had a boyfriend on the
station. 'It was just a thought,' he had said. 'You hardly know
any of us, after all.'

'In a way, that's it,' Kay had said, with one of her concealed
smiles. 'The fact that I don't know any of you to talk to except
you, of course, and if I did, that would somehow spoil it . . .'
Her smile turned into a self-deprecating laugh. 'I know that
sounds pretty silly, but . . .'

'It wouldn't sound silly to them,' Kirby had said, 'they'd
understand perfectly. But since I seem to be the elected
spokesman, suppose it was just me? That wouldn't spoil
anything, would it?'

Kirby let out the clutch, which needed adjusting and snatched a bit, and drove off.

'Where shall it be?' he asked. 'Chelmsford? Or anywhere you like, within reason.' Kay said nothing, and he glanced at her sideways. She was staring straight ahead through the windscreen, as if where to go were a matter of grave importance.

'There's a place not far away,' she said, finally. 'I'll direct you.'

The Packhorse was only a few minutes' drive, but so tucked behind a tangle of country lanes that Kirby had not even been aware of its existence.

Inside, the small, panelled lounge bar was busy, but mostly with civilians, war-prosperous members of the local farming community, Kirby guessed. There were only a couple of other RAF uniforms.

He bought drinks, and they found a table. Chintz-shaded wall lamps cast a subdued light.

'It's like negotiating Hampton Court maze to find this place,' Kirby said. 'How did you come across it?'

'It's miles by road,' Kay said, 'but you can walk here in half an hour from the airfield. There's a footpath across the fields. Well, not in this weather, but it's nice during the summer.'

She had evidently been stationed at Woodley Common for some time. Kirby told her about Ferris's theory of the three 'Ks'. She laughed, and Kirby became aware of how agreeably her face could change.

'It never even occurred to me,' she said. 'Superstition's evidently a fine art as far as he's concerned . . .' Kirby smilingly agreed.

A thoughtful look crossed her face. 'Unless it was subconscious,' she said. 'That could be, I suppose . . . but I don't think so.'

Ferris's other deduction proved to be more accurate. Kay nodded.

'Janet,' she said. 'She's in my hut. She's a telephone operator in Air Traffic Control. She rings through and tells me if you're coming back early, or landing somewhere else.'

'Well, tell her she's doing a great job,' Kirby said. He was about to add 'Like you', but he checked himself. It had to be voluntary, not by arrangement. She had to be there of her own free will, not as the result of any pressure, however oblique. That would break the spell. He was getting as bad as Ferris, Kirby thought. Well, rationally, it was obvious nonsense. A girl's thoughts could have no effect on the progress of an anti-aircraft shell, or the appearance or otherwise of K – King on some German night fighter's radar screen, or whether its cannon shells merely put out an engine instead of exploding in the petrol tanks and frying them all, as had happened on the way to Berlin. The fact remained, however, that he did believe it. He believed it more strongly every time they remained unscathed after each succeeding operation. Or at any rate, he needed to believe it.

Kirby noticed that two of their neighbours seemed to be studying a handwritten menu. He suddenly felt hungry.

'They'll have booked a table,' Kay said. 'The dining room's always full.'

'Let's try,' Kirby said. 'No harm in asking.'

They were greeted with some warmth – or more accurately, Kay was – by a cheery dark man in his fifties who, Kirby later learned, owned the place.

'Hullo, there. Welcome back. Nice to see you again . . . yes, of course I can fit you in . . . that couple over there are just leaving.'

They sat at the table for two, and ordered mixed grill. Wartime mixed grill often usefully concealed a multitude of culinary sins, but then so did most restaurant food.

'You've obviously been here before,' Kirby said.

'That was a while ago.' She arranged her serviette carefully, smoothing it over her lap, glanced at Kirby quickly, and seemed to come to a decision. 'Don't tell your crew this . . .' Kirby promised. 'That's why I picked on K – King. Someone I used to know, his call sign was K – King too.'

'Did you see him off every time as well?'

She looked away, and seemed to be studying the people at

the next table. 'He nearly made it,' she said. 'His tour was almost over.'

'Perhaps he's a POW,' Kirby said, quietly. 'Or lying low somewhere in Belgium or Holland, waiting for one of the escape routes to get him back home.'

'His mother heard from the Red Cross,' Kay said. 'His body had been identified.'

'I'm sorry,' Kirby said. 'I didn't mean to intrude.'

'You're not,' Kay said, calmly. 'But there was a girl who was engaged to a flight sergeant. She used to do it – and he finished his tour. I wished I had too. Well, it was too late for Mike . . . but then you arrived, and when I found that you'd be flying K – King . . .' Her clasped hands parted, opening in a gesture of doubt. 'It can't really make any difference, I suppose. Common sense tells me that.'

'Sensible or not,' Kirby said, 'it helps.' Kay nodded, clasped her hands again, and leaned her chin on them. On the little finger of her right hand was a plain gold band. 'Were you and . . . Mike . . . married?' Kirby asked.

Kay shook her head.

'When he came back, he was going on leave,' she said. 'It was to be then. Parish church booked, and all that. The wedding ring belonged to his grandmother,' she said, inspecting it. 'She must have been tiny. I was going to have it altered. But it fits my little finger.'

The mixed grill featured the expected sausages, but there was a piece of liver as well, and even a slice of bacon. Kirby ate with relish, while he told her something about himself.

Kay listened attentively, nodding and smiling now and then, her expression changing to one of understanding when she heard about his father and brother.

'I'm still not really used to it,' Kirby said. It was easy to talk to this girl. 'Somehow, whenever I go home, I half expect them to be there.'

'I know,' Kay said. 'It's how I feel about Mike. I know he's dead – and yet, he isn't. Not all of him. Up here, in my mind, he still lives, just as he was. And I expect he always will.'

*

Kirby drew up in the lane outside the blacked-out WAAF quarters. Kay, a dark shape beside him, unlatched the passenger door. The chill of the night air entered the car.

'Thanks for tonight,' Kirby said. 'It's been a welcome change to talk to a girl again.'

'I've enjoyed it too,' Kay said. 'I haven't been out with anyone since Mike was killed.'

'Why did you take me to The Packhorse?' Kirby asked.

A kind of exorcism he had supposed at first but he had discarded that one. Kay had no wish to exorcise her dead fiancé.

Kay said, 'I've often wanted to go back. Somehow, I felt it would be all right. You're nothing like Mike, but if you'd known each other, I think you might have been friends.'

'If you'd like to do it again some time,' Kirby said, 'I'd be glad to. I'll leave it to you.'

LACW Kay Dunn walked towards her billet. She felt less lonely. The company of a man she could like as a friend was probably what she needed. She could face nothing more. She liked David Kirby, and he liked her. There was no reason why they should not see each other. He understood that she belonged to someone else.

'Bomb doors closed.'

It was Berlin again. He was tense, strung up, every sense and sensation alert and keyed high. Fifty miles short of the target, he had swallowed another benzedrine tablet. A booster. It had become routine.

Suddenly, one of those feared, thin blue, radar controlled searchlights flicked on to them, and locked into place. Instantly, hunting conventional searchlights converged, coning the aircraft like a helpless rabbit caught in the headlights of a car.

The cold, harsh, man-made glare illuminated the cockpit, lighting up the instruments, Kirby's own clenched hands, the face of Len Bellamy frozen beside him.

Down far below, the muzzles of batteries of anti-aircraft guns swivelled, leaned towards the Lancaster impaled on the searchlights high above, fired, and recoiled. Shell cases ejected. Gunners rammed in fresh shells, and bent away as they fired again. Explosions, fireworks on high, bracketed the tiny moth-like thing.

Kirby saw the expanding flashes as if in slow motion, he heard the explosions, he smelt the cordite, he heard the rattle of shrapnel striking the aircraft.

He had at once, second nature, begun evasive action, but the twisting and turning was useless, and he knew it. He had seen it happen to others caught in the inexorable searchlights, guided by the thin blue one. Every battery within range was pumping shells at the exposed victim, K – King. They would only flutter uselessly for seconds now, before they died.

Eyes narrowed against the glare, Kirby peered through the armoured windscreen. He flinched as they seemed to fly directly through an exploding shell. Fragments spattered, the sound of hail on a corrugated iron roof.

Dimly, he managed to pick out the pencil-slim blue beam. Kirby pushed forward the control column, forcing the big plane into a dive, careless of the protesting roar of the engines, banking to starboard and then port, using aileron and rudder, until the nose was aligned, and they were hurtling down that sinister blue beam.

The plane was shaking, vibrating madly. The altimeter unwound rapidly. They seemed to be diving at the ground almost vertically.

'Pilot to Bomb Aimer,' Kirby said. 'Open fire at the blue one. Now. Fire!' He heard the rattle of the long burst from the two ·303 machine-guns in the bomb aimer's turret, and then it stopped. 'Keep going!' Kirby ordered. 'Keep firing the bloody thing.'

Ted Hollis complied. They swept down the blue beam heading for the ground. 10,000 feet . . . 9,500 . . .

'Flight Engineer, throttle back,' Kirby said. He was sweating, his wrists were aching, as if he were physically pushing the Lancaster down the blue beam towards its source. They were well above maximum permitted speed. The tortured engine note reduced in volume.

They were still embraced by the shrinking cone of search-lights, but as yet the anti-aircraft gunners had not found them again. They damn soon would though.

As the altimeter needle unwound past 8,000 feet, the blue beam flicked off. The enveloping searchlights parted, and wandered hesitantly, lost without their radar controlled guide. Abruptly they were in darkness again. Kirby concentrated on easing the great machine out of its dive without tearing the wings off. Light ack-ack pursued them for a while as they flew over the suburbs and then died away.

'Good work, Ted,' Kirby said. He was breathing hard.

'Bomb Aimer to Pilot, do you think I hit it?' The calm interest of a man unsure if the clay pigeon had descended to earth in one piece or several.

'It doesn't bloody matter,' Kirby said. More likely, the searchlight crew, unused to being machine-gunned by a Lancaster seemingly maniacally intent on diving straight into their site, had simply switched off. 'Pilot to Flight Engineer. Any problems?'

'Flight Engineer to Pilot, everything seems OK.'

'Pilot to Rear Gunner. How's it back there?'

'Rear Gunner to Pilot, OK back here.' 'Fuck me,' Ferris thought. That had been a new experience, to find himself gazing at the stars, first almost floating against his straps, and then his stomach compressed by G forces against his spine as they had pulled out of the dive. 'Fuck me.'

His practised eyes searched the surrounding sky automatically for any dim outline which might appear. 'Jesus. That was bloody nearly curtains!' It was some time since Ferris had thought of Kirby as a sprog skipper.

Kirby screwed up the first two pages of the letter he had started to his mother, and threw them away. He had set out to tell her about Kay, how she was regarded as a mascot, the occasion when they had gone for a drink together. But after a while, he became doubtful, stopped writing, read it through, and decided against.

To explain Kay, and what she meant to them all, even Alan

Russell who had quickly become a convert, meant hinting, at the very least, at the fear that one day they might not come back. Better not to mention it. He started afresh.

The door rattled, and Roy Harrison came in.

'Fit?' he enquired. They were going to pick up Jacko and Don Shepherd, and go for a drink in the village.

'Shan't be a minute.' Kirby shoved his notepad in a drawer, and put his cap on.

'I'm going to be a Daddy,' Roy Harrison announced.

'What?' Kirby stared at him. 'When did this happen?'

'When I was on leave, I should hope,' Roy Harrison said. His face registered something between a smirk and a beam.

'No, I mean when did you hear, you fool,' Kirby said. He shook Roy's hand. 'Congratulations. Bugger me . . .'

'I'd rather not, if you don't mind,' Roy Harrison said. They were both laughing idiotically. 'Had a letter today, second post. All confirmed, date and everything.'

'You with a baby . . .' Kirby shook his head in amazement. 'Wonder what it'll be?'

'A boy,' Roy Harrison said, confidently. 'No question. Men in my family always sire sons.'

'Another Harrison to infest the earth,' Kirby said.

'You mean inherit,' Roy Harrison said.

'Not if he's like you,' Kirby said. 'Well, come on. Stop looking so bloody pleased with yourself. Let's get down to the pub and celebrate.'

'You're driving tonight,' Roy Harrison said. 'Tonight, I intend to get pissed as a newt. In fact, paralytic.'

Operations told on Smithy. His plump face lost its normally florid hue, and became paler and thinner. He rarely appeared in the mess except to eat, and often pushed his meal aside unfinished. He had turned in upon himself, and spent hours on end in his billet just lying on his bed, staring up at the ceiling.

'What happens to an officer who goes LMF?' Roy Harrison wondered.

'Don't know,' Kirby said. 'They can't take away the King's commission the way they rip off a sergeant's stripes.'

'Court-martialled and cashiered, I suppose,' Roy Harrison said. 'Poor sod. They should have made him an instructor. Watching him, it's like cruelty to dumb animals.'

Roy Harrison had settled in well, and gained Wing Commander Norgate's approval. He viewed Smithy with compassion but from a position of some superiority. Roy Harrison knew with absolute certainty that he was going to be around when his son was delivered. The unborn child was a talisman.

545 Squadron was part of the diversionary force attacking a secondary target in south Germany, which made a pleasant change from Berlin, especially since the defences seemed to be thoroughly confused that night, and they met very little opposition. Except, evidently, for Flying Officer Graham Smith who was posted missing.

There was widespread sympathy for him in the mess. It seemed especially bad luck to buy it on such a relatively easy operation. Hopes were expressed that Smithy and his crew might have been able to bale out, and could be still in one piece. Roy Harrison nurtured a private suspicion that Smithy was very safe indeed, having decided to fly on from the target rather than back. Roy had a hunch that Smithy had landed in Switzerland, and was even now safely interned for the duration. It was not entirely unknown for crews who could no longer endure the ceaseless strain of one operation after another to adopt such a course.

However, people were so busy discovering good qualities in the missing Smithy that he did not mention his suspicions. It would have been like guffawing in church.

'Where's Arthur?' Kirby enquired. 'He never turns up any more. Where the hell does he get to?'

It was one of the nights out for the crew in the village pub. Ferris's smile was sly and knowing.

'He's trying to keep it dark,' he said. 'But I've had my

suspicions for a long time. I finally managed to winkle it out of him.'

'Keep what dark?'

'You remember that first night in the pub in Chelmsford, when prize prick Maurice Howard was chatting up some Wrens?' Kirby nodded. 'Arthur fell for one of them,' Ferris said. 'Hook, line and bloody sinker. That's where he sneaks off to on his own. Chelmsford. He's potty about the silly bitch.'

'Which one is it?' Kirby could hardly remember the girls' faces now. There was one tall one . . . another was much shorter . . .

'The dumpy little bint,' Ferris said. 'And you know what?' he chortled. 'Her name's Georgina. Would you believe it? Imagine that! Arthur trying to get his hand up the skirt of some toffee-nosed piece from Cheltenham called Georgina.' Ferris roared with laughter.

The Wrennery was only half a mile from the pub, but the quiet lane was dark and lined with trees and hedges. Arthur Wood always saw Georgina safely indoors, before he walked back down the lane to catch the transport to Woodley Common.

They were walking side by side, but not touching. Arthur's feelings about Georgina were wholly romantic, and unspoken. He treated her with the care and respect which others might have lavished on a piece of fine porcelain, and would have been appalled by Ferris's coarse interpretation of his intentions.

Arthur Wood was disturbed, and growing angry. They had passed a bunch of squaddies, cheered and noisy with drink, dim shapes in the blackness under the hedgerows. Arthur Wood, embarrassed, had lengthened his stride, but when the squaddies finished urinating, they fell in behind, passing remarks which set Arthur's ears burning.

'Ignore them,' Georgina said, softly. 'They'll get tired of it.'

Probably they would have done. But Arthur Wood's common sense deserted him, as the leering voices from behind continued.

'What's she doing with a turd of a flight sergeant?'

'I thought Wrens only let officers poke 'em.'

'She must be desperate for it.'

Something in Arthur Wood snapped. He stopped dead, and swung round, fists clenched.

'Shut your filthy mouths, you scum, and clear off,' he said into the darkness, his voice choked with fury.

The dark shapes moved close to Arthur Wood, and encircled him. There were four of them. The fatuous, beery levity vanished in an instant, and was replaced by surly, threatening hostility. The voices were suddenly quiet and deadly.

'Did you call us scum?'

The one nearest to Arthur Wood stabbed a finger at his flying badge.

'Listen, mate, I don't care how many times you've been to Berlin. No one calls us that.'

Arthur Wood was still shaking with anger, but he also perceived that he had made a serious mistake. Now that they were close to him, he could not only smell the beer, he could see that the berets they wore were red, and he could also make out the shape of their cap badges. He was facing four men who belonged to the Airborne Division, which took a considerable and justified pride in its own lethal abilities. No one in their right mind got into a fight with Airborne troops.

'You walk on ahead,' he said to Georgina in a low tone which was as controlled as he could manage in the circumstances. It was liable to start any second, and when it did these bastards would half kill him. He could see no way out of that and, when it happened, he would prefer Georgina not to witness it.

He was utterly bewildered by what happened next. Georgina took his arm, and hugged him close to her. When she spoke, her clear voice was well modulated, and precise. Ferris was right about one thing. Georgina's accent was decidedly upper class.

'I'm terribly sorry,' she said to the looming shapes. 'We were only married today, and we've just come from the reception. I'm afraid my husband has had too much to drink.'

Georgina was not only an ingeniously rapid thinker, she

carried complete conviction. The befuddled squaddies did not doubt her ladylike assertion for a moment.

The nearest and most aggressive one shifted on his feet.

'That's all very well,' he complained. 'He still had no call to talk to us like that.'

'You're absolutely right,' Georgina said. 'He would never have said such a thing normally but, as I say, he's been celebrating a little too much. I can only ask you to accept my sincere apologies.' The four shapes stared back at her uncertainly. It was still touch and go.

'We've only got twenty-four hours, before he goes back on operations,' Georgina added, for good measure.

'Leave it, Eddie,' one of the others said. 'He's not worth it.'

'Come on,' Georgina said to Arthur Wood. 'Lean on me.'

She turned him round, still gripping his arm tightly, and they began to walk away.

Eddie was not wholly satisfied. He had an obscure feeling that justice had not been done. Two of them wandered away, but Eddie and the other one followed behind for a while. Eddie and his mate were now speculating about the delights of the first night of marital bliss awaiting Georgina.

Arthur Wood could stand it no longer. He swung round, Georgina still clinging to one arm like a limpet, and raised his free clenched fist.

'Oh, fuck off, you,' he roared. Even as the words came out, Arthur Wood was astonished at himself. He was one of the most peaceful and docile men alive.

Paradoxically, Eddie was content. He had needled this flight sergeant into obscenity in front of his posh young bride. Honours were even.

'Only just married and he talks like that,' Eddie said, laughing derisively. 'Effing and blinding in front of his wife already.'

'That's the RAF for you.'

'Right. Dead common.'

But they were retreating now. The voices grew more distant, and faded away.

Arthur Wood and Georgina walked on arm in arm. Georgina said nothing. Arthur could think of nothing to say.

They turned into the grounds of the Wrennery, and approached the front door. Formerly it had been a large, rambling Victorian house, set in acres of ground on the outskirts of the town. Arthur Wood had been inside once, when the Wrens had held a dance there.

Georgina guided him away from the entrance, and across a lawn.

'Look at our apple tree,' she said, coming to a stop. 'The first blossom has just come out. Can you see it?'

Arthur Wood could see her upturned face as she gazed up at the branches. He kissed it. For a few moments, her arms were round his neck, and her lips opened, hesitantly. Then she drew back.

'You mustn't kiss me like that, Arthur,' she said.

Arthur desisted at once. He stood holding her close against his body.

'I wish all that had been true,' he said at last, 'what you said to those soldiers.'

Her face detached itself from his chest, and looked up at him.

'Do you mean that?' Georgina asked.

'Of course I mean it,' Arthur Wood said. 'It's all I ever think about.'

'Well, why didn't you say so before, you idiot?' Georgina wanted to know.

She made no further complaint about the way he kissed her.

Arthur Wood ran down the dark lane like an Olympic half miler, partly because he did not want to miss the transport and be stranded in Chelmsford, and partly in case Eddie and his mates had had second thoughts, and decided to hang about for a while. In that case, when they saw the happy bridegroom departing, they would take exception to being deceived, and act accordingly.

Arthur Wood felt that his only hope lay in taking them by surprise, and bursting through, before they realized that the running figure was him. If the transport had gone, of course, that would only delay matters.

But there was no sign of the soldiers. The transport, bottom gear growling, was moving off. Hands reached out, and strong arms hauled him over the tail-board, to the accompaniment of cries of encouragement, and cheers.

Arthur Wood sank breathlessly on to the floor, his back against the tail-board. The swaying mass, packed sardine-tight into the 15cwt, broke into song.

> *'I don't want to join the air force,*
> *I don't want to go to war . . .'*

Arthur Wood sat as the truck bumped towards Woodley Common, and the voices roared out one ditty after another.

Arthur Wood was confused, and more than a little bemused. But one thing he was reasonably certain of.

It seemed that Arthur Wood had become engaged to be married. He suddenly grinned broadly, and joined in the current chorus.

> *'Oh, be kind to your web footed friends,*
> *For the duck may be somebody's mother . . .'*

In the Flight Office, Arthur Wood fidgeted restlessly. His eyes were fixed on the notice board. The rhythm of his heartbeat was unsteady. He was praying that the flight commander would not appear, and pin up the piece of paper which would mean they were flying that night.

In that event he might be able to get into Chelmsford. Arthur Wood did not want to fly, he wanted to see Georgina.

Kirby was sitting reading Richard Hillary's book, *The Last Enemy*. He had read it before, but had felt impelled to go back to it. It seemed tragic that a man who could write so movingly, having suffered in and survived the Battle of Britain, had later met the last enemy he referred to in the title, death, and been killed on operations.

Roy Harrison wandered in, and touched Kirby's shoulder lightly. Kirby looked up.

'Can you come outside for a minute?' Roy Harrison asked.

A mild westerly was blowing. Roy Harrison leaned his back

against the hut, cupped his hands, lit a cigarette, and handed Kirby a letter.

The letter came from a Stalagluft, via the Red Cross. It began:

'*Dear Mum,*
Just to let you know I am safe and well, so you can stop worrying. When you have read this, please send it on to Frank, so he can tell the rest of the lads . . .'

Kirby looked up. The flimsy piece of paper in his hand fluttered in the breeze.

'Who's Frank?'

'My bomb aimer,' Roy Harrison said. 'They both come from Penzance. Knew each other before. Great chums. Read the rest.'

Kirby read it.

Smithy's plane had been attacked by a Junkers 88 on the way back, and one engine knocked out.

'*The skipper tried to nurse her back, but we had lost a lot of height, and then another engine started playing up . . .*'

Smithy had given the order to bale out. He had remained at the controls, keeping the Lancaster steady, but inexorably losing height all the time.

'*We all got out and landed safely, but by the time the skipper jumped, he was too low, and his 'chute did not open. The Germans were out looking for us, and they found his body, but he was dead . . .*'

Kirby's eyes travelled to the conclusion of the letter.

'*We would all like his wife to know what he did. We are being well treated, and things are not too bad at all.*

> *All my love,*
> *Walter.*'

Kirby folded the letter.

'I expect the CO'd like to see this,' he said. 'Shall I give it to him?'

'Up to me,' Roy Harrison said. He took the letter. His face

was stony. 'Shit,' he said. He dropped his cigarette, and ground it savagely underfoot. 'Shit. Shit. Shit.'

Kirby stared at him.

'What's the matter with you?'

Roy Harrison shook his head wordlessly, and walked off towards Squadron Headquarters.

Only one military decoration was ever awarded posthumously, the VC, 'For Valour'. Had Flying Officer Graham Smith survived, he would almost certainly have received the DFC, but it was not thought that his action, although highly commendable, justified the highest award of all.

Chapter Fourteen

Fifteen had been David Kirby's magic number. Thirty was altogether too formidable to contemplate. Getting halfway through his tour of operations was his aim. After that, it would be downhill. The end would be in sight.

The magic number came and went, and was replaced by thirty. One numeral changed for another. The new one seemed as far away as ever. There was nothing downhill about it.

He was now Acting Flight Lieutenant David Kirby. Jacko and Don Shepherd had fulfilled his predictions. Jacko, seemingly without effort, had quickly welded his raw crew into a smoothly efficient team. Jacko's instructor at BFTS had only been half right when he described him as a born fighter pilot. Jacko was a born bomber pilot, too. He was a born pilot, period.

Don Shepherd was not. He was a worrier, privately uncertain of his own judgements. He lacked whatever it was – flair, dash, confidence – which, in Jacko's case, commanded instant respect from his crew.

And yet, for entirely different reasons, Don Shepherd became a highly effective bomber pilot, with one of the squadron's most reliable crews. For all his defects, Don was grimly determined. He faced fear and overcame it. Flying was always an effort for him, his reactions and co-ordination never truly instinctive, but, perhaps because he was careful and cautious by nature, when it mattered, he did not make mistakes.

Probably more important, Don Shepherd was patently decent and honest, and while aware of his own fallibility, he was determined to grit his teeth and see it through come what may. It was to these attributes his crew responded. His very vulnerability, paradoxically, turned Don Shepherd's crew into an efficient one. He was such a nice chap that never, under any circumstances, would they let him down. Don Shepherd was no one's idea of a leader, but he got to the target, he bombed the right markers, and he brought his aircraft home again. Results were what mattered, and Don Shepherd's results were good.

'You were right about those two,' Wing Commander Norgate said to Flight Lieutenant Kirby approvingly.

Wing Commander Norgate was pleased with the instrument which 545 Squadron had become. Among the losses had been wheat as well as chaff, but he believed that the chaff had now gone. Squadron losses had become more infrequent. 545 was now largely composed of hardened, experienced crews, toughened to a sharp edge in the forge over Germany.

They were now ready, he believed, for the kind of task of which he dreamed, and Wing Commander Norgate waited and chafed for the right opportunity to come along. His squadron was too good merely to form part of blunt hammer blows against German cities. They were fit now for the single sharp thrust, some dramatic and unusual operation – whatever that might be.

Wing Commander Norgate kept his ear to the ground through his contacts at Group Headquarters, alert for the first whisper of any special operation being contemplated for which he might press the claims of 545, but to no avail. He racked his brains for some suggestion which he could put up to the AOC, but none occurred to him.

Wing Commander Norgate did not despair, however. He was not a religious man, and considered Bishop Bell of Chichester a meddling fool, but those who prayed to a God of peace and love for victory in war and blessed the tools of human destruction were even more crass. There could, self-evidently, be no such Being. But if He was not there, the Gods of War most certainly were, sardonic, cruel, unpredictable, ruthless, not supernatural but the manifestation of mankind itself, ready to select and reward, in their own good time, those warriors best fitted to further their cause. Norgate had every faith in the Gods of War. His time would come.

Flying in a slow, elliptical, continual corkscrew above the suggested height had become automatic for Kirby, except when in dense cloud.

The method had only really proved itself once as yet, but once was enough. When, crossing into Germany on the way to Berlin they had been intercepted by an enemy aircraft; the corkscrew had uncovered the Junkers 88 which was sliding into position beneath K – King, and Ferris had spotted it in time.

The Junkers 88, unknown to them at that time, was equipped with the mysterious weapon which had such awesomely devastating effects, the one which caused bombers to explode in mid-air for no apparent reason, from no source which could be seen, the one which the RAF feared more than any other because it had not yet been identified, they did not then know what it was.

The device was not only deadly, it was also simple in its conception, and consisted of an upward firing cannon with which Junkers 88s were fitted. Having been guided on to a bomber by Ground Control, the Junkers 88 identified the bomber on its airborne radar, and climbed slowly up from below until it was sitting underneath its prey, undetected, and in position to deliver the death blow from its upward firing cannon, which was called *Schrage Musik*. The doomed bomber crew never even knew their remaining lifespan was measured in seconds.

On that occasion, the Junkers 88 had been thwarted, although Kirby's immediate diving turn to starboard had not succeeded completely. The Junkers 88 had got in one burst which knocked out their port inner engine before they lost him, but they had got back to Manston, and they had survived. That was all that mattered.

Tonight, there was no moon. Below, at five thousand feet, a layer of cloud blanketed most of Europe. High above, another layer blotted out the stars. Flying between the two, the blackness was as dense as any unlit underground dungeon.

Kirby was flying his slow corkscrew. The gyro compass drifted lazily to and fro, a few degrees either side of his course. The altimeter needle drifted lethargically up and down. They were on their way back, having bombed on cloud markers.

In this pitch darkness, the human eye, even Ferris's, was a poor substitute for radar. Ferris was feeling the hours' long strain, his muscles tense with concentration, a dull thud beginning to make itself evident behind his forehead as he searched, co-ordinating all the time with the mid upper gunner, his eyes crinkled, up, down, either side, his head rotating with his turret.

'Christ,' Ferris muttered. He had the unreasoning feeling that he had gone blind. But the fighter which might be out there somewhere, gently manoeuvring into position, would not be blind. It would be guided on to them by its Ground Radar Control Station. Once within range, the Lancaster would appear on its airborne radar screen. Using that blip, it would close up to its firing position.

Ferris was beginning to see shapes which were not there. More than once his hand had travelled to his oxygen mask to switch on his intercom and give his urgent warning, only for him to realize that the shape was a figment of his mind, that he had imagined it. Ferris blinked his eyes rapidly and forced himself to continue his calm, methodical scan, fearful just the same that, on a night like this, even if it was there, he would not be able to make it out until it was too late.

And then, for a fraction of a second, just as he was blinking again, there was a faint, dark silhouette superimposed on the blackness, momentarily discernible only because it had a stealthy movement of its own. Ferris's reaction was immediate. He spoke and rotated his turret at the same time.

'Rear Gunner to Pilot – corkscrew port! Me 110 coming in . . .'

The instant message from Kirby's brain had not even reached his muscles when Ferris spoke again, his voice rising, shrill with anguish.

'I've lost him . . . I can't see him . . . he's gone . . .'

'OK, Rear Gunner,' Kirby said. 'He's overshot us.'

Ahead, the dim, almost imperceptible outline of the twin-engined night fighter was drifting across his windscreen. Kirby eased out of his corkscrew, his eyes fixed on that shape, trying not to lose it.

. He could guess what had happened. The Me 110, closing in on radar, would be expecting its target to be flying straight and level. It had passed underneath Kirby's aircraft. Ahead of him would be a disconcerted Me 110 crew wondering how a blip could suddenly vanish from the radar screen, and hurriedly checking equipment.

Behind the Messerschmitt, they were safe for the time being, but they were falling back. If he was not careful he would lose sight of it.

'Flight Engineer, maximum power,' Kirby said.

Len Bellamy's left hand smoothly slid the four throttle levers wide open. Kirby did not dare to take his eyes off that wavering shape, threatening to melt into the blackness and disappear.

'Bomb Aimer, open fire at him. He's all yours.'

'Bomb Aimer to Pilot, I can't see him . . .'

'He's banking to port, Bomb Aimer. I'm following him. Straight ahead of you.'

Kirby forced the huge, vibrating Lancaster into a turn, striving to align it on the tail of that elusive shape, mere blackness against blackness.

'Bomb Aimer to Pilot, I'm sorry, I still can't spot him.'

Kirby said, 'Bomb Aimer, aim your gun straight ahead, and fire when I tell you.'

The angles of the dark shape shifted and changed. The Me 110 was rolling gently out of its turn to port, and into a turn to starboard. Its Ground Control Station would be assuring it that the bomber was still there. Its airborne radar checked and found serviceable, it was hunting for the target which had unaccountably vanished.

Kirby heaved the Lancaster round in its crazy pursuit of the far more agile fighter. The last time he had done anything like this had been under the blazing blue skies of Oklahoma, striving to align his camera gun sight on the silver target Harvard, flown by Mr Morrissey. Now it was being played out as in some wild delirium, translated into a blackness which was so intense as to be palpable.

'Bomb Aimer, we're right behind him. Centre your guns and open fire, my order . . . now.'

The two .303 machine-guns rattled. Tracer bullets spouted ahead into the inky sky.

The dark shape reared into a steep climbing turn and vanished. Kirby banked in the opposite direction, and dived. The odds were that it would be some time before the alarmed Me 110 pilot collected himself. Being shot at from behind was contrary to all the rules of his game. Still, it was prudent to depart from the area as quickly as possible.

'Bomb Aimer to Pilot, did I hit him? Did I hit him?'

'I don't think so, Bomb Aimer,' Kirby said. 'But we put the fear of God into him. That'll do.'

'I thought I might have done. I thought I saw bits flying about.' Ted Hollis was disappointed.

'You'll be lucky, mate,' Ferris thought, scornfully. 'Mucking about like that up front, you'll be lucky.' Ferris was deeply frustrated. If only *he* had been in the front turret, he would have seen and got the bastard.

David Kirby's crew thoroughly approved of his friendship with Kay Dunn. They asked solicitous questions about her health, they supposed casually that she might be due for some leave pretty soon. Kirby was able to reassure them. Kay was one of those fortunate people who never needed to see a doctor, and although entitled to leave, she had arranged to take it only when and if the squadron was stood down for a spell.

Kirby's crew were pleased and relieved. Their own private good luck charm was in good operational order, and on constant standby.

Avro Lancaster R5992 Self Crew War Ops – Kassel.

Kirby had fallen into the habit of indulging in an additional superstition of his own. After briefing, no matter how great the rush, before every operation he made the initial entry in his logbook. That meant, he hoped, that he would return to complete it. It was an extra genuflection in the direction of whatever fates governed his continued existence or otherwise.

Wing Commander Norgate was not flying that night, and was in the Control Tower when it happened. The Lancaster in front of Kirby received the green from the caravan, the signal that he was clear to turn on to the runway and take off. But the bomber did not move. It sat there, propellers spinning, immobile.

More greens followed, in agitated flashes. The Lancaster remained where it was, barring Kirby's path. Keyed up, he wondered irritably what the hell was going on.

So, as the delay dragged out, did Wing Commander Norgate, who finally came on the R/T from the Control Tower.

'Castle to S – Sugar, you are clear for take off. What's the problem?'

There was no reply. S – Sugar was flown by Flight Sergeant Ken Lambert. He and his crew had completed eighteen operations. Kassel would be their nineteenth. On board, a discussion which had simmered amongst them privately in the Sergeants' Mess for some time was boiling over to a conclusion.

'Castle to S – Sugar, this is your squadron commander. I say again, you are clear for take off.'

Kirby heard Flight Sergeant Lambert's reply. His voice was not quite normal.

'S – Sugar to Castle. Request permission to return to dispersal.'

There was a pause. Kirby could see the whitish shape of S – Sugar's rear gunner's face through the perspex of the turret below and in front of him.

'Castle to S – Sugar, you are cleared for take off. Clear the runway immediately.'

In front, the throttles were opened. S – Sugar began to move forward on to the runway. Norgate's voice acknowledged the obedient response.

'Castle to S – Sugar, good luck.'

S – Sugar moved off down the runway, but at a sedate, even speed with, quite obviously, no intention of getting airborne.

'Castle from S – Sugar,' Flight Sergeant Lambert said. 'Returning to dispersal.' Before Flying Control could reply, Lambert spoke again, hysteria finally breaking through. 'We're not going. Send the service police to pick us up, but we can't go . . . we can't . . .'

The green Aldis in the caravan was now directed at Kirby. S – Sugar had turned off at the first intersection. He manoeuvred his aircraft onto the runway, and lined it up, the flarepath tapering away into the darkness in front of him.

'Crew, stand by for take off. Flight Engineer, follow me on the throttles.'

Kirby's practised hand eased the four throttle levers forward. K – King gathered speed.

Over Germany, banks of cloud rose to 12,000 feet, but above, the skies were clear, and a bright moon hung high. It was a night when the German defences read Bomber Command's intentions accurately. Fighters were waiting on track. It was perfect night fighter weather.

K – King was engaged by a Junkers 88, seventy-five miles short of Kassel. Kirby took evasive action, diving and weaving. Ferris's four machine-guns hammered bullets into the Junkers 88. He saw hits in its port wing and then the Junkers broke away. But K – King was hit.

'Flight Engineer to Pilot, starboard outer's on fire.'

'Flight Engineer, fire extinguisher. Then feather starboard outer.'

K – King had lost a considerable amount of height during the engagement with the Junkers 88. Kirby continued on down, choosing to seek the cover of cloud, while he sorted things out. Anxiously, he watched the flickering flames torn back from the starboard outer engine in the slipstream, but they seemed to be dying away. Blessed cloud groped for and enveloped them. The crew reported no further damage.

'Navigator, position, please.'

'Navigator to Pilot, fifty miles from target.' Alan Russell's voice was calm.

'Flight Engineer, remaining engines?'

'Flight Engineer to Pilot, all OK.'

They were entitled to jettison their bombs at once, and turn back. There would be no criticism, even from Norgate. But the retrimmed aircraft was flying well. They were only minutes from the target.

'Pilot to crew. We've come this far, we may as well go the rest of the way.'

'Flight Engineer to Pilot, she won't climb up again with a full load on board.'

'Flight Engineer, we'll bomb from 12,000.'

'Rear Gunner to Pilot, there'll be a lot of nasty shit around.'

At 12,000 feet, they would be within the extreme range of the light anti-aircraft guns. Ferris was entitled to be worried. Kirby was worried.

'Have to chance that, Rear Gunner. I don't want to lose this cloud.'

But they lost it anyway. As they approached Kassel, the cloud became patchy and fragmented. They could see the markers, the fires boiling, the bombs exploding, the erratic winking of anti-aircraft guns far below.

K – King was turning on to its bombing run when the anti-aircraft shells caught it. The plane lurched and heaved, there was the sound of the explosions, the sickening smell of cordite. And at the same time, a rush of bitingly cold air into the Lancaster, normally heated at the front by warm air from the engines. But K – King went on flying, and the controls seemed to be unaffected.

'Pilot to crew, anyone hurt?'

'Navigator to Pilot, we're OK here, but there's a fire in the wireless compartment. Dealing with it, Mid Upper's helping.'

'Flight Engineer, give them a hand.' Len Bellamy sidled from his seat, and moved out of Kirby's range of vision. He could smell the smoke now. 'Bomb Aimer, are you OK?'

'Bomb Aimer to Pilot, bloody cold. Got some holes in the perspex down here.'

'Rear Gunner?'

'Rear Gunner to Pilot, OK back here so far. I can see a hell of a lot of fighter activity behind us, though.'

'Worry about that later. Bomb Aimer, fuck photographs tonight. Let's just bomb and get out of it.'

Kirby wondered what was happening in the wireless compartment. He could still smell the stinking smoke of an electrical fire.

'Bombs gone.'

Kirby turned away at once. 'Bomb doors closed.'

The main stream were four thousand feet above them now, and there were no Stirling squadrons in the bomber force tonight attracting fire over the target itself at their altitude.

'Navigator, how's that fire going?'

'Navigator to Pilot, coming under control.'

Kirby had already selected the nearest sailing lump of broken cloud, and was heading towards it. A flurry of light ack-ack came uncomfortabiy close, he heard that spatter like hail, but then the cloud temporarily embraced them.

'Navigator to Pilot, fire's out.'

'Good work, Navigator. What's the damage?'

K – King emerged from cloud, crossed a canyon of clear air, and entered the main bank which should provide cover all the way home. Kirby let out a deep breath. Len Bellamy slid back into his seat.

'Navigator to Pilot, damage report is, all navigational equipment U/S, and the radio's completely burned out, no R/T no W/T, nothing.'

No airborne radar, no link with ground beacons, not even any way of securing bearings as they approached home. Kassel was on the banks of the Rhine, deep in the south of Germany. They were entirely dependent on Alan Russell's skill in navigating by dead reckoning, without any aids, without any sight of the ground.

'Give me a course, Navigator.'

'Navigator to Pilot, you can steer three five five to be going on with.'

The compass and direction indicator were still working, thank God. Kirby settled on 355 degrees.

'Bomb Aimer to Pilot.' Ted Hollis sounded apologetic. 'Could someone come and give me a hand? I'm bleeding a bit, and something's wrapped round my foot. I'm stuck here. Can't move.'

'Flight Engineer, go and get him out.' Len Bellamy left his seat again at once. Kirby was shivering continuously in the savage cold. 'Bomb Aimer, how bad is it?'

'I don't think it's much. A piece of flak in my arm when that shell hit us. I've shoved a field dressing on it, but it won't stop bleeding.'

'Why the hell didn't you say so at the time?'

'I could still press the tit. Didn't seem worth it.'

'We'll soon fix you up, Ted. Let me know if Len needs any help.'

Kirby concentrated on flying an accurate, steady course, and waited. His watch told him that it was only just over four minutes, but it seemed like hours before Len Bellamy plugged into the intercom from somewhere behind him.

'Flight Engineer to Pilot, there was a chunk of metal wrapped round his ankle. I managed to free him, and move him back to the main spar. I've fixed up a tourniquet on his arm, but it'll need loosening now and then.'

'Pilot to Flight Engineer, does he need morphine?' Morphine ampoules were part of the equipment carried on board.

'He says not. I don't think it's too bad.'

'Try and make him as warm as you can, Flight Engineer. There's a long way to go yet. Then you take over the front turret. Navigator, keep an eye on Ted, please, and loosen that tourniquet at intervals.' They might be unlucky and run out of cloud. Kirby wanted to make sure that the aircraft remained fully defended all the time.

'Navigator to Pilot, understood.'

They were reasonably safe in cloud, but Kirby wondered how accurate the forecast wind was. Unless it was spot on, they could be steadily drifting many miles off track.

'Navigator to Pilot, I need to get a star shot.'

'Rear Gunner to Pilot,' Ferris said, ominously. 'There'll be fighters sitting above this cloud, and I don't fancy our chances on three engines.'

'Navigator to Pilot,' Alan Russell said, 'if I don't get a good fix, we could miss England, never mind Woodley Common. Give me thirty seconds, and I'll get you home.'

Kirby weighed the risk of exposing themselves to night fighters, against those of flying blind for hours and possibly ditching in the North Sea, with negligible chances of being picked up.

'Thirty seconds, Navigator,' he said. 'Quicker if you can. Be ready. Climbing now.'

He gave the three remaining engines full power. Without its bomb load, K – King was capable of a slow, laborious climb. Alan Russell would have to identify two stars and take a bearing on each in order to secure a good fix. It was asking a lot within seconds.

K – King heaved itself into clear air. Kirby lowered the nose, skimming above the cloud, cotton wool sheets spreading as far as the eye could see. Against that background, illuminated by the baleful, silver moon on high, the Lancaster would stand out as clearly as an insect crawling across a white bedspread.

'Rear Gunner to Pilot, something at around fifteen thousand, flying across our track, about five miles behind.'

'Has he seen us yet, Rear Gunner?'

'Don't think so, but he soon will unless he's fucking blind.'

'Mid Upper, have you got him?'

'Mid Upper to Pilot, enemy aircraft in sight,' Arthur Wood said. 'Could be an Me 110. Can't see any more though.' Kirby too was anxiously scanning the quadrant of sky he could see.

'Pilot to Flight Engineer, how about you?'

'Flight Engineer to Pilot, nothing in sight from down here,' Len Bellamy said from the bomb aimer's front turret.

They flew on in the full glare of the moon. Time had expanded. Seconds dragged by like minutes. Half a minute was eternity.

'Mid Upper to Pilot,' Arthur Wood said. 'That aircraft's changed course.'

'Rear Gunner to Pilot,' Ferris said, sharply. 'Definitely a 110, and he's seen us. Coming down like the clappers.'

'Navigator to Pilot, I've finished,' Alan Russell said.

Kirby shoved the control column forward without any regard for finesse. The nose lurched down, and K – King slid back into the shelter of cloud.

'Navigator to Pilot,' Alan Russell said, 'continue your descent. Predicted cloud base is two thousand feet. I'm aiming to bring you in over Gorleston.'

K – King broke cloud. Below was the dull plateau of water. Ahead was a dark, transverse line.

'Coast ahead,' Kirby said. 'Flight Engineer, back up here, please. I'll need you for the landing. Navigator, how's Ted doing?'

'Gone to sleep,' Alan Russell said. 'Believe it or not.'

'Bloody typical,' Ferris thought. 'Dozy bugger.' He watched the North Sea recede, the thin line of foaming water on the beaches, the blacked out town of Gorleston-on-Sea as it slid underneath his turret. He switched his intercom on.

'Rear Gunner to Navigator,' Ferris said solemnly. 'Well done, chum. I'll never call you a fucking conchie again.'

Squadron Leader Abel was posted missing, presumed killed during the running series of engagements with enemy aircraft which they had all encountered on the flight to and from Kassel. Wing Commander Norgate regretted his loss but, considering the opposition the squadron had met, one was not too bad.

It was the action of the crew which was alive and well, Flight Sergeant Lambert's, which really hurt him where it mattered most.

For any member of 545 Squadron to go LMF would have been a direct personal insult as far as Norgate was concerned. For an entire crew to go LMF, and an experienced one at that, was unbearable, a tragedy which could ruin all he had striven for, precisely the wrong way for 545 Squadron to come to the attention of the AOC.

Norgate sought for some way to divert the limelight from the wretched, unspeakable Lambert, who had treacherously betrayed his commanding officer, and focus it elsewhere on some achievement so remarkable in the AOC's eyes that it might far outweigh the act of cowardice which would otherwise hold centre stage.

Happily, Wing Commander Norgate felt, there was one conveniently to hand. He was glad to find from Air Vice Marshal Farleigh's reaction that he was right. Possibly the AOC too had a vested interest in one of his squadrons acquiring credit rather than raised eyebrows.

'You were quite right about Alan Russell, David,' Wing Commander Norgate said, largely. 'My doubts were misplaced. He's being recommended for the DFC, and your bomb aimer for the DFM.'

'I'm glad,' Kirby said. 'They deserve it.'

'And you're being put up for the DFC as well, of course,' Norgate added.

Kirby was slightly surprised. It was pretty unusual for several members of the same crew to earn, or at least receive, immediate awards on the same operation. Such was exactly what had been in the forefront of Wing Commander Norgate's mind when he constructed his glowing tributes.

'Well, naturally, I'm pleased,' Kirby said. 'Thank you, sir.'

'A most gallant and determined effort. A credit to the squadron.' Norgate's smile expressed considerable relief. 'I quote the AOC. His exact words. I thought you'd like to know.'

'I only wish Ron Ferris could be included as well, in some way,' Kirby said. 'He drove off the Junkers 88, and that's not the first time . . .'

'I know what Flight Sergeant Ferris wants, far more than any gong,' Norgate said. 'Leave that with me. One more thing, David. Now that Squadron Leader Abel's gone, I'd like you to take over "A" Flight.'

Norgate's original suspicions concerning David Kirby had

receded to the back of his mind. Kirby had become a first-class pilot, and attracted the approving attention of the AOC more than once. Apart from that, he was the senior of the remaining flight lieutenants. He was next in line.

Ted Hollis was in sick bay. His right arm was bandaged and in a sling, but he was not in bed. He was sitting in a chair, sucking an empty pipe.

'Apparently it just nicked the artery,' he said. 'But it's nothing. This lot's coming off tomorrow. I hear we're getting some leave.' Kirby nodded. 'It'll have healed by the time we get back,' Ted Hollis remarked.

'Here. Present from the crew.' Kirby produced two ounces of tobacco, and a box of Swan matches. 'Even Ron Ferris chipped in. Said that after Kassel, he didn't mind contributing to your thousand quid any more.'

'Oh, thanks. Would you mind? A bit awkward just now.' Kirby took the pipe, and filled it. 'Not too much,' Ted Hollis said. 'You get a better smoke that way.'

'Lasts longer too,' Kirby said. Ted Hollis grinned amiably, took the pipe, adjusted the tobacco with his thumb, and held it between his teeth while Kirby lit it for him.

'You've been put up for the DFM,' Kirby told him.

'Me? What for?' Ted Hollis's moon-like face registered honest astonishment.

'Although wounded when approaching the target, Flight Sergeant Hollis did not report his injury, but continued to direct the aircraft on its bombing run with coolness and courage . . .' So, in part, ran Wing Commander Norgate's recommendation. Flight Lieutenant Kirby had, 'when attacked by enemy aircraft seventy-five miles from the target, and despite the loss of one engine, continued with his attack, and displayed great resolution and determination.' Flying Officer Russell's eventual citation spoke of his decisive action in extinguishing a serious fire, and commended him for 'an exceptional feat of navigation'.

'The DFM, eh,' Ted Hollis mused, reflectively. 'That's funny.' He puffed on his pipe stolidly. 'Funny peculiar, not ha ha,' he said. 'The first time the squadron have bombed Kassel, right? Well, in our time anyway.' Kirby nodded. When Ted Hollis did get going, he could be long-winded and prone to circumlocution. Still, considering the guts he had shown, the least he deserved was an attentive audience. Sick Bay was centrally heated, and it was hot and stuffy. Kirby swallowed a yawn. 'Before the war, I was a skilled man,' Ted Hollis wandered on. 'Earned good money, too. But I didn't like working during the summer, so come the warm weather, I'd get myself the sack. Check the foreman, or something. Go on the dole. Walk in the country. Lie in the sun. Go fishing. Once the nights started drawing in, I knew I could always get another job. I paid my insurance stamps the rest of the year,' Ted Hollis explained. 'So I reckoned I was entitled to the dole during the summer.' Kirby nodded with a show of deep interest. He had no idea what his bomb aimer was on about, if anything. 'Anyway,' Ted Hollis resumed, 'in 1938 I decided to go abroad, see a bit of the world for a month. Would you believe it, they wouldn't give me my dole for that month, down at the Labour Exchange?' he enquired, aggrieved. 'Still, that's another story.' Kirby was relieved to hear it. 'I took a boat trip down the Rhine,' Ted Hollis reminisced. 'Met this German girl. Eva. We wrote to each other during the winter, and in '39, June it was, I went back. We got engaged. The *Daily Express* was saying there'd be no war this year, next year, or any other year. I always used to read the *Express*.' He examined his pipe. 'Sorry. It's gone out,' he said.

Kirby struck another match, and held it over the bowl. Blue smoke swirled and rose.

'That's better,' Ted Hollis said. He puffed contentedly, while the last weeks of peace passed in review behind his blank eyes. 'Eva should have come back with me,' he said finally, 'but we arranged that she'd come over in October and we'd get married then. Bad timing, as it turned out. Her home was in Kassel. She took me to meet her parents. So for all I know, I could have got the DFM for killing her. Funny that, isn't it?' His gaze shifted, and focused on Kirby. 'Perhaps I'll go back when this lot's over,' Ted Hollis said. 'Find out. Just out of interest.' He scratched his ear with the stem of his pipe. 'She's probably married to some storm trooper by now,' he said. An agreeable thought struck him. 'Here,' he said, 'I get twenty quid with my DFM, don't I?'

One of David Kirby's school friends was home too, now a captain in the Royal Artillery. The long delayed Second Front, he said, would definitely happen during the summer. The whole south coast area seemed to be full of American troops. They were everywhere. Off duty, they scoured the pubs, bidding, so it was related, five pounds and even an unheard of ten pounds, for a bottle of Scotch. This generated considerable resentment among thirsty regular customers, deeply critical of such lavish expenditure and who, unable to compete, divided their criticism equally between overpaid Yanks and money-grubbing landlords.

When he was not with his friends, Kirby lounged about the house, his mind empty. He could not even be bothered to read. He went to bed early, and lay in bed late. He slept, and slept, and slept.

Something happened to Squadron Leader David Kirby during that ten days leave. When it was over, he did not want to go back. He wanted to return to the days of his boyhood, to the time when he was a child, taken care of, looked after, no need to think.

He watched himself playing a part for his mother's benefit, an activated dummy, smiling, with no cares, casually reassuring her, promising that he would see her again soon. The dummy was empty, there was nothing inside it. Certainly not David Kirby.

He sat on the train as it travelled to London, his eyes closed against his fellow passengers, his stomach leaden. At Waterloo Station he queued endlessly for a taxi to Liverpool Street, lifting his suitcase and shuffling forward now and then as the minutes passed. Finally, he reached the head of the queue, and stood there for more minutes. A taxi appeared.

'No one else,' the taxi driver instructed other anxious

applicants behind Kirby who were going in that direction. 'This is my last job. I'm going home after this.'

The cab driver was in a hurry. Kirby watched the bomb sites of the city race by. Perhaps the taxi would be involved in an accident cutting in front of a bus . . . perhaps, in the collision, Squadron Leader David Kirby would be injured . . . a broken leg . . . a fractured arm . . . an ambulance would take him to hospital . . . he would stay there, for a week . . . two weeks even . . . no need to make any decisions . . . no need to do anything . . . just lie there . . . safe . . .

David Kirby paid off the taxi at Liverpool Street Station. He walked to his waiting train. All the compartments were full, even the first class. He squeezed into a corridor, and sat on his suitcase.

Squadron Leader David Kirby now knew that he would never complete his tour of thirty operations. He knew that he was going to die.

It was to be, in Ferris's words, a monumental piss up, to celebrate Kirby's promotion and his own. For Wing Commander Norgate had accurately diagnosed Ferris's deepest ambition, and seen that it was fulfilled. Ferris wore, with swaggering pride, the service dress of a warrant officer, tailor-made of barathea, the same in every respect as an officer's, save for the cloth crown rank markings on his sleeves.

Kirby's precise air force rank was now somewhat complicated. As far as he could work it out, he was a substantive flying officer, a war substantive flight lieutenant, and an acting squadron leader.

'Who gives a shit,' Ferris said, practically, 'so long as you've got two and a half rings, and you're getting a squadron leader's pay?' Ferris himself, as a warrant officer air gunner, was now in receipt of twelve shillings and sixpence a day. His new if, to his mind, overdue status had engendered a momentous decision.

'Quite right, Mr Ferris,' Kirby said, gravely using the form of address to which Ferris was now entitled, even from the highest-ranking officers in the land. He lifted his glass. 'And here's to you, Mr Ferris.'

Ferris grinned, and stabbed a finger at the ribbon of Kirby's DFC.

'Right,' he said. 'And what's more, I'll have one of those one day, too.'

Warrant officers decorated for gallantry, like commissioned officers, received the Distinguished Flying Cross.

Ferris withstood the barrage of noisy badinage from the rest of the crew with a superior smile.

'You'll see,' he said, loftily. 'Anyway, I've persuaded the landlord to dig out a bottle of whisky for us, and it's on me.' His crew mates cheered lustily. 'If you'll shut your faces, I'll tell you why,' Ferris said. 'Now that the RAF have finally seen fit to give me my due, the finest rank in the air force, than which there is no better . . . oh, for Christ's sake belt up,' Ferris bawled, above hoots of derisive laughter. 'I'm trying to tell you that I'm getting married, and you silly buggers are all invited.'

The grins of the group turned into puzzled expressions.

'I didn't know you had a girl, Ron,' Kirby said. 'You've never mentioned her.'

'Of course I've got a girl,' Ferris said scornfully. 'I'm not a fucking pansy. Known her since I was at school.'

'I thought you were poking that WAAF in stores,' Len Bellamy said.

Ferris regarded Len Bellamy with surprise.

'I'm not talking about poking,' he said. 'I'm talking about getting married.'

'Your wife's going to be a bit frustrated, isn't she?' Alan Russell enquired.

'Oh, don't be so fucking silly. You know what I mean.'

Ferris made a point of asking Kirby to help him fetch the tots of whisky.

'Hang on, skipper,' Ferris said, as Kirby was about to start ferrying the glasses. 'Something I want to ask you. Whether you'd be our best man.'

Kirby was quite overwhelmed. Ferris could bestow no

higher honour. It was the ultimate way in which he could indicate his respect, and Kirby was moved. It was the finest compliment this rough, foul-mouthed little man could have paid him.

'I'd be glad to, Ron,' he said. 'Thanks for asking me. And I wish you both all the best, you know that.'

Ferris nodded.

'Great,' he said. 'Now there's something else, and this is dead private.' His voice was low, and Kirby moved closer, trying to hear him above the hubbub of bar noise. 'It's about Arthur,' Ferris said quietly. 'He's always been twitchy, as you know, throwing up every time we land . . .'

'He told me he gets air sick,' Kirby said. 'Though I suppose if that was true, he'd be sick in the air.'

'It's reaction,' Ferris said. 'He's terrified. Well, all right. Who isn't? But since he got engaged to that Georgina bint, it's got a lot worse. When he knows there's an op on, he sits in the mess and he can't stop shaking. He hides behind a newspaper, pretending he's reading it, but he's not. He's sitting there crying. I mean that. Tears running down his face. I've seen him.'

'Oh Christ,' Kirby said. 'I should have seen this coming. I didn't know it was that bad.'

'That's why I'm telling you,' Ferris said. 'I don't hold with bastards who go LMF, you know that, but that's not how it is with Arthur. Once up there, he's got all the guts in the world. But on the deck, waiting for it, he's in fucking agony. He's crucifying himself. I reckon he's had enough, skipper. Buggers like Norgate and me, it's different. What the fuck would we do if there wasn't a war on? We'd be nothing, sod all. But Arthur can't live with it, especially now he's found this girl. He's been up there, he's done it, he's earned a bloody medal, even though he hasn't got one. Thirty ops for blokes like you and me, that's all right. Maybe for Arthur, twenty's enough. Why not? Thirty's only a bloody rule, a number conjured up by bastards who don't have to do it. Well, there's always a way round any fucking rule. Isn't that right, skipper?'

*

Kirby had suggested a breath of fresh air. They stood outside
the village pub. Twin cigarettes glowed and faded in the
darkness. Inside, a sing-song had developed.

'The MO's a decent sort,' Kirby said. 'If someone's not fit
to fly, there's nothing wrong with that.'

'But I am fit to fly, skip,' Arthur Wood's voice said, beside
him.

'That's up to him,' Kirby said. 'If he says "no", that's it. If
you like, I can have a word with him. Just sound him out,
that's all. Let you know what he says.'

Arthur Wood inhaled on his cigarette. Somewhere in the
village a door slammed. A dog started yapping.

'I don't think so, skipper,' he said at last. 'I know I get a bit
twitchy, but I'm all right once we take off.'

'No one's arguing about that,' Kirby said. 'That's not what
I'm concerned about.'

'Yes, I know. It's not that I don't appreciate the thought,
skipper, because I do.' The pale blur of Arthur Wood's face
turned towards Kirby in the darkness. 'No one else knows
about this, do they?' he enquired anxiously.

'No one,' Kirby lied.

The butt end of Arthur Wood's cigarette arced through the
air as he flicked it away. Sparks showered. 'I'd rather see it
through. Packing it in now, it wouldn't feel right.'

'Well, that's fine, Arthur,' Kirby said, cheerfully. 'I just
wanted to make certain how you felt about things. Anyway,
we'll make it, all of us. You take my word, chum. Bloody hell,
I'm not going to miss your wedding. Mind you, you'll be so
hung over, it won't be true. If I know Warrant Officer Ron
Ferris, he'll make sure you get paralytic the night before.'

Arthur Wood laughed.

'Georgina'll understand,' he said. 'You'll like her, skip.
She's smashing. Why don't you come into Chelmsford one
evening, and meet her?'

'You're on,' Kirby said. 'Come on. Let's get back. We're
missing good drinking time.'

Arthur Wood pushed open the pub door, and slid back the
heavy blackout curtain which hung inside. Squadron Leader

David Kirby, DFC followed. You hypocrite, Kirby, he was thinking. He hardly noticed the wall of sound, the collective rendering of 'Balls to Mr Bengelstein'. You lying, hypocritical bastard. He elbowed his way through the bellowing crowd and, willingly assisted by Warrant Officer Ferris, DFM, he set out to get drunk.

It was a freak of a day, blue skies, sunshine, warm still air which belonged to summer, rather than early spring. They had driven at random, parked on the fringe of a small wood, strolled through the trees, the bright patches of bluebells, found a footpath which led they knew not where, and followed it.

The footpath left the wood, ran between some fields, over a couple of stiles, and emerged on the banks of some narrow, anonymous river. They crossed the shaky wooden footbridge, wandered downstream, and came to a point where the water, gushing over a miniature weir, formed a pool between the energetic little waterfall and a transverse shingle bank, where the river was only a few inches deep.

Kay's legs were bare, her sleeves rolled up. She was fishing, or at least dangling a safety pin on the end of a piece of string which was tied to a slim branch from one of the willow trees. The safety pin was baited with a compressed, doughy piece of bread, the remains of a paste sandwich.

Kirby too had discarded his tunic and tie. He was lying on the bank, eyes closed, his hands behind his head, his face angled towards the warm, benevolent sun.

Kay Dunn hauled the safety pin from the water.

'I felt a tug then,' she announced. 'And the bait's gone.'

'Probably got caught on some reeds,' Kirby murmured, drowsily.

Kay glanced at him. Lying there, his eyes closed, his face had assumed that cast which she had noticed recently when he thought she was not looking at him. It was an expression which filled her with both sadness and helplessness. Instinctively, without being told, she knew where its origin lay. If he was wearing it and caught her eye, his face changed at once, lifting into a smile, his eyes brightening as he made some inconsequential remark, cheerful again, young again.

Kay made another pellet of bread, teased it on to the tip of the open safety pin and watched the line of string drift downstream as she lowered her makeshift hook into the water.

Kirby's body was relaxed and at rest. The continual rushing of the river over the tiny weir was soothing, the sun caressed his face, he was only half conscious. Numbers stealthily crept into his inactive mind. Twenty-two, eight to go . . . no, the last one had not counted, twenty-one, nine to go . . .

He concentrated his attention on the sun, bright enough to veil the inside of his eyelids a dull red. The numbers dissolved, circled, and returned, gently edging into the periphery of his remaining consciousness. Nine left . . . there had been no easy ones to the Pas de Calais for some time now . . . it could be nine to Berlin . . . Kirby banished them again. Without them, sleep was close.

He heard Kay's voice, seemingly far away, almost lost in the murmur of the river.

'It's so warm, it's not true. I'm going to have a paddle. There won't be any more days like this for ages.'

'M'm.' He was drifting deliciously. Small sounds blurred, and lost their individual identity. The numbers had gone away. He was at peace.

The small, startled cry brought him awake. He sat up, blinking in the sun. Kay was wading from the shingle bank towards the deeper part of the pool. Her uniform skirt and shirt lay on the grass beside her shoes, tunic and stockings.

She caught sight of him, and laughed breathlessly.

'Oh. It's like ice.'

Her shoulders were ivory above the water. She ventured into a cautious breaststroke, her head held back, high and erect, the effect clumsy and laboured.

Kirby clasped his knees and watched her.

'You swim like a dog,' he said.

'I'm trying not to get my hair wet,' she gasped. 'It's lovely though.'

Kirby laughed.

'It sounds like it,' he said. 'Apart from the chattering of teeth.'

'Oh . . . that's enough . . .'

She circled, found her feet, waded back to the shingle bank, and scampered ashore. She was wearing her brassière and pants. Her wet brassière clung to her breasts and was nearly transparent. Her pants dated back to the days before she joined the Women's Auxiliary Air Force. WAAFs who were fortunate enough to possess two or three carefully hoarded pants of the civilian, feminine variety, only wore the heavy, unbecoming, if warm and practical, issue knickers, universally known as passion killers, when on duty.

Kay sat beside him on the grass, happily breathless.

'Oh, that was wonderful.'

'If you like catching pneumonia,' Kirby said. 'I think you're mad.'

'I shall soon dry off in the sun.'

'It's not that hot. Here. The best I can do.' He handed her a clean, folded handkerchief.

'Thanks.' She mopped her arms and shoulders, her waist, her legs. 'One sopping wet handkerchief. Never mind.' She spread it out on the grass beside her, and lay back.

No one could fail to be conscious of the brown nipples underneath the damply transparent brassière, of the small swell of her belly, of the way her pants were clinging to her, of the long, shapely legs. Kirby forced himself to think practical thoughts.

'You're still shivering. Put my tunic on.' He reached for the tunic, turned with it in his hand. Kay's green grey eyes were looking up at him seriously.

'Just hold me,' she said. 'If you don't mind.'

Kirby lay down. She turned towards him, lying on her side. He put his arms round her. They lay in silence. After a while, she stopped shivering. The silky skin of her smooth back under his fingers became warm. Kirby had also become conscious of the solid, pounding thumps of his heart, of her cheek against his, of her soft breathing.

Kay moved one arm, and put it round his neck, her fingers touching his neck. Her lips brushed against his.

Kirby drew his head back, studying her face. Her eyes were gauzy soft.

'You could make love to me, David,' Kay Dunn said. 'If you want to.'

There seemed to be something in Kirby's throat. He swallowed. At this time, in this place, he wanted nothing else.

'I want you to,' Kay said. 'I very much want you to.' She stroked his face, and smiled at him. 'I know about you, David Kirby, how you feel about people, how you feel about everything. It's just today, because I'm fond of you, and I think you like me. Because we're here, because we're together, because we can at least have something. Just that. No more.'

Kirby sat up, and pulled his shirt over his head. He wriggled out of his trousers and underpants with relief. He was hard and upright.

He turned and looked at Kay. She was lying, her hands by her sides, her eyes closed. His gaze travelled up her body, long thighs, the tufted mound of dark hair, full breasts, nipples erect. His stomach turned over. He bent down and kissed her properly for the first time.

They kissed and touched each other, their fingers explored, he could feel her heart racing too in tune with his. Her arms tugged him gently. He moved in answer, the sun was on his back, his face buried in her sweet scented hair.

'Oh, David,' she whispered, '. . . David . . .David . . . David . . .'

She was moving underneath him, he was all sensation, a myriad sensations, and as her arms tightened, locking him, and she began to gasp open-mouthed, he came rushing into her in a bursting, fiery climax.

They lay looking at each other, smiling now and then for no apparent reason, not saying very much, almost absurdly pleased with themselves and the other. After a while, interest kindled once more, and they moved together by mutual unspoken consent, a warm, open greeting, like two old friends meeting each other again.

Later, they noticed that the freakishly warm sun was declining, and a chill was entering the air. They dressed, and wandered, hand in hand, back across the wooden footbridge in search of, first the car, and then somewhere to eat.

Squadron Leader David Kirby, DFC, had quite forgotten that he was going to die.

Chapter Fifteen

The logistics of the strategic bombing offensive were formidable. The arithmetic was brutally simple. After the 3·7 per cent losses incurred during the 1,000-bomber raid on Cologne, the German defences became more effective. Losses increased and, for a period, were around 10 per cent.

Had the Germans been able to continue to inflict such casualties, the price would have been too high. Neither machines nor crews, who required lengthy training, could be expended at such a rate, the offensive would have wavered, weakened, and come to an end.

In an effort to avert this danger, in order to try and reduce the heavy toll being taken by German night fighters, new techniques were introduced. The attacking bombers flew in compact streams to swamp small areas of the defences. Aircraft dropped 'windows', small tinfoil strips, to confuse the enemy radar screens. Carefully planned diversionary raids carried out at the same time made it harder for the Germans to assess which was the main target, and assemble their night fighters accordingly. Pathfinder aircraft marked the target, improving bombing accuracy.

Bomber Command losses declined to around 4 per cent, and sometimes less. But if 'only' 4 per cent losses were sustained on each raid, by the end of a tour of thirty operations, every squadron would have lost all of its original strength and more.

Statistically, no crew commencing a tour of thirty operations would ever finish its tour. Statistical quirks, ability, experience, luck, gave rise to exceptions. Some crews died on their first flight over Germany. A few survived one tour and were lost on their second. A small handful came through two tours.

But most were destined to become part of the casualty figures, the crews of those aircraft which had 'failed to return', to be announced on the BBC by newsreaders in measured tones, at some point during their first tour of thirty operations.

The great majority of the young air crew of Bomber Command never completed their first tour. That was what 4 per cent losses meant. Such was the inexorable but simple arithmetic of the strategic bombing offensive.

The eye travels down the stiff pages of the battered log book which belonged to Squadron Leader David Kirby, DSO, DFC, the laconic, stereotyped entries, the record of one man's war from first dual flight to the final, incomplete entry. They can be counted, as David Kirby counted them. Berlin recurs time and again. The twenty-second operation on which he flew was to Berlin. The aircraft number has changed again. The badly damaged Lancaster which he brought back from Kassel had been replaced.

Avro Lancaster   R6135   Self   Crew   War Ops – Berlin.
8000lb plus incendiaries. Full moon.
Good visibility. Heavy casualties, but
not   a   scratch.   Excellent   target
photograph.   8.15

On the same night, Leutnant Horst Krieger's Me 410 was part of a small Luftwaffe force which attacked Hull. The port of Hull was bombed more frequently than any other British city bar London.

The Me 410, yet another brainchild of the brilliant Doctor Messerschmitt and his brilliant team, was the German equivalent of the Mosquito. Its fuselage and wings were constructed of metal, and not plywood as were those of the Mosquito, but it flew equally high and equally fast. Fortunately for the British, there were few Me 410s in service.

Leutnant Horst Krieger flew across the North Sea, and

dropped his bombs on Hull. In the Me 410, it was an easy mission. At the height he was flying, the anti-aircraft guns could not reach him, and his speed made him virtually impervious to night fighter interception.

Leutnant Krieger was a skilful and experienced pilot, with the Knight's Cross, and a long string of operations behind him. In the RAF, he would have been at least a squadron leader, and probably a wing commander, but the Luftwaffe was not so free in bestowing high rank upon its air crews.

All the way across the North Sea, Leutnant Horst Krieger had been listening in on his R/T to the continued exchanges between the ground controllers and the night fighter pilots who were harassing the returning RAF bombers. It was clear that the attack on Berlin had been exceptionally heavy.

Leutnant Horst Krieger was a Berliner. He had recently been on leave. His home had been destroyed. His parents had been dug out alive, but his fourteen-year-old sister was dead. His mother and father were now living with his grandparents in their two-roomed flat. Leutnant Krieger had not been on leave for some long time. He had been appalled by the devastation, the condition in which people were continuing their existence. It was hard to credit that so much of a capital city could be reduced to ruins.

Leutnant Horst Krieger decided not to return home high above the North Sea. The full moon was altogether too tempting. He descended in a wide circle over the sea until he was flying low, below British radar, recrossed the coast, his navigator map reading easily by the light of that brilliant moon, and flew south towards East Anglia, where most of Bomber Command's aerodromes were concentrated. Given a piece of luck, he thought the risk was worth while. He judged that he should arrive over the area roughly when the RAF bombers were returning.

Leutnant Horst Krieger was skimming low towards Chelmsford when he picked out the runway lights. The next second, he saw the silhouette of the Lancaster, its undercarriage down, on its final approach.

Leutnant Krieger banked slightly to the right, and then

eased to the left, overtaking the Lancaster now, and on its tail. He fired one burst from his forward-firing cannon, saw the shells strike home, banked steeply, flew over Woodley Common, and was gone.

Kirby and his crew had climbed out of their transport, and were walking towards the debriefing room. One moment there was the steady roar of the four engines of the Lancaster on finals. The next a single burst of cannon fire. A plane thundered overhead. The crash as the Lancaster fell into the fields short of the runway, the immediate explosion of the fuel tanks, the gushing, ugly, leaping hell of flames and smoke. They watched the conflagration helplessly. Dry-mouthed, they wondered who it was. Who it had been. Finally, they went inside to complete their night's work, and be debriefed.

Not much later, they learned that it had been Stan Jackson, and that there were no survivors. Ferris's creased face was taut with anger.

'Chalky should have known better, the stupid bastard,' he said, his voice vicious with frustration. Flight Sergeant Chalky White had been Jacko's rear gunner. 'Thought he was safely back home, and fucking relaxed. Yawning his bleeding head off, thinking about crawling into his bloody pit, I'll bet. Well, he'll have a fucking long sleep now, and serve him right. Jesus Christ, he knew the score. Why couldn't he keep his fucking eyes peeled?' Ferris stamped off into the night, still boiling with fury. Chalky White had been one of his drinking companions in the Sergeants' Mess. Ferris had liked Chalky White.

David Kirby undressed slowly, and got into bed like an automaton. Jacko, the natural pilot, had run what was probably the best crew in the squadron, except perhaps Wing Commander Norgate's. If it could happen to Jacko, it could happen to anyone. There were no exceptions.

Warrant Officer Ferris was married in the village church.

'Me, I don't believe in all that crap,' Ferris explained. 'But she wants it.'

The squadron had been given a seventy-two-hour pass.

Ferris's bride was a plain, peaky-faced girl. Ferris thought she was Cleopatra. After the ceremony, they adjourned to the pub, which Ferris had hired for the reception. Kirby had done his bit with the ring. After his more or less obligatory speech, in which he sincerely wished them every happiness, he slipped away. Roy Harrison had gone home to his pregnant wife by train. The 1933 Ford 8 was available. The petrol tank was half full. There was one two-gallon coupon left, valid until the next rationing period began.

They had no destination in mind. They were intent merely on leaving Woodley Common behind, slanting away from that concentration of aerodromes, the towns and villages where the streets and pubs were full of RAF or American uniforms.

Kirby simply followed the bonnet of the shaking little car, turning into winding lanes at random, anywhere which promised empty countryside, some feeling of timeless tranquillity.

They found it at an inn, deep in Derbyshire. 'The Crown', sheltered on a lonely crossroads, looked inviting, and had accommodation. All around, the dales rolled magnificently into the distance, intersected by small, lively streams. There was scarcely a human habitation in sight. Apart from the small sounds of a nature oblivious to the war, the rustling of newly green leaves in the cool breeze, the twittering of birds, there was silence. Visually, at least, the war had not invaded this place. It had been like this, unchanged, for centuries.

They explored briefly, walking through the formal, well-kept gardens at the rear of the inn, climbing to the top of the nearest gentle rise, but it was growing late, there was plenty of time at their disposal – two whole days left – and they strolled back, and into the dining room.

After dinner, they sat in the bar, furnished with Windsor chairs and stout wooden tables. Polished horse brasses hung everywhere. The ceiling beams were festooned with them. A blazing log fire burned and crackled in the massive inglenook fireplace. Its comforting, embracing warmth was welcome. That freak of a day which was almost hot, the product of an unusual 'high' bringing southerly air across the country, had long since gone, and been replaced by the more customary 'low', with winds from the north-east.

'The Crown' dated back to the eighteenth century. Built as a coaching inn, travellers heading north, a journey measured in days, had once climbed down from their stage-coaches as night fell, stiff, weary and hungry, glad of the prospect of rest, sustenance, and a comfortable bed for the night. The following morning, with ale and a heavy breakfast sitting in their stomachs, they had heaved themselves back on to the stage-coach, a fresh team of horses harnessed between the shafts, and set off on the next stage.

There must have been some houses within a mile or so though, or perhaps a village, tucked, invisible, into some fold in the hills. During the evening, the bar filled with men who grunted greetings to each other, and exchanged remarks in broad accents about people and subjects familiar to them, mystifyingly incomprehensible to an outsider. They were all middle-aged or elderly, their women-folk left at home, men who made dry jokes with weathered, straight faces, laconic, inward men, who used words as though they were rationed. They glanced briefly at the two strangers in the corner, but after that they considerately ignored the young squadron leader and the slender WAAF sitting beside him.

The bedroom doors were of solid oak, with heavy wooden latches, and had served their purpose for nearly two centuries. David Kirby had taken two rooms when he booked into the inn. He had no right to take anything for granted and did not.

But only one of the rooms with the wide, soft beds, was ever used. They fell asleep in each other's arms, and when it was morning, Kay was beside him. She would blink and stretch and smile.

'Morning.' Her voice still husky with sleep. 'Is that rain?' Lifting herself to listen. 'It'll soon stop.' She was always confidently optimistic.

The renewed sight of her full breasts filled him with wonder, a natural beauty as splendid and moving as any glorious sunset. He would stretch out a hand and trace their contours delicately, caressing the warm softness. They would decide not to get up for a while yet.

During the day, they walked. They walked, and walked, and walked, tramping for miles across the dales. And they talked, easily, without constraint, with no invisible barriers between them.

Kay seemed incapable of seeing a stream without feeling impelled to take her stockings off, and paddle in it.

'You have a cold water fetish,' Kirby told her.

Kay collected wild flowers. She knew all their names, and catalogued them for Kirby's benefit. He nodded, and promptly forgot them. Later, she pressed some of them in a book, and kept them.

They were together in a fragile bubble of time, Squadron Leader David Kirby, DFC and Leading Aircraftwoman Kay Dunn. They shared no past, no future. The present they inhabited was detached and separate. Within it they drew temporary comfort from the other's being and presence, a man and a girl who knew affection and companionship in an isolated loop line which led nowhere, who might remember each other with gratitude when they resumed the main tracks of their own lives.

Kay hoped to resume her education, eventually, and go to art college.

'I was offered a place, but I felt I should join up instead . . .'

'Then what? Paint impressionist pictures or something?'

'I'm more interested in abstracts. I shall probably end up in some advertising agency, doing cartoons about people beaming fatuously over hot drinks at bedtime.'

'You'll probably get married instead.'

'I don't think so. I can't imagine it anyway.'

'Well, I shall look at the adverts, and wonder if you did them.'

'I wonder what you'll be doing? Civil aviation probably. People are bound to fly a lot more after the war, and with all your experience . . .'

'Fat chance. One thing there'll be no shortage of is pilots.

There'll be hundreds for every job going. They won't want people like me.'

'Don't be such a pessimist.'

'I'm not. I'm a realist. God knows what I shall do. There's nothing else I know, except flying. And banking,' he added. He smiled. It was hard to believe that he had ever been a bank clerk.

In Kay's company, the future became tangible. His forebodings vanished. He could not only talk about 'after the war', he could visualize himself living in it.

'We'd better go back,' Kirby said. 'That rainstorm's coming our way, Kay. Come on. Don't start picking flowers again.'

'I shan't be long. Anyway, I like the rain.'

It was over. Kirby threw the bags on to the back seat and climbed in beside Kay. He took the direct route back to Woodley Common. They had cut it fine, and were leaving at the last possible moment.

He dropped Kay outside the WAAF quarters. She took her bag, pressed his hand, and looked at him. Suddenly, there was absolutely nothing to say except, 'Well . . . see you, David.'

He gave her the smile which had to be consciously constructed.

'See you, Kay,' he said, smiling, and drove off. The next time he saw her, she would be a figure in the darkness, lifting her hand as he took off.

He parked outside the Nissen hut, walked into his room, and unpacked automatically. In Derbyshire, not only had he forgotten, better than that, he had looked at his six remaining operations, and been able to contemplate them as six flights from which he would return. That had gone.

The very sight of the Lancasters at dispersal had been enough. Six was too many. One was too many. The next one was when his turn might come, as it had come for Squadron Leader Gale, for Warrant Officer Harding, for Ralph Whitney, for Smithy, for Squadron Leader Abel, for Jacko.

The hours of forgetfulness in Derbyshire had vanished as though they had never existed.

*

The duties of a flight commander were not onerous. There
was no administration involved. That was done by Squadron
and Station Headquarters. With the help of a small orderly
room staff Squadron Leader Kirby was responsible for the
allocation of aircraft, ensuring that they were air tested, for
servicing and refuelling. In short, it was his job to get aircraft
into the air in time to do *their* job and he carried it out
efficiently.

His private score, which rarely left his mind, rose to 28.
Only two to go. Only two more pieces of luck, that was all he
needed now. That was not too much to ask for. That was
possible. The balance had tilted in his favour. Christ, he would
need some really bad luck now, to buy it on one of only two
ops. The lead in his stomach weighed less, and often disappeared altogether. He was practically there. He had nearly
made it.

Squadron Leader Kirby looked at Daily Routine Orders in
shocked disbelief.

The brief, uncommunicative notice announced that 545
Squadron was to be withdrawn from operations for special
training.

The crews of 545 were delighted. For some unspecified
period, they did not have to fly over Germany. Rumours
abounded. Tropical kit had arrived in the stores, they were
going to India . . . no, no – from someone with superior
information – it was to be the Middle East where they would
support the Allied armies bogged down in Italy, which sounded
like a soft touch after Berlin . . . they were to be converted into
a Pathfinder Squadron . . .

They really couldn't care less which of the rumours would
turn out to be true, if any. There was to be a respite during
which the mincing machine over Germany would function
without them. That had to be pure bonus, an unexpected gift.

Kirby felt otherwise. Keyed up for those last two operations,
he wanted to get them behind him, and quickly. Within a
week, it could have been all over. Instead, he had to hang
around, with that crucial number stuck at 28. Inside his head,

he swore and blasphemed, he cursed whichever unknown fool was responsible.

Squadron Commanders' Conferences took place regularly at Group Headquarters, once a stately home, now inhabited by a bustling staff of planners and clerks, alive with telephones and teleprinters. Nissen huts linked by asphalt paths disfigured the gracious lawns.

At those conferences, the course of the air war was outlined, policy explained, special problems identified. The squadron commanders were there to contribute, as well as to be put in the picture. Their operational and command experience could lead to useful suggestions being offered.

Wing Commander Norgate had sat through that particular conference, the one which was a turning point. They were sitting in what had formerly been the library, now the conference room. It was the final session. The senior air staff officer, Air Commodore Whiting, was addressing them. The air officer commanding, Air Vice Marshal Farleigh, sat beside him on the dais. The subject was the Second Front.

'. . . I cannot indicate a date, gentlemen, but you will be aware that it cannot be long delayed. The Germans know that too, and they are waiting for us. For the invasion to succeed, complete command of the air by day will be essential. Failing that, the entire landing would be at risk. Provided we only have to deal with conventional fighters, we can expect to attain air superiority, but the Messerschmitt 262 is another matter altogether, and the Chiefs of Staff are deeply concerned about the threat to our invasion forces which this aircraft poses . . .'

The existence of the Me 262 was well known. It was the first operational pure jet aircraft. It could outfly and outfight any allied plane in service. A mere handful had attacked a Fortress formation, broken it up, and wrought havoc, with no loss to themselves, either from the massed ·5 machine-guns of the Flying Fortresses, or from the escorting fighters. The Me 262 was far and away the most formidable aircraft flying. The RAF also knew that the Me 262 was being prepared as a night fighter, equipped with the latest radar, which would make even the fast Mosquitoes their prey, let alone lumbering Lancasters and Halifaxes.

'. . . it is not known how many Me 262s are in squadron service,' the SASO was saying, 'but it must be assumed that the Germans are making every effort to produce as many as they can, as fast as they can. Clearly, we in Bomber Command would dearly like to interfere with the production of such a powerful and menacing weapon, but no single manufacturing centre can be identified. It is probable that none exists. Production is almost certainly dispersed in many small centres. We ourselves, of course, improvised in this way when the main Spitfire factory was knocked out in 1940. Garages were used, laundries, anything which would house machine tools, and production continued unhindered. The Luftwaffe were left with nothing to bomb . . .'

Wing Commander Norgate was paying close attention. Instinct told him that out of this could come something of supreme personal importance. And yet, if there was 'nothing to bomb' . . .

'. . . also, in many respects, the Me 262 is a very simple aircraft,' the SASO went on. 'Wings, fuselage, and so on, could be built virtually anywhere. Advanced engineering, or high skills, would not be required . . .'

The genius of simplicity then, lay in the design, Norgate reflected. And it was too late to interfere with that.

'This of course does not apply to the jet engines,' the SASO continued, 'the conception of which is simply enough, and familiar to us too, although I'm afraid we are some way behind as regards getting a similar machine into service, but the construction requires machine tools and skills of a very high order. Now, gentlemen, a great deal of activity has been observed – here.'

Norgate's eyes followed the pointer. The tip touched the map, and rested on shaded contours deep in the mountains of Southern Bavaria.

'The valley is called Ascheraden,' the SASO said.

A blown-up aerial reconnaissance photograph was displayed. The pointer moved precisely over it.

'It is heavily defended,' the SASO said. 'Considerable numbers of both light and heavy anti-aircraft guns. The floor of the valley is extremely well camouflaged. Something important is going on there, gentlemen. Intelligence reports lead us to believe that it is *here* that turbine blades for the Me 262's jet engines are being manufactured. If we could find some way to knock that out, we would stop the production of the Me 262 dead in its tracks.'

There was a pause for thought. It was apparent to all of them, Norgate included, that to attack such a target by night would be a waste of bombs. The target area was little more than a few hundred yards across. Norgate's mind raced furiously. Among the wide range of bombs which the Lancaster could carry was the 8,000lb armour-piercing, and *that* was fully ballistic. Even at night, it might be possible to deliver such bombs on the target . . . but no. *This* target would be a complex of buildings, workshops where the turbo fans were made, supply facilities, workers' accommodation . . . AP bombs would be no use. Blockbusters would be required to achieve maximum devastation for such a widely spread target, and they had no ballistic characteristics and, even carefully aimed, could land a mile or two miles from the aiming point . . .

Someone asked the obvious question.

'Sir, the Eighth Air Force would be capable of hitting it. I take it that has been considered?'

It was the AOC who replied.

'You're quite right, Harold. It has. But the Fortress can't carry heavy enough bombs to destroy machine tools in one attack. They'd have to go back time and time again. Losses would inevitably be very heavy. Our American friends are quite ready to accept such losses, in view of the importance of the target, but the difficulty is that the first raid would betray our knowledge of its importance. The Germans would up sticks and move at once, and then we wouldn't know where the devil they were.'

The discussion continued for a while, and ended without any conclusion being reached.

Wing Commander Norgate did not contribute. His whole body was rigid with excitement. He took out his handkerchief, and wiped the palms of his hands. They were damp with sweat. There was no more than a misty, half-formed idea in his mind, but that was enough. He knew that this was it. This was what he had been waiting for.

When the conference ended, Norgate waited until all his colleagues had climbed into their cars, and set out for their respective stations. Then he asked for a brief note to be placed before the AOC. The note requested an immediate interview, and included the word 'Ascheraden'.

Norgate smoked one cigarette after another while he tried to turn that hazy notion into something more practical, straining to anticipate likely objections. He really needed more time, but his guts told him that the moment was now.

Forty-five minutes later, he was sent for. Norgate went in and saluted.

'Sit down, Barry,' the AOC said, pleasantly.

'Thank you, sir.' Norgate removed his cap, and sat in the chair in front of the AOC's desk. Air Commodore Whiting was there too.

'Something occurred to you since the session ended?' the AOC enquired.

'Yes, sir.' Norgate began to speak. The idea was still not entirely clear in his mind. He was more than half improvising as he went along, alert for the expressions on the two men's faces. Air Commodore Whiting's told him nothing. The AOC gazed at him steadily. His lips pursed.

'We don't want 1942 all over again, Barry,' he said.

'It wouldn't be, sir,' Norgate said, injecting confidence into his voice. 'The Rose turret is available now. We'd time the raid so that we flew back under cover of darkness,' he said, recalling in time the previously tried tactic. 'Simultaneously, we'd need carefully planned diversionary raids by the Eighth Air Force, of course, to draw away any likely fighter opposition all the way along our route, but given that, we should stand a good chance of avoiding interception entirely.'

'You couldn't bomb from below 10,000 feet,' the AOC

objected, referring to the awesome power of an 8,000lb bomb's explosion. An aircraft flying any lower would be included in the destruction caused by its own bomb. 'From that height, you'd never hit the target.'

'These are only very hurried, rough sketches, sir,' Norgate said. 'The detail may not be right, I'm not a draughtsman. But I'm sure such a modification would be possible. It just needs sufficient commitment by the experts.'

He handed the pieces of paper to the AOC, who glanced at them briefly, and passed them to Air Commodore Whiting.

'We'd also carry liquefied petroleum jelly bombs, sir,' Norgate said, coolly, containing his excitement, as though it were part of his plan. It had just come to him. The master stroke. 'After dropping our cookies, we turn, dive back into the valley, and burn what's left.'

'A manoeuvre like that would take several minutes,' the AOC observed neutrally.

'There'll be all hell let loose on the ground from the 8,000 pounders, sir,' Norgate argued. 'They won't know what's hit them. They won't be expecting us to return to the target. We blow it up! And then we burn it!'

'Put your plan on paper for me, please, Barry,' the AOC said. Wing Commander Norgate stood up, and replaced his cap. 'Soon, if you possibly can,' the AOC said. 'If such an operation were to be considered, it would take time to mount. There's very little time at our disposal. I can say no more than that.'

One highly important thing had been left unsaid. Wing Commander Norgate said it. 'Sir, should my suggestion prove to be feasible, I would very much hope that the operation might be carried out by 545 Squadron.'

The AOC gave Norgate his agreeable smile.

'Let me have your paper on the subject, Barry,' he said.

The AOC watched the trim, spruce wing commander, with the composed, rather sharp face, and the eyes as pale as pack ice, as he saluted and left. The AOC studied his senior air staff officer.

'You're not convinced, John,' he supposed.

'It flies in the face of long established policy, sir.'

'Well, I'm not convinced yet either. But circumstances alter cases.'

'Given the dates for the invasion which the Supreme Allied Commander is considering, sir, we only have a few weeks at our disposal. Quite apart from the risk factor, are these modifications even possible? Mounting an operation calling for such a high degree of inter-Allied co-operation would be extremely complex. We'd need Fighter Command. The weather would have to be exactly right. Wing Commander Norgate skated over all that.'

'Oh, that's forgivable, at this stage,' the AOC said. 'He's come up with something. He's keen to have a go. I like that. The problems you mention, John, it's our job to look at those.'

'Fair enough, sir. But the training alone would take weeks, if we're not to have another disaster.'

'Given the earliest possible invasion date, there's enough time,' the AOC said. 'If it stands up to examination, we'd get all the facilities and effort we need. General Eisenhower wants the sky over the landings full of Allied fighters, not Me 262s. Having proved their worth, the Germans must be building up their strength of jets, and holding them back for the invasion. They'd be mad to do anything else. It's one hell of an important target, John, Ascheraden.' He looked at his watch. 'Let's go and have a drink.'

The two men stood up.

'We'll see how Norgate's idea shapes up on paper,' the AOC said. 'The risks have to be acceptable. I haven't bought it yet by a long way. But it's worth considering. No one's come up with anything else.'

Wing Commander Norgate wrote several drafts before he was satisfied. Each one was shorter than its predecessor. His aim was to reduce it to a few, brief, businesslike, numbered paragraphs, in which there were no superfluous or ambiguous words, and each one was essential The final version was sent to the AOC at Group Headquarters by despatch rider, marked TOP SECRET.

At Group, planners and specialists worked round the clock. From Wing Commander Norgate's two-page plan, a multitude of files sprouted, each dealing with a specific aspect, all TOP SECRET. The air officer commanding held meetings with his bombing experts at which representatives from industry, specialists in ballistics were present; with his senior navigation officer; with his senior gunnery officer; with all those who represented the many different disciplines which would be involved. The files grew in number, offshoots from offshoots, and became thicker. A firm shape began to emerge. The AOC held a final lengthy meeting with Air Commodore Whiting. A summary of their conclusions was submitted to Bomber Command.

Shortly afterwards, the AOC was summoned to an urgent meeting at Bomber Command Headquarters. Also present, as well as the high-ranking British officers, was a general from the United States Eighth Air Force.

Wing Commander Norgate, DSO, DFC and bar, DFM would have been gratified, had he known of the turmoil of activity which had resulted from his two pages, but he did not. All he knew was silence. A dozen times, he put in a call to the AOC and cancelled it. Good sense told him that he would receive a decision in due course. But the waiting was agony, worse than any operation over Germany.

He had almost given up hope when he received a brief telephone call of congratulations from the AOC, followed by a signal.

Wing Commander Norgate read the signal time and again. He sat for ten minutes, alone in his office, before he summoned a clerk, and dictated the brief notice which would appear on Daily Routine Orders.

He had done it. He had brought it off. As far as Wing Commander Norgate was concerned, the most difficult part was behind him. Discerning a half chance, seizing it, and convincing the powers that be, that was what was beyond most men. And he had achieved it, the near impossible. All that remained was the execution of the operation itself.

Compared with the monumental difficulties, successfully

overcome, of initial conception and securing the go-ahead, Norgate faced the raid itself with a calm expectation close to equanimity. He knew without doubt that, under his leadership, his crews would get there, and achieve complete and outstanding success.

545 Squadron could do it. He would damn well make certain they did it.

Chapter Sixteen

545 Squadron's mood of cheerfulness began to seep away as soon as their special training began. They found themselves flogging round Great Britain on 1,000 mile flights, at low level, in daylight, and in close formation.

None of the pilots had carried out any formation flying since they were at training school, and then in aircraft considerably more manoeuvrable than the heavy, four-engined Lancasters.

Not surprisingly, the initial results were ragged, to put it mildly. Pilots sweated at the controls. The main difficulty, they all found, lay in making the relatively small yet precise adjustment of power necessary to maintain position in the formation. Until they got it right, they were either over-running each other, or under-shooting, and struggling to catch up again. There was the continual and imminent risk of mid-air collisions.

Wing Commander Norgate barked irritable orders in the air on his R/T, and hectored them at debriefings, after they had landed. He behaved like a man possessed.

Slowly, their formation flying began to improve. As it did so, Wing Commander Norgate offered no encouragement, but turned the screw, leading them down to lower and lower heights.

From five hundred feet, they progressed downwards, to two hundred and fifty feet, and finally even lower, until they were hugging the contours, thundering along at tree top level.

They were told nothing, but they did not have to be told. It meant flying underneath enemy radar, by daylight. Discontent simmered and grew. They had been trained as night bomber crews. The Lancaster was designed to operate by night. They were being required to fly in a manner in which they were not experienced, and for which neither crews nor machines were properly fitted. Night bombing was their trade. What the hell was going on?

All the initial euphoria had long since evaporated by the time they watched dummy, modified 8000lb bombs being loaded. When they took off this time, the briefing included a new tactic. Having flown at low level for hours, they jinked their way through the mountains of Wales, still at low level. As they approached the target, a deep, precipitous valley in Snowdonia, they climbed to 10,000 feet, and carried out a bombing run, releasing their modified dummy cookies, aiming at the small camouflaged area in the valley far below.

As soon as their bomb doors were closed, 545 Squadron regrouped in a wide, sweeping, diving turn, and hurtled down into the valley where, the mountain peaks towering above them, they released more, smaller dummy bombs on to the target area. It was a complicated manoeuvre, which they practised many times. After they left the target area, 545 closed up once more into close formation, and threaded their way back through mountain valleys at low level.

Although Wing Commander Norgate was never satisfied and criticized them all at every debriefing in a distantly scathing fashion, the crews knew that they were becoming increasingly well drilled. As men whose trade was flying, they could not help but derive instinctive satisfaction in overcoming the new and challenging demands being made upon them. It was a good feeling, knowing that they were flying better and better on each practice sortie. It was the type of operation for which all their growing new skills were to be required which was the deep, unresolved nagging worry in all their minds.

Wing Commander Norgate had become completely unapproachable. Obsessed with the standards which he had set for his squadron, he was either blind to the simmering discontent or, if he did detect it, his only response was to drive them on harder and harder. He refused to discuss the object of all this special training, and brushed questions aside, or more often simply ignored them.

' "Theirs not to reason why . . ." ' Alan Russell quoted sourly, after yet another fruitless attempt to raise some of the problems which they could all see.

'Don't waste time with things which don't concern you,' Wing Commander Norgate had snapped. 'Let me do the worrying, that's my job. Flight Sergeant Shepherd . . .' And he went on to berate Don Shepherd for lagging behind during that critical second diving attack on to the target area, which had meant that it subsequently took Shepherd several minutes to catch up with the remainder of the squadron, and move back into close formation.

'Theirs but to do or die.' David Kirby found the comparison discomfitingly apt. Like the Light Brigade, they were to charge into some valley, 'guns to the right of them, guns to the left of them', a fragile spearhead attacking some unknown far away objective, without explanation and, as far as they could tell, without any adequate protection, or reasonable chance of emerging alive.

The crews of 545 Squadron were not fools. Whatever their boyhood ambitions might have been, war was now their business. The Royal Air Force was not a democracy. It was their job to obey orders. The deadly trade of night bombing had become familiar to them, and they accepted the risks. But they had been snatched away from that, they were being honed for something else. They were facing the unknown. They did not expect to be told much, they well knew that they could not be told much, but they badly needed reassurance, which could only come from their commanding officer. Wing Commander Norgate did not provide it.

On the other hand, even if they did not know the details, there was a considerable amount which the crews of 545 Squadron could work out for themselves from the nature of their special training. The unknown target was in mountainous country, deep inside enemy territory, which they would attack in daylight, having flown for several hours over hostile country at low level. Even if they eluded the Germans on the way out, once the target was bombed, the enemy would know where they were, and would be waiting for them on the return trip.

'I reckon it's somewhere in Lower Saxony,' Alan Russell guessed.

'It sounds to me like bloody Augsberg all over again,' Roy Harrison said, glumly. Roy had lost faith in the talisman of his unborn child. As a guarantee of continued good luck, that would not stand up to anything like Augsberg.

During the afternoon of 17 April 1942, twelve of the first Lancasters to come into service had crossed the Channel at fifty feet. Six were from 44 Squadron, and six were from 97 Squadron. The formation was led by Squadron Leader Nettleton of 44 Squadron. Each aircraft carried four 1,000lb GP high explosive bombs, fitted with eleven-second delay detonators. The target was the MAN diesel engine works at Augsberg. In broad daylight, they were to fly some 1,000 miles across France and Germany.

They crossed the enemy coast safely, the Luftwaffe having been drawn away by Boston bombers and a large force of strafing fighters, but the aircraft from 44 Squadron became detached from those of 97 Squadron. Due to the need to conserve fuel on such an extended sortie, the latter group, which had fallen behind, made no attempt to catch up. Briefing had allowed for separate attacks if circumstances decreed.

When well into France, Squadron Leader Nettleton's six aircraft, now well ahead of the 97 Squadron formation, were intercepted flying at tree-top level, by a number of Messerschmitt 109s and Focke Wulf 190s. Four of the six Lancasters were shot down before the fighters withdrew due to lack of fuel.

The two surviving Lancasters, although damaged, reached their objective, and bombed the target factory. As they began the run-out, one was shot down by anti-aircraft fire.

Squadron Leader Nettleton, now alone, set course for the return journey.

Soon afterwards, the six aircraft from 97 Squadron

approached the target, went in at roof-top level, virtually in
line astern, and bombed the target. Two were shot down.

On 28 April 1942, the *London Gazette* announced the award
of a Victoria Cross to Squadron Leader John Nettleton. On 4
January 1943, he was promoted to wing commander (acting).
On the night of 12–13 July 1943, he was killed during a raid
on Turin.

British press propaganda reports made much of the 'vast
damage' achieved in the attack on the MAN works at
Augsberg, but in reality only seventeen of the 1,000lb bombs
dropped actually hit part of the engine factory, and five of
those failed to explode. The effect of the raid was that 3 per
cent of the machine tools in the whole plant were put out of
action. Of the twelve Lancasters which set out to bomb this
objective, seven failed to return; of the eighty-five men who
took off, forty-nine were 'missing'.

Since the Augsberg raid, Lancasters had not so far been used
again in daylight for, it seemed to the crews of 545 Squadron,
very good and obvious reasons.

Anxiety swelled into discontent. Grumbling grew into something approaching rebellion.

'Why won't he say anything, unless it's fucking suicide, and
he knows it?' Warrant Officer Ferris demanded. He was
referring to Wing Commander Norgate, and glowering at
David Kirby in his place. 'I've never known anything like this,
skipper. It's bloody insane.'

Kirby shook his head helplessly. Norgate had cut himself off
from his flight commanders, and paid them no more heed than
any sergeant pilot. But the crews of 545 Squadron were not
brainless automatons. They were all highly individualistic
young men, they were not exempt from fear, they had to
believe and have faith in *something* – usually themselves, and
the reliance they could place on the other members of the
crew. But this was clearly to be a squadron operation, in which
they would be led by a man who was giving them nothing.
Fear was beginning to be present in the very air they breathed,
and if they took off not only afraid but convinced that few

would return, then the operation would certainly be a disaster of frightful proportions.

Kirby conferred with his fellow flight commander, Squadron Leader Jack Lucas, who was also concerned about the groundswell of angry cynicism, which could so easily turn into despair. They agreed to hold an informal meeting of squadron pilots in 'A' Flight Office, timed when there would be no clerks present to overhear, and Norgate would be safely elsewhere.

The bitter bewilderment which emerged was worse than Kirby had anticipated. It was only when he suggested that the two flight commanders should see Norgate together and acquaint him with the feelings of the squadron that the mood became calmer. All the pilots were sure that their crews would be happier if they knew that something was being done.

At the appointed time, David Kirby made his way to Squadron Headquarters. They had arranged to meet early for a quiet last-minute discussion about how best to present their case. Lucas was not there. Kirby waited. The minutes dragged past. Finally, a message arrived. Squadron Leader Lucas was flying, air testing his aircraft. Kirby went into Norgate's office alone.

'Whatever this is about, Kirby, kindly be brief,' Wing Commander Norgate said curtly. 'I'm trying to prepare for a meeting at Group.'

He stared at Kirby intently, but he wore the expression of a man who may have been listening to what was being said, but was not hearing it. After a while, he moved restlessly in his chair, and broke in.

'You're wasting my time,' he said querulously. 'I'd have thought it was obvious that half your questions can't be answered yet. As for the rest, you can take it for granted that any snags which have emerged will be ironed out. Do you think they haven't been spotted already and acted upon?'

'Then I suggest you have a chat to the squadron and explain that,' Kirby said. 'Take them into your confidence, treat them as responsible individuals.'

'You're either being impertinent or stupid, Kirby,' Wing Commander Norgate said, coldly. All his latent suspicions of

David Kirby were rising to the surface again. 'I don't regard my crews as children who need patting on the head, and their hands held at every turn. Their job – and yours – is to fight a war. This is the air force, not a kindergarten.'

'You haven't understood, sir,' Kirby said. 'Morale in the squadron is about as bad as it can be. If you're not aware of that, I think you should be.'

'*You* think I should be,' Wing Commander Norgate repeated. 'It seems I have more faith in this squadron than you. I'll tell you what *I* think, Kirby. I think you'd rather complete your tour with a couple of nice soft trips, and you're getting jumpy. I think it's your morale I should be concerned about, not that of the squadron.'

'I don't give a damn what you think,' Kirby said, tartly. 'If you don't believe me, talk to Jack Lucas, talk to Warrant Officer Ferris, any of the crews, come to that. Find out how they feel for yourself.'

Wing Commander Norgate laughed.

'You sound like a union official bleating about the feeling on the shop floor,' he said, contemptuously. 'This pointless discussion is over. Kindly tell the adjutant I want to see him on your way out.'

'If you refuse to listen, you leave me with no alternative,' Kirby said. 'I request permission to see the station commander and seek an interview with the air officer commanding.'

'Don't talk like an idiot,' Wing Commander Norgate told him. 'Go away, Squadron Leader Kirby, and for God's sake try and pull yourself together.'

His face flushed with anger, Kirby went straight to Station Headquarters. Without permission, he would never get near the AOC. Only one man on the station was in a position to make Norgate see sense.

The station commander, Group Captain Vesty, was a regular officer, who had been wounded when flying Hampdens in the early days of the war, and was no longer fit for operational flying. He was well liked, known affectionately as 'the old man', and was regarded as such, being all of thirty-seven years old.

He treated Kirby with cordial consideration, listened sympathetically, but explained that he was obliged to support Wing Commander Norgate. However, he promised to have a quiet word with Norgate himself, and see if the crews' apprehensions could be allayed.

'Leave it with me, David,' he said, kindly.

If quiet words with Wing Commander Norgate were exchanged, they had no discernible effect. If anything, his cold, manic intensity only increased.

Sixteen Lancasters with a somewhat unusual configuration were delivered to Woodley Common. On the same day, the station was sealed off. All leaves and passes were cancelled. All personnel, air crew and ground staff alike, were confined to camp until further notice.

Ferris studied the hump-shaped dome with the twin, ugly-looking machine-guns, which had replaced the normal mid upper turret.

'Rose turrets,' he said. 'Fitted with two point fives. At least no fighter's going to be able to stay out of range, and lob cannon shells at us.'

There was a note of disconsolate regret in his voice. It would not be Ferris who would be behind those lethal guns. He would still be in the rear turret, with its four ·303 machine-guns, effective when a fighter had to come in close, but not at long range.

The mid upper gunners of 545 Squadron, Arthur Wood among them, spent hours on the gunnery range, familiarizing themselves with the heavy ·5s. This was followed by aerial practice so that the mid upper gunners could get used to engagements at longer range. At first, they fired against drogue targets towed by Defiants and Martinets. Then came fighter affiliation exercises, when Spitfires made not only curve of pursuit but head-on attacks while the gunners in the Lancaster formation tried to align their sights on the fighters hurtling towards them. This was carried out at a dangerously low level for the attacking Spitfires, but although there were some close calls there were, mercifully, no accidents.

The new Lancasters had been further modified to carry

extra fuel, making nearly three thousand gallons in all, which did nothing to reassure 545 Squadron about their eventual destination.

Late on during their special training in the new Lancasters, Wing Commander Norgate led the squadron across the airfield when they returned, still in close formation, and at low level, which suspiciously resembled some sort of fly past, and led to instant rumours that the AOC had arrived at Woodley Common, and was watching. If so, it was an informal visit. There were no parades or inspections.

But in the Officers' Mess that evening, a large group of very senior officers was clustered around the bar. Group Captain Vesty and Wing Commander Norgate were in respectful attendance, doing the honours.

Kirby studied the faces belonging to all the top brass from a distance. He had never seen the air officer commanding, and had no idea what he looked like. But when a gap momentarily opened in the bunched group of uniforms, and then closed again, he caught sight of the air vice marshal's rank markings.

He gave Roy Harrison a dry smile.

'Worth a go,' he said. 'Never get another chance.'

'You'll get shot,' Roy Harrison predicted.

'Now or later, what's the odds?'

Just the same, Kirby's heart was bumping as he walked across the ante-room towards the bar. Air vice marshals did not expect to be buttonholed by squadron pilots, and he had no reason to suppose that this one would take kindly to it.

Their backs to him, none of the group of staff officers saw him approaching. He skirted them, and got as close to the AOC as he could before he spoke.

'Sir,' he said, loudly. 'May I speak to you, please?'

The AOC's head turned. He looked surprised or displeased, or both.

'My name is Squadron Leader Kirby, sir. A lot of us are unhappy about this operation we're being trained for, and I'd like to ask you . . .'

Kirby got no further. The group closed protectively around the AOC, cutting him off from Kirby's vision, and he found himself being hustled away by Wing Commander Norgate and some unknown staff officer, a group captain.

'Go to your quarters, Kirby, unless you want to find yourself under arrest,' Wing Commander Norgate said. His voice was quiet and controlled, but ice cold. His eyes were blazing with fury. 'You'll be dealt with tomorrow.'

Kirby walked back to Roy Harrison, and a number of other junior officers who had been watching.

'You've done all you can,' Roy Harrison said, consolingly. 'Brick walls won't listen, and that's it.'

'Suppose we give them a song, Roy,' David Kirby said.

'Right,' Roy Harrison said. He sat down at the upright piano.

Kirby looked at the others.

'One that even stone-deaf bastards ought to be able to hear,' he said. They nodded. Alan Russell grinned.

Roy Harrison struck up the tune, banging the keys as if he were wielding a sledgehammer. At the tops of their voices, they bellowed out the words.

> *'I don't want to join the air force,*
> *I don't want to go to war.*
> *I'd rather hang around Piccadilly Underground,*
> *Living on the earnings of a high born lady.*
> *Don't want a bullet up my arsehole,*
> *Don't want my bollocks shot away.*
> *I'd rather live in England,*
> *Lovely, lovely England,*
> *And fuck all my bleeding life away,*
> *Gor blimey . . .'*

The same ditty, the same words, with 'army' instead of 'air force' had served their fathers, hoarsely defying impending fate, as they had trudged, rifles slung, packs on backs, in long unending columns towards the front lines in Flanders, towards the slaughter of the Somme and Passchendaele.

Without warning, Roy Harrison stopped playing, the singing ceased. Silence fell. Kirby turned. An air commodore was approaching. Roy Harrison stood up. They all came to attention.

'Squadron Leader Kirby,' Air Commodore Whiting said, 'the AOC wishes to speak to you at once. He's in the billiard room.'

'Yes, sir,' Kirby said.

The senior air staff officer jerked his head in a nod, and walked away. Kirby followed. He passed the bar. None too friendly eyes studied his progress. Behind him, Roy Harrison and the others began to bawl another song which formed part of the squadron repertoire.

> 'Cats on the roof tops, cats on the tiles,
> Cats with syphilis, cats with piles,
> Cats with their arseholes wreathed in smiles,
> As they revel in the joys of fornication . . .'

Kirby closed the door of the billiard room behind him. Air Vice Marshal Farleigh was knocking snooker balls around the table. Wing Commander Norgate was watching him.

Kirby crossed to the table, and stood to attention. The AOC tried to cut a red into one of the centre pockets, and failed. He laid his cue on the table, straightened up, and glanced at Kirby.

'A bit out of practice,' he said. 'Do you play?'

'I prefer billiards, sir,' Kirby said.

The AOC turned to Wing Commander Norgate.

'This young officer seems to have something to say,' he remarked. 'I think I should hear it – in your presence, of course.'

'As you wish, sir,' Norgate said. His face might have been cast in cement, and was much the same colour.

'Let's make ourselves comfortable,' the AOC said. 'Kirby, bring up a chair.'

The AOC and Wing Commander Norgate settled themselves on the leather bench seat flanking the billiard table. Kirby set up a folding chair, and sat facing them.

'Well, Kirby, you wanted to speak to me,' the AOC said. 'You say you're unhappy about something. A point your song was intended to reinforce, I imagine,' he said dryly. 'Now's your opportunity to tell me why. Go ahead. I'm listening.'

Kirby told him. He avoided any mention of poor squadron morale. Why, when it came to the point, he should feel loyalty towards Norgate, he was by no means sure, but he did. Norgate was, after all, the squadron commander, and a brave man, and he, Kirby, was not only one of his officers, but one of his flight commanders. What was worrying the squadron crews was the important thing, not dropping Norgate in the shit.

Air Vice Marshal Farleigh listened with close attention. His searching eyes never left Kirby's face. He did not interrupt, neither did his expression change, or give any indication as to what he might be thinking.

Air Vice Marshal Farleigh was in his early fifties, a little portly, more than a little bald, the remaining half circle of white hair resembling a monk's tonsure. His gallantry decorations had been won during the Great War, when he had flown at first, observation planes, and later Handley Page 0/400 bombers. A distinguished pilot, he would have commanded the first squadron of Vimy bombers to go into service, but the war had ended before that – at the time – formidable aircraft could be used. The Vimy was designed to bomb Berlin, and it was in a modified Vimy that Alcock and Browne flew the Atlantic non-stop for the first time ever in 1919.

Air Vice Marshal Farleigh was the best type of regular RAF officer. Often obliged to make hard and difficult decisions, he had never forgotten what it was like to be a squadron pilot. He could be hard, but he was never callous. He could be ruthless, but he was never unfair. He was always conscious that, while Bomber Command now had the right machines for its task, it took men to fly those aircraft to their targets and back – men who, to Air Vice Marshal Farleigh, now seemed little more than boys.

Kirby came to the end of his catalogue of doubts and guesses.

'. . . well, that's about it, sir. The operation must be on soon, or we wouldn't be confined to camp. And yet those modified dummy cookies are useless. Either the nose cones or the tail fins keep falling off. We'll never be able to deliver them accurately from ten thousand feet. We just haven't been hitting the target during practice, due to those wretched bombs failing, and that's without opposition. As to that, well, the Rose turrets'll help us defend ourselves, but only one squadron, sixteen aircraft . . . well, I've said all that, sir. It's been tried before, and we know what happened then.'

He fell silent. The silence spun out until it seemed to be endless. Air Vice Marshal Farleigh appeared to be thinking.

'Let me tell you as much as I can,' he said at last. 'And if that is too much, I rely upon your discretion.'

'Of course, sir,' Kirby said.

'The bombs first of all. You're quite right. The first modifications were not successful. Ballistics experts have been working non-stop on further modifications. A special unit has been testing them. I am satisfied that if you go – *if* I say – your cookies will be fully ballistic, and capable of hitting the target from a bombing height of ten thousand feet. Fair enough?'

'Yes, sir,' Kirby said. There was something about this calm man which carried conviction, complete faith in anything he said.

'However, those bombs have to be delivered. If we can achieve it, all of them. On the target. They're of no use to the war effort if they explode in some field aboard a shot down aircraft. You, and perhaps your friends, seem to have Augsberg very much in mind. I'd like to think that we've learned a lot since Augsberg.'

It was the mildest of reproofs, but Kirby felt his cheeks grow hot.

He said steadily, 'We only know about our training, sir. Apart from penetrating even deeper into Germany, it seems like a re-run to us. I'm sorry, sir, but . . .'

'Don't apologize,' the AOC said. He seemed to be amused. 'I'm not going to ask you where you think the target is in case you shock me with the right answer. Now then, the Rose turrets. Thirty-two point fives firing in unison should serve as a useful deterrent for any stray fighter you accidentally encounter, but that's all we have in mind. The object is to arrive over the target without being intercepted at all.' Kirby's dubious reaction to that must have been expressed in his face. 'To that end,' the AOC went on, 'not only will massive fighter sweeps be mounted so that you may cross the enemy coast undetected, but large formations of the United States Eighth Air Force will be carrying out attacks on targets in Germany during that period of time while you are flying towards your objective. The Fortress attacks will be in strength, and their targets carefully chosen so as to suck away, as it were, enemy fighters, and leave you unmolested. We think it likely that the Luftwaffe will be more concerned with heavy raids on cities than with any reports they may receive about a few Lancasters whose destination will not be clear to them.'

Kirby stared at him. They all knew it was something big, that had been obvious from the beginning. But none of them had imagined for one moment that it was *this* big, certainly not Kirby. To commit several hundred American aircraft to a series of simultaneous raids, merely to ensure that one squadron of Lancasters reached its target . . .

'Yes, Kirby,' the AOC said quietly, 'the target is that important. Your track has been most carefully worked out with the object of avoiding opposition so far as is humanly possible and, of course, so as not to reveal your final destination to the enemy until it is too late. The operation will be timed so that, having reached your objective, you will return under cover of darkness. *But*, everything has to be right before you go, and especially the weather. We need a combination of certain weather conditions, and if they do not occur, the operation will not be authorized. If and when you learn what 545 Squadron's target is, you will understand how essential it is that it should be destroyed. Nevertheless, the risk must be acceptable. This is not some desperate last throw, and I would not countenance it for a second if it were. I am only interested in a well planned operation, with a good chance of complete success. Even if you do get the go, after your take off, progress will be continually monitored from Group, and if I am not satisfied with the way things are going, I shall have no hesitation in recalling you at once. Do you have any further questions?'

'No, sir,' Kirby said. He felt a surge of trusting warmth towards this quiet, incisive man. 'May I pass on the gist of what you've said to the other chaps?'

'No you certainly may not,' the AOC said, decisively. 'Under no circumstances.' Air Vice Marshal Farleigh was privately rather taken with this young fellow's moral courage and forthrightness, even if his actions would have been unthinkable in the pre-war regular air force. Still, like nearly all operational air crews, the lad was really a civilian at heart, and one made certain allowances, if not many, and all this should have been dealt with long before by Wing Commander Norgate anyway. The AOC was distinctly annoyed with Norgate. On the other hand, 545 Squadron was the chosen instrument, that was now irrevocable, and its commanding officer, Wing Commander Norgate, was entitled to his AOC's full support. Air Vice Marshal Farleigh was quite accustomed to squaring the circle. 'The remainder of the squadron will be put in the picture by your squadron commander – properly – when the time is right, and not before,' he said severely, although choosing his words with care.

'Yes, sir,' Kirby said. He stood up, and came to attention. 'Thank you, sir.'

'One moment,' Air Vice Marshal Farleigh said. The system he lived and breathed by called for a dressing down here and now, in front of Norgate, for Norgate's benefit, even if a mild one. 'Your name has come to my attention more than once, Squadron Leader. You have an excellent record, and I'm glad to have had an opportunity to talk to you, although I wish it had taken place under other circumstances. There is a right and a wrong way to do things, and you've chosen the wrong way. You have a fine commanding officer, who has done a first-class job in bringing the squadron to a peak of readiness. I would have expected you to know that he would deal with your forebodings in his own good time.'

Wing Commander Norgate stared straight ahead, his face expressionless. David Kirby wondered for a fleeting moment if there was not a certain degree of irony in the AOC's words, if the crinkled gaze directed at him did not contain some knowing amusement. If so, it vanished, and became intent and serious.

'A great deal depends on 545 Squadron, Kirby,' Air Vice Marshal Farleigh said. 'Good luck.'

'Thank you, sir,' Kirby said. 'And if we do go . . . well, we'll all do our best.'

'I know you will,' the AOC said quietly.

Kirby about turned and walked to the door. The AOC watched him in silence until the door had closed behind him.

'Quite wrong of him, of course,' he said. 'Still, I think he's got the right stuff in him, even if he did jump the gun. A promising young officer, I feel. You made a good choice in selecting him as a flight commander.'

'Thank you, sir,' Wing Commander Norgate said.

The AOC rubbed his cheek reflectively.

'Barry,' he said, 'it's not for me to tell you how to manage your squadron, but I would like you to clear up this business at once.'

'I will, sir,' Wing Commander Norgate said.

'Good,' Air Vice Marshal Farleigh said. 'I suggest you run over all those points raised by Squadron Leader Kirby with the whole squadron. Tomorrow, I think, don't you?'

'Yes, sir,' said Wing Commander Norgate.

'Quite easy for a man with your powers of persuasion,' the AOC said dryly, 'to put them all in the right frame of mind. However, if after that you still detect any undue worry, kindly let me know at once.'

'Of course, sir,' Wing Commander Norgate said.

'Otherwise,' Air Vice Marshal Farleigh said with abrupt and bleak finality, 'I am finished with this matter.'

Secretly, Norgate would gladly have throttled David Kirby, very slowly, and with the utmost pleasure.

But Wing Commander Norgate was a realist. His personal feelings about Kirby were profoundly unimportant, compared with the clear, if superficially tactful, signal which he had received from his air officer commanding, in whose eyes

Norgate had made a mistake. Certainly it was through Kirby that the AOC had formed this opinion, and Norgate spent a few vindictive moments brooding on the fact, but not very many. That young man's turn would come in due course, Wing Commander Norgate would ensure that. He savoured the thought briefly, and then dismissed it in favour of what mattered, behaving as his AOC had indicated he should.

The crews of 545 Squadron listened to the address which they received from their CO, and despite his stiff, stilted, awkward delivery, they were impressed and heartened.

Norgate could, and did, get through to his men when he made the effort even if, in his heart of hearts, he regarded it as an exercise for weaklings, not fighting men. Even so, the look of resolve which began to harden the faces of the young air crews sitting before him induced a feeling of distinct gratification.

There was more than a little of the actor in Wing Commander Norgate, and if this was what the AOC wanted then by God he could do it as well or better than the next man. His performance grew in stature as he went along. By the time he said, 'Any questions, chaps?', they were ready to follow him anywhere.

Ready, if not precisely eager. There was another side to the coin which they did not fail to perceive. Massive diversionary raids, all the care and precautions were, indeed, reassuring in the extreme. They also indicated what a spectacularly dangerous operation it would be, should anything go wrong. But Norgate had, belatedly, done his job. He left them steeled and keyed up, grimly accepting the absolute necessity of all their special training.

Two days later, on Thursday evening, it was announced that seventy-two hours' leave had been granted. Woodley Common was no longer sealed off. Some of the ground staff would commence their leave on Friday, the remainder, including the air crews, at 12.00 on Saturday.

There was only one explanation for this relaxation of all the tight security. The operation had been called off. The crews of 545 Squadron received the news with no regrets. The Officers'

Mess and the Sergeants' Mess were cheerful places Friday evening.

'Who wants to be a fucking hero?' Warrant Officer Ferris enquired, which accurately summed up the general mood. It was all over. Back to normal. Kirby thought about his two remaining operations when he returned from his seventy-two hours' leave with the calm confidence of a man contemplating the routine. A couple of familiar night ops seemed nothing, not any more, not compared with the risks he would have faced, along with the rest of the squadron, had the special operation gone ahead.

At 07.30 the following morning, Kirby was shaken awake by his batman with a cup of tea.

'Put it down,' Kirby mumbled drowsily.

'Briefing at 11.00 hours, sir,' the batman said.

'What?' Kirby rolled over, and stared up at the airman. 'We're due to go on seventy-two hours' leave.'

'Everyone's confined to camp again, sir,' the batman said. 'All crews to assemble for briefing at 11.00 hours.'

Chapter Seventeen

Perhaps the Spitfires which flew high over Germany and France collecting meteorological information had recorded unexpected changes in weather patterns and the operation had been hurriedly reinstated. Or perhaps some over inventive fool in Air Staff Plans had come up with the idea of a phoney 72-hour leave to distract attention from the final preparations in case any faint whiff of its possibility had somehow leaked out. The crews of 545 Squadron did not know which. All they knew was that they were going.

Briefing took much longer than usual. When they emerged from the briefing room the mood was one of grim determination. Now they understood the full reason for all those weeks of preparation, and why this particular target was so important. Something which might have a direct bearing on the invasion of Europe itself . . . that was worth doing. There were no more doubts, no remaining reservations. They had been trained to get there, and get there they would.

Out on the airfield, the modified Lancasters were being fuelled and bombed up. The crews made their final preparations. Alan Russell and the other navigators had the most to do. They were not to fly straight across France. Their track was to be a series of apparently erratic dog legs, designed to avoid defended and heavily populated areas, and Luftwaffe fighter bases.

Wing Commander Norgate would lead the formation, but the squadron would not follow him 'blind'. The navigators in all aircraft would map read individually and maintain their own plots. The leader might be shot down. If Norgate was lost, Squadron Leader Kirby would take over the lead. If Kirby was shot down, Squadron Leader Lucas . . . and so on. The formation would close up, and continue towards its target.

Map reading was not easy at very low level. The navigators would fly beside the pilots instead of in their usual compartments, from which they could see little or nothing. The bomb aimers would assist with the map reading. After take off, the flight engineers would travel in the navigators' compartments, available for any tasks which might arise until they were required up front again.

Under no circumstances were aircraft to become detached from the formation, or make separate attacks. They carried plenty of fuel, even for such a long sortie. They listened to and absorbed all the meticulous planning and information, and gained heart as it became clear that the painful lessons of Augsberg had been learned. The wireless operators would be able to receive coded morse messages from Group Headquarters, which might convey further information, or different orders, but between the aircraft of the formation there was to be absolute radio silence to avoid betraying their presence to German listening posts. There would be no R/T exchanges until they were over the target when it would no longer matter. Until then, communication would be by Aldis lamp, morse signals flashed and received by the wireless operator/air gunners from their mid upper turrets.

Kirby snatched a few hurried moments to write in his log book. Avro Lancaster R6248 Self Crew War Ops – Ascheraden.

He gazed at the few words for a brief moment, and wondered how the remainder of the entry would read. Or indeed, if he would ever open his log book to make it. Then he returned the log book to its rack, and hurried back to the figure of Alan Russell, bent with his navigational instruments over a series of maps and charts.

Take off was timed for 16.00 hours. Transport dropped the crew of K – King off beside their waiting Lancaster. Overhead, two thousand feet above them, was an unbroken sheet of cloud. The overcast extended across the English Channel, and over most of France, where it was expected to be lower, with outbreaks of rain limiting visibility to a few miles. Over Germany, however, the forecast was for broken cumulus cloud, allowing accurate visual bombing by formations of the United States Eighth Air Force, while in the mountains of southern Germany, visibility was expected to be good, with little or no cloud over the target of Ascheraden. Such was the combination of weather conditions for which Air Vice Marshal Farleigh had been waiting.

It was time to climb on board and start the engines. Ferris was scanning the airfield, his forehead knotted in a frown. His eyes travelled around the perimeter track, and rested on the humped Nissen huts of the distant WAAF quarters, half concealed in a clump of trees.

'Where's Kay, skipper?' he asked.

'Yes.' Arthur Wood glanced at his watch. 'Cutting it a bit fine, isn't she?'

David Kirby had known that this moment would inevitably arrive.

'She went on leave last night,' he said, offhandedly.

Five pairs of serious eyes were focused on him. Len Bellamy, who had been a little distance away, moved closer, in case he had misheard.

'You mean she doesn't even know? She won't be here?'

'I was supposed to meet her in London an hour ago,' Kirby said.

None of them said anything, but their faces were eloquent enough. Twenty-eight times Kay Dunn had been there to watch them take off. Twenty-eight times she had been waiting for them to come back – and they had. Now, on their twenty-ninth and most difficult and dangerous operation, she was not there. And, immediately, they were convinced that this time they would not come back.

It might be irrational and silly, mere superstition, but it was how they felt. The belief was etched in the tiny lines around eyes and mouths.

'Well, that's it then,' Ted Hollis said.

Kirby said, 'When I don't turn up, she'll guess what's

happened. She'll be thinking of us, just the same as if she was here. The odds are she'll come back. She'll want to be at the end of the runway as usual when we come in to land tonight.'

'That's right,' Ferris said, with false heartiness. 'Comes to the same thing, really. Doesn't make any difference.'

'Be funny though,' Ted Hollis said. 'Not seeing her here.'

Whether the grave nods from the others were in agreement with Ferris or Ted Hollis, Kirby could not tell. Either way, it did not matter. Ferris himself did not believe in his own optimistic assertion, that was patently obvious, much less the others.

They had to be shaken out of it. Brooding over the inner conviction that this was a sign from some implacable fate that their luck had run out was not the mood in which he wanted the crew of K – King to take off.

'Now listen you lot,' he said, his face as hard as his voice, 'it doesn't mean a thing. There's nobody pulling any bloody strings. We've made our own luck. We've always got back in one piece because we're a damn good crew. The rest is all crap. I know it, and so do you. It's like a baby getting used to a bloody dummy. Some time, he's got to do without it. Well, now we fly without it, for Christ's sake, so I don't want to hear any more about where Kay Dunn is, because it doesn't matter a sod. Come on. Let's get going. And I'm coming back in one piece. You bastards can please yourselves.'

Kirby heaved himself on board K – King. His crew followed, a little sheepishly, but in a better frame of mind, he could tell that. Len Bellamy responded crisply, as Kirby snapped his way through the all too familiar starting procedure. Another part of David Kirby found time to wonder why, if he had spoken the truth as he lambasted his crew, he had taken the trouble to make that hurried initial entry in his log book, even though he had known then that Kay Dunn would not be seeing them off. A last despairing appeal to the gods for mercy?

Very soon, Squadron Leader David Kirby, DFC, would be too busy for any such thoughts. But as he awaited his turn to take off, something told him, as surely as if he were a seer who possessed the gift of prophecy, that K – King was doomed.

The spell had been broken. They would not be coming in to land at Woodley Common that night.

K – King received the green. Kirby inched the throttles open.

'Pilot to crew, stand by for take off. Flight Engineer, follow me on the throttles.'

The heavily laden Lancaster used up nearly all the runway before it finally gained sufficient speed to drag itself reluctantly into the air. By then, Kirby's premonition had left him. Thereafter, concentrating as he was on flying and the task before him, it did not recur until the very last moments.

The squadron moved, with the practised skill they had acquired, into close formation, flew low over southern England, and dropped down almost to sea level as they left the coast behind them. Fifty feet below, the grey waters of the English Channel heaved monotonously as they thundered along.

Somewhere above that blanket of low cloud and to either side of their track, lost in the increasingly poor visibility, were the several hundred aircraft from Fighter Command which had been, and still were, carrying out extended sweeps and intensive strafing of coastal positions. 545 Squadron saw none of them, but the fighters had done their job. The squadron crossed the French coast without incident, apparently undetected, and turned at once on to the first of the many dog legs before them.

545 Squadron roared deeper into France, and deeper. Whoever had painstakingly worked out their track had earned his pay, and more. They flew low across fields and woods, lifted over rolling hills, followed gentle valleys, but only now and then did they glimpse so much as a village to port or starboard, and there was not a sign of the Luftwaffe. The only opposition came from a couple of startled small columns of German vehicles on the move. Harmless bursts of small-arms fire were directed at them as the squadron roared close overhead – but then they were gone.

Their presence would be reported of course, but by the time those reports got through they would be many miles away, following yet another of those deceptive seemingly random dog legs. France was a big country, much bigger, more widely spread than England with far more open countryside, but even so, the way this ingeniously winding track had been worked out . . . it was bloody marvellous. If it went on like this, it would be a doddle!

They penetrated further and further south. It could have been a training exercise. Confidence grew by the minute, confidence in themselves, in the squadron, in their authoritative leader, in the success of the operation.

Kirby could feel the adrenaline racing, his optimism rising, and little of that was due to the benzedrine tablet he had swallowed before take off. Like the others, he was riding high on his own skill, the squadron's unopposed progress across enemy territory. Early days yet, of course . . . less than halfway there . . . just the same . . . Christ, they were going to make it . . .!

Three benzedrine tablets had been issued to each crew member on this occasion in view of the lengthy flying time involved. Kirby thought about taking the second one, with the easy calm of a man wondering whether to have another piece of chocolate, and decided to postpone it for a while. Perhaps in about half an hour . . . yes, that would be about right. The third, he would swallow as they approached the target. That should gear him up nicely for the long haul back under cover of darkness, when fatigue would be an additional enemy. He remembered how much he had enjoyed low flying across the peaceful, deserted Ozarks of Arkansas. Up to now, it was no worse than that . . . it was practically fun . . .

At Group Headquarters, Air Vice Marshal Farleigh had access to much information which 545 Squadron did not have. Air Commodore Whiting was beside him. They sat on a raised dais, overlooking an improvised plotting table on which the progress of the operation was being recorded.

An overhead electric clock indicated the time. A WAAF plotter, working in shirtsleeves, spoke quietly into her headset now and then, and moved counters with a long, wooden rake.

Occasionally, telephones rang, and one of the other officers watching the proceedings answered. Message slips were written out. One or two were considered important enough to reach the AOC.

The counters indicating the strafing British fighters had long since been withdrawn. 545 Squadron was a single counter which was moved steadily along its laid down track at its predicted ground speed. To the east, counters of a different colour indicated the American Flying Fortress formations. Others showed the estimated strength, as reported by the Fortress crews, of the German fighters, Focke Wulf 190s and Messerschmitt 109s, which were engaging the American bombers in mid-air battles.

A brigadier from the United States Eighth Air Force was also there. He watched the AOC's face as a message slip reached him. Air Vice Marshal Farleigh glanced at it, caught the brigadier's eye, and returned his expressionless gaze to the plotting table below, directing it at 545 Squadron's estimated position.

Air Commodore Whiting had made deep inroads into the packet of cigarettes beside him. He took another and lit it with a gold lighter, a gift from his wife. He inhaled deeply, and looked sideways at his AOC. For a moment, he was tempted to speak, but he held his tongue. Air Vice Marshal Farleigh could see what was going on for himself. It was too soon yet.

545 Squadron crossed the loop of a small river, and banked in gentle unison, turning on to the next dog leg.

'Navigator to Pilot.' Alan Russell's voice crackled in Kirby's earphones. 'We're dead on track, but that forecast wind was miles out. It's shifting and strengthening as we go along. I've checked the drift three times on the bomb sight.' They were contour flying. Alan Russell could identify their position, but since they were not steering steady courses, accurate dead reckoning navigation did not apply. 'I have an estimate of the new wind speed and direction coming up, but it'll only be approximate.'

Kirby lifted his own folded map, glanced at it, and shot a

look at the face of his watch on the inside of his left wrist, his eyes constantly aware of the formation around him. He settled back, relaxed, almost cheerful as he made his rough mental calculations. More good news coming up. The fates were on their side after all.

Leading Aircraftwoman Kay Dunn had met three trains at Liverpool Street Station before, her heart bumping apprehensively, she had telephoned her friend Janet at Woodley Common.

Running to the booking office, she had bought a ticket, and then just missed the train she wanted. Unable to face waiting for the next, she had caught the first one which would do, a stopping train to Bishops Stortford. From Stortford she could get a taxi – 'Dear God, let there be a taxi there.' She would only just have enough money, but that did not matter. Nothing mattered but getting back to Woodley Common. If only she had not decided to go and see her parents, if only she had waited for David Kirby . . . she would have known . . . she would have been there . . .

She sat in the dirty, uncomfortable carriage as the slow train huffed and squeaked on its leisurely way.

Leading Aircraftwoman Kay Dunn blinked several times and stared out of the grime-encrusted window. She was silently praying, 'Please God' . . . 'please God' . . . 'please God' . . . over and over again. 'Please God . . .'

More counters were moved on the plotting table, another message slip passed to the AOC. Air Commodore Whiting resisted the temptation to light another cigarette, and fiddled with his lighter instead.

Air Vice Marshal Farleigh folded his arms. He seemed not to be looking at his senior air staff officer.

'Well, John?' he enquired. 'You seem to be anxious to say something.'

'I don't think there's anything to be gained from waiting any longer, sir,' Air Commodore Whiting said. 'The weather over Germany isn't what we expected. We can't alter that.'

Instead of the anticipated cumulus cloud, two groups of Flying Fortresses had encountered dense banks of cumulonimbus cloud, 'thunder cloud'.

The hammer-headed cumulonimbus rose to over thirty thousand feet, well above the laden Fortresses' ceiling. They could not fly over it, and they dare not attempt to fly through it. The vertical up and down currents inside cumulonimbus clouds could be so terrifyingly fierce, rising to over one hundred miles an hour, that they would not only break up any formation, but the bombers themselves, too. The two groups of Flying Fortresses had been obliged to turn back, well short of their respective primary targets. They had reported little fighter opposition.

'As far as we know, the weather over Ascheraden is still suitable,' Air Vice Marshal Farleigh said.

His SASO well knew what his role in life was, in these circumstances, and he played it.

Air Commodore Whiting said, 'The two Fortress groups which have turned back were designed to draw enemy fighters away from 545 along the southerly part of their route. Those fighters will also have turned back. They may not even have been committed. We've no way of knowing, but there's been less than expected fighter opposition . . .'

'I know that, John,' the AOC said.

'The final decision is yours, of course, sir,' Air Commodore Whiting said. 'But I feel it should be borne in mind that, if 545 Squadron continue, are intercepted, and suffer heavy losses, we'll have lost any chance to try again. They are the only squadron trained for this task.'

'There may be very little time left to try again,' the AOC objected. 'All the signs are that D-Day can't be long delayed now.'

'We can only guess about that, sir, but my own is in about two weeks or so,' Air Commodore Whiting said, softly. 'The right weather conditions may recur during that period, in which case we'd be ready. The other factor which exercises me is that the deeper 545 are allowed to penetrate, the greater the possibility that the Germans may deduce what their target is.

If they're recalled too late, we risk giving away our intentions. I do feel, sir, that the decision should not be left any longer.'

'I'm sure your advice is sound, as always, John,' Air Vice Marshal Farleigh said. 'I'm reluctar.t though, I must say. So near, and yet so far.' He stared down at the quietly efficient scene, the counters on the plotting table, the WAAF and the group of officers. In his mind, he saw 545 Squadron roaring low across France, he visualized the actions German Fighter ground controllers would be taking, the instructions Luftwaffe fighter pilots might be receiving. Air Vice Marshal Farleigh took in a deep breath, and let it out. 'However, I'm sure you're right, John,' he said. 'You never know. We might get another bite at the cherry. Very well. Send the signal.'

Arthur Wood deciphered the coded morse message.

'Wireless Operator to Pilot. It's the recall signal.'

Kirby was leading the second vic of Lancasters, in position behind L – London. He waited for the flickering Aldis lamp from Norgate's mid upper turret to confirm the recall signal, for one wing of Norgate's aircraft to dip slightly as it entered the gentle bank which would take the formation through 180 degrees on to a reciprocal course.

L – London flew on steadily, straight and level, as though nothing had happened. The waiting was only measured in seconds, but it seemed endless.

'Pilot to Mid Upper. Perhaps his wireless is on the blink. Query if he's received the recall signal.'

Ferris sat in his turret, the French countryside streaming backwards, close beneath him. Not for a second did he stop searching the low cloud above in case a fighter should descend through it, the vague, misty semi circle around them, thicker in some places where showers of rain were falling. Such conditions comprised a shelter for the squadron on an operation like this, but Ferris was not sorry they had been recalled. Flying by daylight like this still seemed unnatural. He preferred the darkness, when his abnormally acute night vision would usually give him a moment's edge over any incoming enemy aircraft.

Kirby had spent many hours at his Initial Training Wing learning to read morse code signals from an Aldis lamp, but like the other pilots, navigators and bomb aimers, he had only been required to reach the basic standard of six words per minute. The rapid flicker from Norgate's mid upper turret was much too fast for him to decipher.

'Mid Upper to Pilot,' Arthur Wood said. 'Message from L – London reads, "Recall signal not applicable due to changed circumstances. Hold present course." '

Wing Commander Norgate had decided to ignore the recall signal. Kirby saw the Aldis lamp in front, angled now, as it repeated the message to Lancasters on either side of him. Probably every aircraft in the squadron had flashed the same query.

'Now he thinks he's bloody Nelson,' Warrant Officer Ferris thought rebelliously. He flicked his intercom switch. 'Rear Gunner to Pilot. What the hell's going on?'

'Pilot to Rear Gunner. We've been experiencing a different wind. Not a head wind as forecast, but right up our tails. We must be eighty miles further on than Group imagine. They won't know that.'

'Rear Gunner to Pilot. We can't know why Group's fucking recalled us, either.'

As the commander on the spot, Wing Commander Norgate was entitled to disregard the recall signal, provided new and unforeseen factors had emerged of which his air officer commanding was unaware. There was a weighty condition. Subsequent events had to prove him right. If he was wrong, he would be finished.

'Pilot to crew,' Kirby said. 'The CO has every right to use his own judgement. In his place, I think I'd have done the same thing.'

Air Vice Marshal Farleigh was waiting for the recall signal to be acknowledged by L – London. Plotting continued. The Fortress formations were returning to the UK but until the awaited brief coded morse reply was received, the counter symbolizing 545 Squadron was not yet being moved in the generally northerly direction, along the different series of dog legs which had been laid down at briefing, to be followed in the event of a recall which necessitated a homeward flight in daylight.

The American brigadier had lit a cigar, and was thoughtfully surveying the counters indicating his Fortresses. All their targets had been worthwhile, aimed at disrupting German internal communications as a prelude to the rapidly approaching D-Day. The two groups forced back by cumulonimbus cloud had bombed secondary targets instead, which had formed part of *their* briefing. It had been a good day's work, even if the primary objective had not been achieved. He was wondering now what the final losses would be. Assuming that 545 Squadron got back more or less in one piece, he supposed they would have to do it all again if they were lucky enough to get another weather forecast which would contain all the necessary components. It was getting a bit late in the year for such another piece of good fortune, but they could only hope for the best. The American brigadier thought of the raids planned for the US Eighth Air Force in support of the Allied armies once a bridgehead had been established, and shifted uneasily as he contemplated what Me 262s could do to Flying Fortresses and Liberators.

How many of those god-damned jet fighters did the Germans have up their sleeves – just waiting to unleash them?

Air Vice Marshal Farleigh had asked for and received coffee and sandwiches. An immense effort had been mounted to enable just one squadron of Lancasters to reach its target. The AOC silently cursed those unexpected Cunimbs which had necessitated recalling 545 Squadron, but he did not regret his decision. He was very well aware that this operation had gone up to Cabinet level before it had finally been authorized. Far better to be obliged to account for a delay than a potential disaster, a waste of massive resources and a specially trained squadron. Wing Commander Norgate might have come up with the original conception, but Air Vice Marshal Farleigh had become its proponent. The can was firmly attached to him now, not Wing Commander Norgate.

Much better for 545 to try again, given the right weather. Air Vice Marshal Farleigh stared at the electric clock, blind to what it was saying. Had they overlooked some other possibility? Was there some different permutation of weather conditions more likely to occur at this time of year which would suit the respective air forces of both allies, and enable them to commit 545 Squadron against the valley of Ascheraden once again?

The face of the clock moved into focus. The AOC felt all his muscles become tense. Why the delay? Why no acknowledgement?

It *must* have been received. The wireless on one aircraft might be U/S, but not on board sixteen. There must be some other explanation, and Air Vice Marshal Farleigh did not like the one which occurred to him.

He thought again about those cumulonimbus clouds, which could have caused a gigantic line squall, which in turn would bring about a dramatic wind shift. Was that it? Because of that, did Norgate intend to . . .? Air Vice Marshal Farleigh ordered the recall signal to be repeated.

'Navigator to Pilot,' Alan Russell said sharply. 'We should have turned forty degrees starboard on crossing that railway line.'

Ahead, L – London flew straight on, its wings parallel to the ground. Kirby waited until it was plain that Wing Commander Norgate had no intention of altering course.

'Pilot to Mid Upper. Signal that we should have changed course.'

The rapid exchange of messages by Aldis lamp took place.

'Mid Upper to Pilot, message from L – London reads, "Dog leg cancelled. Follow me on present course. Will resume laid down track later".'

'Oh, shit,' Warrant Officer Ferris muttered to himself. 'Now what, for Christ's sake?' Ferris did not like all this. Ferris was used to flying as a member of one crew in one aircraft when there were occasions when *he*, in effect, assumed command.

'Rear Gunner to Pilot, Me 110 coming in. Corkscrew

starboard!' And the skipper bloody did as he was told and unhesitatingly corkscrewed starboard, no messing, pronto. This time, they were in the hands of some other bugger who was going his own sweet way and all they could do was follow. Ferris chafed restlessly. He did not like all this at all. Glumly, never ceasing his scan for enemy aircraft, Ferris popped his second benzedrine tablet into his mouth.

In L – London, there had been a difference of opinion, curtly ended.

'Pilot to Navigator, I intend to omit this dog leg, and fly straight on.'

'Navigator to Pilot.' It was the squadron navigation leader who was sitting beside Norgate on this occasion. 'Briefing was specific. Under no circumstances are we to depart from the laid down track.'

'Pilot to Navigator.' Wing Commander Norgate's tone was clipped and decisive. 'Those German ground units will have reported our presence long ago, but we've gained a lot of time, due to the change of wind. I want to capitalize on that. If we leave out the next dog leg, we'll be nearly an hour ahead. The sooner we reach the cover of hills and mountains, the better.'

'Navigator to Pilot, our original track was designed to avoid opposition. Flying straight on is a considerable risk.'

'Pilot to Navigator,' Wing Commander Norgate said. 'I've given you my orders.'

Wing Commander Norgate had not replied to the repeated recall signal, nor its successors. There was no point. He knew what he was doing. When they got back, the target successfully destroyed, his actions would be approved and applauded.

Kirby glanced at his map, his eye traversing the features which lay ahead until they rejoined the briefed track. Soon after that, they would make their turn which would take them around the border of Switzerland. Their new course would not take them near any towns. Norgate was extremely experienced, and certainly no fool. Kirby could guess what his CO had in mind. Reaching the cover of high, broken ground, and getting to the target as quickly as possible. It was one of those chances a daring leader might take. If it came off, it was a brilliant decision . . .

'Mid Upper to Pilot. Three Focke Wulf 190s about four miles at three o'clock, low. Must be an airfield there. Two on finals, one on its cross-wind leg. I don't think they've seen us.'

Kirby glanced sideways quickly. He was only just able to pick out the two fighters coming in to land, floating, dark shapes under the dull overcast. The third, the one on its cross-wind leg, was a silhouette against the cloud, but it was heading away from them.

In front, L – London was descending. Kirby and the remainder of the formation followed. Norgate had seen the enemy aircraft too. He led 545 Squadron down until they were practically skimming the tree-tops, aiming to keep the camouflaged Lancasters – from the Germans' point of view – against a background of rolling countryside of fields and woods, hoping to avoid the formation being silhouetted against the overcast should any hostile eyes chance to glance in their direction.

As far as Kirby had been able to make out, the airfield was of grass, with no runways. He took another quick look. The two leading Focke Wulfs were approaching the perimeter fence, undercarriages still down. He could see a few huts scattered about, but no large buildings. Probably some newly established base, as yet unmarked on RAF maps. There seemed to be no other aircraft on the ground.

'Go on you bastards, land,' he thought. 'Land!' The third Focke Wulf was turning on to its final approach.

Instinctively, Kirby shrank down in his seat, hunching his shoulders, as though by so doing he could hide himself from those formidable aircraft, the best propeller-driven, single-engined German fighter in service. The formation was still thundering on, apparently unnoticed. The airfield was slipping behind them. The long mass of Kirby's port wing obscured it now, and he could no longer see it. Dear God, perhaps they were going to get away with it . . .

'Rear Gunner to Pilot, two Focke Wulfs overshooting.'

Ferris watched the two ominous shapes as the pilots gave

their engines full throttle and, instead of landing, flew parallel
to the ground and a few feet above it. He saw their wheels rise
and slip back into their wings.

Leutnant Guenther Wolf and his wing man Oberfeldwebel
Hermann Weigand had been scrambled with the remainder of
the newly arrived squadron but had failed to make contact
with the Fortress formation towards which they were directed
by Ground Control. Adverse weather, it seemed, had forced
the Fortresses to turn back.

Leutnant Guenther Wolf had not seen the Lancaster formation, but Flying Control had radioed its presence as he was
about to commence holding off. Leutnant Wolf concentrated
on making a smooth, safe overshoot in the heavy fighter with
its high wing loading, as soon as the staccato voice crackled in
his earphones. He knew without checking that Hermann
would be doing the same. Wolf trusted his wing man implicitly,
with good reason. Leutnant Wolf and Oberfeldwebel Weigand
were veterans of the daylight air war against the Americans.
Between them, they had twenty-nine confirmed kills, nineteen
Flying Fortresses and ten Liberators.

What the devil Lancasters were doing so far south and in
broad daylight, Leutnant Wolf had no idea, but it would be a
pleasure to deal with a few Lancasters instead of a Fortress
formation, with its massed banks of long range .5 machine-
guns.

Leutnant Wolf had been in training when Augsberg took
place, but he knew all about the losses which the anti-aircraft
guns and a few fighters had inflicted on those twelve Lancasters. One would have thought the British would have known
better after that.

Undercarriage up, gaining speed nicely. Leutnant Wolf
checked his fuel, put his Focke Wulf into a gentle climbing
turn to starboard, and looked for the Lancaster formation. It
took him a few seconds to locate it. The Lancasters were well
camouflaged, and were hugging the ground, almost invisible.
Only the movement of the aircraft against the ground below
gave them away at this distance.

Leutnant Wolf put his Focke Wulf into a lazy turn, confident that his wing man would be there, in position, following, a manoeuvre which would take him behind and across the formation, while he studied it before deciding on his method of attack. Automatically, he had already scanned the sky in search of any accompanying fighter escorts, unlikely though that would be at this distance from England. There were none. He was just able to count the Lancasters now. Sixteen of them. A squadron.

Feldwebel Freidrick Gottschalk, the pilot of the third Focke Wulf 190, had been on local flying. He had just been posted to the squadron on completion of his flying training, and had yet to fly on operations.

Feldwebel Gottschalk had not seen the Lancasters, but he heard the snapped report from Control on his R/T. He saw the two Focke Wulfs ahead overshoot and climb away. Feldwebel Gottschalk abandoned his approach, and followed. He was just twenty years old. He had been introduced to Leutnant Wolf and Oberfeldwebel Weigand, and had found himself shyly tongue-tied. He regarded the two men, with their impressive string of kills, with something akin to hero worship, and yearned to be like them.

Feldwebel Gottschalk's heart was pounding madly, but it was an agreeable sensation. He was in a state of high excitement. Chance had benevolently offered him his first kill on a plate. Perhaps more than one! The Lancasters had no answer to his powerful cannons, which were fully loaded. Even during his advanced training on Arado 98s, that aircraft's two forward firing machine-guns had always been loaded and ready for use when flying. Unlike the RAF, the Luftwaffe had to make do without the benefit of an Empire Air Training scheme where pilots learned to fly far from the war. The Luftwaffe's training was always liable to be interrupted by hostile action.

Feldwebel Gottschalk searched anxiously, and for some time in vain, for the reported Lancaster formation. When he finally glimpsed the squadron he could hardly believe his luck.

The planes were to his half left, out of range, but in a perfect position for him to turn in on that diving curve of pursuit which he had practised so assiduously at flying school.

Feldwebel Gottschalk banked his Focke Wulf steeply, pushed the nose down, and gave her full power.

'Rear Gunner to Mid Upper,' Ferris said. 'Focke Wulf coming in forty-five degrees starboard.'

'Mid Upper, got him,' Arthur Wood said. He aligned the sights of his .5 machine-guns on the enemy fighter, growing in size as it swooped towards the formation, and waited until it came within range.

Leutnant Guenther Wolf, as soon as he was close enough, had immediately recognized the significance of the unusual mid upper turrets with which the Lancasters were equipped. Followed by his wing man, he crossed behind the squadron's path, making sure they remained out of range of those heavy .5 machine-guns, turned until he was flying parallel with the formation, and eased his throttle wide open to overtake it. This would have to be a head-on attack.

From the corner of his eye, he caught sight of another Focke Wulf which was diving towards the Lancasters as though there were no danger.

The damned fool! The stupid idiot!

Feldwebel Gottschalk was closing on the formation fast on his precise curve of pursuit. Carefully co-ordinating aileron and rudder so that his aircraft did not skid, he eased the nose round, and watched his illuminated gunsight as it traversed the formation until it was aimed ahead of the leading aircraft. Allowing for the relative speed of his cannon shells and the target, it was his object to hit the Lancaster he had picked out in the middle of the formation, and then pull on his stick and turn away before he was within range of the defensive .303 machine-guns. He knew that his deflection was good . . . no, it was perfect . . .

Feldwebel Gottschalk heard the first words of Leutnant

Wolf's barked, urgent warning just as he pressed the firing button.

Feldwebel Gottschalk achieved his first kill and died at the same moment.

Arthur Wood opened fire in unison with the fifteen other mid upper gunners. The Focke Wulf exploded in mid-air like a bomb going off.

Warrant Officer Ferris could only watch impotently, and take no part.

Then he saw that the Lancaster immediately behind had been hit, and was falling back. Its two inner engines were on fire. Trailing flames from both engines, it finally stalled into a clump of trees. Trees and aircraft vanished in a gigantic explosion as its 8,000lb bomb went off. Ferris flicked his intercom switch.

'Rear Gunner to Pilot, J – Johnny's gone. What's happened to the other two Focke Wulfs?'

'Pilot to Rear Gunner.' So Wilf Tully and his crew had bought it. 'They're staying out of range, and overtaking us.'

Old hands then. Buggers used to screaming towards formations of Flying Fortresses. Ferris's spine was prickling. His back was towards where the action would be. There was nothing he could do save perhaps catch a glimpse of one of them as it belted overhead, and loose off a futile burst after it. What a hope! Still, if anything happened to K – King he would only be aware of it for a few seconds at most before the explosion took him into eternity. But there was no consolation in that. If he was going to get his, Ferris would rather see it coming. He touched the hard shape of the cigarette case in the breast pocket of his battledress for luck. The one which his girlfriend, now his wife, had given him.

The remaining fifteen aircraft of 545 Squadron had changed formation fractionally. They were now slightly stepped to give the mid upper gunners a clear field of fire against fighters making head-on attacks.

The two Focke Wulfs would be obliged to fly several miles

ahead of them before being able to make their turn on to a course which would enable them to intercept.

Kirby watched them as they drew ahead, turned into dots, and then vanished from sight. At the same moment, L – London's port wing dipped as Wing Commander Norgate led the formation into a turn. He was hoping that the two Focke Wulfs would either miss the formation completely on its new course, or expose themselves to the .5s as they adjusted their line of attack at the last moment.

Kirby saw the two dots as they reappeared. They had climbed until they were just underneath the cloud base. They were some distance to starboard, thanks to Norgate's manoeuvre, but evidently not taken by surprise, the bastards. Kirby saw them execute a smooth S turn which brought them head on to the squadron, and the shapes grew larger with startling speed.

There was nothing Kirby nor any of the other pilots could do but stay tucked into close formation and rely on the gunners. But the two Focke Wulfs were coming in on a shallow dive, throttles wide open. With the formation and the fighters flying directly towards each other, the closing speed was nearly six hundred miles an hour, close to the speed of sound at ground level.

Kirby watched the shapes grow larger, he saw the winking flames as their cannons fired, he flinched instinctively as it appeared that they must crash head-on into the formation – and then they were gone.

It was more miles before Leutnant Wolf and Oberfeldwebel Weigand were able to complete their turns and begin to overtake the formation again. Guenther Wolf glanced at his fuel gauges with some anxiety. He thought there was enough left for one more pass.

He was pleased to note that the first one had been as effective as he had hoped. He flew past a roaring furnace of fire and billowing smoke which had once been a Lancaster.

Another Lancaster had dropped back behind the formation, pluming smoke. Leutnant Wolf wondered if it needed finishing off, but even as he considered the idea the bomber's port wing erupted into a sea of flames. That one was finished too. Leutnant Wolf flew straight on, his wing man in position. With any luck, they could bag one more each.

Thirteen aircraft of 545 Squadron closed formation, filling the gaps. The two experienced Focke Wulf pilots repeated their head-on attack.

This time there was only one evident result. The subsequent German combat report read, 'the bomber reared suddenly, almost like some creature in agony, stalled, plunged into the ground, and exploded.'

Arthur Wood and the other mid upper gunners fired continuously during those all too few seconds while the Focke Wulfs were within range, and before they had gone.

'Mid Upper to Pilot, one of them's hit. Smoke coming from his engine, but no flames.'

'Burn you bastard, burn,' Warrant Officer Ferris breathed.

Chapter Eighteen

Leutnant Wolf and Oberfeldwebel Weigand switched roles. Wolf was now the wing man, shepherding his companion back towards the airfield, anxiously watching the thin stream of black smoke, alert for the first trace of flames.

Oberfeldwebel Weigand was reluctant to bale out. He had throttled back as far as he dared, but while his engine was missing ominously now and then, it picked up almost immediately each time, enabling him to maintain a safe if slow flying speed. The cylinder head temperature was rising, but had not yet reached danger point. Oil pressure had dropped but seemed to have stabilized. He told Leutnant Wolf on his R/T that he thought he could nurse his aircraft back home. Just the same, he opened his canopy in readiness, in case he did have to jump.

It was ironic that he should have sustained damage during an attack on such a relatively small formation. But there had only been the two of them, the sky had not been full of hurtling fighters to confuse and disperse the gunners' fire, as it was when several squadrons carried out their attacks on massed American formations. Also, hugging the ground as they were, the Lancasters had limited the Focke Wulfs' freedom of manoeuvre. They had been forced to pull up and pass over the squadron, providing the gunners in those mid upper turrets a few extra moments' firing time.

It was extremely annoying though, to have been hit during an engagement with what should have been easy targets, and Oberfeldwebel Hermann Weigand was not anxious to compound his misfortune by abandoning his

Focke Wulf unless he really had to. If he could get his faithful, familiar machine down in one piece, the engine could be changed in no time. Oil pressure was dropping again though, if slowly, and the temperature rising, but the airfield was coming up. Oberfeldwebel Weigand decided to come in high, switch off his engine, and make a glide approach and landing. He lowered his undercarriage, and felt the 'clunk' as the wheels locked into position.

Leutnant Guenther Wolf circled slowly overhead, and watched helplessly. He saw the propeller of Weigand's aircraft slow until it was windmilling gently. At the same time, he saw the first streaks of flame emerging from the cowling. He saw the flames grow, licking back towards the cockpit as Weigand held off, searching for the grass with his wheels. He saw the wheels touch and, as the Focke Wulf slowed down, rolling across the grass with agonizing deliberation, he saw but could not hear the 'whoosh' as the remaining fuel and petrol vapour in the tanks exploded. He saw the figure of a man jump from his cockpit, run for a few yards, and fall to the ground. The man was enveloped in a sheet of flame.

Leutnant Guenther Wolf circled the airfield, landed, taxied to dispersal, and switched off. Fire tenders surrounded the burning Focke Wulf. A few yards away a heap of foam had extinguished the flames which had embraced Oberfeldwebel Hermann Weigand. Men were dragging something black along the grass, a charred and unrecognizable object.

There was a foul taste in Leutnant Guenther Wolf's mouth. Hermann Weigand had not only been his wing man, they had become as close as brothers, closer.

Ground staff were already refuelling and re-arming his Focke Wulf, and Leutnant Wolf walked away towards the hastily erected hut which served as a crew room. During the engagement, he had heard Ground Control divert the remainder of the returning squadron, somewhere above the overcast, in search of the Lancaster formation. But they would be running low on fuel, and would be able to spend little time on the hunt before turning back. The Lancasters were flying away from the airfield, and would certainly have changed course by now to avoid detection.

Leutnant Wolf doubted if they would find the Lancasters, but at least the entire area was now on the alert. He wondered what the eventual British target was. Toulons perhaps? Did they intend to bomb the powerful French fleet lying at anchor in the harbour there? Was that it?

He entered the crew room, and began to write out his combat report. One thing was certain. Wherever those Lancasters were heading, they had to come back again.

Squadron Leader Lucas did not know what had struck his starboard outer propeller. His aircraft had sustained no discernible damage otherwise. Possibly flying debris from the Lancaster in front, as it had fallen back after being hit, perhaps a stray cannon shell which had failed to explode. He could not account for it, but the fact remained that the shimmering disc was no longer 'clean' and even. It appeared to have an ominous bulge in it, and the engine was running roughly.

Squadron Leader Lucas did his best to continue. With the aircraft beginning to vibrate, he reduced power on the defective engine and increased it on the other three, but it soon became apparent that the condition was worsening. The whole starboard wing was visually taking up the vibrations. If he went on like this, that lousy prop would tear the engine from its mountings.

Lucas feathered his starboard outer propeller, and began to drop back behind the formation. The Aldis lamp flickered from L – London: 'Good luck.'

Ferris watched as Lucas began a slow and careful turn on to his new course.

There was an emergency plan for a failure at this stage, and Lucas would divert, either to Southern Italy, Malta, or North Africa. Ferris guessed that he would try for Malta, but he did not much fancy Lucas's chances, alone, on three engines. And at some point, poor old Jack Lucas would have to climb, still in daylight, in order to jettison his bomb load.

Eleven aircraft of 545 Squadron droned on in close formation. They skirted Switzerland, and began to cross the Black Forest, flying in the troughs of unending tree-clad valleys. The cloud was starting to break up, as predicted. Far ahead, were occasional shafts of sunlight. Eleven aircraft flew on, unopposed, left the Black Forest behind, and began to work their way through the mountains of Southern Bavaria, leading towards Austria.

Spirits, depressed by the certain loss of four aircraft and the twenty-four men they had contained, together with Lucas's unlikely chance of surviving, slowly began to lift again. The most anxious scrutiny of the clearing skies failed to reveal any Luftwaffe fighters. The Germans had lost them. They did not know where 545 was, and had not deduced their destination. If it went on like this, by Christ they were going to get there! They were going to make it!

The overcast had vanished, and been replaced by high, broken cloud. Above the distant mountain peaks before them were blue skies. As they passed over a particular road bridge spanning a gorge, thirty minutes' flying time short of the target, Wing Commander Norgate led his formation into a slow climb. By now, they had burned off approaching half their initial fuel, but they had set off with much more petrol than usual and, with bombs aboard as yet, the Lancasters were still heavily laden. The climb was deliberate and laborious. As he retrimmed the aircraft for its climb, Kirby remembered his third benzedrine tablet, and took it.

Ten thousand feet above the valley of Ascheraden meant that they would be flying at some thirteen thousand feet above sea level. The crews clipped their masks into place, and began breathing oxygen.

The formation levelled off at bombing height. From L – London's mid upper turret, the Aldis lamp flashed its signal. The formation widened, drifted apart, and reformed into a well spaced out line astern, one of the frequently rehearsed manoeuvres. They would not bomb as a squadron, releasing their bombs when Norgate's aircraft did, 'follow my leader'. Each Lancaster was responsible for the accurate aiming of its own modified 8,000lb bomb.

Alan Russell assured Kirby that they were precisely on track but, as he looked down at the jagged peaks rising from the maze of valleys below, Kirby could not help wondering whether they would be able to find and identify the heavily camouflaged valley of Ascheraden now that they must be practically within sight of it. From this height, everything down there looked much the same. Perhaps they had already overflown it.

Far ahead now, Wing Commander Norgate's aircraft banked into its final turn, and on to the bombing run. One after another, the following Lancasters also turned, maintaining position relative to the aircraft ahead.

There was no mistake in navigation or final identification. Had there been any doubt about the position of the valley of Ascheraden, the abrupt eruption of exploding anti-aircraft shells would have dispelled it.

Kirby watched the ferocious, sudden barrage, appalled. They had been warned that the valley would be heavily defended, but none of them had expected this. How many guns did the Germans have down there for God's sake?

'Turning on target . . . running up . . . bomb doors open . . .'

Kirby caught sight of Norgate's aircraft, miraculously unscathed. He saw the great bomb leave the bomb bay, and angle into its downward path. The next second, his view was obscured as the Lancaster behind L – London turned into a giant fireball. Oh, Christ . . . was that Roy Harrison . . .?

He could not tell. Due to the aircraft which were missing from the formation, the bombing order on the run up had changed. No time to think about that now . . .

'Right, right, steady . . . left, steady . . . steady . . . steady . . .'

Exploding flashes all around them, the stench from the billowing smoke . . .

'Bomb gone.' Ted Hollis, unruffled as ever.

K – King shuddered. They had been hit. Still flying normally though. Engines OK.

'Bomb doors closed.'

Kirby pushed the control column forward and went into the controlled, diving turn, practised so frequently. Astonishingly, they had survived that awful barrage. He glimpsed a Lancaster to his right with only half a wing. It keeled over, and entered into a stately spin.

Kirby caught up with Wing Commander Norgate, as he had done many times over the mountains of Wales. Other Lancasters overtook until the formation was complete. Arthur Wood reported that it comprised eight aircraft.

Roy Harrison was one of them though. Kirby saw him quite clearly as Roy moved past and into position. Kirby gave him a relieved thumbs up, and received the same signal in reply.

The remnant of the squadron had levelled off. Norgate led them in a wide sweeping turn, ready for the final dive into the valley of Ascheraden to release their liquefied petroleum jelly bombs, and burn what was left. Norgate's master stroke. He flew as calmly, as ice coolly, as if this were just another practice sortie over Wales, as if they did not have to enter that valley again, the valley of Ascheraden, and his surviving crews followed, clinging to his aircraft, flying with the same precision.

Many minutes passed before the complicated aerial manoeuvre was complete and they were heading back towards the valley, now at a much lower level. This time, there was no doubt about where the valley of Ascheraden was. A great cloud of black smoke was mushrooming from it.

Wing Commander Norgate remembered his words to Air Vice Marshal Farleigh. 'They won't know what's hit them.' He visualized the terrible confusion, the panic which must be reigning under that evil pall of smoke. On this final bombing run, the anti-aircraft gunners would neither be able to get a clear sight of them, nor bring their guns to bear.

Mountain peaks now either side of him, Wing Commander Norgate eased his control column forward and led his formation on that dive into the valley itself, to release their remaining bombs, the ones which would burn and obliterate whatever was left.

The formation was much looser than on their outward flight across France, close enough to deliver an almost simultaneous paralysing punch, far enough apart to avoid the risk of mid-air collision as they flew across the top and partly through that billowing mushroom of black smoke and dust, and also so as to present a scattered target to such small-arms fire as numbed surviving enemy soldiers might be in any condition to direct at them.

What eight aircraft of 545 Squadron encountered was not random bursts of small-arms fire. As they dived into the valley of Ascheraden towards the smoke, Kirby saw, as did the others, the multiple flashes from seemingly countless points on either side of the valley to the right and left of them, indicating something which had not formed part of their briefing, something which Intelligence had not known.

Christ, they've got gun emplacements on the mountain sides . . . rapid firing cannon and heavy machine-guns . . . we're flying straight into their bloody gun muzzles . . .!

Eight aircraft of 545 Squadron flew into the terrifying gauntlet of cannon fire. On board the Lancasters, the gunners blazed away, guns chattering continuously, in an effort to distract the German gunners.

Fire erupted and swept back from two of Roy Harrison's engines. Steadily, his aircraft flew straight on. A cluster of bombs curled from its bomb bay. Then his Lancaster exploded in mid-air, a ball of fire.

There was nothing to be seen of the ground below. All they could do was bomb the smoke.

'Bombs gone.'

K – King juddered, hit again. Tracer was curling at them from all sides. Kirby pulled his goggles down over his eyes, shoved the control column forward, and deliberately flew into the black pall just below. He coughed and retched and tears streamed from his eyes as the stinking smoke entered the Lancaster, but at least the gunners could no longer see them. It was better than those murderous cannon shells and tracer bullets.

The smoke had penetrated his goggles, and he pushed them up on to his flying helmet again and wiped his eyes continually, straining to perceive the instruments on which he was flying during his blind progress. He prayed that his last visual recollection had been accurate, that he was flying towards the broad gap which formed an exit from the valley, and not the side of a mountain.

Abruptly, they were flying in clear air, blue skies and sunshine above, the smoke behind them. Kirby wiped his eyes again, momentarily dazzled by the bright light, and searched for any other survivors.

There were two aircraft straggling ahead . . . no, three. A fourth was disappearing into a different valley, whether having turned into the wrong one or crippled, he could not tell. Kirby opened his throttles to catch up with the three aircraft ahead, and called for a damage report.

K – King was badly hit. There was a gash fifteen feet long in the fuselage to the rear of the navigator's compartment. The port inner engine was not running smoothly. Arthur Wood did not answer.

Kirby told Alan Russell to see what had happened to Arthur Wood. He needed Len Bellamy beside him. Keeping that port inner engine going was the important thing for the time being.

Alan Russell felt vomit rise into his throat. With an effort, he swallowed it. Arthur Wood's face was parchment white. His eyes were standing out. His face was contorted, his mouth open wide, lips drawn back, teeth showing. Alan Russell was glad that he could hear nothing above the thunder of engines. Arthur Wood, perched in his cramped gun turret, was screaming in agony.

'Flight Engineer to Pilot, it could be just an occasional blockage in the fuel line. It might work itself out.'

The port inner's rev counter was flickering now and then, but the temperature and oil pressure gauges read normal. Kirby eased back the throttle lever controlling the port inner engine a little, and the flickering stopped. He made up the small loss of power by advancing the other three throttles, and retrimmed to counterbalance the slight tendency of the aircraft to turn as a result.

He needed as much power as he could get in order to catch up with the three aircraft in front, which had now joined up in formation. Once K – King was tucked in behind, he could reduce power, nurse his port inner along even more gently. Kirby had no desire to straggle along on his own. Darkness was some considerable way off yet. The Germans would know all about where 545 Squadron had been now, and the Luftwaffe was quite capable of working out possible return routes. Four aircraft might stand a chance. For a moment, he wondered which ones were formating either side of Wing Commander Norgate. Then he wondered why he should assume that it was Wing Commander Norgate who was leading them. Something, however, told him that it was. That man would always come through. It would be the VC for Wing Commander Norgate all right.

The three aircraft in front were drawing closer. Norgate must have reduced speed to allow him to overtake. What in God's name was taking Alan Russell so long?

Kirby tucked in behind the low flying V formation. He glanced at the aircraft identification letters. Don Shepherd was on Norgate's starboard wing. Warrant Officer Douglas Boyce was on his port. And it was indeed Wing Commander Norgate in the lead.

'Navigator to Pilot, the mid upper turret's a mess, flak damage everywhere. Arthur was in awful pain. I've given him morphine.'

'Pilot to Navigator, do you need a hand to get him out?'

Len Bellamy would take over the mid upper turret. Kirby wanted K – King to be fully defended.

'Navigator to Pilot, the turret's no use. The rotating mechanism's jammed. I've tried it.'

Alan Russell, still shocked, gazed up at the figure of Arthur Wood, hunched behind his guns, the muzzles of which were pointing up at the sky.

'Navigator to Pilot,' he said shakily 'I can't see where he's been wounded, but it's bad, and at least he's a bit quieter now. We'd have to pull him about to release him and . . . perhaps we should leave him where he is, for a while.'

'Pilot to Navigator, I want him out now. Make him as comfortable as possible behind the main spar, parachute on. Flight Engineer, you help and then keep an eye on Arthur. If the morphine wears off give him some more, but don't overdo it. Just enough so that he's not in too much pain. I don't want him to pass out completely.'

Kirby was trying to think ahead, and assess possible contingencies. Once night fell, the small formation would be able to break up, climb into the blessed cover of darkness, and return individually. But even then, there would still be a long way to go. If they were lucky enough to make it that far, they could still get unlucky and encounter night fighter opposition. He could rely on Ron Ferris, but even Ron was not a miracle man. If they were hit again, K – King could surely not absorb much more punishment. Kirby might be obliged to order his crew to bale out, and if so he wanted Arthur Wood out of his turret, chest parachute clipped on, and conscious enough to pull his ripcord.

Skimming the trees, the four Lancasters recrossed the Black Forest where they left the dangerously clear skies behind. As they reached and began to fly beneath the blanket of low cloud, it was nearly as comforting as crawling into a warm bed on a cold night. Invisible on German radar, they were now shielded from visual detection by any Luftwaffe fighters flying above the overcast. As the unseen sun slowly descended, visibility at ground level was decreasing. In patches, it was already little more than two or three miles. Map reading became increasingly difficult, but Alan Russell, who was now beside Kirby, confirmed that Wing Commander Norgate was leading them along precisely the right track laid down for that section of their return flight, which it had been anticipated would be carried out in daylight.

The four aircraft skirted Switzerland once more, and crossed back into France. But now they were paying the price for the change in wind which had enabled them to arrive over the target early. By now, it should have been night, they should have been able to climb up through the cloud layer into relative safety. But it was not, and they could not. Beneath the overcast, it was becoming decidedly murky, but above the sheltering cloud it would be much brighter. For some time yet, they must continue to hug the ground.

And, for nearly an hour, K – King's port inner engine had been playing up more and more.

It was now certain that the variations in revs had been due to something considerably more serious than any temporary blockage in a fuel line. Somewhere under the engine casing, a bullet or shell fragment must have penetrated.

Kirby adjusted his throttles, trying to take the strain off the defective engine, but the time came when, in order to remain in station, he was using undue power on the remaining three, and when he cautiously inched the port inner throttle lever a fraction wider open, the engine banged and backfired unpleasantly.

The engine temperature was no longer normal. It had been slowly rising for some time, as Kirby flicked anxious glances at it, and was now approaching danger point. The oil pressure needle too was moving, falling very slowly, but steadily.

Arthur Wood seemed to be reasonably comfortable, and Kirby had told Len Bellamy to come up front. In his heart, he already knew what Len would say.

'Flight Engineer to Pilot, it's too risky to keep it going.'

'Pilot to Flight Engineer, we only need another half an hour, perhaps less, before it's safe to climb. We can shut it down then.'

From the mid upper turret of L – London in front, came the flicker of the Aldis lamp directed at K – King, uncannily bright in the gathering gloom, much too fast for any of them but Arthur Wood to read.

'Oh, Christ,' Kirby muttered irritably to himself. 'Pilot to Bomb Aimer, ask L – London to repeat the message, and slowly this time.'

Ted Hollis had been armed with the Aldis lamp in his front turret. When the reply came, it was deliberate enough for Kirby to read for himself.

'K – King, you are falling behind. Stay in formation.'

It was only a matter of yards, but Norgate's alert crew had noticed and reported the fact to him.

Kirby took one more look at his engine instruments, but it was useless, and he knew it. His ears told him without the instruments. His port inner was no longer giving forth a steady or even an unsteady beat. It sounded as though it was grinding itself to pieces.

'Flight Engineer to Pilot, much longer and she'll seize up and catch fire.'

'Pilot to Bomb Aimer,' Kirby said. 'Inform L – London I am feathering port inner.'

Ted Hollis clicked the trigger of the Aldis lamp methodically. There was a delay before the reply came. To his left, the unnerving racket came to an end. The port inner propeller stopped spinning, and assumed a stationary, upright position. The three aircraft in front began to draw away.

Wing Commander Norgate sat for a few moments, skilful hands and feet automatically guiding L – London, as the aircraft thundered low across trees and fields. Practised eyes assessed the cloud above, turning black now, the diminishing area of dim daylight ahead. For a matter of seconds, he was tempted, but all his instincts rejected the notion. Reluctantly, he instructed his wireless operator/mid upper gunner what to say.

Kirby translated the signal as it flashed from the receding Lancaster.

'Dark soon. Good luck. See you back home. Well done.'

Kirby watched the three bombers as they drew away, further and further towards the tantalizing gloom ahead where cloud merged into the ground. He estimated that they were about a mile and a half away, perhaps less, when he could no longer pick them out, and they had vanished from sight. K – King was on its own.

Not long left, though. Fifteen or twenty minutes at most. K – King was flying more slowly, but quite comfortably. She was perfectly capable of climbing, minus her bomb load, to ten or twelve thousand feet as soon as it was safe to do so. Fuel was no problem. Soon . . . not long . . .

Perversely though, they appeared to be flying towards a slightly lighter, rather than a darker, area of ground. Oh, God. Was that bloody overcast breaking up?

Kirby had no quarrel with Wing Commander Norgate's decision to leave him behind. For K – King to remain in station, the formation would have been forced to slow down considerably. There could be no question of risking three aircraft and their crews in order to protect one. And the whole formation would have been that much more vulnerable. There was no place in war for any such foolish bravado.

All of Wing Commander Norgate's decisions had been correct today, save one. That one, which would have been an act of cool daring had it succeeded, had proved to be a costly mistake, and led to a useless waste of men and machines. It had meant that only eleven aircraft of 545 Squadron arrived over the valley of Ascheraden, instead of sixteen.

Kirby lifted K – King over a gentle, rolling fold in the ground. It was definitely a little lighter, not much, but a little. He could see where the thinning layer of cloud was breaking up. Still, nightfall would take care of that. Only an extra few minutes . . .

Kirby spared a thought for Arthur Wood. He recalled the single occasion when he had met Georgina, over a meal in a Chelmsford hotel, the open, simple adoration in Arthur's eyes as he looked at his girl. Well, although he was seriously wounded, he was still conscious according to Len Bellamy. Kirby hoped that was a good sign. Within a few hours, Arthur would be safe in hospital. They'd look after him there, fix him up. One thing, Arthur Wood would almost certainly not have to fly any more. No more crying behind a newspaper for Arthur. No more heaving his guts up on the grass after they had landed.

It occurred to Kirby that *his* tour was not over. This was only his twenty-ninth. He still had one more to go.

'Rear Gunner to Pilot, two Me 109s crossing our track . . . I don't think they've . . . no. They're turning towards us. They've seen us.'

Chapter Nineteen

Ice chilled Kirby's spine. His hands controlled K – King unthinkingly, as if he were momentarily mesmerized. Mid upper turret out of action. Only Ferris's four .303s against the cannons of the fast, manoeuvrable Me 109s. This was it. They were done for.

'. . . hang on . . .' There was puzzlement in Ferris's voice. '. . . they're going bloody slow for 109s . . . they're not! . . . they're Arado 98s . . . and the silly buggers want to have a crack at us . . .' He was positively gleeful. 'Just keep flying straight and level. Keep her steady.'

Arado 98s were dual control advanced trainers, which rather resembled Messerschmitt 109s in appearance. In the dull, uncertain, fading light, Ferris had, for a moment, seen what he was afraid of seeing.

He was no longer afraid. He sat in his turret and watched them. The corners of his lips were lifted in a smile of pleasurable anticipation.

Two student pilots from some *Fliegerschule*. Probably taken off for a stint of night flying. Saw a Lanc on three engines, and thought they'd make a name for themselves. What? With two piddling little machine-guns each? Stupid sods, Ferris thought, contemptuously. 'They're even too fucking green to come in from different angles. Look at them. Following each other. Queueing up for it. Should still be in bleeding nappies, both of them.'

His gunsight was aligned on the leading Arado 98. When its size in the sight indicated that it was within range, Ferris opened fire. His four machine-guns hammered in unison.

The nineteen-year-old Luftwaffe student pilot lived just long enough to realize that his flying controls were no longer functioning. A second later his aircraft flew into the ground and exploded.

The second trainer veered away sharply, and fled in alarm. Ferris eased his turret round, and sent a long looping burst after it. Missed. The second Arado 98 had been out of effective range, but Ferris was disappointed. 'They'll never believe this,' he thought. An Arado 98. It would be a good joke in the mess. Most of the silly buggers were too ignorant even to know what an Arado 98 was, much less what it looked like. Ferris was proud of his aircraft recognition. He studied books of aircraft silhouettes for pleasure.

Hauptmann Rolf Meuller had been air testing his Junkers 88, when he saw an explosion in the gathering dusk, and flew over to investigate. He circled the burning wreckage. Certainly that of a small aircraft, but he could not tell which type. He was easing out of his turn when he fancied that, curiously, he had glimpsed something moving across a field some distance away. He turned again, towards the point where he thought he had seen this odd phenomenon, or possibly optical illusion.

Hauptmann Meuller had seen many Lancaster bombers, as well as Halifaxes and Stirlings, although until now by moonlight or as dark shapes in the night sky, before he added, or failed to add, one more to his tally of kills.

Hauptmann Meuller was the commanding officer of his squadron, a man who had flown Junkers 88s through the many modifications of that versatile aircraft. He had flown the bomber version in support of the German armies when they invaded Russia in June 1941. Later, when Bomber Command's assault on Germany gathered strength, he had converted on to the night fighter variety, still, at that time, a 'clean' aircraft.

Now, his Junkers 88 sprouted aerials and antennae from its nose, tacked on like the afterthoughts they were, to serve all the radar equipment. The protrusions interfered with the Ju 88's flying characteristics. It was not an easy aircraft to handle, although Hauptmann Meuller no longer noticed. To him, it was second nature. His Junkers carried powerful forward firing cannons as well as machine-guns in the turret behind his cockpit. Hauptmann Rolf Meuller was credited with nineteen confirmed kills.

As soon as he identified the moving object as a camouflaged Lancaster hugging the ground, he had noted the idle engine. He had also registered the unusual mid upper turret, and the two .5 machine-guns.

Hauptmann Meuller was cautious as well as experienced, which was probably why he was still alive. The night air war was a deadly one on both sides. Luftwaffe night fighter casualties were high. Rolf Meuller had lost count of the number of times he had taken off to play his part in the defence of German cities against the British bombers. The one he was looking at though would never bomb Germany again. Hauptmann Rolf Meuller would make certain of that.

Warrant Officer Ferris had reported the Junkers 88 as soon as it had appeared over the burning wreckage. He was still watching it, his turret and guns aimed futilely at the Ju 88, well beyond the range of his .303s.

'Rear Gunner to Pilot, this one's an old hand. He's holding off out of my range, and sizing us up.'

Frustration born of fury and despair knotted Kirby's stomach in spasms. Against the cannons of a Junkers 88, K – King was a mere sitting duck. Darkness was falling like a slow curtain around them, but there was still sufficient light for the Junkers to hold off, out of range of Ferris's .303s and fire those cannons with impunity whenever he chose. Another five minutes, and they would have been safe. Just five minutes . . . perhaps even less . . . between two and three hundred seconds, no more . . . if they could only survive for a mere two or three hundred seconds . . . then he could use the darkness of night to lose the Junkers 88 which Ferris could see behind them, and Kirby could not . . .

He eased the control column forward, and took the Lancaster even closer to the ground hurtling underneath him only a few feet below. All he could do was make the German's target as difficult as possible for him, and ensure that K – King was never silhouetted against the slightly lighter overcast above. On three engines, K – King was flying at 145mph indicated air speed. She was still capable of evasive action. With all that additional gear tacked on its nose, the Junkers 88 was not an especially manoeuvrable aircraft. Playing for time measured only in seconds, they still stood a chance, if a thin one.

'Pilot to Rear Gunner, I'm going to try and use this failing light to lose him, when he attacks.'

'Rear Gunner to Pilot, understood.'

No one better than Ron Ferris to rely on. Their lives had rested on Ferris's acute judgement, his eyes, his hands often enough before now.

Hauptmann Rolf Mueller had completed his examination of the Lancaster. There was a gash several metres long on one side of the fuselage. There was no gunner in the mid upper turret with its .5s, which in any event his cannons outgunned. The bomber was hugging the ground, almost clipping occasional tree-tops.

Hauptmann Meuller adjusted his throttles and, as he moved into range, lowered the nose of his Junkers 88 and aligned his gun sight on the Lancaster.

'Rear Gunner to Pilot, corkscrew starboard!'

Instantly, Kirby pulled up K – King's nose. He was flying so low that had he not done so his starboard wing would have struck the ground. At the same moment he flung the aircraft into a steep, banking turn.

Kirby had been continuously assessing the features racing towards him, ready to use whatever was available to left or right while, neck prickling, he awaited Ferris's barked command.

His turn took K – King round and behind a low hill which was topped by a clump of trees. As he straightened out, he heard Ferris open fire.

Hauptmann Meuller found his cannons firing at empty space.

The Lancaster's manoeuvre had caught him unawares. As his Junkers overshot the hill he heard bullets striking his aircraft. But while the British gunner's aim had been good, he had been firing from extreme range, and had also been unlucky. The bullets merely beat a staccato tattoo on the Junkers 88's armour plating and bounced off.

Hauptmann Meuller turned starboard as steeply as he dared, and searched the ground over which the Lancaster should be flying. There was no sign of it.

'Navigator to Pilot, try and keep flying in a generally northerly direction as much as possible.'

'Pilot to Navigator, let's lose this bastard first. Just keep track of where we are the best you can.'

'Rear Gunner to Pilot, he's picked us up again. He's turning.'

Arthur Wood was propped against the main spar, aware of the weight of his chest parachute, and also that the morphine was rapidly wearing off.

His intercom was plugged in, he heard the exchanges, he knew what was going on. After the rattle of gunfire from the rear turret, he had felt K – King bank steeply again and yet again as the skipper tried to elude the Junkers 88, to fly a course which the hunting German aircraft would not expect or detect.

Sweat was running down Arthur Wood's face. His teeth were clamped tight. The unbearable pain was building and intensifying remorselessly. His head rolled like a pendulum from side to side, and he began to moan in agony, 'Oh, Jesus . . . oh, please Jesus . . . no . . . no . . . dear, sweet Jesus, please . . .'

'Rear Gunner to Pilot, he's coming in again. Be ready.'

Arthur Wood left his intercom switch off. He could not plead for more morphine, not now, not yet. Arthur Wood gave himself up to an eternity of unending, excruciating torment in a private, personal hell of his own.

'Rear Gunner to Pilot, corkscrew port!'

*

This time Hauptmann Rolf Meuller was ready, but just the same the Lancaster's evasive action was so sudden that his answering turn was a fraction late, and again his cannon shells were off target and exploded in a field, so many firecrackers.

It was now clear to him what his quarry was trying to achieve, and in the gathering gloom, Hauptmann Mueller realized, the contest was not as uneven as it had initially appeared.

On this occasion, however, he had not overshot. He completed the turn which would bring him nicely on to the bomber's tail, and stared at the French countryside ahead of him in disbelief. The Lancaster had disappeared. Such a thing was impossible. But it had. The four-engined bomber was nowhere to be seen.

'Rear Gunner to Pilot, bloody marvellous. He's turning the wrong way. He hasn't got a clue.'

Night was falling fast. Most of those seconds had ticked away. Perhaps the Junkers would give up. K – King was flying so close to the tree-tops that Ferris could see the receding top branches lashing to and fro in the Lancaster's slipstream.

Hauptmann Rolf Meuller had the benefit of other pairs of eyes besides his own. His navigator and his gunner were also searching for the Lancaster which had suddenly become invisible, although it could not be.

It was his gunner who finally saw it. Hauptmann Meuller turned through more than ninety degrees, as directed, although even then it took him several seconds before he was able to pick the bomber out for himself.

His lips moved in a twitch of appreciation which he could not suppress. He knew now how the Lancaster had apparently vanished. Immediately after taking his successful evasive action, the Lancaster pilot had at once turned again, deliberately, to overfly a large wood against which the bomber's camouflage, in this poor light, was nearly perfect.

Hauptmann Meuller's fellow feeling for the RAF was decidedly limited. He had seen too much of what their bombs did, killed too many of them, too many of them had tried to kill him.

Nevertheless, what this fellow was exhibiting was superior flying of a very high order indeed which a pilot as skilled and experienced as Rolf Meuller was obliged to acknowledge and respect. What was more, he could well get away with it. Hauptmann Meuller was very well aware that if the unknown Lancaster pilot could bring off one more successful evasion, the odds in the developing, deepening gloom would swing and be in his favour and not Meuller's.

Rolf Meuller experienced a thrill of pure exhilaration, akin to that of the hunter who finds that his prey is no easy kill but exceptionally wily and cunning with every chance of making its escape.

Ahead, though, Rolf Meuller could see that the wood came to an end, with flat, open country to the right and rising ground to the left. He opened his throttles and altered course slightly, anxious to drive his quarry away from possible cover and towards exposed ground. Controlled excitement coursed through his body. By God, the fellow flying in front of him was an adversary well worthy of the final kill!

'Rear Gunner to Pilot, corkscrew port!'

Kirby reacted immediately. K – King's nose lifted, he banked steeply towards the rising ground. There was only one possible path he could take, short of crashing into a hillside, and he took it.

'Navigator to Pilot!' Alan Russell's voice was agonized. 'You've flown into a valley!'

K – King roared along the floor of the wide, shallow valley. Visibility was now so bad that Kirby could not see when the valley came to an end.

'Rear Gunner to Pilot, he's following us.'

Kirby did not dare to attempt to climb out of the valley. To do so, even if the Lancaster could make it on three engines, would mean losing speed and expose K – King to the Junkers' cannons.

He began to take erratic evasive action, peering ahead, praying for the end of the valley to come into sight.

Hauptmann Rolf Meuller was flying a little higher. He could see that, while the Lancaster had not turned in the direction he had wanted, chance was on his side. The bomber's unpredictable twists and turns still made it a difficult target, but the valley was shaped like an inverted V, and was becoming narrower.

Soon, even though the Lancaster pilot was using all the available width, his wingtips almost brushing the hillsides, its movements were becoming more and more confined as it flew on into the funnel ahead of it.

There was no escape for the bomber now. Tracer erupted from its rear turret, a last despairing attempt by the gunner to distract Meuller, but he was out of range of the Browning .303s which were falling short, harmlessly, and Hauptmann Rolf Meuller ignored them.

His sights were aligned on the Lancaster. A hail of cannon shells struck K – King.

Warrant Officer Ferris was granted his wish. He saw it coming, the flicker of flames from the cannon muzzles, a fraction of a second before one of the first shells penetrated his turret, passed through the cigarette case in his breast pocket and exploded inside his rib cage. The shells blew away half the turret as well as Ferris, and damaged the tail plane.

Squadron Leader David Kirby heard explosions, smelt stinking smoke, saw one engine erupt into flames, knew that his rudder had gone slack, and that K – King was losing flying speed.

In the few seconds which remained, his actions were reflex. Ahead, a few feet below the mortally crippled K – King, the floor of the valley was an uneven field. He throttled back on all three engines, and as K – King shuddered towards its final stall, he heaved the control column back, attempting to achieve as soft a belly landing as possible, his reactions as purely instinctive as those of a driver trying to control a suddenly skidding car.

Hauptmann Rolf Meuller saw his shells strike home. He saw the flames belch from one engine, he saw the Lancaster's final agonized lurches before it belly landed. The aircraft bounced and skidded across a field, flames spreading from the burning engine on to the wing itself. At the far end, the Lancaster crashed into a clump of trees, and exploded in a boiling mass of fire and awful incinerating heat.

Hauptmann Meuller flew over the blazing wreckage, turned, and came back for a second look. What had been a Lancaster bomber was a roaring furnace of flames. Hauptmann Rolf Meuller set course for his base, and radioed the shot down Lancaster's position. A detachment from the Wehrmacht would arrive eventually, and search the fragments, which would still be smouldering hours later. They would be wasting their time. Nothing could survive that terrible holocaust of fire.

Hauptmann Rolf Meuller flew home reflecting that this would take his score of kills up to twenty, which was not only a nice round figure, but the one which would almost certainly ensure his Knight's Cross.

Twenty was the magic number of kills, the point at which a Knight's Cross was pretty well automatic.

Hauptmann Rolf Meuller savoured the thought. He wanted a Knight's Cross. It was a considerable distinction. It meant something.

Chapter Twenty

The Allies had landed in Normandy, and eventually crossed the Rhine. An American advance patrol was cautiously working its way forward as a misty dawn was breaking, when a voice called out in English, and a gaunt figure with cropped hair, clothes ragged and torn, stood up in a patch of long grass, and lifted its hands above its head.

The voice called out in English again, and the American sergeant considered shooting the creature there and then. Tales were circulating about English-speaking Germans who attempted to infiltrate the American lines with suicidal sabotage and assassination in mind.

His carbine trained, the American sergeant's finger caressed the trigger. Maybe, though, someone would want to interrogate the bastard first. He sent the unkempt individual back to the temporary battalion headquarters located in the half-destroyed village from which retreating Germans had been ejected two days earlier. There, the military police found that he wore no dog-tags, pushed him around a bit, and threw him into a cell in the small, one-time German police station, where he continued to protest his unlikely identity with growing hoarseness and profanity.

Forty-eight hours later, an intelligence officer from the Royal Air Force arrived, and was ushered into the cell. The intelligence officer, Flight Lieutenant Brewer, was armed with a good deal of information from Air Ministry in London such as date and place of birth, parents' full names, schools attended, former civilian employment, service postings and so on, which no German impostor could conceivably have known.

Within a few minutes, Flight Lieutenant Brewer had established that the man sitting on the bunk was indeed the person he claimed to be, and when and where his aircraft had been shot down.

'Would you like a cigarette?' Flight Lieutenant Brewer asked, relaxing. He lit it for the man, and noted his torn fingernails, the heavily calloused hands, the dirt deeply ingrained into the skin. 'Keep the packet.' The man broke into a fit of harsh coughing as he inhaled. 'I suppose that's the first one for a long time.'

'Tastes awful. Perhaps I'll give up.'

'Do you want to tell me the rest now? We can leave it for a while, if you'd rather.'

'No, let's get it over with. My first recollection is being in a sort of barn. A French peasant had seen the crash. He found me, "many metres from the burning wreckage," he said, in a clump of bushes. Marcel Fournier his name was. The last thing I remember was the aircraft skidding across a field, and hitting a clump of trees. I can only suppose that the nose came off, and I was thrown clear.'

'Were there any other survivors?'

'No. Monsieur Fournier said that the Germans had combed the wreckage when it cooled down, but there was practically nothing left except chunks of twisted metal. They assumed all the crew were dead. Monsieur Fournier persuaded the local doctor to come and treat me. Most of this they told me later. I don't remember much. I was badly concussed, delirious a lot of the time, dislocated shoulder, fractured tibia, cuts, abrasions, that sort of thing. The doctor wanted to send me to hospital. Apparently, I shouted at him . . . said I didn't want to be handed over to the Germans . . . but I don't remember that. Anyway, he agreed to treat me where I was, in this barn place, as best he could. That was bloody brave of him . . . helping an RAF evader he could have been shot . . . I wish I could remember his name . . .'

'We'll find out. Don't worry about it.'

'Marcel Fournier and his wife too, of course. They were risking the firing squad, hiding me like that.'

'If all this took place in France, how the devil did you end up in Germany?'

'Well, it was a long time before I really knew where I was, began to feel better. By then, the Allies had landed in Normandy . . . I think they'd taken Paris . . . I'm not sure. Then we heard that the Americans had landed in the south of France as well. I could walk all right by then, my schoolboy French had improved a lot, talking to the Fourniers. There were rumours circulating about the Resistance, but the Fourniers had no contact with them. I decided to set off south, either try and fall in with the Maquis, or get to the Americans.'

'Why didn't you just sit tight where you were, and wait?'

'I wish I had now. At the time, I was feeling pretty fit again, no one dreamed that France would be cleared of Germans as quickly as it was. Besides, all the lectures about evasion, getting back to England if at all possible, it gets to be ingrained . . . a sort of conditioned reflex, I suppose. My uniform had been burned, of course. Monsieur Fournier gave me some of his clothes, and more money than he could spare. They lived in poverty by any standards, poor devils.'

'They'll be repaid. We'll see to that.' Flight Lieutenant Brewer was making notes.

'I buried my identity discs. Travelling in civvies, they were no protection. If I got caught I stood to get shot as a spy anyway. Sorry, I keep forgetting who I'm talking to. You know all that better than I do.'

'It's all right. So you started walking. But with no papers presumably?'

'As I've said, the Fourniers didn't have the kind of contacts which could provide false papers, and nor did the doctor. But my French was quite fluent by this time, I reckoned it was good enough to bluff most Germans. I had some yarn ready should I be challenged. For a while, it was easy. Hardly any Germans around at all. I suppose I got a bit over-confident. Started walking by day. Made much better time, no trouble at all. Finally, I was approaching a little market town. It was getting late. I'd run out of food. I had a good look round but there wasn't a German in sight. I decided to buy something to eat in the town, and lie up for the night the other side of it. In the square, everything was so normal, it could have been peace-time. Pavement cafés, men gossiping over bottles of local wine, all that. Next second, before I knew what was going on, three German lorries had blocked the exits from the square, and soldiers had jumped out. They rounded up all the men at gunpoint, me included, and shoved us in the lorries.'

'What were they doing? Taking hostages?'

'That's what it looked like. We drove all night. Didn't stop until it was daylight. We expected to be lined up and shot. But the Germans just told us to relieve ourselves, and then herded us back on board again. My lorry was stinking by that time. Some of them hadn't been able to wait. The Germans wouldn't say what it was all about. Just told us we'd find out when we got there.'

'And where did that prove to be?'

'Germany. The tarpaulins were kept closed. We must have crossed the Rhine but I don't know when. We were handed over to the *Volksturm*, given picks and shovels. From then on, no more lorries. When we weren't digging, we walked.'

'You'd been rounded up for forced labour,' Flight Lieutenant Brewer supposed. 'What were you digging? Gun emplacements? Machine-gun nests?'

'That's right. Dig. Fill sandbags. Heave them into place. Start at dawn, work all day. March on to wherever we were to sleep that night. Usually, locked in barns, or village halls, schools . . . sometimes in the open though. The rations got steadily worse, in the end mouldy bread and a kind of greasy gruel . . . hard to keep the filthy stuff down . . . the guards did a bit better, but not much . . .'

'How did you find the *Volksturm*?'

'What you'd expect. The last dregs the Germans could dig up. A few old reservists but mostly fourteen- or fifteen-year-old boys who got more and more frightened and trigger happy . . . they shot two Frenchmen . . . no, three . . . not the same day, different days . . . they were suposed to be trying to escape . . . I think the poor bastards just had diarrhoea . . . we all did at one time or another . . . the feldwebel in charge was in his fifties. Fought in the Great War. Had the Iron Cross. Until the early nineteen-thirties, he worked on the German railways. A steward in restaurant cars. Then he became superintendent in charge of a block of flats in Hanover. Sort of a caretaker, I suppose.'

'A bit more than that, in all probability,' Flight Lieutenant Brewer observed. 'Most of them were active Nazis. People who kept a close eye on the residents, and reported any so-called subversive attitudes to the Gestapo.'

'That could be. He was a hard-looking bastard. He spoke good French, from his railway days, I imagine. His vocabulary was much better than mine. The French chaps covered up for me, but . . .'

'Yes, I was going to ask you about them.'

'They'd realized from the start that I wasn't French, of course. When they knew I was English, they closed ranks, protected me, spoke up if I didn't know what to say. They were marvellous. But as time went by, this feldwebel always seemed to be looking at me, picking me out to talk to. The time came when I was convinced that he'd guessed, he was having fun, amusing himself, playing a game until he decided to shoot me.'

'I should imagine your appearance was rather different to the others, anyway, complexion, and so on.'

'Exactly. They were nearly all much darker than I am, looked exactly what they were, French countrymen. One day . . . well, only four or five days ago, come to think of it . . . we were marched through a town for the first time. I say a town . . . there was virtually nothing left of it. Bomb craters, burned out shells of houses, piles of rubble everywhere. The feldwebel called a halt. I was looking at the devastation . . . it was incredible. I was bombed during the German Blitz, but it had been nothing like that. Then I saw that people were still living somewhere under the rubble, living there like rats. Gaunt women, old men, skinny, dirty children. There was a standpipe. Perhaps the water was only turned on at a certain time of day. They came crawling out of the rubble with jugs, basins, buckets. Filled them with water. I didn't know what

the place was called. I was wondering whether it was one of
the towns I'd bombed, when the feldwebel came and sat beside
me. He waved at all the rubble, and said *"Die terrorfliegers"*. I
pretended I didn't understand. Then he said, "The terror
fliers. The Royal Air Force. They did this." In English. From
that moment, I knew for certain. I said nothing. He grinned
at me, said, "But you do not understand English, of course",
stood up, and shouted out the order to march on. That night,
we were sleeping in the open. We could hear the sound of
artillery in the distance, see the flashes of the guns in the sky.
The advance was overtaking us. I made up my mind to try
and get away, slip through the German lines, before the
feldwebel got bored with his game, and used that rifle he was
always fiddling with. In the middle of the night, I started to
crawl away on my belly. The guns were still rumbling. Very
slowly, very carefully, I kept going until I knew I was clear of
the guards. Just as I was about to stand up, I heard a click. A
rifle bolt. I looked round, and there was the feldwebel with
one up the spout. He stared at me without saying anything,
his rifle aimed at my guts. I said something like "All right. For
Christ's sake get it over with." He kept on looking at me, and
then he lowered the barrel of his rifle. He said, "OK. Try.
Walk." I could hardly see his face, but I thought he was
smiling that peculiar smile of his. I said, "Why? So that you
can shoot me in the back?" He said, "The shooting is nearly
over. One more dead body, what will that change? Go. Walk."
I turned away and started walking. My legs were shaky. I still
expected him to shoot me. But he didn't. So I owe my life to
him as well, that hard-faced German.'

'What was his name? Do you know?'

'Feldwebel Karl Frenzel. Why?'

'Members of the Nazi Party are being rounded up as we
advance,' Flight Lieutenant Brewer said. 'Your Feldwebel
Frenzel could well find himself in the bag, with some nasty
questions to answer. The forced labour gang, and those Frenchmen killed by the *Voldsturm*, even if nothing else. This might
count in his favour. It might not, either, but I'll pass it on.'

*

Ten days later, a Dakota landed at Woodley Common, taxied
up to the control tower, dropped off one passenger, turned,
and taxied back towards the end of the runway. The remaining
servicemen on board were destined for an aerodrome in
Scotland.

Woodley Common seemed to be uncannily deserted. There
were no Lancasters at dispersal. A Hillman car was approaching, a corporal driver at the wheel. It stopped, and Group
Captain Vesty stepped out.

Squadron Leader Kirby came to attention, and saluted. He
had been issued with battledress uniform at an RAF base. His
face had filled out a little, and his hair was starting to grow
again.

Group Captain Vesty returned the salute and then, smiling
broadly, pumped Kirby's hand warmly.

'Welcome back, David,' he said. 'Good to see you. As you
may gather, Woodley Common's being run down. Let's go to
my office and have a natter, old chap. We all thought you were
dead.'

He guided Kirby towards the waiting car.

'How many made it back, sir?' Kirby asked. An airman had
brought coffee. Group Captain Vesty had listened attentively
while Kirby related how he had survived.

'Five,' the station commander said. 'Squadron Leader Lucas
crash-landed at Malta, though two of his crew were killed.
Wing Commander Norgate, Flight Sergeant Shepherd, Warrant Officer Boyce, all with no casualties. And Flying Officer
O'Connor, who lost you over Ascheraden I believe, he
sustained severe damage on the way back, ditched in the
Channel, and the Air Sea Rescue people picked up him and all
his crew in their dinghy the following morning.'

It must have been Paddy O'Connor whom Kirby had
glimpsed flying along the wrong valley from Ascheraden.

'Wing Commander Norgate got his VC, I suppose?'

Group Captain Vesty said, 'Between ourselves, the AOC
was not well pleased with certain aspects of Wing Commander
Norgate's conduct during the operation.'

'He was right to ignore the recall signal.'

'Possibly,' Group Captain Vesty said. 'But he also ignored strict orders not to deviate from the laid-down track, and lost four aircraft as a result. On the other hand, the final attack was led with great gallantry, which thoroughly merited recognition. Barry Norgate received a bar to his DSO.'

Kirby sipped his coffee. Norgate would not have been pleased about that. A bar to his DSO was not what he had coveted.

'As soon as the AOC heard you were alive,' Group Captain Vesty said, 'he recommended *you* for the DSO, David, most strongly. I think you can take it for granted that you'll get it.'

Kirby stared at him.

'That sounds rather like an oblique slap in the face for Wing Commander Norgate,' he said, slowly. 'Giving one of his flight commanders the same award.'

'Oh, I doubt if such an idea crossed the AOCs mind,' Group Captain Vesty said, innocently. 'You deserve it. That's what counts.'

'Where is he now? Commanding a station?'

Group Captain Vesty shook his head.

'545 Squadron was never reconstituted. The surviving crews were posted elsewhere. Wing Commander Norgate had made it known that he was anxious to apply for a permanent commission later on. He was sent to the Staff College.'

'He'll get one then,' Kirby said. 'Open Sesame, after that. The sky's the limit.'

Group Captain Vesty pursed his lips thoughtfully for a moment. 'As one of my old boys, David, I know you'll respect a confidence. Yes, the Staff College is for officers thought to be potentially capable of achieving high rank in due course. Wing Commander Norgate didn't fail – that would be most unusual – but while he's a first-class squadron pilot, when it comes to command he has certain weaknesses. I understand that, when he finished the Staff Course, his assessment wasn't too promising. I doubt if he'll be refused a permanent commission but in the peace-time air force he'd drop in rank – we all shall – probably to flight lieutenant. Personally, I wouldn't expect him to rise higher than squadron leader before he retired. I think *you* might do very much better, David.'

'Me, sir?' Kirby queried blankly. He was thrown.

'You've had a good war. A young squadron leader with the DSO and the DFC, you could have a bright future as a regular officer. Haven't you considered it?'

'No, not really, sir,' Kirby said.

'Well, give it some thought. You'll have plenty of time. You'll be going on a thoroughly well deserved long leave.'

'I suppose that old Ford's not still around? The one Roy Harrison and I shared?'

'The car was disposed of, along with the rest of your personal effects, by the Board of Adjustment, when you were posted presumed killed. The proceeds from the car were divided between your respective next of kin. Mrs Harrison had a son, by the way.'

'Roy was certain it would be a boy,' Kirby said.

'If you want some transport to get you to the station and so on, pop down to M/T, and get yourself a car and driver. I'll give them a call, tell them you're coming.'

'Thank you, sir,' Kirby said. He was thinking again, as he often did, of the barrage over the valley, of the final dive into that smoking hell when Roy Harrison's aircraft had caught fire and exploded. 'I'm told that no Me 262s were encountered during the invasion,' he said. 'At least we clobbered Ascheraden.'

'Photo reconnaissance revealed heavy damage,' Group Captain Vesty said. 'But I'm afraid that wasn't the reason for the absence of Me 262s over the battlefield.'

'We must have had something to do with it,' Kirby said.

'In the last few weeks, a number of high-ranking Luftwaffe officers have been captured and interrogated,' Group Captain Vesty said. 'Their various accounts concerning the Me 262 tally. Hitler was obsessed with attack at all costs. The defensive concept was alien to him. He had intervened personally, and ordered the immediate conversion of all Messerschmitt 262s from fighters into bombers. Such a modification takes time. The Luftwaffe had lost its jet fighters. They'd been grounded.'

Kirby stared at the station commander for several seconds, and then laughed out loud.

'So a squadron was wiped out . . .' He tried to stifle his unnatural laughter. '. . . for nothing. Hitler had already done the job for us.'

'We weren't to know that at the time, David,' Group Captain Vesty said, gently.

Kirby made some enquiries when he left Group Captain Vesty's office, but Leading Aircraftwoman Kay Dunn had been posted, the clerk knew not where. The records had been packed into tea chests.

Kirby sent a telegram to his mother. She had already been informed that he was alive after all, as soon as Flight Lieutenant Brewer had confirmed Kirby's identity.

He was shocked by his mother's appearance. She smiled, and even hugged him fiercely, while she blinked back the tears she never ever shed, but she had turned into an old woman. Hers had not been a good war, whatever that might be.

Then she set to busily, unpacking for him, attending to the meal which was cooking, fussing generally, refusing to allow him to do anything for himself.

Kirby was still not accustomed to the taste of palatable food, and he ate hungrily, while she watched him with a pleased smile. Apropos of nothing at all, she said, 'Why didn't you ever tell me about Kay Dunn?'

Kirby had been reflecting on the virtues of an early night. Surprise dispersed his incipient tiredness.

'How do you know about Kay?' He had never mentioned her name to his mother as far as he could recollect.

He listened, and learned that Kay had written to Mrs Kirby when he was first posted missing, affirming that she was sure David was still alive, a letter full of hope and encouragement.

Later, when he was presumed killed, Kay had visited his mother several times.

'. . . I don't know how I'd have got through without her . . . I just wanted to die . . . she was heartbroken too, but we sat talking about you for hours and hours, and she'd tell me all the things you'd done together, and even made me smile again . . .' Kirby wondered if Kay had really told his mother all the things they had done together. '. . . Such a warm-hearted girl . . . I really came to love her . . . this is a letter I had from her a while ago . . . read it . . .'

Kirby took the letter. He found the concern and care for his mother which it contained inexpressibly moving.

The Recruiting Office in Dorset Street was still in business. Men were registering for their call up. A flight sergeant, his gleaming boots and buttons an ornament to any parade ground, snapped to attention.

'I'm on leave, Flight,' Kirby said. 'I have to telephone RAF Oakington, at once, if you please.'

'Certainly, sir. Use the phone in this office. I'll have you put through at once, sir.'

Kirby held on until he received a reply from the station switchboard, and asked for the parachute section. When he was connected, he said, 'LACW Kay Dunn, please.'

'Who wants her?' The man's voice at the other end was surly.

'Squadron Leader Kirby. Who the devil might you be?'

'Hold on, sir.' The voice was hurried and no longer surly. 'Won't keep you a moment, sir.'

Kirby could hear voices in the background, a man's and a girl's. He could not quite make out what was being said, but there seemed to be some sort of disagreement going on. Finally, the man must have moved closer to the receiver, and Kirby heard him say, 'Tell him yourself. It's nothing to do with me.'

There was another long pause before the receiver was lifted.

'Yes? Who is that?' The voice was hard and antagonistic.

'It's David. Is that you, Kay? Kay? . . . Hullo . . .?'

'David? . . . Is it really you? . . . Oh, my God . . . I thought you were dead, my darling . . .'

'Hey, hey . . . don't cry, please . . .'

'I thought it was some sort of dreadful joke . . . someone playing a cruel trick . . .'

'I'm sorry, I didn't think . . . my mother told me all you'd done . . . your last letter to her was from Oakington . . . I just wanted to tell you I was all right . . . I didn't mean to upset you . . .'

'I'm not crying now, I'm laughing, honestly . . .' She was rapidly becoming calmer. 'What happened to you? I kept on hoping your mother would hear from the Red Cross, but when she didn't, and you were posted presumed killed . . .'

'Not now. When I see you. I'm on a long leave. Could you wangle a few days?'

'I've got two weeks' leave coming up. I'll have to go home first, it's my twenty-first birthday. Could you come to that? Would you like to, I mean . . .'

'Yes, of course, but if it's a family occasion . . . I wouldn't want to intrude . . .'

'Don't be an idiot. My parents'll be delighted . . . they've heard so much about you . . .'

They arranged when to meet, and where. Kirby hung up, and walked out of the office. The flight sergeant was emerging from another door. He came to attention respectfully, but there seemed to be sly amusement lurking somewhere on that immobile face. Kirby wondered if he had been listening in on an extension.

'Everything all right, sir?'

'Everything's fine, thank you, Flight.'

'Very glad to hear it, sir.'

'You don't know me, do you, Flight.'

'No, sir. Haven't had the pleasure, sir.'

'You have, you know,' Kirby said. 'You were here when I came in years ago. I said I wanted to volunteer for air crew, pilot training. You told me I didn't have a hope – because I hadn't been in the Air Training Corps.'

'We all make mistakes, sir,' the flight sergeant said, un-ruffled. 'Good luck, sir.'

'And you, Flight,' Kirby said.

David Kirby walked along beside the park, and crossed London Road at the Titanic memorial in memory of the crew

of that ill-fated liner, most of whom had been Southamptc
men.

Weeds and grass covered the bomb site where had once
stood the Central Library he had haunted in his schooldays,
borrowing books weekly, reading voraciously. He must start
reading again. There would be plenty of opportunity now.

He walked past the Cenotaph, the stately monument to the
men of Southampton killed in the First World War, countless
names inscribed upon it. Would there be more Cenotaphs
built all over the country? Yet another Remembrance Day?

At the Junction, he stood waiting for a tram or a bus to
Millbrook, whichever came along first. The rubble from the
bombed buildings which spread all the way along Above Bar
to the Bargate and beyond had been dug out and removed,
revealing gaping, grass-grown cellars beneath, around which
protective plank fences had been erected. Somewhere, among
all that, his father had died.

Far away, in another country, so had his crew, Ron Ferris,
swearing, aggressive, proud of his warrant officer's uniform,
not long married. Alan Russell, a pacifist at heart, his ambition
to become a teacher, and who would have made a fine one.
Ted Hollis, placid, unassuming, his object, never realized, to
accumulate a thousand pounds. Arthur Wood, living constantly with fear and so braver than any perhaps, who had
found a simple, constant love, and experienced the agony he
had feared before the end. Len Bellamy, rocklike, the regular
airman who had joined the RAF in the days of peace and
unemployment, in search of security and a pension.

And Roy Harrison, closer to Kirby than even his own crew.

Kirby could find no reason why he should be breathing the
crisp, clean air, with a life before him, and they should not.
There was no logic, no merit, just luck. He was no more
deserving then they, but they had paid in full, while he had
not. In the years ahead, perhaps, he would always harbour a
lingering feeling that he had received a gift which he had not
wholly earned.

Don Shepherd had made it too, even more unlikely in a
way, the pilot to whom flying had never come naturally, and

been a constant effort. Kirby wondered where Don
was now . . . he must find out, and look him up . . .
was approaching. Kirby moved the few yards to the
top, jumped on board, and climbed on to the top deck.
ere were others he should go and see. Georgina, to whom
he would lie, and swear that Arthur Wood had been killed
instantly . . . Roy Harrison's widow . . . it was right that she
should be told of Roy's final act of courage when, his aircraft
burning and doomed, he had flown on steadily and dropped
his bombs . . .

The ageing bus jolted forward, its worn bottom gear
whining. Kirby watched the parks go by, green and well kept.
Very soon, the air raid shelters, unused for years, could be dug
out and replaced by smooth grass, as though they had never
been there.

Kirby began to consider what to buy Kay Dunn for her
birthday. He thought of the many evenings they had spent
together, of the river bank, the inn in Derbyshire. Late, but
not too late, he knew what he had not been able to perceive at
the time, and had only fully recognized in the last twenty-four
hours the nature of his true feelings for her and, given the way
she had spoken on the phone, how deep hers were for him.

If she was nearly twenty-one now, he mused, she could only
have been nineteen when he first met her.

It occurred to him that he had a birthday in the near future
too.

Quite soon, Squadron Leader David Kirby, DSO, DFC,
would be twenty-three years old.

Postscript

To my knowledge, the distinguished historian John Terraine was the first to make the point with such precise clarity when, in his book *The Smoke and the Fire*, he wrote: 'One of Churchill's primary preoccupations . . . throughout the war was the avoidance of mass British casualties. The national haemorrhage of World War 1, and its cost to British greatness, weighed heavily on English minds and inevitably affected strategic thinking. Churchill's addiction to . . . strategic bombing was in part the product of the British past . . .

'. . . And here lies the . . . irony . . . One of the aspects of the First World War, especially on the Western Front, that had so appalled Lloyd George . . . and Churchill, was the loss of officers, the flower of the nation, the natural leaders of the rising generation. The total number of British officers killed during the First World War, including the Royal Navy and the RAF, was 38,834. The total number of aircrew of Bomber Command, exactly the same type of men, killed during the Second World War was 55,573 . . .'

During World War Two, RAF Bomber Command lost a total of 10,724 aircraft, of which 6,931 were heavy bombers including 2,232 Halifaxes, and 3,832 Lancasters.

The United States Eighth Air Force, which flew from the United Kingdom and formed the daylight component of the bombing offensive, also suffered cruelly, losing 4,754 B17 Flying Fortresses and 2,112 B24 Liberators out of total losses of 9,057 aircraft, most of the remainder being fighter escorts.

44,472 air crew of the United States Eighth Air Force lost their lives.

More than 100,000 British, Commonwealth and American air crew of RAF Bomber Command and the United States 8th Air Force were killed, all physically fit young men who were also able to comply with the exacting standards required of air crew.

Such was the cost, such was the price which was paid.